DOUBLE-CROSSING THE BORDER

A SEDUCTIVE TALE OF LOVE AND GREED

SARAH LAUER NAKAWATASE

Black Rose Writing | Texas

ISBN: 978-1-68513-686-4
LIBRARY OF CONGRESS CONTROL NUMBER: 2025940799
PUBLISHED BY BLACK ROSE WRITING
www.blackrosewriting.com

Printed in the United States of America
Suggested Retail Price (SRP) $22.95

Double-Crossing the Border is printed in Minion Pro

To all the small moments that, when strung together over years, make up a life.

Thank you, Beverly, Josefina, and Saburo, for zillions of perfect moments.

You three are pure magic!

Praise for
Double-Crossing the Border

"The novel starts with a bang and continues to deliver surprising twists all the way to the conclusion. In the process, it provides a timely look at immigration, different cultures, and the common threads of love, family, and ambition that run throughout humanity."
–Travis Tougaw, author of the *Marcotte/Collins Investigative Thrillers*

"*Double-Crossing the Border* is a dual timeline, sweeping epic of a story that is equal parts cautionary tale and sweet romance."
–Gail Ward Olmsted, bestselling author of the *Miranda Quinn Legal Twist* series

"Nakawatase delivers a cross-cultural tale of intrigue about a couple in turmoil. Both know what they want. Neither knows what they need. Only one of them will discover what really matters."
–Cam Torrens, bestselling author of the *Tyler Zahn suspense* series

"In *Double-Crossing the Border*, Nakawatase weaves a complex tale of how the search for a lost fortune plays out in Mexico during the revolution and reaches into present time. Some want to keep what they've amassed, others want to claim these treasures as their own, some seek love and security, and some just want to survive."
–Karen K. Brees, author of *The WWII Adventures of MI6 Agent Katrin Nissen*

"Sarah Lauer Nakawatase's *Double-Crossing the Border* is a captivating historical novel full of vivid storytelling and a powerful exploration of family and resilience."
–Kate Laack, author of *While the Coin is in the Air*

"Betrayal and suspense wind stealthily through the pages of *Double-Crossing the Border* with such intrigue, it's hard to put down."
–Lucille Guarino, author of *Elizabeth's Mountain* and *Lunch Tales: Suellen*

"Sarah Nakawatase has a wonderful grasp for bringing the goods to her reader. *Double-Crossing the Border* is a brilliant and clever love story that brings the reader into a new culture."
–Paul Jantzen, author of *Sour Apples*

"Looking for love and intrigue, you'll find it all in *Double-Crossing the Border*. Author Sarah Nakawatase hits the bullseye in her latest novel."
–Christopher Amato, author of *An Authors Dozen: Thirteen Short Stories*

"Sarah Nakawatase is one of those rare – and enviable – writers who couple an innate bent for storytelling with a lyrical style."
-Lea O'Harra, author of the *Inspector Inoue Thriller* series

"Strap in and be prepared for a cross-cultural immersive wild ride that takes you through dual timelines—with a span of 100 years! Nakawatase is a masterful storyteller as she weaves a tale of romance, betrayal, loss, and reinvention."
–Joelle Babula, author of *Infidelity Rules*

"*Double-Crossing the Border* tells a tale of love versus greed in an international and intergenerational puzzle revealed at the perfect pace."
–Lena Gibson, award-winning author of the *Love and Survival* series

"Sarah Nakawatase knocks it out of the park with *Double-Crossing the Border,* a sensational story that has it all—intriguing mystery, steamy romance, and buried treasure. Nakawatase's elaborate plot will pull readers into a gripping dual timeline as they follow complex characters who need to untangle both their past and present to find who they really are."
–Hannah McNamara, author of *Gut Instinct*

"Double-Crossing the Border is a fun and exciting read filled with rich historical details, complex characters and tons of action."
–Karen E Osborne, best-selling author of *Justice for Emerson* and *True Grace*

"Nakawatase flexes her storytelling muscles in this adventurous romance that spans across time, national borders, and the thin lines between both ambition and greed and love and hate. Double-Crossing the Border is two tales that twist and turn into one amazing epic you will not be able to resist."
–Lorna Hollifield, award-winning author of *Bright Little Girls*

"The story blends suspense, romance, and intrigue, both historical and present day, with richly drawn characters, vivid settings, and a twist-filled plot. A captivating read for fans of cross-cultural sagas and storytelling filled with tension and meaning."
–A.J. McCarthy, bestselling author of the *Charlie and Simm* mystery series

DOUBLE-CROSSING
THE BORDER

Chapter 1

Jalisco, Mexico 1910
The Hernandez Castañeda Ranch

Catalina pulled her crocheted shawl higher over her shoulders against the crisp morning air. Nestled in the mountains of Jalisco, she sat in the courtyard of her vast estate, and the wrought iron table and chairs mirrored her rigid posture.

"Luisa?" she called across the courtyard and watched as their young housemaid slipped through the tiled archway of the hacienda's grand cloister, cutting through the moyotle bushes bursting with pungent flowers. Tubular blossoms painted orange stains on Luisa's skirt as she hurried toward the breakfast patio to meet the lady of the house.

"Please gather the children for breakfast," Catalina instructed Luisa without looking up, then unfolded her cloth napkin embroidered with vibrant flowers, guiding it lightly as it fell onto her lap.

Quick and silent as a fox, the housemaid turned and vanished into the shadows cast by the pillars that blocked the morning sun, leaving her mistress alone at the breakfast table.

Catalina waited under the heavy branches of the ciruela trees, laden with clusters of golden fruit, admiring the life she had built for herself. Endless rows of blue agave clung to the mountains, climbing the rocky slopes until sharp, succulent leaves met the sky. Clouds hung low in the valley, enjoying their time before they would be exiled by the heat of the day. High stone walls encircled the main house, offering protection from animals and marauders alike. The walls, a symbol of strength and affluence, shielded them from the day-to-day tasks of the mountain folk who labored on the hacienda. Catalina had married into wealth. She played the lady of the house flawlessly, supporting her husband, and grooming her children to continue their life of luxury.

The children's laughter reached her first, bouncing off the stucco walls as her two daughters came rushing down the corridor from the east wing of their home. They spilled onto the patio, smiling and catching their breath. Luisa looked on, patiently waiting to attend to the needs of her mistress.

"Hi, Mama!" Her youngest daughter, Ivette, bent over, guarding the cramp on her side. Whether it was from sprinting down the hall or laughter, Catalina didn't know. Wildflowers woven throughout Ivette's hair wilted, in need of a drink.

Daria, aged fourteen, smoothed her dress as she approached the table. Coal-black hair tied into a braid fell past her waist. "Good morning, Mother."

"Good morning, girls." Catalina waited for her children to sit before beginning the morning meal. She noticed some brittle pieces of grass stuck in Ivette's hair besides yesterday's flowers, but didn't comment. Instead, she closed her eyes, shook her head, and motioned for Luisa.

The housemaid approached the breakfast table, hands folded neatly in front of her, and waited. Only one year older than Daria, Luisa had been in the Castañedas' employ for years. She knew their habits and preferences, making her irreplaceable.

"Where is Vicente?" Catalina addressed the young woman.

"I'm sorry, but I don't know. I haven't seen him this morning."

No information. "Well, thank you, Luisa. We have everything we need." Catalina waved her away, and the housemaid ducked into the kitchen. Out of sight, but within earshot—never more than a stone's throw away.

This time, Catalina directed the question toward her children. "Do you girls know where your father is?"

Ivette scooted her chair closer to the table and took a long gulp of fresh-squeezed orange juice from a tall, slender glass. "I saw him riding out to the fields earlier." She wiped orange juice from her mouth with the back of her hand.

"Use your napkin," said her mother. "What time did he leave?" Catalina waited as Ivette bit into a piece of sweet bread stamped with swirls of sugar.

"A little after six thirty, Mother." Daria answered for her little sister, who was taking her time, savoring the sweet sugar crystals.

"Luisa?" Catalina called the housemaid to the table once more.

She appeared at Catalina's side, carrying a ceramic serving plate brimming with huevos rancheros—scrambled eggs smothered in a red chili sauce. Steam rose from the warm platter.

"Have Nesto saddle a horse for me." Catalina knew she wouldn't be able to eat anything without talking to Vicente first. It wasn't out of the ordinary for him to get an early start, but it wasn't like Vicente to miss desayuno. They ate their meals together.

"Yes, señora, right away." Luisa placed the heavy dish on the table and obediently made her way down the hill toward the stables. Catalina appreciated her housemaid's sense of urgency as she moved swiftly on the cobblestone path, cutting through the hibiscus trees with their petals tightly curled, still asleep at dawn.

"Where do you think he is?" Daria asked her mother.

Catalina knew Daria deserved an explanation—the truth. Her quinceañera was rapidly approaching, and a lot more than directing the kitchen staff went into being the lady of an estate. So much of it was political. Sometimes, Catalina felt the only thing harder than building wealth was holding on to it.

"Things are changing, Daria." Catalina scooped some huevos onto her plate with a wooden serving spoon, even though her stomach indicated she could not eat them.

"How do you mean?" Daria's eyes narrowed as she waited for her mother's response. "What's changing?"

"It's the revolutionaries. They're cropping up all over the countryside, persuading the ranch hands to revolt. This land …" Catalina paused and held her hands out. The mountains on the horizon rested in her palms, an illusion created by distance. She imagined the mountains slipping through her fingers like the dusting of sugar crystals onto sweet bread. "Our land has been in the family for generations, but there are people who think our land belongs to them. They're threatening the natural order of things."

"The natural order of things?" Daria parroted her mother's phrase and waited for her to continue.

"You know how we're in charge, and everyone works for us and has to do what we say?" Ivette chimed in with a confidence no seven-year-old should rightfully have.

"Keep quiet and eat your breakfast," Catalina reprimanded, then turned her attention back to Daria. "It's only a matter of time before these revolutionaries and their ideas infiltrate our ranch hands, if they haven't already."

"What if they have? What's going to happen to the ranch?" asked Daria.

"We'll talk more later," said her mother, glancing toward Ivette. "I'll catch you up on everything that's been happening on the neighboring properties. I've never heard of anything quite like it, even before I married your father."

Catalina had put the conversation off, mostly to shield her younger daughter from topics she couldn't yet handle. She had probably left Daria with even more questions, but her eldest didn't press her for any more details. Instead, she joined Ivette, grabbing a concha from the plate of pastries.

After watching her daughters eat breakfast, Catalina rode into the agave fields, unchaperoned, hoping to have a private conversation with her husband. There were things he wasn't sharing with her, but why?

The dark-brown mare picked its way through the sharp leaves of the agave plants, its hooves leaving divots in the parched earth. Catalina flicked the reins with sweaty palms, sending the horse into a gallop that matched the pace of her accelerated heartbeats. Dust took flight in Catalina's wake and came to rest on the folds of her dress. As she descended the mountain, she spotted Vicente in the valley below. He towered over most men thanks to his Spanish bloodline, making him relatively easy to identify, even at a distance. He was engaged in conversation with a man in the valley who looked like Nesto's cousin, Gaspar. Would she get her chance to talk to him alone? Would he think her foolish for riding into the fields, interrupting him as he worked? As the ranch owner, he had the right to skip breakfast or any other meal as it pleased him, but she knew him well. Theirs wasn't just a marriage match. They cared for one another and their two girls. The gnawing in her stomach, which had kept her from breakfast, was still trying to tell her something. She just wished she knew what it was.

"It's time to clear these fields," said Vicente, pointing at the surrounding mountainsides. His broad shoulders and midnight black mustache lent credibility to his words. He waved to Catalina as she approached them, then continued to give directions.

Today, they would begin harvesting the mature fields of blue agave. Sturdy leaves shot out like fireworks from the dense bulbs that anchored the plants to the ground. The end of each leaf brandished a spike that could skewer exposed skin. These menacing leaves would be hacked off with machetes, and the tremendous bulbs carted off on the backs of donkeys to be roasted and fermented.

Gaspar nodded in understanding, mounted his horse, and rode to deliver the instructions for harvest to the obreros waiting in the mature field beyond the ridge. Catalina seized her chance to speak with Vicente alone.

Her husband smiled and took the reins to her horse. He guided Catalina and the mare to a water trough and tied the animal with enough slack to take a drink.

Catalina climbed down from the mare and stood in the field, looking up at her husband. "Vicente?" The clomping of hooves had stopped, but her heart raced on. Should she question him?

"What is it, Catalina?" Worry crept into his eyes. "Is something wrong with the girls?"

"No, the girls are fine." She wrung her hands together, unable to keep them still, like two fish in a shallow pool. "It's just … what we talked about the other day. I was worried about you." Catalina glanced around. They were still alone. "Have you heard any more about what happened in Las Pintas?"

"Only what we heard yesterday," he responded, taking her hands in his. "That's why I'm out here this morning. I want to keep a close eye on things."

His reassuring words didn't have their desired effect. "Over half of the mature fields at Las Pintas burned before the rain put out the fire," Catalina countered, averting her eyes to the ground, picturing a blanket of ash accumulating on their fields like snow on the peaks of Toluca.

"Thank God for the rain." Her husband raised his arms to the heavens. "It's the dry season. There should have been no rain."

Catalina responded with gravel in her vocal cords. "I know."

"We'll have these fields cleared in less than a week," said Vicente, surveying the expansive ranch with its lines of blue touching the horizon in every direction.

"Just don't bring in any extra help. That's how it happened in Las Pintas. They brought in new workers, and they were the Zapatistas who set fire to the fields. We know Gaspar and Nesto and all the rest. No one new … okay?" Catalina looked into her husband's dark-brown eyes, trying to hide her fear.

"Cati, I wouldn't let anything happen to you or the girls." He pulled her close and held her. The buttons on his shirt pressed into her cheek.

His embrace would have calmed her nerves under normal circumstances, but wasn't doing anything to ease the persistent gnawing in her stomach. Catalina pushed back from his chest. "How can you guarantee nothing will happen to our family or to our ranch?"

"Look. I'm going to be out here for the entire harvest, and if I see anything unusual, I'll put a stop to it right away." He placed his hand on the gun hanging from his hip. "Don't worry. I've been running this ranch for years. I know the men, and I know the land."

He drew her into his chest again and held her, longer this time—tighter. She exhaled slowly, feeling the safety she craved from his arms. "I trust you, Vicente."

"You should," he whispered, stroking her hair, "but you're needed at the house, and I'm needed over the ridge." He moved his hands to her shoulders, stepped back, and went to untie the mare. He looked over his shoulder. "I'll see you at dinner. Okay?"

Vicente adjusted the bridle, waiting for her to agree. In all the years she had been married to him, she had never known him to be fearful of anything, and today was no different. She agreed they would see each other at dinner and accepted the reins, but before her husband let go of the leather straps, he caught her eyes once more.

"I love you, Cati. You have nothing to worry about." His words came with a self-assured smile.

She knew he truly felt this way. He would do everything he could during the harvest to maintain order, and she would watch over their daughters. With nothing more to say, she lifted herself into the saddle and kicked her heels into the horse's sides. "I love you, too." The wind swallowed her words as she returned to the ranch house at a gallop.

That evening, Catalina lay awake thinking about everything they had to lose, everything that needed protecting. Warm currents of air blew through the open windows, past the lacy curtains, carrying the musky smell of freshly cut agave, when Vicente came into the room. He approached the bed with his muscular arms and tanned chest. She needed his strength.

"When do you think all of this will end?" She wanted him to say it would be okay, just like he had earlier in the fields. She needed to hear it again.

"It can't last much longer. El Presidente Diaz won't allow it to continue. I hear the military is organizing troops to stop the revolts. Everything we have will be secure again. You'll see, mi amor."

"I hope so." Catalina curled her knees up, folded her hands together, and tucked them under her pillow.

Vicente climbed into bed next to her. "How were the girls today?"

Catalina realized she'd forgotten to fill Daria in on what had happened in Las Pintas, but was glad she hadn't. She didn't want Daria to lie awake and worry about something over which she had no control. "The girls are fine. They spent the morning in class and the afternoon in the gardens." Catalina consciously tried to release the tension in her neck and felt her head sink a little farther into the pillow.

"I love you so much, all three of you." Vicente tilted her chin up and kissed her lightly on the lips. "Come here." He opened his arms, and she snuggled into him. In his protective embrace, she drifted to sleep before her mind started cycling through the what-ifs.

Catalina awoke to the smell of smoke. She pushed herself up in bed. Disoriented from sleep and the unexpected smell, she rubbed her face, taking stock of her surroundings. A thick haze filled the air in their bedroom. Catalina massaged her eyes again, which didn't help to clear her vision.

"Vicente, wake up!" She grabbed his shoulders and shook him hard, then tore off the covers and ran to the window. The blue agave fields burned bright orange and yellow, with billows of smoke rising into the morning sky. She coughed, pulled her nightgown over her nose, and turned to face her husband—still in bed. "Vicente!" The cloth muffled her voice. "What should we do?"

The look on his face changed from surprised to knowing. He rushed to her side, placed his hands on her waist, and stared through the window at the charred fields.

"What should we do?" she repeated, but already knew the answer—the girls. They had to get Daria and Ivette to safety, but panic had welded her feet to the floor where she stood watching the destruction.

Vicente spun her around so quickly she almost lost her balance. "You need to get the girls! I'll get the horses ready!" He pointed toward the door. "Go!"

Catalina darted down the corridor to rouse their daughters, tripping over her nightgown, almost falling through the threshold of their shared bedroom. The view from their children's window looked as though nothing was wrong. The fields to the east had not caught fire yet. Catalina shook Daria by the arms and told her to get dressed, now! She circled around to Ivette, lifting her out of bed.

"What's going on?" Ivette asked through a curtain of sleep with her arms wrapped loosely around her mother's neck. She rested her head on Catalina's shoulder.

"I need you to follow every direction, mi amor. Do you understand?" her mother asked.

"What's happening?" Ivette raised her head from her mother's shoulder, more alert.

"We have to leave the ranch," said Catalina. "No more questions. We'll all be fine. Now, everybody, come on."

Ivette had gotten so big. Catalina put her down and clasped her hand as she led both girls along the corridor, through the gardens to the stables, stopping only to fill a gourd with water from a metal pump around the backside of the barn.

•   •   •

Vicente burst through the heavy, wooden doors of his wife's dressing room and rifled through the drawers of her vanity where she kept her jewelry. Ribbons and chains knotted together as his large hands mixed the contents of the drawers. He ran his fingers around the perimeter of each square compartment, then began pulling the drawers completely out of their units, dumping his wife's possessions onto the floor. Fastened to the underside of the top left drawer, he found a drawstring bag. Vicente inserted his finger into the bag, loosened the strings, and poured its contents onto the cupped palm of his hand. An assortment of gems with three large rubies tumbled out, throwing their fiery reflections across the smoke-filled room. He dropped the gems back into the bag, along with some tangled gold and silver chains he haphazardly scooped from the floor. Precious stones in hand, he ran for the stables.

A cloak of smoke covered the barn, and Vicente fumbled with the buckles as he saddled his two fastest mustangs for Catalina and his daughters. His wife and children arrived in the barn with their bedclothes pulled over their noses, but it wasn't helping. They coughed as Vicente lifted his little girls onto one horse—Daria in the front and Ivette in the back. Catalina passed Daria the water-filled gourd and mounted the second horse.

"Where is *your* horse?" Catalina studied her husband with red, watery eyes. Tears traveled down her cheeks, but it was hard for him to tell if they were from the smoke or fear.

He stood straight with his mouth set in a firm line beneath his black mustache. "I'm going to stay and put an end to this."

"We're not leaving without you! The ranch … everything is too far gone. We need to leave!" His wife looked down at him from her seat in the saddle, and he could see now that hers were tears of love and desperation, but this wasn't the time for emotion. It was a time for action, for a show of strength.

"Papa," shouted Ivette, "we need you!" Their youngest daughter started to climb down from the horse, but Daria caught her by the arm.

Ivette's small voice had penetrated the cloud of rage that enveloped her father, but it wasn't enough to change his course of action. "Go with your mother, preciosa." He squeezed her tiny hand, then secured the gem-filled, leather sack in the saddlebag.

"Cati," he said sternly, "you have to go now, and don't argue. Ride west. Then follow the coast north. I'll send word to my cousin in Nayarit to intercept you at the border. It's a two-day journey."

Vicente watched as Catalina grabbed the reins with feigned confidence, preparing to lead their girls through the swirling clouds of white smoke, out of the ranch, and into the unknown. He smacked the horses, and the mustangs carried his most precious possessions into the distance. How could he send word to Nayarit faster than they rode on the mustangs? He couldn't. They were on their own.

His family crested the hilltop and disappeared. Vicente's gaze lingered briefly on the space left behind, then he turned to saddle a horse for himself. He would ride into the fields and find whoever had done this. Seated high on his mount, Vicente spurred the horse toward the stable doors, but the animal stopped when a dusty ranch hand stepped onto the threshold, barring his exit.

"Nesto," said Vicente. "Come. Ride with me to find whoever's done this."

Nesto's feet remained firmly planted, his shotgun at his side, pointed downward along the length of his leg.

"Nesto? Are you all right?" Vicente's voice held concern for a man who had worked the ranch with him for years. "We can set this right. Come with me."

Nesto said nothing, but raised the shotgun, training his sights on the haciendero.

Vicente had misread the situation. "Nesto, you've been with this family for years. You don't want to do this." His horse danced in place and snorted. The tension between the two men had set the beast on edge.

Vicente's onetime friend held the gun steady, undeterred by his words. "You're not in a position to tell me what to do anymore. We're taking *our* land back."

"Who's 'we?'" asked Vicente, looking into a pair of eyes that had once been so familiar, but were now the eyes of a stranger. He spurred the horse, and the animal paced forward.

Bang! A deafening shot rang out in the barn, blowing a hole through the ceiling. Debris rained down and Vicente's horse reared up, sending the haciendero tumbling to the stable floor. He coughed and scrambled on his hands and knees, away from the horse's wild kicks. On his feet again, Vicente faced his attacker, keeping a wide stance—ready to move.

He approached Nesto on foot this time. Straw clung to his trousers, and he held his hands out to the side in plain sight—nonthreatening. "I've never mistreated you. Why are you doing this? You've been like family."

"Family?" Nesto laughed. "You have your family, and I have mine, but *we* are not family. You and your family live a life of prosperity, while my family and I subsist on beans and tortillas. I send my daughters into the dry mountains to collect cactus leaves while your family eats ciruelas from the trees on your patio."

Vicente drew closer, still holding his hands out, angled down, ready to grab a pistol from his holsters.

"Stop right there!" Nesto repositioned the shotgun. "It's your turn to listen. Your Daria has three hundred people coming to her quinceañera in a few weeks … three hundred. How can you have parties like that while the families who work on your ranch have to save for months just to buy a few candies for their children at Christmas?"

A crowd of ranch hands gathered behind Nesto as he continued to inform Vicente about how things really were on the ranch. "I'll never be able to give my family what they deserve, no matter how hard I work. The government and the haciendros own the land, and the people of Mexico have no way to better their own lives."

"Nesto, please don't do this."

The mob grew—filled with unknown faces. They were not the faces of the men and women who worked the fields year in and year out, but the faces of revolutionaries, just as Catalina had warned him. Everything was closing in on him—the smoke, the mob, and the betrayals. Crackling flames devoured his life's work on the other side of the wooden walls, but he was safer out there than inside. Vicente dashed toward the back of the barn.

He pushed the sliding door, but it didn't budge. He tried again, leaning into it this time—still nothing. With his hands balled into tight fists, he banged on the door, answered only by the clanking of chains. His foot slid from under him on the dirt floor littered with straw, and in the few seconds it took him to reach the front entrance again, the horde had chained it shut.

The wildfires drew nearer, and the horses, penned in their stalls, paced and whinnied. Smoke snaked into the stables through the walls' wooden planks, but instead of carrying the heady scent of the agave fields it smelled of burning pine.

He reached for his pistols, but his hands met empty holsters. In his haste to find the rubies, he had neglected to bring his guns. A chorus of cheers and shouts erupted from the crowd gathered around the barn, overtaking the roar of the blaze and the popping of burning planks.

"Nesto! Don't do this!" He banged on the walls and shouted, but the rioters and the fire drowned out his cries for help. Either that, or his words meant nothing to them.

Vicente scratched at the wooden boards. He should have gone with his family, but it was too late. Splinters snapped off, lodging themselves under his nails. He dropped to the ground and clawed at the packed dirt. Beads of sweat fell from his forehead, hitting the earthen floor. The smoke irritated his eyes, and tears flowed down his face, mingling with sweat as he frantically scratched at the ground. His hands would not get him out of there, but a shovel hung on the tool wall. He stayed low and crawled to retrieve it, sputtering and coughing as he went. When the handle was within reach, he grabbed it. On contact, the calloused skin of his palm sizzled. He let go as the searing pain traveled up his limb, and a single twist of steam rose from his blistering flesh.

Vicente rolled onto his back, cradling his hand close to his chest. Cries of rage and frustration escaped his lips as he lay there with his face contorted in agony. He closed his eyes, blinking back the pain, and when he opened them again, flames danced inside the barn. Shifting columns of orange and blue lapped at the walls, traveling along the overhead beams, and sending the horses into next-level fright. Vicente's horse jumped and kicked—moving everywhere, but the hissing and spitting of the blaze swallowed its pleas for help. Thick air, saturated with heat and smoke, hummed as the inferno gathered strength through every gust of wind and every plank consumed. Vicente didn't see it coming when his horse planted a hard kick squarely on his collarbone. He rolled into a side-lying position, staring at where the barn met the earth, and watched as the flames devoured the wall. This would be his grave. Trapped inside the barn, his only salvation would be to pass out from smoke inhalation before the flames reached him. He propped himself up on his elbows, thirsty for oxygen, coughing and choking against the smoke.

Chapter 2

Adam
Baltimore, Maryland
Present Day

A rusty, metal construction sign banged against the temporary chain-linked fence surrounding the muddy lot. Stopped backhoes and yellow Bobcats sank into the saturated ground. Adam parked on a patch of gravel and stepped down from his SUV, leaving the engine running. Cars whipped by on the city streets, spraying the sidewalks with foul water churned up from the scattered potholes. This soggy lot on Fleet Street would be the future home of Anderson Financial's eight-story office building, but the rain had slowed their progress. He was two weeks behind schedule and would need to make up for lost time.

In a pair of work boots, Adam squelched his way to the trailer, turned mobile office, to grab an extra set of blueprints. Halfway there, the rain picked up again, and he thought about the umbrella lying in the passenger seat. He wrapped his coat tighter around his somewhat pudgy waist and quickened his pace, sliding in the mud. At forty-three, Adam was still considered a good-looking man by conventional standards. Dark-brown hair framed his strong facial features, but he had adopted the figure of someone who sits at a desk for a living. As a project manager, he spent most days in a warm, dry office behind a laptop, only making his site visits on Fridays.

The local Doppler showed the rain expected to clear that afternoon, but he needed a plan to get the project back on schedule. Heavy grading equipment sat idly under a gray sky. It would be days before the ground would be suitable for leveling again, but these working conditions were out of his control. He would have to focus on completing the interior faster and under budget, which brought him back to the blueprints. Inside the trailer, Adam spotted the plans on top of a singular, wobbly desk. He rolled them up, tucked them under his jacket, and started toward the truck, dodging puddles as he went.

A vibration inside Adam's jacket pocket signaled he had a text—Sammie. *Hey there. Are we still getting together tonight?*

Sammie was a graduate student at the Bloomberg School of Public Health in downtown Baltimore—lean and gorgeous, with wavy, blonde hair that fell halfway down her back. They'd met when Empire Commercial Builders was renovating a library for JHU. He had completely forgotten about their dinner plans, preoccupied with the Anderson job.

I'm sorry, but I won't be able to meet you tonight, he texted as raindrops hit the screen. Images of her spread out on her bed played in his mind, and he shook his head, trying to recenter his thoughts on the project at hand.

Adam had been with Empire for years, and it was time for him to take the next step, but he needed to deliver on this build. Yesterday's conference call with the client had not gone well, and significant progress would have to be made this week. No one would ever consider him for a senior project manager position if he couldn't handle a midsize job like the Anderson building.

OK, she texted back.

That was too easy. He would call her and make sure everything really was "okay." After a few seconds of searching for a signal on the rainy lot, the phone was ringing.

"Hey, Adam."

Her voice held no undercurrent. Adam was used to having to decipher his wife's true meaning from the words she used, but college girls were different.

After Adam's long pause, she asked him if he was all right.

"Oh, yeah, I'm fine … I just wanted to apologize for canceling our plans." Not that he was invested in her feelings, but he wanted her to feel respected, or at least happy enough to continue their arrangement.

"No worries," she assured him. "Right after I got your text, I made plans to meet some friends. So it all worked out."

It was good that she wasn't mad at him, but he could have done with a bit of disappointment. "Where are you guys going?" Adam asked, curious to see what kind of invitation could put her in such a good mood after canceling their dinner plans.

"Some Latin dance club in Fells Point."

He heard her rummaging through something in the background. "Are you going with Angie?" She and her roommate, Angie, usually went out together.

"No, I'm going with Justin and some other friends."

The phone slipped from Adam's hand and landed in the mud. Rain funneled into his jacket and onto the blueprints when he bent down to get it. "Damn!" He pried the phone from the thick sludge and brushed beads of water from the drawings before they soaked into the paper.

"It's not like that." The shuffling in the background stopped. "Justin and I are just friends now. You know how it is."

Adam did know how it was. Sammie was going out with her ex-boyfriend. His reddened ears would have given his true feelings away, but she was none the wiser over the phone. "It's fine. I'm just on site right now. I'll have to let you go."

"Okay."

There it was again. Just an "okay," but this time, he would let it go. His blueprints weren't *okay*, and he had to get back to work. "I'll call you later." Adam waited for her to hang up first.

Back in the truck, he turned on the defogger. Muggy air filled the vehicle, and he was careful not to tear the plans as he unrolled the damp prints to dry on the front seat. Over the weekend, he needed to uncover all the cost-saving interior changes he could find, but before that, he had a company event to attend that night. And where was Mark? His field manager should have been on site.

"Call Mark," Adam said. The field manager picked up on the second ring.

"What's up, Adam?"

Adam shrugged off his jacket. "I'm on site at Anderson. Where are you?"

"I didn't think you'd be by today with all the rain."

Of course, Adam was coming today. He always did his site visits on Fridays, no matter the weather. "Look, Mark, we have to catch up with each other on Monday and go over the new timeline for Fleet Street."

"Are we pushing everything back a few weeks?"

"Absolutely not." It was the exact opposite. "I'm going to figure out how to trim some time from the interior build-out. I took your blueprints from the trailer, but I'll drop off a modified copy on Monday. We can go over the changes." Mark was silent.

Adam glanced at the time—three o'clock. Fridays were never long enough. He still had to stop by the office before heading home to get ready for the company dinner that evening. "Mark, are you there?"

"I'm here. Is there anything I can do to help?" Mark usually said all the right things but rarely followed through on anything outside of his basic job description.

"Yes, actually, there is." Adam picked small chunks of dried mud from his screen. "We'll need to recover some of the time we've lost due to the inclement weather, but you've got to be present. Do you know what I'm saying?"

"Yeah, I'll be there on Monday."

That wasn't what he'd meant. "Mark, I'm going to need you to extend the workday once we get to the interior build-out, but you'll need to rotate the guys so we don't give any overtime. I'll have everything for you on Monday."

"Like I said, I'll be there."

Sometimes, Adam wasn't sure if Mark was playing him or if things just went over his head. "I'll see you Monday morning."

"Yeah, boss. Have a good weekend." Mark signed off.

Adam would be working all weekend, but if that's what it took, he was willing to put in the time. As a senior project manager, he wouldn't have to make any more of these site visits, and he could get rid of the work boots he kept in his car.

Adam had just put the truck in reverse when he received a text from Sophie, his wife. *Don't forget about the Empire dinner tonight.*

He hadn't forgotten, but he had so many things he needed to do before dinner, and with all the rain, traffic would be hellacious. Standing water had blocked his usual route through the city that morning. *I'm running late. Could you bring my suit and black shoes and meet me at the venue tonight?* He texted back.

We're not going to ride together?

Obviously not. That's what he had just said. Why did she always ask questions when she already knew the answer? To make him feel guilty, of course. He was so tired of their relationship, or maybe just bored. Either way, it was easy enough. All he had to do was survive one more of his company's dinner events with Sophie. In the next few days, he would finally work up the nerve to leave her. At least that's what he had been telling himself for the past year. It wasn't his fault. She was the one who'd changed. Had he given it his best? Of course, he had. They'd been together for eleven years, at any rate.

Will you bring them? He texted again, refocusing on immediate concerns.

She waited almost ten minutes before sending her reply. He was halfway to East Fayette before she texted, *Yes. I'll bring them. See you at six?*

Rain poured down in sheets, and he waited until he'd reached the office to send his reply. She would most likely read too much into that, too. At least Empire had a parking garage. Adam took the elevator to the third floor, blueprints in hand. He had a couple of hours to catch up on work before meeting Sophie at the hotel.

•　　•　　•

As promised, Sophie met him in the parking garage of the Omni Hotel that evening wearing a form-fitting, below the knee, black dress, showcasing her trim, athletic form. Sure, their marriage was stagnant, but he could always depend on Sophie to follow through. Adam snatched his suit from his wife and performed a quick change in a public restroom beside the elevators.

"You look pretty good," said Sophie when he joined her outside the elevators.

"Thanks. You, too," he offered without actually looking at her.

The married couple stepped off the elevator that had carried them from the parking garage to the lobby. "Ugh," said Adam. "There's Eileen. Just smile and pretend you're having a good time."

"But I am having a good time."

"Sure you are." Adam laughed as they fell in line behind Lisa, VP of Finance.

Bob and Eileen stood at the entrance to the banquet hall, greeting guests as they arrived.

"Hi, Lisa," said Eileen with a broad smile, stretching her leathery skin. "You look wonderful! I've got you at table two with the sparkling pomegranate juice." Eileen gave the pregnant VP a warm hug.

Lisa smiled at the interfering hostess. "Everything looks great, Eileen. You did an amazing job putting this all together."

"It was nothing." Eileen beamed with the compliment. Or maybe she was just overly tan from their trips to the Caribbean.

Arm in arm, the VP and her husband made their way to table two. Adam thought he heard Lisa whisper "boundaries" as they walked away. It was Adam and Sophie's turn to step up and say hi to the president and his wife.

"Hey, Adam. Good to see you," said Bob, shaking his hand as if he hadn't just seen Adam at the office earlier that day. "It's nice to see you too, Sophie."

"You as well, Bob. Eileen." Sophie acknowledged them both and waited for what Eileen might say next.

The boss's wife took Sophie by her hands and squeezed. "I love your dress."

Adam glanced at Sophie to make sure she was playing the part. Yup, she was smiling. Good.

"It's a beautiful color on you." A brief pause, and Eileen dove right in. "Tell me, how long have you and Adam been together now? I mean, it shouldn't be long before the two of you are starting a family."

Definitely need some boundaries here, thought Adam, while continuing to smile. "It's been eleven wonderful years, Eileen." He put his arm around Sophie and pulled her close. He still had dirt under his nails.

"Aren't the two of you so cute." Eileen pressed on. "So, any plans to fill up that new house of yours?"

Adam saw Sophie biting her tongue. He and Sophie had just had this discussion—again—last week.

"Our house isn't so new anymore." Adam grabbed the reins, strategically avoiding the discussion about family planning. "Sophie's given me a list of home improvements she wants done. This lady keeps me too busy to even think about kids—maybe in the future."

"Oh, sure," said Eileen. "Everything in its own time."

She released Sophie's hands, and with that, Adam thanked them and led his wife to table two, next to Lisa and her husband. All senior management was at table two—a good sign.

Bob had inherited the company from his father, who had grown it substantially from what he had inherited from Bob's grandfather—a true family business. Now, Empire boasted over five thousand employees nationwide, but the home office was still based in Baltimore, and everyone important was at *his* table.

Sophie leaned in and whispered to Adam. "Did you mean what you said about kids in the future?" She touched her husband lightly on his forearm.

Was she serious? He was just trying to be polite to his boss's nosey wife. The last thing he wanted was for Eileen to come poking around in his business. Adam ignored Sophie's question and whispered back, "I don't know how Lisa will manage once the baby's born. She works some pretty long hours." There, he had successfully avoided the question while the background music played loud enough to block their whispers from their neighbors.

Adam took a roll from the bread basket in the center of the table and broke it open, releasing a puff of steam. When his phone vibrated, he saw a picture Sammie had sent from the Latin club. She and a handful of friends were at the bar doing tequila shots, and he wished he were there instead. Sophie kept glancing at his phone, which was turned over on the table, so he put it back in his pocket. The serving staff moved smoothly through the venue and set small garden salads in front of each guest. Adam doused his with creamy dressing, drained his glass of wine, and ordered a beer. He leaned over and spoke into Sophie's ear. "I hate these things."

"Who sent you a picture?" Sophie asked.

It was going to be one of *those* nights. "What?" Adam pretended not to know what she was talking about. He just needed her to be supportive and polite, to hold his hand in front of Eileen. How would picking a fight at the dinner table make him look?

Luckily, Bob approached the podium before their conversation went any further. Adam looked at Sophie and then up at Bob, silently conveying they would need to take this up another time.

"Hi, everyone," Bob began. The dining room quieted down. "Thank you all for coming." He paused for effect, holding his index cards. "I know you're probably wondering why we put this dinner together. We usually only gather like this around the holidays, but my wife, Eileen, and I just wanted to thank all of you for the outstanding jobs you do for Empire."

On cue, the guests clapped for their host. As he continued his speech, the serving staff circulated with Cornish game hens stuffed with herb-infused rice and steamed vegetables. They set two small birds in front of the pregnant VP as a joke, and Adam caught Sophie glancing in Lisa's direction. Maybe this *wasn't* the perfect table for them.

"It's no surprise that we've been courting several offers from some of the largest commercial construction companies on the East Coast," Bob continued. "Our numbers are strong, and our products are solid. Thanks to everyone in this room, we've built a reputation for honesty and quality." Bob paused, and the room clapped accordingly.

While the guests applauded, Bob dropped his next index card, and it slid under the podium. He bent to get it, but it was out of reach. "Oh well." He held his hands up and tossed the rest of his cards onto the podium. Good-humored laughter swept across the room, and after everyone had quieted down, he moved forward.

"What I wanted to say is that we'll be expanding *internationally* as a company. We've partnered with Apex Development. Now, I know this has always been a family company, but if you're not growing, you're moving in the opposite direction, and we all know what that means. International expansion is the next logical step, and our first job with Apex will be in Mexico."

More applause, but this time, people were excited, not just going along with things. This was news to everyone. It was huge! Adam bit his lip to keep from grinning. He had come to the dinner with aspirations of becoming a senior project manager, but why stop there?

"We are also offering stock options to those who are interested," said Bob.

Lisa and her husband whispered to each other. She had probably known about this for months as the VP of Finance. The tiny chicken on Adam's plate remained untouched. Bob was talking about money, expansion, and career advancement opportunities. This wasn't just some stupid party. *Come on,* Adam thought, *get to the point. Who's it going to be?*

"So," Bob said, "Kevin, our Senior Project Manager, will be the first to represent Empire Commercial Builders internationally! Congratulations, Kevin. You've been with Empire since the beginning, or at least since my beginning as president. You've been an integral part of our growth and our high quality standards. My father trusted you, and so do I."

Applause filled the hall. Adam clapped out of necessity but felt inwardly outraged. Sure, Kevin had been with the company the longest, but Adam's profit margins always exceeded Kevin's. What the hell was Bob thinking? He stopped listening after the big announcement and focused on his dinner. At least the rice was good—aromatic.

●   ●   ●

The following morning, Adam arrived at work half an hour early. Empire's new flexible scheduling policy allowed him to swap Wednesdays at the office for Saturdays. He spent most of the day billing clients and approving invoices from subs that had piled up on his desk.

That afternoon, a shadow fell across his paperwork, cast by Mr. Greenberg standing in the doorway to his office. Outside of work, he was Bob, but here they addressed him as Mr. Greenberg.

"Adam, could I see you in my office?"

"Absolutely." Adam folded his laptop, rose from his desk, and followed Mr. Greenberg down the hall into his office. The view wasn't much. A two-story McDonald's stood across the street, bordered by vacant, brick row homes.

"Adam, I know what I said at last night's banquet, but I want *you* on the job in Mexico." His boss sat behind a large, mahogany desk and motioned for Adam to take a seat on the leather couch opposite the desk.

"What?" Adam ran his hand through his hair several times. "I thought that was Kevin's job." He reached back, feeling for the sofa, and sat.

"Yes, but listen," said Mr. Greenberg, his eyes widening ever so slightly. "Comp Zero is an important client. Their company is also expanding, and they want to work with only one developer on *all* of their new infrastructure."

"So, what you're saying is ..." Adam trailed off.

"My wife and I noticed Kevin came to the company dinner alone last night. Eileen did some asking around and found that he and Emily are getting a divorce. My wife is a very smart woman, and she pointed out that it may not be wise to send a newly single man *south of the border*, as she calls it, and I agree with her."

Had he really just said that? Adam tried not to look offended and wanted to explain how inappropriate that sounded, but knowing where this discussion was leading *his* career, he opted for silence. Besides, you can't change people, especially people like Mr. Greenberg and Eileen.

"How long have you been married now, eight, ten years, something like that?" Mr. Greenberg asked, casually leaning back in his chair.

He had not been paying attention to their conversation last night. "Eleven, sir."

"Right. Ten, eleven, same difference. Are you interested in the job?"

"Absolutely!" Adam didn't hesitate to answer, rarely consulting *his* wife about anything. "Thank you for the incredible opportunity!" He opened his mouth once more to gush over the assignment but held his words in, letting a brief pause occupy the space instead. He didn't want to appear too eager to abandon his other responsibilities with the company. "But what about my other jobs, like Fleet Street?"

"I'll let Kevin handle those. I need you on site in Guadalajara Monday morning," said Mr. Greenberg. He glanced at his cell phone. "It's already two o'clock. I'll let Kevin know about the reassignment. You start packing, and check your email for the flight information."

Mr. Greenberg had gone to find Kevin, leaving Adam sitting on the couch in disbelief. He couldn't go home just yet. Even though almost everything was electronic, each job still had paper files and he would have to get those from Kevin. He gave Mr. Greenberg some time to deliver the news first.

•   •   •

Adam stepped into the Senior Project Manager's office, where Kevin stared blankly at his computer screen. "Hey, Kevin. I'm just here to pick up the files."

"I'm fine with the reassignment." Kevin opened his file cabinet and thumbed through the hanging folders. "This doesn't have to be awkward."

"Of course. I mean, we get paid no matter which projects we're heading up, right?" Adam put his hands on his hips and waited for Kevin to locate the correct folders.

"It just pisses me off how it happened."

So Kevin really wasn't fine with it, Adam thought.

"How can one woman, who's never worked a day in her life, have so much control over what happens in this company?" asked Kevin.

It was a fair question, one that Adam had thought about many times, usually after one of Eileen's comments about starting a family. It was none of her business and had nothing to do with business.

"I don't know," Adam replied, keeping it short, even though he really did know the reason. Eileen came from old money. His boss had inherited the company from his father, but he still had to work. Eileen's money did the work for her. Mr. Greenberg would never let her go, and would do whatever it took to keep her happy.

"She's just so intrusive!" Kevin raised his voice, and his hands stopped paging through the folders.

Kevin would not let him off that easily. Adam's only path to the files was through this conversation. He pulled the glass door to Kevin's office closed. "So what happened?" Adam didn't sit, hoping it would be a short story.

"She found out Emily and I are getting divorced."

"Your situation isn't that uncommon," said Adam. He took his hands from his hips and crossed them in front of his chest—closed body language.

"That's not all of it." Kevin forged ahead.

"Okay. So what happened?"

"Well, Eileen went through all of Emily's social media posts. Emily had changed her status to single and was posting inspirational quotes and all that stuff, but that's not the creepy part." Kevin paused.

"Creepy part? What do you mean?"

"This should be illegal, but it's not." Kevin slammed the file drawer shut. "Eileen made a fake online dating account and found my dating profile."

"Oh, shit," said Adam, covering his mouth with his hand in surprise. Kevin had always seemed so dull.

"Yeah, 'oh, shit,'" Kevin agreed. "The things she was saying to me were so out there—sexual stuff, you know. I thought I had met someone sort of exciting. Then, the next thing I know, Eileen is on the phone with Emily!"

"What the—" Adam realized how lucky he and Sophie had been in their dealings with Eileen.

"I love my wife, Adam. I'm being serious. I was just trying to have a little fun. It wasn't the first time I'd stepped out of the marriage, but we'd gotten past that."

Maybe he and Kevin had more in common than he'd thought, but he sure wouldn't share any of *his* personal details with anyone if this was how things would play out.

"Be good to Sophie, Adam. You never know how much you'll miss someone until they're out of your life for good."

Adam had heard enough. "How about those files?" Kevin passed him the documents.

"Thanks, Kevin, and good luck." Files in hand, Adam left to pack, thinking about breaking things off with Sammie as he drove home. He would be in Mexico for months, so it made little difference if they stayed together or broke up. Armed with this new information about Eileen, he didn't want to give her any reason to have Mr. Greenberg take him off the project.

Chapter 3

Adam

Adam tossed his computer case onto the sofa at home and flopped down next to it. Sophie's car was gone. Great. He would have some time to work on the spreadsheets for Apex. Adam opened his computer and scrolled to the top of the report—completion date, September fifteenth. That was achievable. He was sure he could make it happen, but wasn't sure how he would fare with Sophie for five months in Mexico. Here in the US, she had her business and her family. It would be just the two of them in Mexico. No doubt she would make him feel guilty for the hours he'd be working. Well, it didn't matter how he felt, because he wouldn't give Eileen any ammunition. Sure, he had been messing around with Sammie, but he hadn't been dumb enough to create a dating profile. He and Sophie had gotten by together for eleven years, and he was confident they could do it for five more months. Not much could change in that amount of time.

At half-past seven, Sophie walked through the door with her leather design bag draped diagonally across her shoulder. Adam was still on the couch, checking his email.

"Guess what," she said, sitting beside him.

"Just one second." Adam held up an index finger as he finished typing a response with the other.

She sat back, crossed her legs, and pulled the thick strap of her bag over her head. "The Richardsons went with my design." His wife tried to make eye contact. "They especially loved the layout for the mosaic at the bottom of the fountain. Want to see it?"

"Just one more second," said Adam, never looking up.

"Never mind." Sophie headed toward the dining room, where Adam had set the table for dinner. "What's all this?"

Okay, now he *had* to break away from his computer, or his plan would never work. Adam closed his browser and joined her in the dining room. "I made us dinner."

"I can see that, but when did you have time for all this?" She smiled at him.

Smiling was good. "I got it delivered from the Amish market. So I guess I didn't *make* it, but I ordered your favorites—strawberry cheesecake and seared-to-perfection veal chops—just for you."

"That was nice of you." Genuine appreciation filled her soft, green eyes. "Thanks for taking care of dinner. We have a lot to celebrate today, with the Richardsons signing the contract and all."

"No problem. We both deserve to celebrate." She had provided him with an excellent lead-in to his news.

"What do you mean? I thought Fleet Street was turning into a money pit." Sophie placed her bag in the corner beside the china cabinet.

"It was … or it is, but that's not my news," Adam responded. "I'll give you the condensed version, but just know that Eileen was behind the decision again."

"What did she do this time?"

"They reassigned me to the Comp Zero job in Mexico—the one from the other night with Apex Development." Adam waited for her congratulations, but she just looked at him. He couldn't tell what she was thinking. "You're coming with me!" He held out his arms, introducing the surprise. "They sent two plane tickets and made accommodations for both of us. It'll be like an extended vacation."

"So this celebratory dinner is all about you?" Her eyes narrowed, and her smile disappeared.

"Well, yeah, kind of. I mean, sorry … I wasn't trying to gloss over your signed contract. I'm glad they went with your design, but let's be logical. We both know I make more money. It's the smart choice for us to go to Mexico together. You know what we're up against with my boss."

Her smile returned, but he had to be careful. It wasn't her real smile. The hair on his neck stood on end as he waited for what she would say next.

"What about *my* career?"

Adam tried to formulate an acceptable response. He didn't want to walk into any traps.

"Just because I'm not making more money than you now doesn't mean my business isn't growing. How dare you bring that up! I thought we had both agreed on me quitting my job with the county and growing the plantscaping business. I thought you believed in me."

"I do believe in you. You know I do." He hadn't expected things to go in this direction. "It's just that things are happening for me right now. We can't ignore this opportunity."

"Why should I put my life on hold to go with you? What would *I* be doing there?"

Adam knew it was a rhetorical question and let it hang in the air between them.

"Well, thanks for the invitation, but no." Sophie left the room, disappearing upstairs. The scent of her coconut hair cream lingered in the dead space where she'd been standing.

"Do you mean no to Mexico or no to dinner?" Adam called up the stairs.

"You don't care enough about either to come *upstairs* and ask me," she shouted back.

Moments later, Adam entered their bedroom. "Sweetie, I do care. I've always cared about you." She had begun to change clothes, and seeing her in her underwear and no bra was turning him on. Her daily jogs had kept her in great shape. "Come over here."

"I don't want to be anywhere near you right now, Adam."

He was tired of hearing that, and yet he still wanted her. Ignoring what she had said, he pressed on. He was used to initial rejection and usually got his way, eventually. "Come to dinner." Adam tilted his head. "Or, we could skip dinner and go straight to bed."

"Are you psycho? Where've you been for the last ten minutes? Clearly, you haven't heard a thing I've said since I walked in the door."

He needed her on board and decided to play it—the baby card. "Look, Sophie, we've been together for a long time. I hate to say this, but maybe Eileen has a point. Maybe we should grow our family."

"You can't be serious!" Sophie glared at him with dead eyes, knocked his hands away, and went to retrieve her robe hanging in the bathroom. "I've been practically begging you to have a baby for years and the first time having a baby stands to advance your career is when you want to have one? It doesn't work like that, Adam."

Adam stood in the center of their bedroom with his hands at his sides. "Then how does it work? You tell me. What do you want me to say?"

"I can't tell you what to say! It has to come from you!" Sophie tied her robe.

"All I know is that I want to be in this marriage with you, and I do want to grow our family." There—his thoughts, just like she wanted.

"Do you?" Sophie descended the stairs, rapidly distancing herself from her husband.

"Where are you going?" He honestly didn't know and followed her down the stairs.

She approached his cell phone on the couch, and then he knew. Sophie picked it up.

"Put it down!" he shouted.

"No." She held the phone up to his face, unlocking the device. "Let's see who keeps texting you."

He grabbed both of her wrists, too hard, but she had already pulled up the thread. "Who's Sammie?"

"She's no one." Adam wasn't lying. She *was* no one to him, but she wouldn't be no one to Sophie.

"You think I'm stupid?" asked Sophie, holding the phone in one hand while both hands turned a reddish purple in his grasp.

He forced himself to calm down, silently counting to three. "No, I don't." He was at her mercy and let go of her wrists. He needed her to come with him.

"Well, I'm not going to be stupid anymore. I know she isn't the first, Adam." Sophie dropped his phone on the carpet and crossed her arms tightly.

He said nothing, biting his lip and stalling for time. Saying the wrong thing now could ruin everything. The only problem was that he had no idea what the right thing to say was, not after all this.

"So that's it," she said. "Nothing. You have nothing to say. No sorry? No excuses?"

Adam maintained his silence.

"That's exactly what I thought. You don't care, and maybe you never did." Sophie pointed at the door. "You can leave now."

"You can't kick me out!"

"This is not the time for you to tell me what I can and can't do, not with these marks on my wrists." She held her arms in front of her.

Adam examined her wrists. He hadn't meant to grab her that hard. His fingers had left red marks that would probably bruise. "Just let me pack for Mexico. I can stay at a hotel near the airport."

"Stay wherever you want, but you need to leave. I'll give you five minutes to pack before I call the police."

After closing the front door, Adam's feet remained fixed on the porch as the evening's events raced through his mind. The good thing was that neither one of them had mentioned divorce. They could come back from this. No one had to know they had separated. Was this even a separation? Also, how would anyone know Sophie wasn't in Mexico with him? If anyone saw her in town, he could explain that away. She had a business and would have to travel back and forth. Yes. He would go to Mexico, give her some time to cool down, and then make things right. He could hold this sinking ship together for a little longer until Comp Zero was complete.

Chapter 4

Sophie

"I can't believe I wasted so many years of my life with him!" Sophie paced back and forth in her bedroom, talking to Harriet on speakerphone. "It's not losing *Adam*, but the loss of eleven years I'm mourning."

Harriet owned the property next door to Sophie's childhood home and had watched her grow up—one of the few who knew the baggage Sophie carried. "You haven't wasted your life," Harriet assured her. "These past few years have been a learning experience."

"You don't have to make me feel better." Sophie held a framed picture of their honeymoon in Aruba. What a joke. "This relationship, this marriage, was my mistake. I wasted so many years on a man who never truly cared about me." She threw the photo onto the hardwood floor, but it didn't break.

"Sophie, you know you and your sister are like my own daughters, and I love you. What you're feeling is normal, but you have to cut yourself some slack. You've been this way since you were a little girl. You're too hard on yourself."

"I'm just so angry. Nothing I do is good enough." Sophie squeezed her hands into fists. "How did we go on the way we did for so long?"

"It takes two people to keep a marriage alive, honey. You've always been good enough. Even if your parents couldn't see it back then, even if Adam couldn't see it, I've always seen it, and you are enough."

Sophie listened to the rhythmic drags Harriet took on her cigarillo—one of her skinny cigars that smelled of everything from cloves to peaches. As she listened, she pictured Harriet on her front porch, watching her and her sister play in the yard, always with a thin wisp of smoke drifting toward the sky. Her whole life, Harriet had always known how to make her feel better, but her current situation was beyond repair. Sophie's marriage was over, and with her marriage went the chance to build the family she had wanted from as early as she could remember.

"How long has it been since you've slept, sweetie?" Harriet asked.

"I don't know. Last night was terrible. I was too stressed to sleep, and I was at the Richardson job all day." Sophie plopped onto the bed and sighed. "There's this overwhelming feeling of guilt right in the center of my stomach, but I'm not the one who should feel guilty."

"No, you're not."

There it was again, the familiar long pause. Sophie imagined the orange embers at the end of the cigarillo and wondered which delicious smell was swirling around Harriet. Maybe all of her wisdom came from the endless pauses she took with those cigarillos amid every conversation.

"Sophie, I know many people who wish they could change things about the past, but I never met one person who's been able to do it. When you look back, you're looking in the wrong direction. Turn your head around and start looking toward your future. There are so many years left for you to do exactly what you want to do, and holding on to these negative feelings is only hurting you."

"How do you always know what to say?" Sophie lifted the picture from the floor and placed it face down on the dresser. "Enough about me, though. What's been going on with you? Have you been looking toward your future?"

"I'm glad you asked, because I have. I'm writing again."

"Oh my God, Harriet, that's great." Sophie pictured her smiling. "You need to send me what you have so far."

"Well, we're not there just yet, and you've got a lot on your plate right now." Harriet didn't like to hold the spotlight for too long. "I know it's probably too soon to say this … but after some time passes, things will seem better."

"I want to move on. I do, but I can't." Sophie slouched, not knowing what else to say.

"You could just be overtired. Why don't you try to get some sleep and we'll talk about it some more later?"

"That sounds like a good idea." Sophie lay down on top of the comforter in her clothes. Sleep would help everything. "Goodnight, Harriet."

"Bye, honey. Love you."

•　　•　　•

Sophie arrived at work early the following day. Helen Richardson had contracted her to restore the grounds of a historic waterfront colonial on the Baltimore Harbor. A substantial amount of money had gone into renovating the place. From the foundation to the roof and everything in between, the entire building had needed attention and refurbishing. The courtyard would be Mrs. Helen Richardson's last project, and she hovered on the second-story balcony to oversee the progress, always with a book in her hand.

Helen looked on as Rigo laid the mosaic tiles on the bottom of the fountain. Rigo had pieced together dozens of mosaics, his experience ensuring there would be no mistakes.

"Is she still pretending to read up there so she can keep an eye on me and make sure I don't steal anything?" asked Rigo as Sophie passed him some more tile pieces.

"Yup." A hint of a smile played across her face, the first one since her fight with Adam.

"She makes me feel like I just got out of prison or something." Rigo aligned a tile square. His deep-brown eyes focused as he built the ornate pattern she had designed.

"Don't pay her any attention. Everything looks fantastic. I can't believe how fast you're moving." Sophie looked on as her design came to life under Rigo's skilled hands, one glistening ceramic square at a time.

"Not fast enough." He nodded toward Mrs. Richardson.

"Don't worry about her. Let her watch you. She just might learn something about real work." This lady was so ridiculously inappropriate and had been since they'd started the job. Her behavior around Rigo was absurd to the point of humor, only it wasn't funny.

"Thanks for saying that." Rigo glanced up from his work. "It gets kind of old, you know?"

Actually, Sophie didn't know. "I can only imagine."

"It's nice to see you smiling." Rigo changed the subject, continuing to fit the pieces together.

"I took a jog this morning. It always helps me recenter."

"I'm glad to hear it."

She could tell he meant it. Rigo listened to her, unlike Adam, who blindly agreed with her until their conversations fizzled out. Sophie didn't know how she could have gotten through the last few years without Rigo.

"Pass me some turquoise, triangular pieces, will you?" He held his hand out for the materials.

"Sure. Here." She pressed the tiles into his palm, feeling his calloused hands against hers.

"So what did Adam do this time?"

Sophie sat beside Rigo on the cement wall and told him what she had found on Adam's phone, leaving out the part where he had grabbed her wrists.

Rigo shook his head. "Wow, unbelievable. No, actually, I believe it." He stopped arranging the tiles and raised an eyebrow at Sophie. "Tell me for real, though. Are you surprised?"

"What do you mean by that? *Am I surprised?* Of course, I'm surprised. I didn't know any of that was going on." The feigned incredulity felt like an ill-fitting mask on her face. Truthfully, she'd had her suspicions, but didn't want Rigo to think she was the kind of person someone could walk all over.

"Okay." Rigo dropped the conversation and gave the fountain his full attention.

In the midmorning sun, Sophie sat contemplating the last few days. She didn't know how he did it, but Rigo always saw everything coming. How could he have seen this? The real question was, how could she have missed it? Maybe she had just been lying to herself, subconsciously looking the other way out of convenience and complacency. "How did you know about his cheating?" she finally asked.

"I don't think we should get into any more of this today," he said calmly. His voice held no judgment.

"You're probably right." Sophie eyed the balcony where Helen Richardson lingered, her suspicious gaze boring a hole into Rigo's back.

•　　•　　•

After dark that evening, Sophie pulled into her driveway. Without showering, she changed into an old pair of gray sweatpants and a T-shirt, then poured herself a glass of merlot and stretched out in the lounge chair on her patio. It was the only place where she could relax, the only place that didn't remind her of Adam.

Bower vines swallowed the wooden pergola, and a stone sink flanked the stainless-steel grill. She stared into the bushes, sipping the burgundy liquid. When the night air turned cool, she rose to collect a down comforter from the linen closet and the bottle of wine from the kitchen counter, returning to her post on the patio.

Clouds passed over a crescent moon, smiling down on her like the Cheshire Cat, laughing at where her life had ended up. She looked away from the taunting moon, and her thoughts turned to Rigo. Even though they talked all the time, she didn't know as much about his personal life as he did about hers. He had a way of redirecting the conversation back to what was happening in her life, just like Harriet.

Too bad he was off-limits. She pictured his chest muscles moving under his work T-shirts and had to remind herself not to go there. He worked for her. Plus, she was a married woman. Some marriage it had turned out to be. This last fight with Adam had been different. A permanence surrounded their parting ways. She had kicked him out, and their marriage was over. Why not allow her thoughts to rest on someone kind and handsome like Rigo while she knitted herself back together?

The vibration of her phone drew her out of her thoughts—a call from her sister. "Hey, Megan. What's up?" Sophie poured herself another glass of wine.

"I wanted to see how you were doing. I haven't heard from you this week."

Sophie knew better than that. Harriet had asked Megan to call and check on her. "I know Harriet asked you to call."

"Okay, she did, but that doesn't mean I don't want to hear what's going on with you. I guess a lot has changed since the last time we talked?"

"A lot!" Sophie paused before elaborating. "You know what? No. Nothing has *actually* changed." She was seeing things clearly, taking stock of the last few years through an unfiltered lens.

"What do you mean?" her sister asked. "Harriet said Adam was cheating on you."

"What I mean is exactly what I said. Nothing's changed. The only thing that's different is that I'm aware of what's been going on. It's not like this just happened. It's been happening."

"I guess that's one way to look at it." Her sister waited for her to continue.

"I don't know why I didn't push harder for the truth," said Sophie. "Maybe it was just easier to believe he was working late at the office. It sounds so stupid now that I'm saying those words out loud—*working late at the office.* Isn't that everyone's excuse when they're having an affair? He couldn't have bothered to come up with something more original?"

"Sophie, you know I never liked him."

"I know. You've always been very clear about that."

"But I never wanted any of this to happen to you. Whether or not I ever liked Adam, I always wanted the best for *you*."

Sophie set her wineglass on the concrete slab. "I know. I just got tired of hearing it from you."

"Is that why you haven't been up to see me?" Megan asked.

Her sister lived in Pittsburg. True, Sophie hadn't made the trip to see her in years, but that didn't mean she hadn't seen her at all. Megan came to all the holiday parties at Harriet's house.

"What we need to do is get you hooked up with someone new." Megan wasn't wasting any time.

Sophie didn't want to offend her sister, but it had only been a few days. "I think I might need a while longer before you start setting me up, Megan."

"Fine, I get it. Seriously, take all the time you need. Just know that I'm here for you, and I'm still in touch with a lot of our friends from high school. Some of those guys are single, too."

"High school?" Now Sophie was offended. "Please don't fix me up with anyone who went to our high school."

"Only trying to help."

"It's just been … a lot." Sophie pulled the comforter higher and tucked it under her chin. "What do you think about all of those scuba trips Adam took? I mean, he has that display case with his artifacts and that Spanish coin, but those could be fake. Do you think he was really meeting other women instead of going on those dives?"

"Now you're thinking how you should have been thinking the entire time, but no, I think his stupid obsession is real. Remember Neil?"

Sophie closed her eyes, conjuring a remote picture of one of Megan's many exes. "Okay, yeah. I remember him now. He's the one who always prefaced everything he said with the phrase 'that being said.'"

"Yes!" Megan laughed out loud. "He's the 'that being said' guy. You got it. Anyway, he and Adam went on one of those expeditions together one time, and let me tell you, Adam is obsessed. Neil said he was just going to have a good time—beers, burgers, time with the guys—but Adam was relentless about his grids and dive times. Neil even showed me a video of Adam blowing up at the captain for making a wrong turn."

"I'll probably be wondering about everything he's ever told me now. If he lied to my face while he was cheating, he could have been lying about anything."

"True, but I wouldn't focus on that. What did Harriet say?"

"You know exactly what Harriet said." Sophie brought her arms out and flopped them on top of the comforter. "She's the reason you called me. Remember?"

"Well, I'm glad I did, aren't you?"

"Yeah. It's probably good for me to talk about it."

"Keeping everything inside isn't good for you, Sophie."

The bottle of wine ran dry long before their conversation, and it was after midnight when Sophie wished her sister a good night, falling asleep outside on the patio.

Chapter 5

Adam
Guadalajara, Mexico

Sophie hadn't used the plane ticket, and Adam hadn't mentioned it to anyone. It had been a few weeks, and no one had asked about Sophie yet. He figured he was in the clear. Sammie had broken things off with him a couple of days after he had left, not wanting to bother with a long-distance affair. Adam knew she didn't need him. She was young and beautiful—using him just like he'd been using her, and now they were both done using each other.

He was adjusting well to the differences between the two countries. In the US, his workdays began at six, but in Mexico, they started at nine, and he would enjoy it while he could.

With a rudimentary understanding of the Spanish language, Adam could get by, but Empire had hired Carlos, a bright, young site supervisor, who did all the translating. Carlos helped Adam not only with the language barrier but also with understanding the cultural differences. Anything Adam didn't understand, Carlos was right there to explain. He wished his field managers in the US were half as efficient.

When Carlos invited him to the mango fair, held in his childhood village, Adam hadn't refused. The fair had started as a celebration of the maturation of the mangos that grew wild in the region but had evolved over time. He had been secretly hoping for an invitation, having heard the tradesman talk about the event on the Comp Zero site all week. It would be Adam's first trip out of the city.

•   •   •

Adam had been waiting a little over an hour when Carlos pulled up to the curb in a 2002 Chevy Malibu. Grupero music spilled from the sedan, playing as loud as its tired speakers could manage. In dark-blue jeans and a long-sleeved, western shirt, Carlos looked like he was going to a rodeo. Adam questioned his own choice of khakis and a polo shirt as he got into the back seat.

"I'm glad you decided to come," said Carlos, glancing over his shoulder. "It'll be nice for you to see more of Mexico."

"I appreciate the invite. It's been a long time since I've been to a fair."

The site supervisor pulled away from the curb, throwing Adam's head against the headrest. It wasn't Carlos's driving skills but the age of the vehicle that made for an unexpectedly jerky ride through the streets of Guadalajara. His wife sat in the passenger seat, and Adam rode beside a young boy in the back. Both of them appeared unbothered by the bumpy ride.

"I think it'll be fun for you. We go every year." Carlos adjusted the rearview mirror to see Adam. "This is my wife, Amelia, and that's Joaquín beside you."

A sharp left jolted Adam's shoulder into the door panel, and he braced himself with the handle. "Nice to meet you."

"Mucho gusto." Amelia nodded kindly.

"Say hi to Mr. Adam, Joaquín," Carlos instructed his son.

Joaquín turned his head away from the newcomer to look out of the car window.

"Joaquín is very shy," explained Carlos.

"That's all right. I'm going to look out my window, too. There's a lot to see out there, right Joaquín?" Adam got no response.

They drove over a pothole, which lifted everyone a few inches off their seats except for Joaquín, fastened securely in his car seat.

"Do you like Grupero?" asked Carlos.

"What's that?"

"That's what we're listening to."

It was still hard for Adam to distinguish between genres of music in Mexico. For him, the sounds blended together, but he didn't want to be rude. "It's pretty good." Adam couldn't decipher the lyrics, but a lot of brass was coming through.

Carlos turned up the radio and held his wife's hand. The couple exchanged a look Adam and Sophie had never exchanged in all their years of marriage.

They rode out of the city and wound through the mountains north of Guadalajara. Adam let go of the handle. The countryside slipped past his window—the Sierra Madres silhouetted by the setting sun. As the city lights faded, his window to the Mexican countryside turned black. With no streetlights to illuminate the mountain roads, Carlos relied on his headlights alone, winding their way to the fair. As they neared the village of San Cristóbal, they passed over a narrow bridge.

"Oh my God! What's that smell?" said Adam. He wasn't sure if he should roll his window up to shut the smell out or keep the window down so the smell wouldn't get trapped inside the vehicle.

"Sorry, I forgot to warn you," said Carlos. "It's the water." Amelia made eye contact with her husband, wanting to know what was wrong.

"What's going on with the water?" Adam asked, stifling dry heaves.

Joaquín peeked over his car seat and laughed at Adam's noises.

"Nada más que huele el río, mi vida." Carlos explained Adam's outburst to his wife before answering his question.

"No one knows for sure. Industrialization, I guess. It hasn't smelled right in fifteen years. It's sad." Carlos paused. "When I was a kid, my brothers and I used to swim in this river while my mother washed our clothes."

Adam couldn't imagine that. He couldn't even imagine breathing through his nostrils at this point.

"It's not as bad as it seems," Carlos assured him. "The entire river isn't like this, just this section, and it doesn't smell at all in the wet season."

How could anyone get used to the smell of stale sewage baking in the sun? Adam lifted himself off his seat and glared over the guardrail. Foam backed up behind boulders, breaking the river's surface.

"It gets better after the dry season," said Carlos. "It's a shame the mangos mature at the hottest and driest time of year."

"Why haven't they moved the fair to another location?" asked Adam. It only made sense.

"Who knows?" Carlos shrugged, keeping his hands on the wheel. "This is the worst part, crossing the river. It's not as bad in the village. You won't even notice the smell after a while."

Adam let it drop. He was their guest and grateful for the night's diversion. It was getting lonely going home to an empty townhouse every night after work since he had been in Mexico. He didn't want to offend Carlos or his family.

They turned off the main road onto the cobblestone streets of San Cristóbal. Multicolored lights from the fair shone in the valley below, and the main road sloped sharply downward, splitting the village in two. At the end of the road towered an overloaded Ferris wheel, and barely visible behind all the blinking lights, tucked next to the church, was a graveyard—small and silent.

Amelia stepped from the family car and unbuckled Joaquín from his car seat. She passed the little boy to Carlos as some of their friends came to greet them. Even with many more years of Spanish class, Adam could never have kept up with the rapid-fire conversation, and he wasn't going to try.

"Come and join us," said Carlos, waving Adam over to the group.

"That's okay," said Adam, holding his hand up. He let Carlos know he would not be responsible for translating that evening. "Go have fun with your family. I'll walk around and explore on my own."

"Okay, whatever you like. We'll be by the rides if you change your mind."

"I'll be fine. You guys have fun." Adam signed off with a casual wave.

On his own, Adam strode down the hill toward the festivities, passing groups of friends, couples, and families. He didn't need anybody else to have a good time. With plenty to do, he just needed to loosen up a bit. Ahhh, a beer tent. He could get behind that. Adam sat at a pop-up table under the tent and ordered a Sol. Even after dark, the air in San Cristóbal retained the heat from the day. The surrounding mountains killed any breeze that might have provided some relief. He sipped his beer, feeling the cold liquid travel down his throat.

The drinks relaxed him. It wasn't so bad, not having Carlos at his side. He could figure things out on his own. With his hands in his pockets, Adam continued his stroll downhill toward the line of vendors where a man was making potato chips. His sign read Papas. The vendor shaved slices of potatoes into a pile, then dropped them into a large pot of boiling oil, extracting them with a long, metal strainer. A sprinkle of salt and a few shakes of hot sauce finished the treat. Adam ordered some papas for himself, using a combination of broken Spanish and hand gestures.

As he crunched on the chips, he thought another drink might go well with the salty snack and headed back toward the beer tent, passing through a flood of latecomers as he climbed the hill. Adam emerged on the other side of the crowd and sat across from a strikingly beautiful woman under the tent. Without Sammie or Sophie, he was free to meet whoever he wanted. Adam pulled out his phone to check the time, trying to appear casual. Before he could think of something to say, the mystery woman asked him a question.

"Y te hablas Español?"

Adam's eyes explored her full lips as she spoke. "Um, I only speak a little Spanish. Could you speak slower?"

"How … about … like … this?" She gave him a smirk and crossed her legs under the table.

Familiar words had never sounded so out of place, and his ears embraced these sounds they'd been craving. "You speak English?" Adam hadn't expected it. This would make things so much easier.

"Yes, I learned it in school. And how about you? How is your Spanish?"

Adam held her gaze. Shiny locks of raven hair cascaded over her shoulder and her almond-shaped eyes sparkled, reflecting the lights from the fair. "Un poquito solamente. Palabras para el trabajo más o menos." He only knew a little Spanish—mostly construction vocabulary.

"I think we'd better speak English."

What a snarky comment. He liked that. She had said it without saying it. His Spanish was bad, but he already knew that. "English it is. I'm Adam." He set the bag of chips on the table and extended his hand to her. "It's nice to meet you."

"Marisol." She accepted his outstretched hand. "Mucho gusto."

After their official introduction, the server approached their table. "¿Qué quieren tomar?" He asked for their order from underneath the brim of a cowboy hat. A tight, cotton shirt proudly displayed his biceps, but he wasn't competition—too young.

Marisol answered for them, having already established Adam's limitations with the language. "Quiero una horchata, por favor," said Marisol. The young man acknowledged her order, and she turned to Adam. "You should try the horchata."

"What is it?" Adam was willing to try anything, but needed to know what he was getting into first.

The server let Marisol explain. "It's a traditional drink made from rice, milk, and cinnamon."

"Sure. Why not? Make it two horchatas." Adam laid fifty pesos on the table, the equivalent of three dollars. "It's good to try new things, right? Tell me, though, are you here alone?"

"Yes and no," was all she said.

Vague. What the hell did that mean? She was difficult to read, and her accent made it hard to pick up on the nuances of language that would ordinarily offer some insight. Adam pulled another papa from the bag, then offered one to his new companion.

"No, thanks," she said, "but I'm curious. How did you end up at the mango fair? It isn't exactly a tourist attraction." Marisol rested her back against her chair, waiting for his response.

Okay, change of subject. They were talking about him, which was fine. "I'm here on business."

"At the mango fair on business, what do you sell?"

"I'm actually in Guadalajara on business." He corrected himself. "I'm a project manager for a commercial construction company."

"So you build things." The server placed the drinks on the table. Marisol politely thanked him and took a sip of her rice drink.

"Well, *I* don't do any of the building," Adam clarified. "Our company manages construction projects. We submit the bids and manage the work done by the subcontractors." He could smell the cinnamon wafting from his drink.

"Really? Which project are you managing here in Mexico?"

"It's a corporate headquarters for an international software company in the city."

Interest pooled in her brown eyes. "I think you may be working with my cousin."

Cool beads of condensation slid down their glasses, and Adam tucked a napkin under his glass. "Who's your cousin?"

"Carlos Valdez."

What were the odds? He had only met a handful of people so far, too few for any of them to know one another. "You probably won't believe this," he told her, "but I came here with Carlos and his family tonight." He waited for her reaction, but she showed no surprise.

"That's not as crazy as you might think. Everybody knows everybody in los ranchos. Carlos is my mother's brother's son. My full name is Marisol Valdez Avila, but you're stalling." She pointed at his glass. "Take a drink."

"Yes, ma'am." As instructed, he took a sip. It was a little sweet for his taste, like drinking watered-down ice cream, but he said he liked it. He didn't want to be rude. "You never answered my question before. Are you here alone?"

"Why don't we walk around the fair?" Marisol offered.

She had sidestepped the question again. Whatever. He would let it go. She wasn't wearing a ring, but then again, neither was he. "Let's walk." Adam left another fifty pesos on the table. He admired her skill as she navigated the cobblestone streets in high heels. "What would you recommend we do first?"

"Do you dance?"

He hadn't meant that. "I was thinking about trying some more of these carnival creations," he suggested, nodding at the vendor scooping helado.

"Not a dancer," she said. "You're interested in food—anything else?" She waited while he thought.

"How about taking a ride on the Ferris wheel?" He wouldn't mind getting closer to Marisol. The seats weren't that wide, and he pictured himself snuggly pressed against her curvy hips.

"Sounds good to me. I wanted to go that way, anyway."

They continued down the hill. Marisol held her arms out here and there to balance herself on the uneven path, and Adam soaked in the new sights and smells as they walked. The scent of grilled chicken filled the air, and well-manicured fruit trees occupied every break in the walkways. It was nice to be out, doing something outside his normal routine.

"What's that?" he asked, pointing at dry, orange shapes that puffed up when fried in oil.

"Those are chicharrones," said Marisol, touching a hand to her smiling lips. She looked over her shoulder at him. He had fallen behind her in the crowd. "You're so funny."

"What do you mean?" Adam took a few quick steps to catch up.

"I have to explain things to you like I have to explain them to my nieces and nephews."

"Thanks," he said. "So now you think I'm annoying?"

"I didn't say that." Her deadpan delivery gave him pause, but she continued in a friendly tone. "I am having fun with you, though. It's interesting how different things can be from one country to another. For example, what are you wearing?" She looked him up and down.

What was *he* wearing? What was *she* wearing? Why would anyone wear five-inch heels to a smelly festival with cobblestone streets? Carlos had been wrong. The smell wasn't *as* bad, but it was still very noticeable.

From the top of the Ferris wheel, black mountains blended with the night sky under an umbrella of stars. The two of them made the most of their unanticipated connection, riding the scrambler and eating ice cream. Adam won Marisol an enormous teddy bear by knocking down a stack of cans—after seventeen tries. When they found themselves close to the graveyard, his new friend pulled him aside. Marisol backed up to the rock fence and used the palms of her hands to push herself up, then swung her legs over the piled stones and hopped down on the other side.

"Pass me the bear." She held out her hands.

"What are you doing?" Adam whispered.

"Just pass me the bear." She motioned for him to hand it over. "My heels are sinking in the dirt."

Adam passed her the teddy bear, and she carried it to a cluster of small headstones. Marisol laid the bear next to an assortment of weatherworn trinkets lining the grave markers, said something Adam couldn't make out, then joined him once again. This time, she unlatched the gate from inside the yard so she wouldn't have to climb.

"What did you say in there?" Adam asked, peering over the fence, trying to decipher the etchings on the stones.

"Just a prayer."

"Oh." Adam wasn't a Catholic.

"I know that might have seemed a little strange to you. I should've explained, but I'm used to everyone knowing everything in this small town."

He'd never lived in a small town before. "You don't owe me any explanations," said Adam. They had just met, and it was her business.

"Well, everyone else knows. So why not you, too?" She wrapped her arms around herself. "I am here alone." She had finally answered his question, but he'd figured as much. "But,"—she kept going—"I wasn't always alone. My three sons are buried here."

He looked past the rock fence, still unable to read the names on the grave markers. "Oh, I'm sorry. I had no idea …"

"How could you have known? It's okay—really."

She wasn't upset with him, but he felt the need to apologize. Only, it's challenging enough to find the right words for a subject like this with a long-time friend, let alone someone you just met. Adam looked past the twinkling lights reflected in her eyes, catching a glimpse of the dark space behind them. "I'm so sorry, Marisol."

"Me, too."

All around, kids laughed, music played, and people danced, but where they stood next to the cemetery, a quiet sadness rested its silent hands on their shoulders.

"I'm surprised," Adam said, filling the dead space between them. "You look so young. I never would have imagined … three sons?" He gestured for them to sit on a wooden bench next to the stone wall.

Marisol accepted his offer. "Yes. Three. I was married once. My husband and I had three baby boys. Unfortunately, as you can see,"—she pointed over the fence—"none of them lived—all were stillborn."

Adam still couldn't see. The lights from the fair made the graveyard seem even darker. He couldn't see any names or dates, but would take her word for it. The thought of dead babies buried beyond the fence had extinguished the flame of childlike excitement generated by the fair. This time, he changed the subject.

"Your cousin, Carlos, has been a great asset on the jobsite. His language skills are incredible, and he knows his way around every trade."

"Thanks," said Carlos, walking up behind them with his wife and son.

Just in time, thought Adam. The story about her sons had been too much.

"Sorry to cut your time short, but Joaquín is sick. We have to take him home." Amelia held their toddler in her arms. His face looked pale.

"Of course," said Adam, quickly standing. "Is he going to be all right? What happened?"

"You know kids," said Carlos. "Sometimes it comes on fast. We were on the Ferris wheel, then he had some helado, and after that, the helado came back up. He'll be okay."

"I'm ready when you are," said Adam. "It was nice meeting you, Marisol. Maybe we could get together sometime."

Carlos's wife shot her husband a look. "¡Vámonos pues!"

"Sometime sounds good," said Marisol. She turned to Amelia. "Ojalá que todo estará bien con Joaquín."

Adam followed Carlos to the car, sensing the urgency in Amelia's voice. He rode next to little Joaquín, who was growing sicker by the minute. When the stench of the river hit the boy as they passed over the bridge, all bets were off. Vomit—all over Adam's khakis. The kid had eaten tacos and potato chips in addition to the helado. Warm, partially digested food soaked through his pant legs, and he tried not to let the boy's parents see the look of disgust on his face. Carlos's wife offered him her shawl to mop it up and apologized profusely in Spanish. Adam would ride by himself next time.

Chapter 6

Sophie

Sophie woke up freezing on Saturday morning. Cold dew drops covered the steel arms of the lounge chair. When she sat up, her oversize comforter knocked over the empty wine bottle, sending it clanking against the concrete patio. What she needed was a hot shower and a cup of tea. She left the soggy comforter outside. Under a stream of hot water, she flexed her tingling fingers as the heat chased the cold from her bones.

Down in the kitchen, wrapped in her terry-cloth robe, Sophie cupped a heavy mug filled with Lemon Zinger tea, but she couldn't sit around all day feeling sorry for herself, not while Adam was in Mexico doing … whatever. Why not work? It's not like she had anything better to do. Mrs. Richardson would be glad to have the job finished ahead of time. All they had left was the plant shopping. She had to do something, and working seemed like a productive rather than self-destructive choice. So she called Rigo.

•   •   •

The vibrating hum of the company truck preceded him as Rigo rounded the patch of azaleas in bloom at the end of the Richardsons' driveway. He pulled up beside the fountain and stepped down from the cab.

Sophie met him by the truck. "I thought I'd ride with you to the nursery."

Rigo stood with his thumbs in his pockets, involuntarily flexing his triceps against the taut fabric of his T-shirt. "I figured you would. Are you ready to go?"

She told him she was and climbed into the passenger side. Rigo was so positive, making everything easy, always working with her—never against her.

"Where to today?" He put the truck in reverse, but kept his foot on the brake. "You should put your seat belt on."

She pulled the belt over her shoulder. "Let's go to Leroy's, since we're already in the city."

Rigo waited until he heard the click of her belt before taking his foot off the brake. One long, vinyl seat spanned the length of the cab underlaid with industrial springs. Sophie was acutely aware of the jiggle in her breasts as they bounced up and down, headed out of the driveway. She wondered if Rigo noticed.

Leroy must not have heard them pull up. Sophie and Rigo stepped into the small shed where the aging proprietor huddled next to his space heater. Every time the machine swiveled, a current of air would ruffle his stacks of papers.

"What's new today, Leroy?" Rigo asked.

"Shit! Why're you always sneakin' up on me?" Leroy pulled on a second jacket and led the two of them outside. "It's cold today." Leroy was always cold.

"You're going to burn this place down one day." Rigo reached into the shed and paused the swivel function on the space heater.

Leroy blew into his hands and rubbed them together. "I just got a shipment of low-growing succulents that'd be great for a rock garden." He arched an eyebrow, tempting a purchase.

"We're looking for more color," said Sophie. "Something full and bright, but able to withstand the frosty nights we're still having."

"We're all trying to withstand these frosty nights." Leroy shuffled and steered them slowly to a row of flowers hidden behind stacked pallets of stone. Sophie estimated Leroy was approaching eighty. He stopped in front of an assortment of proud petals, standing tall in the cool morning air. "How about some flowering perennials like these white daisies and purple pansies?"

Sophie paced along the hidden line of flowers. "They look great. What do you think, Rigo? Mrs. Richardson might like them."

Rigo hesitated before answering. "I don't think she likes anything. I'm glad we're getting this job over with today."

Wow. He never said things like that. Mrs. Richardson must've really gotten to him.

"So what d'you think?" Leroy chimed in. "Is this lady gonna like 'em or not? It's cold out here."

"We'll take them all," said Sophie.

"Okay then. I'll go get the invoice ready." Leroy returned to the shed to fill out the paperwork.

Rigo loaded the truck while Sophie paid the bill. Three hundred dollars for a stake bed full of flowers and shrubs. That's why she came to Leroy. The nurseries in the suburbs would have charged twice as much.

"Hey, Leroy?" said Rigo, leaning out of the truck. "You want us to bring you a cup of coffee? We're grabbing one across the street."

"You know it!" Leroy called through the window of his shed. "Be right back."

They'd had no plans to get coffee. Rigo had just noticed Leroy struggling with the cool morning and couldn't resist making a kind gesture. How was he still single? Or was he still single? He hadn't mentioned any dates in a while, but that didn't mean there hadn't been any.

The wind blew across the harbor, forming choppy waves that reflected the sunlight as they worked. Mrs. Richardson had found her way onto the balcony, but her book sat idly on the glass tabletop as her eyes tracked the two of them.

"You've been kind of quiet since we got back. Is something wrong?" asked Sophie. "I hope I didn't take you away from any plans, calling you in to work today."

"No," Rigo said. "It's good that you called. You shouldn't be alone after what happened with you and Adam. It's just ..." He moved his eyes toward the balcony.

She knew exactly what he meant. "Look, we're almost done here, but if you want me to say something, I will." Sophie wasn't just saying that either—enough was enough.

"No, don't do that." He shook his head. "It's fine. Plus, it probably wouldn't do any good, anyway."

Mrs. Richardson's phone rang while they were planting daisies. She took the call inside and Rigo cracked his neck, relaxing his shoulders, before rising to collect the rest of the flowers from the truck. He returned, setting the pansies beside Sophie. Dozens of smiling, purple faces swayed in the breeze, blowing inland from the harbor.

"So how's your mom doing?" Sophie liked hearing about Rigo's family in Mexico. He made it sound so beautiful.

"Are you sure you want me to tell you about Mexico today?"

"I'm fine. I mean…it's fine. Yes." They couldn't skirt around select topics forever. "We can just be normal with each other. You don't have to avoid talking about anything with me."

"Okay. Well, my mom just moved in with my abuela in García." Rigo started removing the pansies from the plastic garden trays.

"Which village is that again?" Sophie sat in the dirt, watching the wind blow Rigo's T-shirt.

"That's the one close to Guadalajara."

Guadalajara. That's where Adam's job was. Sophie tried to keep her face from falling. "I thought your mom just redid her bathroom. What made her decide to move?"

"My abuela's getting older, and my mother is her oldest daughter. That's how it works—family first."

He said that so simply, as if taking care of family was like drinking a glass of water.

"Eventually, I'll move back to Mexico to help my mom. My sister won't be able to go because of her husband's business in Alexandria."

"And what about your dad?"

Rigo moved his hands to his hips, watching the waves as he spoke. "He passed when I was young."

"I'm so sorry, Rigo." How could she not have known this? Sophie knew something was amiss with Rigo's father, but never thought he had died. Was she really so focused on herself that she hadn't bothered to find out about this huge part of Rigo's life until now? "What happened?"

"Most people blame it on the ranch." He tore his eyes from the horizon and continued loosening the flowers from the nursery plant pots.

Sophie squinted in his direction. "Did your dad have some sort of accident on the ranch?"

"Not exactly. He wanted to expand the business and purchased a neighboring orchard, but after a year, it stopped producing."

What did an under-producing ranch have to do with his father's death? Sophie broke the root clusters as Rigo handed her the flowers. She waited for him to elaborate.

"As far as my dad could tell, nothing was wrong with the trees." Rigo pierced the soil with his shovel, creating pockets for the flowers. "Before he bought the property, people had warned him that the orchard would bring its owner nothing but bad luck. I guess they were right because shortly after the trees stopped producing, my father died."

"You know, and I know, that bad luck can't kill someone. What do you think really happened to him?"

Rigo stopped digging. "We think it was a burst appendix, but nothing was ever confirmed. It was sudden, and people don't go to the doctor in los ranchos like they do here." Rigo leaned on his shovel, remembering the details of how his father passed. "We tried all the home remedies first—teas, rest, herbal pastes—but he wasn't getting better. The nearest clinic was a day's ride on horseback from los ranchos, and he died less than an hour into the journey."

"Wow … I'm sorry." What else could she say?

Once the trash had been cleared, Sophie surveyed the job one more time—perfect, everything she had envisioned. Helen hadn't returned to the balcony, and Sophie thought it best not to ring the doorbell. She would email the final invoice.

Inside her car, Sophie searched for her phone in her purse when Rigo knocked on her window. She rolled down the glass. "What's up?"

"Would you like to go to dinner with me tonight?"

Her face flushed as she recalled her recent thoughts about him. She didn't think she'd been behaving any differently and certainly hadn't said anything to Rigo.

"I was wondering if you wanted to have dinner with me tonight," he asked again.

"I … already made plans with a friend." This lie came tumbling from her mouth before she'd granted it permission.

"Some other time then." He tapped the roof of her car, turned, and made his way to the truck.

What did he mean by dinner? Was it dinner as friends? Dinner as more than friends? And why had she lied? Sophie pulled her phone from her purse and selected a calming playlist. Why hadn't she said yes to dinner? She had nothing going on that evening. She hadn't wanted to reach out to any friends just yet. If the conversation were to turn to Adam, she wasn't sure what she should say. Were they separated or not? Would they work through this? She wasn't sure she could ever work through it, or if she wanted to. What scared her most was not feeling strongly about it one way or another. They'd been so emotionally distant for so long. She didn't even know if she loved him anymore. It was hard to recall a time when she'd felt … anything for him.

Chapter 7

Esmeralda
García De La Cadena, Mexico
January 1987

Esmeralda pushed her way through the crowded streets of García in her rhinestone studded skirt with her midnight hair looped into a tight bun. The smoky scent of chicharrones traveled on the cool breeze swirling around the small village perched on top of the mountain.

Esmeralda fronted Los Avispones de Jalisco, a traditional Mariachi group, and the deep, rich tone of her voice had earned them the featured spot at the winter festival. Only thirty minutes until they were due on stage, but where were her bandmates?

She wove through the hordes of festivalgoers gathered in the square, headed toward the tallest tree in the village. The mammoth birch stretched its limbs to the sky, shading the people of García year after year. She stood on the brick wall surrounding the tree, scanning the crowd until she spotted them.

"Where have you guys been? And who's this?" Esmeralda gestured to a man with a gray beard whose arms rested on the shoulders of Beto, their trompetista, and Chofo, their guitarista.

"Who? This guy?" Beto pointed at the man she didn't know.

"Yes. *That guy*. Are you two drunk?" She pushed what's his name's arms from her bandmates' shoulders. "Come on." Esmeralda pulled Beto and Chofo toward the stage. "So who was that guy?"

Beto broke into a light jog to keep pace with Esmeralda. "He said his name was James."

She glanced over her shoulder. "He doesn't look like a James."

"I think it's the English name he gave himself in the US," said Chofo as they headed backstage to join the rest of the band. "He said he'd been out of the country for ten or twenty years. I don't remember. Why do you care, anyway?"

"I don't. He just looked familiar, but we see a ton of people at these things." Esmeralda moved on. "You guys need to drink some water."

"We're not that bad," said Beto, giving her a small kiss on the lips.

She pushed him away and thrust a cup into his hand. "Water. Drink it."

By the end of the show, "James" had carved a space for himself, center-stage. The stranger stared up at her, taking swigs from a half empty bottle of tequila. *Ugh, it was going to be one of those nights.* This wasn't anything new. She had dealt with her fair share of overzealous fans before, but to her relief, the man stumbled away after they had finished their cover of "El Zopilote Mojado." Lost, passed out, gone home—Esmeralda didn't care, just as long as he wasn't there.

Applause enveloped the village square, and one lone, loud whistle sailed over the crowd. Esmeralda's chest vibrated from within and she clasped her hands together. This had been their greatest concert yet! She surveyed the audience for anyone who looked important, anyone who could take them to the next level, but all she saw were the men and women of los ranchos.

"That was phenomenal," said Beto, wrapping his arms around her waist and lifting her into the air. "You were hitting everything tonight!"

"She always hits everything," said Chofo, unimpressed.

Esmeralda secured her microphone in the stand and smoothed her costume, taking a bow as the audience continued clapping. "You guys want to get something to eat?"

"Marcos, Manny, and I have plans already," said Chofo as they left the stage. All three glanced at each other, but it was no secret to anyone in the village, even Esmeralda, that the tack shop had a poker table in the storage room.

"I don't know how you guys can blow through your money like that," said Beto as he placed his trumpet in its velvet trimmed case.

"We don't plan on losing."

"No one ever *plans* to lose, Chofo." Beto closed and latched his case. "I have bigger plans for my money."

"We know, Beto. You tell us all the time," said Manny. "If only we could be more like you." Manny finished winding the cords and stowed them in the box next to his accordion.

"My man's going to be a lawyer." Esmeralda smiled at Beto. "And when we move to the city, I'm going to get us better venues and more money for these concerts."

"You won't need money by then if you're married to a lawyer." Chofo smugly pressed his lips together. "Let's go, guys. Beto can stay and hang out with the ladies if he wants to."

"*Lady*." Beto corrected his bandmate. "You all wish you had girlfriends." Hand in hand, Beto and Esmeralda made their way toward the taco truck parked on the far side of the birch.

"I get so hungry after a set like that." The taco vender passed Esmeralda a plate brimming with steak tacos buried in chopped onion, cilantro, and hot green salsa.

Beto's eyes moved between his meal and Esmeralda's. "I can't imagine what you'll eat when you're pregnant."

A hint of a smile danced across her face. "You're assuming I want kids."

"I just thought … that once I'm done with school, and we're living a nice life in Mexico City, I mean, don't you?"

"Of course I do," she said. "I had you going, though."

"That wasn't funny."

"It kind of was." Esmeralda made quick work of her first two tacos. "Listen. I think you should hang with the guys tonight."

"Why? I was being honest back there. I really don't want to lose any money."

"I know, but that doesn't mean you can't have some tequilas with the boys."

"That I could do." Beto stuffed the last of his tamale into his mouth and brushed the crumbs from his hands. "You've convinced me."

"Well, good. You'd better get moving before you miss all the fun. I'm just going to pack up the car."

"I'll help you."

She nodded toward the tack shop. "With the utility cart, I'll be fine. Seriously, go."

Beto deposited his wrapper in the trash and disappeared down the street, swallowed by the swarm of people.

Esmeralda returned her attention to her plate, but she had ordered too much. Unable to finish her last few tacos, she tossed her napkin on the pile of food. "Oh my God!" she gasped.

James was back. He had materialized out of nowhere, taking a seat across from her. "I wanted to tell you I enjoyed your singing tonight."

"Thank you." Esmeralda stood, holding her unfinished meal. "I'm glad you liked it." His eyes held a vacancy that turned her stomach, and the tacos she had eaten threatened to rejoin those still on her plate.

"I do a little singing myself," he said.

Yup. That's what they usually say. "Look, señor," she said, "I appreciate the compliment, but I'm here with someone. You might want to head home."

"That's probably a good idea, but could you point me in the right direction? I'm staying at the Hotel Nuñez."

"Señor, no one's called it that in ten years. Señora Nuñez passed, and it's now the Hotel De Las Montañas." She pointed down the street to where the village met the cornfields. "Go that way."

"Okay. Thank you." He faltered, side-stepped, then regained his balance.

There's always one of these guys. Once Mr. Drunk Festival Fan was out of sight, Esmeralda loaded the wheeled cart with their mics, cords, and her box of costumes. Her bandmates would take their own instruments with them. She pulled the cart along the cobblestone street, wishing she hadn't sent Beto away so soon. The cracks between the stones stalled her cart, demanding great effort with every tug. Ridiculous. Her arms grew tired and Esmeralda veered from the populated main street to the shadowy edge of the cornfield. Grass would be better than cobblestones.

It had seemed like a decent idea, but the local cattle had left deep divots in the soil. In the end, it was no better than the cobblestone streets. Esmeralda heaved, lifting the cart from a large hoofprint, when a man ran by and snatched her box of costumes. *What the?* She whirled around to see who it was. She'd been so focused on pulling the cart, she'd neglected to keep an eye on her surroundings.

The man cycled back, cradling the box in his arms. "Let me carry this for you," he said.

Oh shit, this guy again! "Look, I tried to be nice about it, but you need to back off!" She let go of the cart, and the hair on her arms stood on end. The eyes of drunk men lacked reason, but the stranger's eyes lacked more than that. He stared at her through two empty spheres, out of touch and devoid of emotion. Was he dangerous or just not right? Either way, she needed those costumes. They were expensive. "Give those back to me!"

"Let me help you," insisted the man, slurring his words. He ran into the cornfield with her box of costumes.

Esmeralda looked around for anyone within earshot, but her brilliant plan to pull the cart on the outskirts of the cornfield had squelched that prospect. Every costume in the box had been custom-made for her. This guy was probably just another harmless asshole, she tried to convince herself, ignoring her gut.

"Hey, bring my costumes back! What are you doing?" she called after him and followed James into the cornfield.

James wove in and out of the stalks—wobbly but quick. He stumbled and glanced over his shoulder, making sure she was still following.

This guy was an idiot. "Just give them to me!"

The lights from the festival could not penetrate the corn crop, and the overcast night concealed her view of the thief.

Esmeralda couldn't go any farther. She stopped following the stranger lost among the silent stalks. Going back was her only option. Considering how much the man had been stumbling, her costumes were probably scattered throughout the field. She would go to the tack shop and enlist the help of Los Avispones—The Hornets—relatively harmless alone, but lethal together.

She tromped her way through the field toward the village square. Brittle sheaths from last season's crop crunched underfoot, and she didn't hear him come up behind her. James drew close, forced his fingers through her tightly pulled hair, and swung her body to the ground. Her skull smacked against a rock fence, hidden by the season's lush plants, and the long leaves of maize swallowed the sound of breaking bone.

Chapter 8

Adam

The entire week after the mango fair was devoted to laying the bricks for the Comp Zero exterior. Carlos was a lifesaver on the jobsite, able to motivate the men as Adam could not do. At first, Adam thought he intimidated the men, but now he felt like they were purposely excluding him. Had he done something offensive? Whatever the reason for the cold shoulder, he was glad the weekend had arrived. He'd had problems concentrating on work all week. Every time he looked at Carlos, he wanted to ask about Marisol. They had left in such a rush last Friday he hadn't gotten her contact information.

With the tools locked in the gang box and the laborers gone for the day, Adam decided to ask Carlos where he could find his cousin. They didn't seem that close, but maybe Carlos had her number in his contacts.

"So you like her," said the site supervisor with a wide grin. "She's had a rough time, but she's a good one, Marisol." He pointed at Adam's bare ring finger. "I see you're not married."

There had been a white tan line when Adam had taken his ring off, but after working under the Guadalajara sun, it had disappeared. "I just thought it would be nice to get together with someone who speaks English. You know, for some company on my day off."

"Got it. I won't say anything else." Carlos held up his hands, and Adam knew he wasn't buying any of it.

"Well, do you have her number?"

"It's been a while since I've been to her ranch—too long, but last I heard, she didn't have a phone or power."

How could someone not have a phone? "Do you have her address?"

"I'll just tell you how to get there. Your GPS may not get a signal in the mountains."

"Hold on a second." Adam jogged to his SUV, returning with a clipboard of invoices and a pen to take down the directions.

"You go through las curvas on the same road we took to San Cristóbal," Carlos began. "Keep going north until you come to a village called El Mezquital del Oro. Across the street from that village is a gravel road. Follow the road until you come to the river. You'll find her. They still don't have electricity in parts of los ranchos, so you should plan on going in the daytime."

"Thanks, Carlos." Adam dropped his arm and held the clipboard at his side. "By the way, how's Joaquín doing?"

"Oh, he's doing fine. It was just motion sickness. This was his first year on some of the bigger rides."

Carlos beamed when he talked about his family, but all Adam thought of was the warm contents of Joaquín's stomach on his leg. Why would anyone want to have children? "That's good to hear. I hope you and your family have a nice weekend."

"See you Monday." Carlos set off toward his truck, but turned around. "Just be careful on the roads. There are some sharp turns."

"Will do." Adam nodded at his site supervisor and read over the directions he had jotted down on the back of an invoice—not too complicated. He placed his laptop in the passenger seat, fastened his seat belt, and pulled out of the Comp Zero lot.

Road signs were scarce leaving Guadalajara. The landscape quickly transformed from busy city streets, packed with stores and pedestrians, into rolling countryside. Roble trees—a species of oak—dotted the dry terrain. Foothills grew into sizable mountains, and the road hugged extreme curves. The trash littering the roadsides in the city disappeared, replaced by cacti. Silhouettes of the broad, flat nopal leaves and the towering limbs of the saguaro were etched onto the mountainous horizon.

An hour into the trip, the sun sank behind the mountains, creating an illusion of dusk. In the distance, a controlled brush fire crept along the side of a hill, leaving charred, black earth in its wake. Adam rolled down his window, and in wafted the scent of burning undergrowth mixed with dust, carried on the hot, dry air. He rounded another abrupt curve with no guardrail, felt the vehicle's center-of-gravity shift, and tried to concentrate less on the scenery and more on the road.

From a high branch in a grand magnolia tree, almost hidden by a bend in the road, hung the sign for El Mezquital del Oro, literally translated—mesquite wood of gold. Across the street from the village sprouted the gravel road Carlos had described. If he hadn't been looking for it, he would never have noticed it. Adam turned off the paved road and crunched down the bumpy gravel drive lined with barbed wire fencing. Large limbs had been cut from living trees and thrust into the ground as fence posts. Many of these tree branches had taken root in the ground, transforming themselves back into the trees from which they had come.

Only large enough to accommodate the width of one vehicle, the road demanded Adam pull over to make room for a stake bed truck stacked with wire cages full of chickens. It was a tight squeeze. Narrow driveways stemmed from the loose, rocky roadway, winding their way into the dry underbrush. He didn't know which one to take, so he continued straight as the road angled down, and a small valley came into view. The road ended abruptly at the river, just like Carlos had said.

It had been over two hours since he had left the construction site, and he wasn't sure he could navigate out of the valley without proper lighting. Dirt and gravel had fallen loose from the mountainside, forming piles on the road. The dry season had taken its toll. Without moisture and root systems to tie the ground together, the roads were filling in. They had not been that wide to begin with, and he had noted some steep drops along the way. It wasn't worth the risk. If he couldn't find Marisol, he would have to sleep in the SUV.

Even though the vanishing daylight barred his departure from los ranchos, adequate light remained to explore on foot. He had come this far and wouldn't waste the opportunity to do something new, one of the perks of his assignment in Mexico.

Adam hopped down from the truck and wandered toward the river, which would get much wider in the rainy season everybody said would come. It was hard to imagine rain and tall, green grass in this place. A cluster of mango trees boasted green leaves, but the surrounding vegetation stood dry and brittle, threatening to go up like a matchstick if exposed to the slightest spark. At least he would have something to eat for dinner. Hundreds of soft, ripe mangos littered the ground on the river's edge, emitting a sticky, sweet odor that might have been sickening if not balanced with the earthy scent of parched ground.

Smooth stones clattered under his feet as he walked along the riverbank in the direction of the current. A line of fat, black tadpoles swam downstream, flicking their slick tails. He followed this caravan of amphibians, attempting to clear his mind of deadlines and emails, homing in on the tiny ripples of water generated by these modest creatures.

"Hey, you!" someone shouted from behind, causing Adam to lose his balance on a wobbly rock. He sucked in a quick breath and caught himself with the palm of his hand. It wasn't Marisol, but a man's voice. Adam spun around toward the unknown voice and, seated on a boulder at the edge of the water, was an older man waving him over. With his back propped against the trunk of a tall fruit tree, the elderly man leisurely sucked on a mango pit. Adam hadn't expected to run into anyone other than Marisol and scoured his mind for the Spanish words needed to form an apologetic sentence.

"¿Y qué estás haciendo aquí, joven?" asked the unknown man, smacking his wrinkled lips.

Adam stepped tentatively toward the man, planting his feet in the wet sand. "I'm sorry, but I don't speak Spanish that well. Do you know any English?"

"My English is not good in years. I work in United States for five years, cuando era joven como tú. I forget a lot the English," said the old man, not budging from his spot under the mango tree.

"Well, your English is better than my Spanish." Adam was sure he could understand him well enough.

"What you are doing here?" asked the old man. "What you name is?"

"Oh, sorry, I'm Adam, and I was hoping you could help me."

"What you need?" The man threw the wet mango pit into the sand and started peeling another fruit with a pocket knife.

"I'm looking for Marisol. Do you know where I can find her?"

"¿Cuál Marisol?"

This seemed to have piqued his interest because he looked up from his work with the mango. Adam had never heard the name before. Honestly, how many Marisols could there be around there? He thought of how to describe her to the older man, but before he could speak, the man began rattling off all the Marisols he had ever met.

"There is Marisol de Jesus, Marisol de los Castros, Marisol de Nacho—"

Adam broke in. "I'm looking for Marisol Valdez."

"Oh, Marisol de Christo," said the man, nodding.

"No, she said her name was Marisol Valdez Avila."

"Sí, Marisol married to Christo Avila Nuñez. You looking for Marisol de Christo." The old man attempted to stand, swinging his arms forward, still holding on to his pocket knife and partially peeled mango, but his efforts weren't strong enough to raise him from the boulder.

"I don't think this Marisol is married anymore." Adam corrected the old man. "Do you need some help?" He held out his hand and took a couple more strides closer to the stranger.

"No, no," said the man, waving Adam away. "Ella es una viuda—how you say—widow. Her husband die crossing the border." The man put his knife down and placed one hand on the rock behind his back, pushing himself to his feet. "That what people say. Her husband leave, and no come back for years. Christo go to find work in United States, como yo, but he never come back."

Adam took a moment to assess the old man's balance. Now that he was up, he was doing okay. "Do you know where I can find her?"

"Sure," said the man, pointing at the gravel road. "Follow the road where you come from. Cuando you see to go left or right, go right. She live at the end of the road with her kids."

Kids? Adam hadn't come all the way out there to spend time with a woman who had kids. What about everything she had said at the mango fair—the teddy bear in the graveyard? Maybe the old man had gotten his words mixed up, but Adam wasn't going to call him out on it.

"You understand los directions?" asked the old man, eager to help.

"Yeah, I got it, but it's getting dark." Adam didn't want to chance driving out of the valley that evening. He would have to back up a fair part of the way before he could turn the truck around, and he wasn't interested in trekking up the hill on foot with the rattlesnakes and scorpions. He would stick to his original plan. "Do you own this land? Is there somewhere I could stay for the night?"

"This is the land of my brother." With one hand on his back, the old man straightened his torso and shuffled over to shake Adam's hand. "I am Alberto, and my brother, his name is Javier."

"Is he around? Would he mind if I just slept in the truck?"

"Javier spend most of his time in the city. We are, how you say, retired, but he have many properties. My brother, he went to the college and the university, and work a lot outside the country."

Adam's thoughts returned to how he might climb his way back to the main highway.

"But,"—the old man wasn't done—"we stay here tonight, you and me. Tomorrow morning, I teach you fishing."

Thank God. He wouldn't have to find a way out of there, but the fishing concerned him. Did this river connect with the polluted river running past San Cristóbal? Adam held his cell phone in the air to find out—no signal. He threw up his hands, used to having the answers to his questions at his fingertips. It looked like he would have to wade through conversation with Alberto for the answers to his questions tonight.

Alberto grew nimbler the more he moved around. He started a fire with an armful of bone-dry logs and spread a dusty afghan on the riverbank. The breeze blowing through the valley pulled the temperature down for the night, and Adam watched the fire closely, not wanting a stray spark to ignite the surrounding brush.

"You want some?" Alberto held a full bottle of tequila over his head.

"Where did you get that?" Alberto had all the creature comforts there by the river, having stashed things behind various rocks. "Of course, I'll have some." Adam waited to see where he had squirreled away the cups.

Alberto poured two generous glasses. The distilled beverage helped Adam follow Alberto's broken English as the old man lay on the crocheted blanket, telling stories about the Mexican Revolution and buried treasure.

"I think we have more in common than I would have guessed, my friend," Adam said, helping himself to another glass of the amber liquid. "Here, let me show you some pictures of what I found diving last year." He didn't need a connection to access his photo library, so he handed his phone to Alberto. "Just swipe right."

"What this is?" Alberto held up the phone, showing a picture of an oversize nail caked in a knobby, hard substance.

"Oh, that's a bronze spike from a shipwreck. Most likely from—"

Alberto cut him off. "That's not a treasure." He squinted, holding the screen closer to his face, swiping through the pictures, blinking his eyes as if refocusing his vision might somehow turn Adam's bronze artifacts into gold.

Adam snatched the phone back. His pictures were amazing. "These bronze spikes had been under the ocean for a hundred years, and because bronze is a metal alloy—" Adam stopped midsentence as Alberto got up and walked away from him, headed toward the mango grove.

"Sorry if I'm boring you," said Adam to the old man's back.

"You are the boring one," Alberto confirmed.

Alberto's statement didn't penetrate too deeply. What drove Adam to book these dive trips wasn't the possibility of finding the equivalent of a rusty nail, after all, but the possibility of finding anything from Archer's last voyage. In trying to convince Alberto of the value of the bronze spikes, he may have been trying to validate these costly expeditions to himself.

"What are you doing over there?" Adam called into the blackness as Alberto disappeared behind a mango tree.

A few minutes later, Alberto reemerged from the grove, clutching the front of his checkered shirt, cradling a collection of mangos in the sturdy material. "A menos que, we can eat this gold." Alberto joked about the yellow meat of the fruit. "And, you can tell me what you really looking for."

This old man was smarter than he let on, but what would be the harm in telling Alberto about Archer's last voyage? Who was he going to tell? Adam seriously doubted Alberto would ever be able to make it to the dive site off the North Carolina coast. As Alberto had said, he was retired, destined to live out the rest of his days there on the ranch.

The unlikely pair drank tequila distilled from the blue agave growing wild in the state of Jalisco. They drank and talked until Adam could no longer stand the mosquitoes, retiring to his SUV, tipsy and exhausted.

The next morning, Adam awoke to stale breath and a damp shirt inside the truck. Sunlight beat through the windshield onto his forehead, aggravating a pounding headache. When he opened the door and stepped onto the gravel, stagnant air spilled from the vehicle. Where was Alberto? What time was it? Adam took his phone out—ten o'clock. He touched his hand to his forehead and grimaced. Then he set off in the direction of the current to find the old man. The sun was too bright. Adam kept his eyes on the ground, feeling a little weak from last night's activities, only looking up when he heard Alberto calling to him.

"Adam! Come, I teach you fishing." Alberto steadied himself in the middle of the river, tighty-whities wet and clinging, with a sleek, black catfish in his hand.

"What are you trying to do to me?" Adam's eyes had just been assaulted by the bright light and the vision of Alberto's sagging skin wrapped in transparent undergarments.

"I take a shower and I fish at same time. Get in."

Adam didn't believe anyone could come out of the river *cleaner* than when they went in, but a swim sounded nice. Between the alcohol and sweating it out in the truck, he was parched but wouldn't dare drink the river water. Maybe he could rehydrate by diffusion, soaking in moisture through his skin. He stripped down to his boxers.

The two men walked over smooth rocks, taking care not to slip on the algae, eventually coming to a moderate expanse of still water six feet deep in the center. Just short of stagnant but relatively clear, Alberto referred to this stretch of the river as the chor. Chilly water flowed past Adam's feet and through his toes.

"What about water snakes and alligators?" asked Adam, hovering on the outskirts of the chor while Alberto waded into the middle.

"No snakes, no alligators," said Alberto, still holding his catfish.

"You're gonna lose that fish. Are you going to keep it?"

"Not this one." Alberto turned it loose, and the catfish swam to the bottom of the chor, wriggling out of sight.

"Are you sure there are no water snakes?" Adam pressed. "Have you ever seen one?"

"No chance for snakes and alligators. Snakes are with the mountain rocks, and no alligators."

Adam would have to trust that Alberto knew what he was talking about. Back in Maryland, he never would have gotten into a river this riddled with rocks and boulders. It would have been a haven for copperheads and cottonmouths. As he continued to scan for snakes out of habit, he couldn't help looking for the glint of something shiny hiding among the sandy pebbles. The memories of Alberto's treasure tales from the night before were wrapped tightly in his headache, but the desire to look stuck to him like the lingering emotions from a forgotten dream.

Alberto dove underwater and resurfaced, pushing his gray hair back from his face. "Get in."

Adam decided to let the refreshing water rinse the stale party residue from his body and waded in after his new fishing companion. Gooseflesh formed on Adam's forearms, so he submerged himself and surfaced for air, evening out his exposure to the cold.

"Ready to fish?" Alberto asked, huffing with the exertion of treading water.

"Sure," said Adam. "Why not?"

Alberto led Adam to a half-sunken boulder on the edge of the chor and stuck his arm under the rock. Adam cringed as Alberto felt around under the rock, still thinking that at any moment, the old man would withdraw his arm with a poisonous water snake attached by the fangs, but seconds later, Alberto pulled out a writhing catfish.

"The small fish, they taste good," said Alberto, smiling with pride. He propelled himself to the riverbank and dropped the fish into a tiny pool he'd created from stacked river rocks to keep them fresh. A dozen catfish slipped past one another in the shallow water.

This eighty-year-old man had caught a fish with his bare hands. Adam couldn't let Alberto put him to shame. With a renewed sense of sportsmanship, he set out to catch a fish of his own. Adam successfully emulated Alberto's technique, but after smelling the San Cristóbal river, he was cautious about eating anything from the surrounding bodies of water. Maybe Marisol would want them.

He strung the flipping fish onto a stick through their gills. After retrieving his clothes, he and Alberto walked back to their makeshift camp, and Adam tossed the fish onto the passenger side floor of the SUV. It was a rental. Alberto returned to his spot under the mango tree where Adam had found him the day before, his fish penned and protected in the stone pool for later.

"You remember los directions?" asked Alberto, air drying under the tree.

"Yes, I remember." Adam nodded and thanked the old man. He pulled on his shirt and pants over his damp shorts and climbed in next to the fish. Once thirsty for air, their heaving gills had ceased to move, and the cluster of fish lay motionless on the floor mat.

Alberto's directions brought him to a house made from stacked river rocks, just like the fish corral in the river. Teja—semicircular-shaped bricks—covered the roof, engineered to channel the rainwater off the home. The entire structure was no more than two hundred square feet, but he'd expected as much. What would Marisol do in a larger place with no electricity?

Steam rose from a tin pot hanging over the patio cookfire, and the rolling boil sent pinto beans rising to the surface only to be pushed back down under the scalding water. Marisol looked up from her task, putting down her wooden spoon as Adam came around the side of the house.

"Pásate, Adam." She brought a chair from across the cobblestone patio and set it next to the fire.

Adam moved the chair to the shade of the teja awning, fish swinging on the stick slung over his shoulder. "I thought you might like some fish this morning."

"Thank you. I'm sure my babies will love them. Juanito, Pepito, Luisito," she called.

Babies? Adam froze where he stood as the pendulous fish came to rest dangling beneath the stick. The old man hadn't mixed up his words. Marisol had lied to him at the fair. No wonder she had been there alone. Who would want to spend time with a pathological liar? What a horrible thing to lie about. She'd had him feeling sorry for her, but maybe that was the goal—attention through sympathy. What kind of mother would tell someone her children were dead and then casually call them home for a snack?

Three dogs came rushing up from a narrow ravine behind the house, interrupting his scathing thoughts. Clumpy, matted fur covered the hounds. Encrusted dust hid their coats' color.

They charged in his direction at full speed. Instinctively, Adam dropped the fish, jumped out of their path, and watched as the dogs devoured the catfish caked in gritty earth.

"These are my babies," said Marisol as one of the mangy dogs nuzzled against her leg. "Meet Juan, Pepe, and Luis."

"Are these the kids Alberto was talking about?" Adam felt like a jerk inwardly, but he hadn't said anything out loud. Everything was still good.

She laughed. "Don't believe anything that old man says. It's a joke in the village that these are my kids. My husband and I raised no children, only my sweet dogs. Anyway, there's plenty of fish in the stew I've got cooking." She returned to the pot, and the dogs trolled closely behind, hoping for more scraps. "Alberto's my second cousin on my grandfather's side. He told me you might stop by, so I caught some extra fish this morning."

How early had Alberto gotten up? No wonder he needed a nap before noon.

Marisol took up the wooden spoon again and stirred the stew. "Did you have a nice rest in your truck?"

Word traveled fast in los ranchos. "Sleeping in your truck is never comfortable, but the river was refreshing." Adam settled into his chair, now that the dogs had redirected their attention to the stew.

"I agree. The mountain water is refreshing, and the chor is my favorite place to go. It's peaceful," said Marisol. She abandoned the wooden spoon and wiped her hands on her apron.

She wore a simple pair of jeans and a T-shirt with sandals, the complete opposite of what she'd had on at the fair. Surprisingly, she looked even better without makeup. It rarely worked that way.

"The chor is relaxing," said Adam, surveying the property. Clothes hung on a line tied to a tree weighed down with hundreds of small, yellow fruit shaped like plums.

"You don't look so well," said Marisol with her hands on her hips. "How late did my cousin keep you up?"

It took a moment and a fair amount of brain power to bring last night's conversation into focus. "The details are a little fuzzy. I think we might have finished an entire bottle of tequila. Anyway, we talked for a long time, or at least he talked, and I listened. Alberto told this story about three rubies. Do you know which one I'm talking about?"

"I know exactly the one you're talking about—the Hernandez Castañeda family fortune," Marisol said whimsically, as if she didn't believe any of it, then pulled her chair into the shade next to Adam.

"So they're just stories with no truth to them?"

"You look so sad." Marisol turned down her bottom lip as if she were sympathizing with a child. "When I was a girl, Alberto and Javier would tell the same story to us younger cousins, and we would go off in search of the legendary rubies. Let's just say we never found anything." She tipped her chair back, leaning against the stone wall of the house.

"That's too bad." Adam felt his heart sink just a sliver.

"The stories are plausible and historically accurate, but any treasure that might have been buried around here has long since been unearthed," she said. "All that remains are the stories."

"So people *have* found things in the past?" Adam wasn't sure why he was so interested. He was in Mexico for work. Where would he find the time to scour the mountains of Jalisco for buried treasure? Plus, all of his gear was in the US, not to mention that his tools were meant for underwater excavation.

"My cousins haven't found anything since the 1980s, and it wasn't even that much—a few pieces of silver, if that. I went with them to the Banco de Comercio in Guadalajara once. They were going to show me their treasures, but when they opened the safe deposit box, everything was gone."

"What do you mean 'gone?'"

"Gone, as in not there."

"What happened to the silver?"

"What do you think happened?" She gave Adam the come-on look. "Don't let Alberto rope you in. Whatever they might have found back then wasn't worth the time or the energy they had spent looking for it."

"Don't worry. I'd never be able to leave the construction site long enough to go on a digging expedition." Adam laughed and crossed one leg over the other. "Do you live here alone? I mean, you have your dogs, of course." He'd done it again. He and his big mouth. This was the same type of question she'd been avoiding at the fair.

"I've been waiting for my husband to return home for years—six years."

Well, he hadn't expected that answer. There they were, having another "too soon" conversation, but he resolved to venture out of his comfort zone and actively take part in the dialogue. He was the one who had brought it up, after all; and how do you back out of a subject after someone says what she just said?

"I don't mean to be rude or to pry, but I remember Alberto saying your husband had died." Adam crossed his arms and tilted his chair back in the dry dirt, resting against the stone wall with Marisol.

"If you really want to know, I'm la viuda—the widow. That's what they call me around here." Marisol looked up at the sky and into her memories. It had been a long time since she had relayed this story. Everyone in los ranchos already knew the tale.

"If you're not in the mood to talk, that's fine."

"No, it's okay. I don't mind filling you in." She unconsciously twisted the hair falling over her shoulder in a circle as she brought Adam through the events of her past. "It's been six years since my husband left to find work in the United States. I dropped him off in Coahuila with the guide and haven't heard from him since."

"Why would Alberto have said that he died?" Adam didn't understand.

"That's what everyone thinks, but I know he's not dead. I can't believe I'm telling you this, but everyone else stopped listening to my theories years ago when we held a memorial service for Christo."

"Why did you have a service if you think he's alive?"

"My friend, Rosa, thought it would be beneficial for me to get some closure, but the only thing that came of the service was closure for the rest of the people who knew him. Now, I still feel he's alive, but no one will listen. I never buried a body, but the memorial service buried everyone else's hope he could still be out there."

Adam turned toward Marisol, still leaning back in his chair. "What do you think happened to him?"

"Would you like some stew?" She lowered the front legs of her chair to the ground and stood.

"I won't let you do that again."

"Do what?" she asked, feigning ignorance.

"Change the subject," he clarified. "Just think for a second. You haven't been able to talk to anyone about this in years because everyone thinks he's dead. So talk to me. Who am I going to tell? Maybe it'll help." He didn't stand to gain anything from having this conversation and surprised himself a little after he had made the offer.

"I guess you have a point." She shrugged and continued. "I think he's hiding from me."

"What? I mean, why?"

"Christo and I had three baby boys, all stillborn, like I told you at the mango fair, buried outside the cathedral in San Cristóbal, like you saw. I gave my babies the best possible resting place. I just couldn't give them life."

Adam caught a whiff of the stew, but tried to remain focused on the conversation. "Why would he be hiding?" he asked.

"I could tell Cristo wasn't satisfied with the marriage after the birth of our third son." She busied her hands, ladling fish stew into two bowls. "Our friends were filling their homes with children. Little boys and girls played in their yards while I was preparing meals for two."

"A marriage without children isn't such a bad thing," interjected Adam, thinking about his own situation and preferences.

"Maybe for some, but we grew apart over the years. In the end, before he left, we weren't even talking at mealtimes anymore." Marisol covered the fire with sand, extinguishing the flames while insulating the embers for later use. "Christo decided to look for work in the United States. If we couldn't have children, at least we would have money. When I dropped him off close to the border, I wanted to convince him to stay, but I let him go. If our relationship had been enough for him, he would never have wanted to go."

"I've recently separated myself." Adam didn't want her to feel alone, and this also brought the conversation back to him.

"Oh, where's your ex-wife?" asked Marisol, setting a plastic bowl and spoon on the tree stump beside his chair.

A sleek catfish, head and all, floated in the broth with round pieces of carrot and pinto beans. It smelled fantastic, but how was he supposed to eat it? It still had skin and fins. Adam stalled by continuing the conversation. "She's back in Maryland."

"Do the two of you have any children?"

"No. We'd been talking about it for years, but it never seemed like a good time for children." Adam poked his spoon into the fish's middle section, through its smooth skin, and into the white, flaky meat.

"There's never a perfect time to have a child," said Marisol, "but you may find you've run out of time if you wait too long."

This was something Adam didn't care to delve into. "So do you remember any of Javier and Alberto's stories well enough to tell me one?" Adam asked, changing the subject. He didn't have to have this conversation now like he would have if Eileen had been there. He could just shut it down.

"I remember them all."

She didn't cycle back to children, and Adam was grateful. Marisol had inherited the story-telling gene like her cousins. The details roped him in immediately. Adam listened to her stories while he finished his stew, and the two made dessert out of the yellow fruit hanging from the tree. He and Marisol made plans to meet at her ranch again the following Sunday.

Chapter 9

Sophie

It had been hell finding things to do around an empty house all Sunday. Monday morning had finally come—time to get to work. A young, professional couple had commissioned Sophie to build a courtyard in the backyard of their historic townhome in downtown Alexandria. She'd been working on getting the permit for months. The paperwork had slowly crawled its way through various city departments. Halfway through the Richardson job, the permit had arrived in the mail—approved. She wasn't planning on building anything major, only a stone archway for the entrance to the yard. Still, the historic district was extremely strict with any type of construction, archways included. The city had approved her drawings on the condition she build it two feet shorter than she'd planned.

When Sophie had originally met with the clients, Mike and Amanda Coleman, they had taken her to see what their next-door neighbor had done with his backyard. The Colemans had given her complete creative freedom to do as she wished with the space. The only condition was that their yard be far more impressive than their neighbor's. Those two were competitive to the core, but Sophie would win this competition for them.

Rigo was already on site when Sophie rounded the townhouse, but what was Amanda doing there?

"Good morning." Sophie greeted the client. "I didn't know you'd be off today."

"I'm not *off*," said Amanda, striding to the fence line. Sophie followed. "Look at what Rich has done since you were last here."

All three of them looked over the fence. The Colemans' retired neighbor, Rich, had spoken to Mike and Amanda one evening about how the brown noise from his fountain helped drown out the rumble of the city streets. Rich had also offered them fresh herbs from his garden, which had been the last straw.

"We can work with this." Sophie attempted to assuage the client. "The city's historical society doesn't regulate anything fenced in under seven feet four inches."

"What do you have planned?" asked Amanda, checking the time on her phone. "Give me the condensed version, though, because I need to leave for work. I have a meeting at nine."

"All right, I know a local artist, a stone sculptor. *Your* fountain would not only provide brown noise, but it would double as art!" Sophie waited for a reaction, but Amanda's face gave nothing away as she stood next to the fence in her slate-gray suit.

"Would you prefer any particular type of stone over another?" asked Sophie.

"I'll leave that up to you. You're the professional. I like the idea, and we should move forward with it. Have an updated cost breakdown for me by the end of the week." Amanda adjusted the strap of her computer bag on her shoulder and headed for the back door.

"Absolutely. Done." Sophie tried to keep it short.

"I left the key to the back door in the shed in case you need access to the electrical box or the water valve." Then Amanda was gone.

"She didn't even ask about the price," said Rigo. "How much is that fountain going to cost?"

"Anywhere from eight to ten thousand, I'm sure, and that's a conservative estimate. I found the artist at a trade show last year. But tell me, how did you beat me here this morning?" It had taken Sophie two hours to get there in rush hour traffic.

"My sister and her family only live about ten miles from here. I took the back roads. They're much quicker, but I'm going to grab the rest of the tools from the truck."

"I'll help you," said Sophie as they walked together around the house. The Colemans had an end unit. "You're still living with your sister?" Sophie had thought Rigo would have found his own place by now.

"Yeah. I'm still renting the room. It's not a bad arrangement. She feeds me every day after work, but I'm on my own for breakfast." Rigo pulled the edger from the truck and added gas to the tank.

"It's nice the two of you are so close," Sophie said. "I haven't been to Pittsburg to visit Megan in a while."

"Pittsburgh isn't far from here. It wouldn't be too big of a deal for you to make the drive."

Sophie didn't feel like getting into how she and her sister had different feelings about her marriage to Adam. Rigo had heard it all before, anyway. She pulled a bag of garden soil from the truck, and it landed on the pavement with a thud.

"I'll get those bags," said Rigo, shooing her away.

She agreed to let him take care of the heavy lifting. "Maybe I'll make the trip for Megan's birthday in a few weeks." It wasn't that far, like Rigo had said.

"It's up to you," said Rigo. "But if you do end up going out of town, I won't let any of our jobs fall behind schedule." He stacked a half dozen bags of garden soil in the wheelbarrow and pushed it toward the backyard.

Sophie followed, pushing the edger, thinking about how she and her sister were now in agreement about her relationship, or lack thereof. Adam hadn't tried to contact her since he'd left for Mexico weeks ago, not once. Checking his social media was useless. The last thing Adam posted was a picture of some bumpy spike he had found over a year ago. He obviously didn't care, and if he wasn't going to care, she couldn't care for both of them. Her sister would have said the best way to get over someone was to get under someone new—a true philosopher. Maybe she could use a good dose of Megan, after all.

Sophie reached the backyard, where Rigo unloaded the wheelbarrow. It was time for her to make some changes, to show some initiative in her personal life. She left the bladed machine beside the fence and rubbed the sweat from her palms onto her jeans as she walked across the yard to meet him. "Rigo?"

He let the last bag of soil drop in the yard. "Yes."

"Do you have plans for this evening?" She was doing it, taking her life back.

"I do," he said.

These two words split her newfound confidence in two like a crack running through a concrete foundation. "Oh, that's fine. I was just …" she muttered, turning away from him.

"Hey, hold on." He tilted his head, trying to catch her emerald eyes. "I have plans, but that doesn't mean I wouldn't love for you to join me. Better yet, I'll cancel my plans." He let go of the wheelbarrow, awaiting her response.

"I don't want to take you away from anything."

"You're not. Believe me. You'd be doing me a favor. I was supposed to go out with my friend Nick, but he needs to be studying, anyway."

"Are you sure you want to cancel?"

"He'll thank me for it later, after he passes this exam he's been complaining about. How about I pick you up at six?"

It couldn't be that simple, but just like that, she was going on a date, or at least going out as friends. She didn't really know which one. "That sounds great. Where do you want to go?"

"I have something in mind. It might be a stretch, but I think it's just the kind of fun you need."

His boyish smile accentuated his strong jawline. Sophie couldn't remember the last time someone's smile had caused butterflies to take flight in her stomach. She averted her eyes and, when she looked back at him, he still had the same mischievous look on his face. "What is it you have in mind?"

"It's a surprise."

·　　·　　·

The last time she'd gone out was with Adam to the Empire dinner, the night she had realized her marriage would never be a true partnership. Sophie thought she and Adam had done some reconnecting before that, but nothing had changed. They had no kids, and Adam had no interest in having any.

Sophie had never thought it would be so hard to create a peaceful, normal family life. As simple as it sounded, it was her innermost desire, after her upbringing—to know what it would feel like to come home to unconditional love, smiles, and hugs. She had thought Adam would have been the one to build this life with her, but she had been wrong. Oh well, it was best the separation period had already begun. In less than a year, they would be eligible for divorce. She would visit a lawyer and start the paperwork.

Now, what to wear? How do you dress for a surprise? After showering, she threw on a sundress, applied some light makeup—neutral tones—and gave herself a satisfied nod in the mirror. In the end, she had chosen wisely. Mini golf was the surprise.

•   •   •

"Watch out!" Sophie shouted to Rigo before they had even stepped onto the first hole.

Rigo jumped out of the way, dodging a golf ball one young boy had pelted at another. The two looked like brothers, and their parents were nowhere in sight.

"Why don't we skip ahead a few holes?" Rigo suggested. "For our own safety."

Sophie agreed and followed Rigo to the third hole. They would have to putt over a slender bridge, through a tunnel in a spaceship, and sink the ball on the other side of the spacecraft. "This one looks difficult."

"It's not that hard." Rigo took his stance at the beginning of the hole and lightly tapped his neon-yellow ball, sending it up and through the spaceship.

"You make it look so easy." Sophie placed her ball on the green and tried to emulate Rigo's stance.

"You're too rigid." Rigo folded his arms around her, placing his hands next to hers on the golf club. "Loosen your arms."

"Hey, look, they're boyfriend and girlfriend," taunted one of the brothers while pointing at the two of them. How had they made it to the third hole so quickly?

"Back up, you two," barked their dad.

"They're fine," said Rigo, letting go of Sophie. "Why don't you all play through."

"Are you sure you're okay with that?" Their dad looked relieved.

Rigo motioned for the family to advance. "Absolutely."

"That was nice of you," said Sophie, laughing at the brothers as they continued to drive their dad crazy. Now, they were jabbing their golf clubs into each other's feet.

"They're just having fun." Rigo held out his arm, inviting her back to their golf lesson. "Like I was saying, you just have to keep your arms loose and don't try to crush it. A light tap will get you there."

Rigo let go and backed up, giving her some space. She took his advice and jumped up and down when her ball successfully made it through the tunnel in the spaceship.

"That's great!" He took her hand, and they walked around the spacecraft to play the second half of the hole. "You go first."

As Sophie lined up her second putt, Rigo crossed his arms over his chest, holding his golf club. "So we've been working together for a long time, and I think we've been friends, too," he said.

She shot and missed. "Oh, absolutely, we've been friends. You've been giving me advice for years." She probably should have been paying him for all the listening he'd done.

"But things have been different lately."

The sweat returned to her palms, slick against the putter's grip. Sophie searched for the right reply.

"I've always known a lot about Sophie and Adam," Rigo continued, "but I'm curious about *you*." He gripped his golf club, lining up his shot. "I mean, I already know the smart, driven work you, but I'm curious about the outside-of-work you."

She found her voice again as Rigo's neon ball dropped into the hole. "You're a pretty good putter." A successful deflection. She didn't want him to feel like she was brushing him off. She just didn't know what to say.

He looked at her kindly. "I didn't intend to put you on the spot. I can tell we're both a little unsure of what we're doing here. At least, I'm unsure. But listen, I want you to know I'm not the kind of guy who goes after a married woman. We've always had this connection, you and me. It's no secret you and Adam have been having difficulties for years, but I feel like things are different this time. You're different this time. I guess what I'm asking is … what's going on with you guys *this time*, and please be real with me."

Wow. These were reasonable questions. Sophie had just been so focused on how she felt she hadn't explained what was going on to Rigo in so many words. She and Adam had separated, and she was about to make it official, but it was all so new.

Rigo jumped in, saving her from drowning in a sea of contemplation. "Hey, we're just two people talking. Just a regular guy and a beautiful woman having a conversation. You don't need to get into this now if you don't feel comfortable."

He looked her in the eye, unembarrassed, waiting for her reaction. How bold. He wanted her to know where he stood. Rigo had put himself out there to make her feel at ease. It was sexy, his boyish confidence. He deserved a response, but Sophie broke their eye contact and walked to the other side of the turf to take her next shot.

"You are beautiful, you know," said Rigo to the back of her head.

"Thank you," she said, hiding her emotions by focusing on the game. She couldn't even look at him. What had happened to the new and fearless Sophie? That Sophie came and went, it seemed.

Rigo planted his putter on the turf, resting his palms on the golf club. "So I guess I just want to know what it is we're doing?"

She took a few seconds to pull herself out of the whirlpool of thoughts dragging her under. She should answer his questions, and she would. "I do think you're attractive, and there is no more Adam and I." There. She had said it.

"All right," he said.

To Sophie's relief, Rigo asked no more questions about her marriage, or rather, her divorce. The focus of the conversation moved on to other topics. Lighthearted laughter and sexual tension filled the remainder of the game—typical first date vibes. He had been right. Mini golf was a perfect surprise and just the kind of fun she'd needed.

After the game, Sophie returned her club and walked to the vending machine in the corner of the cashier's hut for a cold water. The young woman running the cash register must not have seen her, but she saw Rigo.

"Rigo?" She said his name as if she knew him.

Rigo set his club on the return counter. "Ava? I didn't think you worked here anymore."

"I didn't, for a while, but things didn't work out at the office—too much attitude from the clients. I can't deal with all that." She tucked her silky black hair behind her ear.

Sophie squeezed her purse strap tighter as she listened to Rigo make small talk with Ava. She stayed hidden in the corner by the vending machine.

"Well, I'm sorry to hear that," said Rigo. "I know you were excited to get the job."

"I was, but I'm with this guy Antonio now." Ava paused.

Sophie knew this pause. Ava was waiting to see how Rigo would react to the news of her relationship, which meant they had been in a relationship, but Rigo didn't bite.

"He owns the Toyota dealership in Silver Spring. He even has a pool at his house." Another strategic pause. "I just fill in here occasionally as a favor to Lynn."

Sophie collected her bottle of water from the vending machine, casually glancing over her shoulder.

Ava put her hands on the counter, leaned toward Rigo, and lowered her voice. "Most days, Antonio doesn't get home until late if you ever want to come for a swim. That is, if you're not seeing anyone right now."

Rigo faltered, unable to come up with a reply.

"It's weird that you're here alone, though. Isn't this where you take all your girls on a first date?"

All of his girls? Sophie marched toward the counter, but stopped halfway there. The heat coursing through her should have boiled the bottled water in her hand, but just like her, the water remained motionless.

Rigo stepped back and brought Sophie into an awkward side hug. "I am here with someone. Ava, this is Sophie."

"Oh, sorry. I didn't know."

Sophie could tell by the way she had said this she wasn't sorry at all, maybe even still expecting Rigo to take her up on the swim.

"It was nice seeing you, Ava, but we'd better get going." He dropped his arm from Sophie's shoulder and reached for her hand.

Sophie let him hold her hand as they left the Putt Hut but let go immediately after Ava could no longer see the two of them. She hadn't wanted to give Ava the satisfaction of believing she had ruined their date.

"Sorry about that," said Rigo. "I didn't know Ava was working here."

"No worries," was all Sophie said. She sat in the passenger seat, looking out the window with her hands folded uncomfortably in her lap.

"So I don't know what all you heard back there, but Ava and I were together briefly about a year ago, around the time you and I were working on the rooftop garden for those apartments in downtown Baltimore."

Sophie said nothing. She attempted to turn down the heat within, trying to keep her blood at a simmer.

"I'm guessing you heard everything," said Rigo, unable to reach her. "I'm sorry. This was supposed to be fun. I should've taken you somewhere new, somewhere I hadn't taken anyone else before, but I thought you would like it. You looked like you were having fun." More silence. "I want you to know I don't consider you to be just another girl. No matter how Ava made it sound, you're different to me. This is different for me, and I hope it's different for you, too."

"It's been different," Sophie said neutrally, which must have stung more than showing her true emotions. He had talked her through enough situations with Adam to know that the calmer she appeared, the more she was hurting. Rigo also knew well enough to let it go for the night.

He walked her to her door. "I guess I'll see you tomorrow?"

"Yeah. I'll see you on site tomorrow." She smiled unconvincingly and slipped quickly through the door.

Lying in bed, she wondered why she had let what Ava had said bother her so much. She thought about how good Rigo had looked in his jeans. She imagined him in her bed, but she would be glad he hadn't been there come morning. Things had not gone so far that their working relationship couldn't return to normal, but was that what she wanted? Truthfully, she didn't know what she wanted, or how she felt. Sophie thought about taking a trip to clear her head, but where would she go? Who would she go with? Maybe she would just visit her sister like she and Rigo had talked about. Why not? It had been too long, and besides, Megan would be very supportive of her impending divorce. She would let Rigo know she wouldn't be in the next morning.

Chapter 10

Adam

Morale among the team was much higher this week than the last. For the first time in years, Adam had fastened a tool belt around his waist. He replaced his khakis with jeans and protected his face against the intense sun with an Orioles cap. His excursion to Marisol's ranch and his little fishing expedition had fueled a renewed interest in working with his hands. It felt good. Adam was piling up scrap metal, exposed during the grading, when Carlos found him.

"Jefe."

"What's up?" said Adam.

"Are you going to the taco stand for lunch today?"

Adam tossed a large piece of rusty metal onto the growing pile. "That's the plan."

"The guys and I wanted to know if you'd like to join us for lunch instead. Diego's wife packed some gorditas and jamaica to share."

Adam stopped, his chest expanding and contracting with the exertion of physical labor. "What are gorditas?"

"They're like flat, round cornbread. I guess that's the best way to explain it," Carlos answered. "They're sweet, and you cook them in an outdoor oven made of stone."

"I'm in." Adam didn't hesitate. He had liked pretty much everything he'd tried since arriving in Mexico. "What's the jamaica?"

"For you … it would be like … a Kool-Aid. I think that's how you say it. It's a red tea brewed from the jamaica flower, and we add sugar," said Carlos.

"Kool-Aid and cornbread, huh? Sure, I'll join you."

It was a night-and-day difference from the feeling he'd gotten from the men last week. Adam thought back to something his father used to tell him as a boy—*to lead by example*. Maybe his father had been right. His example had earned him a lunch invitation, at any rate.

Adam joined the men under the shade tree and removed his hat. Sweat dripped from his temples, and he wiped it off with the back of his hand. Diego passed him a small stack of gorditas on a roble leaf and poured him some jamaica, curious to see if Adam would like the authentic Mexican food. Clearly, Diego didn't know he had eaten a fish with the head and fins still on last week in the mountains.

All eyes were on him, and Adam tried the gorditas—sweet, coarse cornbread with smoky undertones, just as Carlos had described. Flowery hints of the jamaica—hibiscus—petals came through in the tea, not at all like Kool-Aid. He was turning into a true connoisseur of new foods. "Thank you," he said to Diego, smiling and giving the thumbs-up sign.

Assembled under the tree, the crew members laughed at his verdict, but they weren't making fun of him. The tradesmen were happy to see him embracing the food and culture of their country. The men spent the lunch hour talking, eating, and joking with one another. They spoke too fast for Adam to understand, but it didn't bother him. He had his jamaica and gorditas.

•   •   •

Around seven in the evening, Adam arrived back at the townhouse on Calle Orosco, eager for a warm shower. Stacks of purchase orders and pages of emails awaited his return. Working with his hands during the week had taken him away from the administrative aspect of his job as project manager. It wasn't a problem though, because no one was waiting for him at home. This part of being separated was convenient, but a small part of him missed having someone around, just for a bit of company.

Adam removed his work boots and left them by the front door. He plugged his phone in and performed a quick scan of Sophie's Instagram before laying it face down on the console table. Adam didn't know why he continued to check up on her. He had his own things going on and would get his fill of companionship that weekend. He and Marisol had made plans to meet again, and Adam hoped she hadn't forgotten. Without a phone, they had no way of confirming their plans. He would just have to drive to her ranch like the last time and hunt her down.

Inside the shower stall, warm water ran down his body and snaked its way into the drain, washing away the dirt and sweat from the construction site. He stood under the water and thought about Alberto's story about the Hernandez Castañeda jewels, imagining himself combing the mountains with a metal detector and a backpack full of excavating tools.

Marisol had told him, point blank, that he had a zero chance of finding anything, but that's what everyone had told him about his search for Archer's fortune. The artifacts he pulled from his dives would surface, looking like clusters of rock cemented together by hardened mineral deposits, junk to the untrained eye. Adam would soak his finds in a corrosive solution on his workbench in the garage. On the day he discovered the sheen of gold gleaming from one of his congealed clusters, the only person he'd wanted to share the news with was his nephew, Ben. He was the only one who deserved to know, the only one who had never given Adam any shit about the resources he put into his pastime.

He and Ben had been on the treasure journey together ever since Ben's father had passed from cancer the year after he and Sophie were married. It had been too long since he'd spoken with Ben. Two months, maybe. Now, a sophomore in college, Adam hadn't wanted to bother him.

Maybe he would forgo seeing Marisol this weekend and buy a metal detector? The only problem was he couldn't remember the end of the story—too much tequila. Whatever became of Daria and Ivette? More importantly, what had become of the treasure?

Adam stepped out of the shower and wrapped a towel around his waist, but his skin turned clammy as he stood in the bathroom. The water droplets he had just dried had returned, and an uneasy, churning sensation boiled in his stomach. He raced to the toilet and had just lowered his head to the bowl when everything from lunch came right back up—*shit*, he thought, *food poisoning*.

He'd had food poisoning one other time when he and Sophie were on vacation at the beach, and he had ordered a rare steak. The meat hadn't tasted quite right and smelled a little like crab. A couple hours later, he felt just like he was feeling now.

Here it comes again. Adam leaned his head over the toilet, retching until he was sure there was nothing left to bring up. Then the dry heaves started. It was as if his body was trying to turn itself inside out by ejecting his organs through his mouth. *I can't take much more of this,* he thought. Adam grabbed the bathroom trash can and headed to bed. He lay there with an unpleasant taste in his mouth that he couldn't ignore, and returned to the tiled bathroom to swish some water over his acrid tongue. He looked at himself in the mirror, sucked in some of the bottled water, swished it around in his mouth, and spit it into the sink, wishing Sophie were there to take care of him. Adam felt like death and looked just as bad.

Sleep eluded him that night between frequent trips to the restroom and severe abdominal cramping. By the time the sun peeked over the balcony walls, Adam had decided to seek medical attention, but where would he go? He needed to contact home office and see if they could tease out a reputable medical clinic in this foreign country.

An hour later, home office sent him the information for a private emergency clinic in Zapopan. Adam took two precautionary Imodium tablets, pulled on a pair of sweatpants, and left for the clinic. He received some questionable looks from passing motorists, dry-heaving the entire three miles to the Centro Médico de Zapopan, una facilidad de salud privado y lucrativo—a private and for-profit medical facility.

The anxiety he held about seeking medical care outside of the US abated as soon as he entered the building. Inside the clinic, instrumental music played softly in the background, and plush furniture occupied the waiting room. Marble countertops demarcated the reception area, and the front office staff dressed as if for the most important business meeting of their lives.

He must have looked pretty bad because the receptionist paged the clinical staff immediately. Within seconds, an array of medical professionals appeared from the back and escorted him through the double doors to a private room with a hospital bed. His dry mouth begged for moisture, but he didn't want to risk ingesting anything, knowing it would just come right back up. Grateful to be lying down again, the horizontal position helped curb some of the nausea.

"¿Y cómo te sientes?" asked one nurse.

Too sick to process this question, he didn't even try to translate. The room was spinning.

Trained for situations like this, the two nurses started an IV in his forearm, hung a bag of clear fluids from a metal pole next to his bed, and got him undressed and into a gown. His dry eyes burned, so he closed them.

"Solamente una inyección," said the nurse, with a syringe in her hand.

Adam's eyes fluttered open just in time to see the nurse inject him with something. Too weak to care, he closed his eyes once more.

Late afternoon, he awoke to the sound of a man's voice. Adam didn't remember dozing off.

"Hi, I'm Dr. Ortega," repeated the doctor.

Adam focused on the man in the white coat with a stethoscope hanging from his neck. He read his badge: Médico.

"I can't believe you drove yourself here," said Dr. Ortega. "People say, *oh, it's just food poisoning*, but the dehydration that results from the vomiting, diarrhea, and sweating is very dangerous. You were severely dehydrated upon admission."

Dr. Ortega looked at the monitor. Adam's vital signs had improved. His heart rate was coming down, and his blood pressure was back to normal. The doctor took his stethoscope and listened to Adam's chest, then pushed around on his abdomen. "Does that hurt?"

"No," said Adam. "Why do I feel so tired?" He stretched in the hospital bed.

"That's the anti-emetic we've been administering to help with the nausea," said the doctor, sliding his hands into his pockets, "but don't worry. It'll wear off soon."

Adam's eyes closed again. The next time he woke, it was dark outside. *Oh crap!* He had missed the entire workday. Adam sat up in bed and fumbled around, trying to find his phone.

"You're awake," said the doctor, standing in the doorway to his room. "How are you feeling?"

"Much better," Adam responded, still searching for his phone. He had to get in touch with work.

"Here." Dr. Ortega passed Adam his phone. "The nurses had it plugged in over there, charging for you."

"Thanks," said Adam, unlocking the device.

"Don't worry," said Dr. Ortega. "We've been communicating with Empire Commercial Builders. Nothing private, mind you, just updating them on your general condition with the dehydration."

Adam relaxed. "I can't believe I was so out of it. What did they say?"

"You know how it goes. Everyone wishes you the best. They want you to recover, and no pressure to return to work sooner than you feel up to it."

Adam knew how it went. That's what everyone has to say when someone is ill, but if he knew Mr. Greenberg, and he did, he would want Adam back to work just as soon as he could get there, even if he were still feeling like crap. Adam swung his feet over the side of the bed, and a wave of vertigo washed over him.

"Take it easy. Don't move so quickly. It looks like you got a little dizzy just now."

"I did, but I've got to get home. I have work in the morning." Adam held on to the side of the bed to steady himself.

"Look," said the doctor, "it's late. Why don't you stay overnight, try yourself on some bland food and clear liquids, and see how you do?"

It took a moment for the wooziness to resolve. "I guess I could do that," said Adam reluctantly.

"You must enjoy your job," said the doctor, sitting in the armed chair beside Adam's bed. "What is it you do? I've never seen someone so anxious to return to work."

"I'm a project manager for a commercial construction company. There's a lot at stake with this job we're doing here in Guadalajara."

"Really? How so?"

"Well, this is my first job outside the country and our first job with Comp Zero. Everything has to be flawless, from the timeline to the product."

"It's not just that, though. Is it?" asked the doctor, leaning in for the details. "Who is she?"

"Who's who?" asked Adam. *This guy was getting pretty intrusive.*

"I've worked with people for over thirty years," said the doctor. "It looks like you also want to get out of here to see someone. So who is she?"

Adam hadn't realized it himself, but he *was* eager to get out of there for Marisol and los ranchos that coming weekend. How had the doctor known this?

"Sorry to be so direct. This is a private clinic, and you're actually my only patient right now. I'm just trying to make conversation."

"That's okay," said Adam. "You're right. There's this girl I met at the mango fair in San Cristóbal—"

"Wait, wait, wait," said the doctor, holding up his palm. "What were you doing in San Cristóbal?"

Adam could see Dr. Ortega thought it was unusual that he had gone to the mango fair. "A guy on my jobsite invited me."

"You can't be hanging around with people like that," said Dr. Ortega.

"People like what?"

"Let me explain some things to you, Adam. You and I differ from the people who work on your jobsite and the people who live in los ranchos. We have a different lifestyle—money and prestige. Come on now. You can't be seen places like that."

"The fair was kind of fun, and the food was good," argued Adam. He couldn't believe the doctor had come out and said those things so plainly.

"Look where that good food landed you," said the doctor with finality, motioning to the hospital bed and the surrounding facility.

Dr. Ortega had a point about the food. He had just spent all day at the clinic for food poisoning, but it wasn't the food from the mango fair.

"You're scheduled for discharge in the morning," said Dr. Ortega. "You'll be able to get back to work, but instead of seeking out the folks from los ranchos this weekend, why don't you join me for a round of golf and something to eat in the city? I've got a group of professional friends who play golf together every other Sunday."

"That sounds fun, Dr. Ortega, it does, but—"

The doctor interrupted him. "I won't accept any excuses, and please, call me Sebastian."

This guy was extremely pushy, but golf sounded terrific. He hadn't played a single round since he'd left the US. "All right, Sebastian, you've convinced me. I'll meet you guys for golf, but where?"

"Meet me here on Sunday around noon, and you can follow me to the course," said Sebastian. "You'll thank me in the end. Any girl you meet in los ranchos will only be after your money."

Adam ignored that last comment. "Do you get any sports channels in here?" He looked for the remote to the TV hanging in the corner of his room.

"Absolutely. This is a private clinic. Anything you want, we've got it."

Dr. Ortega turned on an American baseball game, and they watched a few innings before he left Adam to rest. The nurse checked on Adam, bringing chicken broth and crackers during the game. Dr. Ortega saw he could keep it down and signed off on his release for the morning.

Chapter 11

Sophie
Christmas Eve, 1997
Catonsville, Maryland

Come here, Megan," Sophie called to her baby sister as she lay beside the Christmas tree on her back. Fallen green needles with brown tips snagged the threads of her holiday dress as she shimmied under the tree.

Megan squirmed between the presents under the evergreen branches until her head bumped the tree stand. She flipped onto her back and waited for further instruction from her older sister. "What are we looking at?"

"Everything." Sophie relaxed her eyes and watched as the kaleidoscope of colors melted together. "Just make your eyes blurry, and the lights will turn into floating circles."

While Megan tried to produce the multicolored floating circles of Christmas magic, Sophie brought her vision back into sharp focus on the biggest present under the tree. Wrapped in shiny, red paper and finished with a white bow, it was the largest present Sophie had ever had. She ran her fingers across the red paper, making a squeaking sound.

When Megan heard the noise, her bottom lip folded down in a pout. "How come your present is bigger than mine?"

Sophie wasn't sure. She hadn't expected it. Their mother had been acting strangely, in one of her cyclones, as their father called them. Their mother had been bringing home armfuls of shopping bags, which Daddy would take right back out to the car. Sophie hadn't been sure she would get any presents at all that Christmas until last week when her mother had come floating into the living room with bags full of unwrapped toys, shooing the girls from the living room so she could wrap the myriad of gifts. Daddy hadn't been home, and so the purchases made their way under the tree. After seeing the gifts, Sophie's stomach bottomed out, like when she was in the car, and her mother would drive over a bumpy road too quickly.

"I may have the biggest gift, but you have more than I do." Sophie tried to appease her little sister.

"I do!" The smile returned to Megan's chubby face, and she pressed her nose against a shiny, glass ornament, eyeing her distorted facial proportions in her reflection.

Tomorrow morning, they would open their gifts. Maybe Sophie could even keep these toys in her room. She thought of her collection of dolls and ponies tucked into shoe boxes in the corner of their neighbor's carport. Her things were always safe at Harriet's.

"What are you girls doing under the tree again?"

From beneath their prickly fort, Sophie saw her mother's high-heeled shoes. Where was she going on Christmas Eve? Sophie's stomach twisted as she watched the lights from the Christmas tree bounce off her mother's patent leather shoes, and her eyes shifted between her big, red present and her mother's feet.

"Come out from under there, girls."

The pine needles had softened her voice, but Sophie could tell her mother was still in a cyclone. As soon as Megan cleared the bottom branches, she was off, darting down the hall toward the kitchen. Sophie tried to follow, but her mother caught her by the arm, jerking her back.

Her mother was wearing her special necklace, the one Daddy hated. A diamond dragonfly dangled from a gold chain around her neck. Maybe Daddy hated the necklace because it was her lying necklace. Every time her mom bent down to talk to her in that necklace, she would lie. Maybe she lied to Daddy in that necklace, too.

"Sophie, hand me the big, red present." Her mother pointed under the tree with her polished nails the color of strawberry milk and waited for Sophie to retrieve the decorated box.

Sophie's heart fell to the floor with a thud, like a pet bird with clipped wings. "My present?" She stared at her mother in the diamond necklace, hoping she would change her mind, or at least pick a different present to take away.

"Yes, your present, Sophie. I don't have all night. Get under there and pull it out. I need it for the party."

Sophie's eyes rested on the smooth, red paper as she listened to the toe of her mother's fancy shoe tapping on the hardwood floor. What party? Her mother had promised them a night of Christmas cookies and milk. They were going to take a family drive around the block to look at Christmas lights. Where was she going? Sophie knew better than to argue, so she got on her belly and reached under the tree, running her finger across the shiny paper one last time before she handed it to her mother.

"When will you be back?" Sophie couldn't stop herself from asking.

Present in hand, her mother paced toward the front coat closet. "I may not be back until the morning, or I may not be back at all," she said matter-of-factly.

Whenever the feeling leaked out of Mom, that's when things were the worst. That's when Daddy called her a wet noodle. When Mom was a wet noodle she didn't care about anything, not even eating. Sophie hoped the cyclone would keep spinning, at least through Christmas. Where was Daddy? Maybe he could stop her from leaving.

"Where are you going, Joyce?" Sophie's dad called from the top of the staircase. He rapidly descended the steps and blew past Sophie, leaving a wake of Old Spice in the air as he made his way to the foyer.

Sophie backed into the corner, behind the Christmas tree. Her voice had disappeared, locked in a box in her throat.

"Leave me alone, Tom!" Her mother shrugged on her long, woolen coat as if nothing unusual was going on.

"I won't let you do this, not on Christmas!" He held her mother's pill bottle in his hands, shaking it like a rattle. Dots of spittle landed in his beard as he tried to come up with the words he needed to save Christmas, but he couldn't find them.

Her mother opened the front door. A blast of cold air washed through the room, blowing through the Christmas tree and tickling Sophie's face.

Her father drew a long breath before he asked, "Joyce, have you been taking your medicine?"

Her mother pulled the door open wider to leave. "I don't need those. They make me feel dead. Is that what you want? Do you like me when I'm dead, Tom?"

"Close the door, Joyce."

Her mother flipped her blonde locks over her shoulder. "I promised Steve I would be over for dinner."

"Steve from work?" Her dad's hands shook, and the pills bounced around in the amber prescription bottle.

"Yes, Steve from work. His daughter is with him for Christmas, and he was nice enough to invite me over."

Tom backed Joyce up against the wall next to the open front door and fumbled with the childproof prescription bottle. The top popped off and half of the small, white pills spilled onto the floor, rolling every which way. A few got crushed under Daddy's shoes as he poured the rest of them into his hand, attempting to cram them into his wife's mouth. "In case you've forgotten, you have your own daughters with you for Christmas." Tom pushed the pills past his wife's painted lips and kicked the front door closed with a bang.

Joyce spit out the pills, her lipstick smeared onto her chin and under her nose. "You're the crazy one! Look at yourself! You need to get yourself under control, and I don't need to be here for this!"

Good, the cyclone was spinning, Sophie thought from behind the tree.

Joyce smoothed her woolen coat and straightened her purse strap. "Besides, Steve has been cooking all day. I can't cancel now," she said too calmly.

Oh no, she's doing the wet noodle. It was hard for Sophie to keep up with her mother's changing moods.

"We're your family! Why would you agree to eat dinner with Steve on Christmas Eve, Joyce?"

Then Sophie's dad got quiet. Her mom stood by the front door, smiling as if nothing had happened. No one moved, but her parents were looking at each other. Maybe her mom would stay and put the red present back under the tree.

Then her dad lunged forward and yanked at the golden necklace, snapping the chain. "Take that stupid necklace off." The dragonfly charm slid across the wooden floor, under the tree, and hit the baseboard beside where Sophie hid.

Her mother let go of the red present, and it landed on the wooden floor with a thump, but Sophie didn't hear anything break inside. Joyce held both of her hands to her naked throat, where the necklace had been moments earlier.

"I can't believe you would do this to me again, Joyce." Her dad dropped to his knees, pawing at her mother's dress like a puppy that had done something wrong, begging for forgiveness.

Get up, Dad. Make her stay. Tell her that's my present. The locked box in Sophie's throat was overcrowded with words that couldn't escape.

"Oh, stop it, Tom!" Sophie's mother opened the front door again. "Be a man, would you?" Her mother stomped out of the front door, not bothering to close it, and her high-heeled shoes clicked their way down the front steps.

Sophie slid down the wall to a sitting position and drew her knees to her chest, holding on to them like dear friends. Her parents had forgotten her again. Her father retreated into the kitchen and Sophie crossed her eyes, watching the lights on the tree, and listened to the clinking of glass bottles as he pulled beers from the fridge. The smell of the turkey baking in the oven grew stronger as the night wore on.

Once the sounds coming from the kitchen had stopped, Sophie crept from behind the tree, past her father asleep with his head on the kitchen table. She turned off the oven, left the turkey inside, and continued to the back porch, where Megan played with Barbies next to the space heater.

"Megan," Sophie whispered.

Her little sister returned from her imaginary world and whispered, "What?"

"Let's open our presents now." The red present was still on the floor next to the front door.

Chapter 12

Adam

On Sunday, Adam met Sebastian for golf, just as they had planned. He hadn't told Marisol he wouldn't be coming, but she didn't have a phone, and his plans had changed. Hopefully, she wouldn't be too upset with him. No matter what Sebastian said about the country folks of Jalisco, Adam found them to be genuine and hospitable. Sure, he and Marisol were from different worlds, but that difference drew him to los ranchos. That, and the folklore of lost treasure, of course. Why couldn't he have two groups of friends? The more people to fill his time now that he didn't have Sophie, the better.

"Buenas," Sebastian greeted his friends as he and Adam neared the tee box. "Adam, this is Luis and Ruben."

"Mucho gusto—nice to meet you," said Adam, having regained his energy for attempting to speak the language. He extended his hand first to Luis.

"Luis works with me at the clinic," said Sebastian. "He and I started the clinic how many years ago now?"

"Three," said Luis. "How are you feeling, by the way?"

"Much better, thank you," said Adam, adjusting his grip on his driver for a practice swing.

"I'm going to take a guess and say you were in for food poisoning," said Ruben. "Am I right?"

"How did you know?" asked Adam, checking his bag to make sure his blister pack of antibiotics hadn't fallen out.

"These guys always have stories from the clinic, and nine times out of ten, anyone from out of town is there for food poisoning," said Ruben.

"You guessed right," said Adam. "Who's up first?"

"That would be me," said Sebastian. "Get ready, because I'm about to kick your asses. The loser buys dinner, just like always."

Sebastian took his stance in the tee box, and everyone else backed up. "Look at that." He shielded his eyes with his hand and watched as his golf ball sailed through the air like a tiny bird, coming to rest in the center of the fairway. "I hope you guys didn't forget your wallets."

"He has a lot more time to practice his golf game since he opened the clinic," said Ruben. "I personally miss getting a free dinner every other week."

"Talk about free time," said Sebastian. "Ruben is a college professor at the University of Guadalajara. He works, what? Maybe … eight hours a week?"

"I'm in lecture eight hours a week. I work much more than that," said Ruben. "I'm a history professor at the University."

"That sounds interesting," Adam said.

"Did anyone even see my shot?" asked Luis. "Or were you all too busy talking?"

"Did *you* even see your shot is the question," said Ruben. "I don't see your ball anywhere."

"It's in the woods," said Luis, replacing his driver in his golf bag. "You guys will have to pick up the pace, or the people behind us are going to get pissed."

"Okay," said Ruben. "It's my shot."

Adam took his swing after Ruben, and rode with Sebastian in his golf cart. "Thanks for helping me out this week."

"No problem." Sebastian smiled. "It's my job, and your corporation has already paid in full."

"Is that why you got into medicine, for the money?"

"No," said Sebastian, laughing. "I got into it for all the right reasons. I wanted to help people and all of that. Luis and I had the same ideas about helping the underserved population of Mexico, but it soon turned into an overworked and underpaid existence."

"I can see that," said Adam, thinking about the living conditions of the people in los ranchos and how much money they didn't have to spend on healthcare.

"Luis and I met in the genetics research lab at the University," continued Sebastian as he drove along the cart path. "We met Ruben in college, too. He was Luis's roommate our first year."

"It's cool how you guys still hang out," said Adam.

"Every other week without fail, unless it's raining." They pulled over, and the doctor took his second shot.

Back in the cart, Adam probed Sebastian for more information. "You had mentioned genetic research back there while we were driving, and I was wondering … the woman from the mango fair … we hung out the other weekend and—"

"Watch out for her," said Sebastian. "Those young girls are just looking for husbands."

"Not to worry," said Adam. "She's not looking to marry me. She's older, and she's already been married once."

"Keep going."

"I was wondering if you might know anything about why she would have had three stillborn sons," said Adam.

"Hey, Luis!" called Sebastian during Luis's backswing. "How long has it been since you've used your genetics background?"

"You can't shake my concentration," bragged Luis. "Years. Why?"

"Let's pull over by the drink cart after this hole," said Sebastian.

Everyone agreed. They would let the group behind them play through. Sebastian ordered four Vampiras—Bloody Marys—for the group.

Sebastian leaned against a laurel tree, Vampira in hand. "Ask Luis the question you just asked me."

Adam did as Sebastian had directed. Luis jumped on the answer.

"First, let me say that it's not *necessarily* a genetic issue." Luis glanced at his partner, who nodded in agreement. "It comes down to the age-old question of nature versus nurture. What this means is the cause could be environmental or genetic."

"You mean there could be something on the ranch that affected Marisol? Maybe something she was eating?" Adam thought back to the fish stew.

"I am *leaning* toward a genetic cause," said Luis. "I only say this because all of her offspring were male. To know anything for sure, your friend would need to be tested."

"What does that involve?" asked Adam. He didn't think he and Marisol were anywhere near close enough to support one another during medical testing. This was getting way too deep for him.

"It's just a simple blood draw," said Luis. "I wouldn't even charge her."

"Really?"

"Really," said Luis. "Ugh, this Vampira is awful. Anyway, I miss using my brain. There are only so many cases of strep throat and food poisoning I can diagnose before it becomes very mundane, albeit lucrative. I miss figuring things out. This would give me a challenge. Bring her by the clinic anytime. I'll leave a lab order with the nurses so you can come even if one of us isn't there, and they'll know what to draw. It's up to you."

"Thanks a lot," said Adam. He tipped back the remainder of his drink. "I'll ask her."

Chapter 13

Sophie

Megan didn't give a shit about what other people thought, at all. Sophie used to be jealous of how freeing that would be. Maybe she still was, but this week in Pittsburg, Sophie would take advantage of it. Not having to worry about bumping into anyone she knew gave Sophie the freedom to enjoy herself without restrictions. She and her sister could dance, say whatever they wanted, and drink whatever they wanted.

Megan answered the door at two in the afternoon, looking like Sophie had woken her up in the middle of the night. "Hey, girl." Megan smoothed her wild hair and peered at Sophie through one eye.

"Late night?" Sophie speculated.

"You know it." Megan backed up and opened the door wider to let Sophie pass. "Do you want some coffee?"

"Sure. I'll take some."

"Great. You make us some coffee, and I'll take a shower." Megan looked at Sophie's backpack with concern. "What's in there?"

"Just my clothes and stuff for the week." Sophie deposited her backpack on the living room sofa and opened the curtains, letting the golden sunlight wash over the apartment. "Where do you keep your coffee?"

"Has it been that long? I've been living here for over two years, and the coffee hasn't changed location. Look in the cabinet next to the fridge. I'll be out in thirty."

As promised, her sister emerged from her bedroom half an hour later, looking effortlessly gorgeous, wearing a pair of wide-legged jeans and a loose-fitting sweater that fell off her right shoulder. Strands of fine hair spilled from a messy bun, and her lips shimmered under a thin layer of pink lip gloss.

"Pass me a cup of coffee. It smells amazing." Megan plucked Sophie's cup from her hand and took a long swallow. "So what do you want to do today?"

"Don't you have to work?"

"I'm remote. As long as I get my stuff done, I can do it whenever."

"Must be nice." Sophie had found yet another reason to be jealous of her sister. "Want to take a walk around the city? It looks pretty outside."

"Have you gotten that boring?"

Sophie didn't know anyone else who could be this directly insulting and have it be okay—natural even, but this nasty comment was well received, and Sophie was excited to hear what Megan had in store for the trip. "So what *are* we doing?"

"First, I know you didn't bring anything current in that backpack of yours." Megan pointed at Sophie's overstuffed L.L. Bean perched on the couch. "You'll need an outfit that requires a hanger for where we're going this weekend."

"And where's that?"

Megan sat next to the backpack. "Well, I was on the bus last weekend and met this guy." Megan eyed her sister with one raised eyebrow, trying to pique Sophie's interest.

"And?"

"So I sat beside this good-looking man. It was the only seat available, so it wasn't weird. I was just scrolling on my phone, and he started a conversation with me." Megan paused dramatically. "Guess who it was."

"The guy?"

"Yes, *the guy*," said Megan.

"Who?"

"Leonard McKenzie." Megan waited for a response. "Leonard McKenzie...?" she repeated, still hoping for some type of reaction. "Ugh. Sophie, where have you been for the past two years, living under a rock?"

"It would seem so because I don't know who this guy is."

"Google him, will you?" Megan rolled her eyes with a sigh.

Sophie did just that. She typed in Leonard McKenzie, an up-and-coming multi-millionaire from Pittsburgh. He grew up on North Hawthorne, went to Pittsburgh University, worked his way through school, and created some computer code used in all the new gaming programs. Now, it was Sophie's turn to roll her eyes. "Why would Leonard McKenzie be riding the bus?"

"We talked about that," said Megan.

"Of course you did."

"He enjoys feeling normal," continued Megan, unaffected by Sophie's sarcasm. She drained Sophie's cup of coffee and poured herself another. "Look. I took a selfie of us together on the bus. We ended up riding all over the city and stopped at this festival on Birch and Third for a craft beer tasting."

"So what does he have to do with our plans for the weekend?"

"He's in town promoting the opening of a club. It's in a rougher part of the city, but his entire premise is to bring working professionals into the lower-income areas to help spur the economy. He's trying something new. It's a social move that aims to bring together the different socioeconomic strata. It also serves as a metaphor for his past and present lives. Big business and humble beginnings coming together. What do you think?"

"It sounds dangerous," said Sophie.

"Come on," said Megan in a whiny voice Sophie had rarely heard her use since they were children. "Adam's in Mexico. You guys are broken up. What's stopping you from having a little fun? A little *danger*?"

Sophie thought about it, and she couldn't come up with a concrete answer.

"It's settled, then. Get your jacket. We're going to get you into shape for the party this weekend," said Megan.

Sophie didn't know what that meant, but she got her jacket and followed Megan out the door.

•   •   •

"Leonard," said Megan. The two of them hugged as if they'd been friends since childhood. "This is my sister, Sophie."

"Nice to meet you," said Leonard.

Sophie thought he was even better looking in person and was grateful for the bountiful grooming appointments her sister had scheduled throughout the week. She felt polished, like she belonged at this party. "Nice to meet you, too."

They walked in together, but Leonard excused himself right away. As the establishment's proprietor, everyone clamored to get a picture with him and shake his hand.

"Well, that's Leonard," said Megan. "We probably won't hang with him tonight. He has to circulate. Let's get a drink!" Megan pulled Sophie along behind her.

Her little sister was used to extraordinarily tall heels, but Sophie was not. She tried to keep up as best she could as they made their way to the bar. The beads on Sophie's dress reflected the lights from the dance floor.

"What do you want?" asked Megan.

"Iced tea, please."

"Seriously. Stop being so *old*!" Megan turned to the bartender. "Two Grey Goose and cranberry juice." The bartender handed Megan the drinks. "Try this."

Sophie took a sip. "That's fantastic! I'll have to be careful with these."

"No, you won't. Tonight's not about being careful."

This is exactly why she loved Megan. Drinks in hand, they ventured onto the dance floor.

Leonard had achieved his goal of blending core city with Wall Street. The Grey Goose drinks were going down too easily by the time Sophie felt confident in her heels. She was getting good out there on the dance floor. The DJ threw it back with some Montell Jordan, and she raised her arms in the air, moving with the music, "—this is how we do it."

"You *are* doing it," said a man in a dark suit, dancing up behind her.

He looked handsome enough. *Who cares? He can be attractive or ugly if he wants. This is a great song!* Sophie's inner monologue was getting drunk. Mr. Handsome or Ugly or whatever had a friend who was dancing with Megan, and the four of them danced and drank until the fabulous lights started making her nauseous. Megan was still going strong as Sophie clumsily dancing her way to her sister.

"Hey, Megan?"

"Hey, Sophie!"

"Megan, I think we should go."

"We're just getting started," said her little sister, with two men now glued to her backside.

"We've really got to go!" Sophie held her hand over her mouth. She couldn't take the spinning lights for one more second.

"Fine," said Megan. Sophie was hitting the wall. "We've got to go, guys, but thanks for the drinks." With that, Megan led Sophie out of the club.

Inside the Uber, Sophie leaned her head against the window, willing the grey geese not to take flight.

"It's fifty bucks extra if you barf back there," said the driver.

"Chill out," replied Megan. "Nobody's barfing."

"Why did I drink so much? I'm not in college anymore. Are we in college?"

"No, sweetie. We're not in college," Megan assured her sister.

"Where's Adam?"

"He's in Mexico, and you're getting a divorce. Finally! Whoo!" said Megan, flinging her arms in the air.

"Where's Rigo?"

"I don't know who you're talking about, sweetie."

"You know. Rigo." Sophie closed her eyes, floating above her body, fighting the overpowering urge to sleep.

"No, I don't know Rigo. And open your eyes. We aren't there yet, and you're heavy."

"Rigo would never say that."

"Again, with the Rigo. Who's Rigo?" asked Megan.

"He's … I love him." Sophie slurred.

"Whatever," said Megan as they pulled up to the apartment. "See, I told you no one was barfing tonight," she said to the driver. She helped her sister to the apartment. What a role reversal. It would have been Sophie helping Megan home in college.

"Here." Megan handed Sophie a pillow. "You're on the couch tonight."

"Thanks." Sophie hugged the pillow against her beaded dress, lost her balance, and fell onto the sofa. "Let's hang out for a while longer, like when we were kids."

"Sophie, I've tried to put that part of my life behind me as best I can."

"Then let's hang out like grown-ups."

Megan snorted out a laugh. "That I can do, but let's switch to coffee. You have a long drive home in the morning."

Chapter 14

Mexico 1910

The possibility of being a widow pushed Catalina's heart deep into her stomach. She held on to her last impression of Vicente, standing inside the barn, his features obscured by smoke. Hopefully, he had made it out.

The fates of so many she cared for were unknown to her. Had Luisa fled? Was she safe, or had she been a part of the uprising? The questions kept coming, but no answers followed. Tiny hands pulled at her skirt, bringing Catalina's thoughts back to the here and now, where she was needed most.

"When is Papa going to catch up with us?" asked Ivette, almost slipping from her seat behind Daria.

Catalina pulled on the reins. Her horse came to a stop but continued to lift its hooves as if it had sensed something in the night. "You can't lean over like that, preciosa. You'll fall." She held her hands out and grabbed Ivette as she transferred from one horse to another, then wrapped her arms around her little girl and squeezed. Ivette looked so much like her father.

"How much longer do we have to ride? I'm getting tired, and it's so dark out here," asked Ivette, snug in her mother's embrace.

The flames that had consumed the agave fields had lit up the night sky as they galloped away from the ranch, but their fiery journey had turned black many hours ago. Catalina lifted the gourd—much lighter. They would need to conserve their water.

"Just a little while longer," she reassured her youngest daughter. The soothing voice on display for her baby girl coated the storm of emotions growing inside her, deceiving like the complete silence one hears while holding themselves under ocean waters as a storm rages above the surface. Catalina's arms and the reins formed a protective circle around Ivette, holding her upright as the horses picked their way through the sparse vegetation in the low light of the waxing moon.

Daria flanked her mother to the right, keeping pace in the arid country spread before them. Her impassive gaze was a testament to Catalina's years of coaching. Hacienderas were the silent leaders of the large estates, choosing their words carefully and guarding their emotions to foster an impenetrable image of strength.

"Where are we going, Mother?" her eldest asked plainly.

Daria could handle the truth, but telling her wouldn't change their circumstances, and even though Ivette had her eyes closed, her little ears were still listening. "We're going to Nayarit to meet your Primo Romualdo. You wouldn't remember him because you were a baby the last time you saw him."

"Primo Romualdo knows we're coming?" asked Daria.

Catalina had done her job, maybe too well. Daria was nearly impossible to read. She knew Vicente couldn't have gotten word to Romualdo ahead of their arrival. This was just something comforting he had said. They had been on their own as soon as they had left the ranch, but it wouldn't serve to share this with her children. People needed to have confidence and hope, and she would let her daughters hold on to both.

"Yes, Romualdo knows we're coming." Whether or not Daria believed her, she couldn't tell.

A curtain of darkness peppered with stars surrounded the travelers. The silent night air carried the labored breaths of the horses and the clatter of their hooves into the distance as they rode, announcing their approach to anyone who might lie in wait.

"How far away is Nayarit?" asked Ivette.

"Just close your eyes and hold on."

Ivette followed her mother's instructions and closed her eyes as the horses tromped on through the night. Daria didn't probe her mother for further information, riding in silence. The rocking motion of the horses came in direct contrast to the adrenaline circulating through Catalina's body, but even more overpowering than this chemical energy surge were the thoughts swirling in her mind—the what-ifs and the whys. She clung to the goal of reaching Nayarit. They would find the ocean and follow the coastline north. They had to go somewhere, and the more distance they put between themselves and the ranch, the better.

Ivette had been fully asleep for miles, no longer pretending in order to eavesdrop, and her tired body rested limply against her mother's. Catalina cradled her baby girl with one arm and massaged a knot from her lower back with the other, the painful spasm demanding she relax her posture in the saddle.

"Are you all right?" Daria tapped her horse with her heels, advancing from her position behind her mother and sister. She had fallen back when they had passed through a thick cluster of brittle shrubs. "Here. Pass her to me."

Daria and her mother transferred the sleepy girl again, providing Catalina with instant relief. She rolled her neck in wide circles and twisted her trunk from side to side, realizing she babied Ivette too much. But this was of little importance in their current situation.

Stars faded, and the obsidian sky turned a midnight blue. Riding through the night without incident had lulled Catalina into a false sense of security. Her eyelids grew heavy, threatening sleep with every blink, and her head fell forward, bouncing back up time and again. Subtle changes in her horse's gait and sporadic snorts went unnoticed, and when a group of men rounded the jagged ridge ahead of them, Catalina had not been prepared.

They must have been camped out, listening to their approach, three of them, all on horseback. Were they fleeing as well? She hoped so, but it was unlikely. Their eyes held no fear, only a calm indifference that told her this was a common practice of theirs. With lifeless eyes serving as the windows to empty souls, these men would not be swayed by emotion. Catalina bit her tongue each time it moved to cry out or plea, knowing a show of strength would be their best defense. Daria mirrored her mother's stoicism.

One horseman drew close enough to speak as the other two hung back. Dressed in a long riding jacket and tall boots, he asked where they were headed. "¿Señora, a dónde va?"

Ivette opened her eyes. "Are we there?" From her place in the saddle with Daria, she looked at the man asking the questions. "Did we find Primo Romualdo?"

"No, preciosa," said Catalina. She shushed Ivette, never taking her eyes off the men.

"Where are you headed?" repeated the man in front.

As he drew closer, the tattered leather and worn trousers confirmed Catalina's suspicions—banditos—a group of marauders, preying on the misfortunes of others.

"We're headed to Nayarit," said Catalina. "Do you know if we're headed in the right direction? We've been traveling all night."

"You're headed in the right direction, but Nayarit is still a full day's ride from here," answered the man. His horse veered to the right, and he yanked the reins, straightening the animal's stance.

Catalina wore a mask of stone, only moving her eyes. She studied their body language and listened closely to the speaker's intonations, trying to gauge how much trouble they were in. "Do you know of any nearby villages?" She hoped her instincts about the trio had been wrong.

"San Pedro is just that way," he said, pointing over the hills to the north. "But information like that doesn't come without a price. What are you ladies carrying with you?"

His smile caused the hair on her neck to stand on end. Catalina held out empty hands, palms facing upward, and kept her voice calm. "We left in such a rush, we have nothing."

The man shook his head and ran his forefinger and thumb over his mustache, smoothing the edges. "You can't expect to ride into a village, seeking food and shelter, if you have no form of payment. You have something of value with you, or you would ride on."

When Catalina didn't respond, he motioned for the other two riders to advance. The two men who had kept their distance spurred their horses, coming closer to Catalina and the girls.

She narrowed her eyes and squeezed her knees together, leaning toward her girls. The hooves of her mount danced over the desiccant terrain, repositioning her between the men and her daughters.

"Check their bags," said the man to his two companions, authorizing their dismount.

Ivette continued to shush, eyeing the strangers as the younger of the two dismounted riders opened the saddlebags on Catalina's horse, ceremoniously dropping their cargo onto the dusty ground. The water-filled gourd slipped from the looter's hands, landing sideways, spilling its life-sustaining contents onto the arid wasteland.

His bowlegged counterpart probed inside the leather bag buckled to Daria's horse. Among extra metal nails and dried goods, his fingers found the small drawstring bag, which he pulled out and tossed from one hand to the other, displaying a toothless grin. "So you don't have anything?" He laughed, appreciating his own sarcasm.

His lips curled over his gums, making it hard for Catalina to assess his age accurately. He loosened the strings and dumped the rubies from the leather pouch onto his open palm, moving his hand so they refracted the early morning light, casting small rainbows onto the gray boulders.

"And that's not all." He clamped his hand around the rubies and dug one bony finger into the bag. On his bent finger dangled an assortment of precious metal chains.

The lead rider nodded, satisfied with the find. "We can accept this." He motioned for the bowlegged man to pass him the valuables. His counterpart obediently put the jewels back in the bag, tied the strings, and threw them over. Before pocketing the goods, the headman withdrew one silver chain. "You'll need something to take with you to San Pedro."

That's all Catalina needed. They would have something to barter with in San Pedro. What good were shiny stones when you were tired, hungry, and subject to the elements? She would have traded the entire ranch to meet her children's basic needs at that moment.

They would mount their horses and depart if this was all these men were after, but Catalina sensed there was more. She watched the speaker and the dismounted horseman exchange knowing looks, communicating without saying a word. The leader gave a singular nod to his associate, and the man who had found the jewelry tore Daria from her horse. He breathed through his toothless mouth and constricted his long fingers around her upper arms from behind.

Ivette screeched as her horse reared up in response to the sudden physical aggression. Her hands gripped the animal's mane, further distressing the beast, but she stayed horsed.

"Do you want the smaller girl, too?" asked the younger rider.

"No, she's too young. She would be too much trouble on the trail."

Catalina jumped down from her horse, lifted her skirt, and ran to protect her girls, positioning herself between Ivette and the man holding Daria.

As the bowlegged man dragged Daria away, Catalina faced a choice no mother should ever have to make. Her legs, weighed down by indecision, remained firmly planted on the sandy terrain as her heart ripped in two.

She saw Daria fling her head backward toward her attacker and heard a loud pop, followed by a gush of blood. Daria's captor grimaced and brought his hands to his nostrils, leaking blood over his curled lips. This gave Daria a chance to make a dash for his empty horse, but before she could pull herself into the saddle, a jarring hit from the side knocked her to the ground. The younger rider lay on top of her. He couldn't have been more than seventeen. After knocking her down, he helped Daria to her feet, holding her in a bear hug, taking care to keep his face out of range.

"I don't want to hurt you," the young man said.

"No!" yelled Catalina, running to Daria's aid. "Let her go! Take the last chain instead! Take me instead!" She clapped her hands and set one of the men's empty horses running into the mountains.

"She's worth much more than a chain or an old woman," the lead rider assured Catalina. "Get back on your horse, and we won't kill you or the young girl." The headman turned to his partner with the bloody nose and pointed in the direction the horse had run. His man set off on foot to catch it, leaving dots of blood in the dirt.

Undeterred, Catalina reached Daria, grabbed one of her hands, and attempted to tear her away from the young man. Tears streamed down her face.

The speaker drew his weapon. "One missing horse, a wounded man, crying and screaming—enough!" He trained his gun on Catalina, then turned, pointing the gun at Ivette.

Catalina froze once more, clutching Daria and watching as he held Ivette at gunpoint. Her feet twitched inside her shoes, unsure of which direction to run. Who needed her most?

"Let me go," said Daria, locking eyes with her mother. This was not a plea to the man who had her arms pinned by her sides, but to Catalina. "Let me go," Daria repeated.

"No!" Catalina shouted through a film of tears. "Let go of her!" Catalina's nostrils flared. She couldn't get enough air.

"We don't make empty threats, Señora." The armed rider waited for Catalina's next move.

Panic-stricken and breathing too quickly, her face began to tingle. Catalina looked behind her where Ivette cried, calling her name, then back to Daria.

"Let me go," her eldest daughter said once more. "I can take care of myself, and Ivette needs you. Let me go."

Catalina's face contorted with grief, but she knew what needed to be done. It was either lose one daughter or lose two daughters. If she returned to her horse and saved Ivette today, she could search for Daria in the days to come. As she made this decision, her heart caved in on itself, folding years of love and nurturing into a knot that sank into a pool of beating, maroon liquid. Now, it was Daria who gave her strength, her confidence proudly displayed as the henchman pulled her backward. Daria hadn't gone peacefully but practically—level-headed in the face of extreme stress. Catalina had no choice but to let her go.

She returned to Ivette and brought her down from her horse. Catalina held her youngest tightly as she watched Daria disappear around the ridge. Ivette sobbed into her mother's chest. Catalina wouldn't go after them today. If she did, it would all be for nothing. She would get Ivette to safety in San Pedro and return for Daria. San Pedro was just over the hills to the north. The riders couldn't travel so quickly that Catalina couldn't catch up with them. She found the silver chain in the dirt and put it in her pocket.

Chapter 15

Sophie

The trip to see Megan had been fun, but Sophie was glad to be home. Mentally preparing to return to work tomorrow, she remembered how she and Rigo had said goodnight after the golf date. She'd been rude. Well, maybe not rude, but noticeably quiet.

With a fresh cup of coffee, Sophie sat at her desk to check her email, finding one of her proposals had been accepted. The new job was a total backyard overhaul in preparation for a wedding, also in Alexandria. After adding the preliminary dates to her calendar, she touched her hand to her forehead. It wasn't warm, but she wasn't feeling quite right—nothing specific, just not right. A slight headache threatened to put a stop to her catch-up day. She couldn't still be hungover. That would be impossible, but the coffee hadn't been the afternoon pick-me-up she'd hoped for. Maybe she needed some water.

Sophie folded her laptop and went to the kitchen to fill a glass. The cold water burned at the back of her throat as she swallowed. Oh! That was painful. She dumped out the glass, turned the tap to warm, and refilled it. She swallowed the water, and the pain was still there. Sophie would have to miss work again. Hopefully, Rigo wouldn't think she was avoiding him. Well, she had been avoiding him at first, but now she was just sick. The night of binge drinking probably hadn't helped anything.

Hey Rigo, I'm going to be out again tomorrow. I've got a sore throat. I'll let you know how it goes with the doctor today. Thanks for all that you do! She had taken the easy way out by texting, but her message was polite and to the point. You couldn't fault someone for being sick.

A thumbs up was all he sent back. She knew he was upset, but what could she do now?

Dr. Bloom logged on to her televisit and diagnosed her with strep throat. The doctor had used a magnifying app to examine her over the computer. No throat culture had been necessary. The white patches at the back of her throat had said it all. She would have to call Megan to let her know. Her younger sister had been drinking after her all week.

Sophie picked up her antibiotics from the pharmacy along with some soup and crackers. When she returned home, she realized she'd forgotten ice cream. Damn. That's the one thing she had to have every time she was sick, but she wasn't about to go out again to get it. The mouse of a headache from earlier had morphed into horses stomping across her frontal lobe. She took her medicine and lay down to sleep on the couch.

Bang, bang, bang. She heard a soft banging. *Bang, bang, bang.* This time, it was louder. Sophie got up to take an ibuprofen and try to chase away the banging in her head, but when she stood, she found her headache was gone. *Bang, bang, bang.* It was coming from the front door. The clock on the microwave read 8:00 p.m. She had been sleeping for hours. Who could be knocking at this time?

She padded to the foyer and looked through the window where a delivery person stood holding flowers, Gatorade, and … ice cream? She hoped that was what was in the brown paper bag swinging below an arrangement of pink roses.

"Thank you," she said after opening the door and taking the goodies from the young man on the porch. "Wait here." Sophie grabbed her purse from the entry table and tipped the delivery person.

Who had sent all of this? Logically, it could have only been one person, but the small kernel of hope in the pit of her stomach waited to pop until she placed the flowers on the table beside her purse and read the note card—*Feel better, Rigo.* He had said nothing and everything with this kind gesture, or maybe he was just trying to smooth things over for employment's sake. She hoped it was more than that. Anyway, there was ice cream inside the bag!

Chapter 16

Adam

Adam left for Marisol's house at dawn, exactly one week late, certain he would find her on the ranch. He parked in front and let himself in through the patio gate hidden between two scraggly crabapple trees. A fluffy chicken perched on a fruitless branch deflated as he passed by, raising its head in alarm at Adam's unfamiliar face. On a short tree stump next to the sloping ravine that led to the chor, Marisol sat squeezing the last drops of milk from the udder of a nut-brown criollo. A frayed rope secured the bovine to a low-lying branch.

He would act like nothing had happened. She might not even mention anything about last weekend. "Can I give you a hand with that?" he asked.

"Do you know how to milk a cow?" she asked in an icy tone. He knew *that* tone well.

"No, but there's a first time for everything." Adam tried to lighten the mood.

"I'm just finishing up." Marisol untied the cow from the branch and smacked it on the backside, sending it scampering away. "So what happened to you last week?"

Avoidance hadn't worked, but he wasn't sure how to explain being an entire week late. A few hours, sure, but a week? "I had food poisoning." There, that was perfect. It wasn't a lie. He just didn't specify when it had happened.

"Oh, I'm sorry. What did you eat?" She didn't wait for his answer. "Are you feeling better?"

"Yeah, I'm all right, but I was in the clinic overnight. Honestly, I don't know if it was this drink called jamaica or these flatbread gorditas." He could see that it all made sense to her now.

"I know exactly which one it was."

"Enlighten me, please." Adam leaned on the branch where she'd tied the cow and waited for her explanation. "I never want to feel like that again."

"It was the gorditas, for sure." Marisol wiped her hands on her vaqueros—jeans—and lifted the bucket of milk.

"But how do you know?"

"Adam, those are made with unpasteurized milk, like what I have in my bucket here." She held it out to him. Inside her semi-rusted, metal bucket swirled warm, pinkish, frothy milk. "I make those all the time. We all do in los ranchos, but it can be dangerous if you're not from around here."

"Mystery solved." He would have to be more careful. "What are you planning to make with this milk?"

"I'm not making anything with it." Marisol handed the bucket to Adam. "Carry this to the far side of the yard and cover it with one of those tin plates. My neighbor makes cheese. He'll be by to pick it up later."

Adam carried the bucket with one hand and lifted his other arm to balance the weight, concerned about the time this dairy product might have to sit in the sun before her neighbor would pick it up. He set the bucket down and covered it with the tin.

Getting all the heavy farm work done before the temperature started to climb was practical. Maybe they could spend the afternoon at the chor, snacking on newly fallen mangos. When Adam returned from dropping the milk off, he made his suggestion.

"I was thinking of something on a larger scale." Marisol asked him what he thought about taking a day trip to Puerto Vallarta, a beach resort on the Pacific coast. "You owe me for being an entire week late."

Her eyebrows had risen with that last remark. Maybe he hadn't fooled her. "I can't help it if I had food poisoning."

"I'm just kidding with you—lo que pasó voló. It's a Spanish saying. Translated, it means *that which is in the past flies away.* So do you want to go to Puerto Vallarta with me or not?"

Adam was glad she was letting it go. Or maybe she was just using him for his vehicle. Either way, he didn't have to do any more explaining. "How far is Puerto Vallarta from here?" Not that it mattered. Imagining Marisol in a swimsuit had been enough to convince him to make the trip.

"If we take the toll roads, we can make it there in less than three hours, but they're expensive." She slid her hands into her back pockets and waited for his thoughts.

"How much?"

"Eight hundred pesos."

"Forty dollars? Is there a different route we can take?"

"There is another road, but it'll take us eight hours to get there."

"You're not serious?"

"Oh, but I am. Most people take the longer route that winds around the mountains, but the toll roads cut right through them with bridges and tunnels."

Adam had already spent a significant amount of time on the mountain roads to get to the ranch that morning and wasn't interested in spending the next eight hours snaking his way through the Sierra Madres.

"Carlos told me you were quite high up in your company. Isn't five hours of your time worth forty dollars to you?"

"When you put it that way, I guess it is." The toll roads would be the difference between driving all day or relaxing on a tropical beach.

"It's settled, then," said Marisol. "Just let me close the gate and change." She ran to the edge of the ravine and dragged a branch studded in barbed wire across the opening where the cattle were penned.

"Sure," said Adam, noting she had not offered to split the tolls with him.

A four-lane highway catapulted them through the mountains to the coast. Fifty kilometers from Puerto Vallarta, they exited the expressway and navigated the narrow mountain roads that would take them to their destination. They wound their way slowly around the dwindling foothills, and a jungle-like humidity replaced the dry heat of los ranchos. Lush trees with thick, leafy vines threatened to obstruct the roadway, and fields of sugar cane swept down the hillsides. Adam had never seen an actual sugar cane plant before. They looked like young corn plants that didn't yet have their ears.

Marisol had changed before they left, but Adam couldn't tell. Other than the dress she had worn at the mango fair, the only things he had seen her wear were jeans and T-shirts, and for the better part of their journey so far, he'd been looking at the back of her head. What was she looking for out the window?

"So what really happened between you and your ex-wife?" asked Marisol, still looking away from him, with her feet propped up on the dashboard.

"It was kind of a slow progression of small things. That's usually how it works," Adam explained, keeping his eyes on the road. "One of the main things we used to fight about was having a baby, or the fact that I didn't want to have one. She was always trying to guilt me into having a family I didn't want, but it's a good thing we didn't have any children. We're heading for a divorce now."

Marisol didn't comment on his share. She wanted children but couldn't have them, and Adam could have them but didn't want them. He shouldn't have said anything about children, but it was too late, so he kept talking.

"I remember we had this connection in the beginning," Adam continued. "Sophie was so fun and spontaneous. That part of her faded over the years, and we ended up in our boring daily routine of work and dinner. I don't see how children could have cured the boredom in our relationship."

"You're getting a divorce because you're bored?"

Adam's face turned a light shade of pink. When she put it like that, she made him sound shallow. "That's not why."

"Sorry, but that's what it sounds like to me."

"I don't think that's a fair assessment."

"Cálmate. I thought we could say anything to each other. Would you rather I start telling you what you want to hear like everyone else in your life?"

"I guess not." He liked skipping over all the pleasant, meaningless chatter and wished more people could handle this type of honesty. "So you haven't heard anything from Christo in six years?"

"Nothing." Marisol pulled her feet from the dash. "Slow down up there." She pointed at a pile of trinkets stacked next to a cross on the side of the road.

"Sure." Adam slowed the SUV to a crawl. "Even if Christo was still alive, though, I don't think I would want anything to do with someone who had wanted nothing to do with me in six years." Fair was fair. If she was going to go there, so was he.

Marisol continued to watch the country slip by through the window. "You can speed up again," she said after they had passed the roadside memorial.

Maybe he had taken it too far. "What were you looking at?"

"I've been trying to read the names on the crosses on the side of the road. One of them might be Christo's."

"I thought you said you were sure he was alive."

"I don't know what I believe anymore. There's nothing worse than not knowing. Anything could've happened to Christo. He *could have* died crossing the border, but he could just as easily have found another woman and moved to Puerto Vallarta. One of these crosses could bear his name or … anything. Not knowing is torture. I just wish at least one of our sons would have lived. My life would have been so different."

Adam felt like a jerk. "I know you're looking for closure with Christo." He eased off the accelerator. "I don't think I can help you with that, but I think I might know someone who could help you learn more about your sons."

"Really?" Marisol abandoned the hunt for Christo's name.

"Last weekend, when I didn't show, I didn't have food poisoning. Well, I did, but that was before. Anyway, last Sunday, I was playing golf with these two doctors, and one of them offered to perform free genetic testing for you to see why your sons would have been stillborn."

Marisol remained quiet. He wasn't sure if she was happy about the testing or mad because he had lied. "I know genetic testing won't bring your sons back, but as you said, not knowing is torture. It may be some consolation to have answers about your children, even if you may never get the answers you're looking for about Christo."

"Thank you," she said, turning to look through the window again.

Now, Adam could tell she didn't care about when he'd had food poisoning. She had much more weighing on her mind, and he gave her time to process. As they neared Puerto Vallarta, the radio struggled to get reception, and they listened to a mixture of Norteño and static. Adam tried deciphering some verses but couldn't translate that quickly.

The jungle thinned as they approached the coast. Well-kept and luxurious, Puerto Vallarta boasted palm tree-lined roads and hotels painted in bold shades of blue, red, and yellow. Sprinkled between the high rises stood large, circular huts with thatched roofs. Through these open-air structures, he could see the tropical waters of the Pacific Ocean.

"Pull over here," said Marisol.

She pointed at one of the thatched roofs, and Adam pulled over as instructed. "Wow," he said. "What is this place?" He parked under a banana tree, with its long, green fruit clusters pointing toward the bright, blue sky.

"These oceanside restaurants have their own private beaches," she explained. "Follow me, but watch out." Marisol ducked under a low-hanging palm bearing the weight of a giant iguana. Its slender tail brushed against Adam's shoulder as he followed her through the parking lot and into the restaurant.

This wasn't just a tiny, thatched-roof tiki bar. As big as a gymnasium and two stories high, the restaurant had ample seating, a stage for live music, and a gift shop. Salty, ocean air swept through the dining area, and the host immediately greeted them.

"Bienvenidos." A young man in a white, button-down dress shirt welcomed them to their day of fun and relaxation.

"Hey," said Adam. "Do you know if any places rent boats around here?"

The young man looked puzzled, so Marisol chimed in to translate. Revelation spread across his face as he waved one of his colleagues over.

A tall and slim man, wearing the same style of button-down, short-sleeved shirt, approached Adam with his hand outstretched. "Hi. My name is Augusto, and I'm the hotel Caliz's concierge." He pointed at the adjacent resort with a lazy river zig-zagging through vibrant flower beds.

"Nice to meet you." Adam shook his hand. "I was wondering if you all rented boats and scuba gear?"

The concierge's eyes lit up at the prospect of making a sales connection. "Yes, sir. When were you planning to go diving?" He looked at Adam and Marisol, assuming they were a couple.

"Today," Adam said.

"We have a few slots open tomorrow," offered Augusto.

"What do you say?" Adam deferred to Marisol. "Want to stay overnight?"

"I can't leave the ranch that long, Adam. I have animals to feed and cows to milk."

Adam told Augusto that wasn't going to work. "We're just in town for the day." It had been worth a try. Banderas Bay was just south of Puerto Vallarta, known to dive enthusiasts for its long history of pirate activity. The adjoining beach was appropriately named Playa de los Muertos—the Beach of the

Dead. Oh well, Adam could book a trip anytime, and he would. Maybe he and Ben would go next spring break.

Today, he resolved to enjoy the trip for what it was, and he and Marisol lounged in resort chairs under the shade of an umbrella, ordering quarter Coronas brought out in buckets of ice. Waves crashed onto the sand, and cumulus clouds cast shadows on the tropical paradise. Patches of dark-blue water contrasted with the turquoise sea, suggesting the existence of a reef, and small, plastic circles bobbed offshore, supporting miles of shark netting. Only three hours ago, they'd been standing in a virtual wasteland whose only moisture could be found inside a cactus.

They drank and watched the surfers. The cold beers went down easily as the breeze from the ocean blew Adam's shirt like a sail. He pulled it off and tucked it under one leg of his beach chair. "Do you come here a lot? This is fabulous."

"Not nearly enough. When you live so close to such a beautiful place, you take it for granted."

"True, very true." Adam lay back and let the ocean air whisper to him as his thoughts drifted.

A Mariachi band warmed up in the restaurant behind them. "La Cucaracha? Really?" said Marisol, rolling to her side and resting her weight on her elbow.

"What's wrong with that song?"

"How cliché. The Mariachis in resort towns always cater to the tourists. If you want to hear some real Mariachi, you've got to go somewhere like San Cristóbal, but you know that. You've been there."

"I'm sorry," said Adam. "Maybe I'm not paying enough attention, but I can't tell the difference."

"Amateur."

Adam took the insult good-naturedly, the way it had been intended. "By the way, where's your bathing suit?" Why would anyone wear jeans to the beach? At least he was wearing shorts.

"I don't have one."

He kept forgetting they were from different worlds. Everyone he knew had at least one bathing suit. "Would you like one?" he offered. "They have some for sale in the gift shop?"

"Where's your suit?" she countered.

"Fine, enjoy sweating out here in your jeans." Adam threw his hands up, then dropped the conversation, disappointed he wouldn't have the chance to see Marisol's curves in a swimsuit. "The last time I saw water this clear was when Sophie and I went to Aruba."

"It *is* beautiful," said Marisol. "Christo and I came here on our honeymoon—not to this exact resort, but we came to Puerto Vallarta." She lay back in her chair and folded her arms behind her head. "Christo was the oldest child in his family, and his parents couldn't wait for grandchildren. My father-in-law sold one of his pigs to pay for the trip. In hindsight, he probably should have kept the pig."

"Here's to keeping the pig." Adam raised his Corona. *What else do you say to something like that?*

Marisol raised her drink and bumped it against Adam's. She began humming along to one of the Mariachi songs.

"I thought you didn't like resort town Mariachi."

"This is different. This is a corrido."

"What's a corrido?" Adam asked, relaxing with his eyes closed.

"Corridos are stories told in the form of songs," said Marisol. "Most of them are based on the truth. This one is by Internacionales de Durango, and it's about a prison."

"What are they saying?"

"This song was written before Mexico underwent a major prison reform. They're singing about a jail in Durango that was notorious for the deaths of its inmates."

"It doesn't sound like it's about anything that sinister." Adam moved his feet in time with the upbeat tempo.

"Listen. This is interesting … and true," she continued. "The guards kept a large, black scorpion they would let loose in one particular cell at night. Not one prisoner had ever survived a night in that cell. The pitch-dark, stone-walled room was a death sentence." Marisol paused for effect.

"The rule was that anyone who could survive a night in that cell would be granted his freedom. The guards gave all prisoners assigned to the cell one last request. Some men chose grilled steak, others asked for cigarettes. Anyway, they would enjoy whatever they'd requested because they knew it would be their last earthly pleasure. Things continued this way until one young man requested a lighter and a sombrero."

"Why would he ask for those things?"

"Just listen." She shot Adam a look of annoyance. "The guards said the same thing. They laughed and asked if he was sure he didn't want to reconsider his request, but the young man would not reconsider, and the guards produced the items. The prisoner waited up all night, standing in the middle of the room, flicking the lighter every time he felt the slightest presence or heard the faintest sound. Eventually, he caught a glimpse of the scorpion and covered it with the sombrero. They found him alive and well the next morning and had to let him go."

"What a strange story to make into a song."

"It has a great melody." Marisol passed him another Corona.

The sun hung high in the afternoon sky. Adam covered one eye with his forearm and drifted off, floating in a peaceful sleep by the ocean. The sun continued its path across the sky, and hours later, the incoming tide woke them as sea water swallowed the metal supports on the lounge chairs. They sank softly into the sand. Adam rescued his shirt from a retreating wave, squeezed out the water, and flipped it over his shoulder. "Want to get something to eat?"

"I'm starving," said Marisol. "Let's go."

Adam and Marisol pressed their way through the powdery sand to the restaurant as the beach attendants ran to save their chairs from the tide. The charred scent of grilled chicken wafted from the fire pit.

"That smells unbelievable." Adam ordered a tall glass of iced water and opened his menu while Marisol went ahead and ordered ceviche and tostadas—potato salad on a big, round tortilla chip.

"Aren't you going to wait for me to order?" Adam held up his menu. "It takes me longer because everything's in Spanish." He pointed at a picture of some savory meat smothered in chopped onions and cilantro. "What's birria de cabeza?"

"That's cow brain."

He folded his menu and placed it on the table. "I think I'll just have the chicken fajitas."

"Excellent choice." Marisol ordered for him. "Un orden de las fajitas de pollo, por favor."

The tender pieces of chicken fell apart in his mouth, flavorful without being too spicy. Good food and good company in a picturesque landscape—if they'd had a dive slot open, the trip would have been perfect.

"Do you think it would still be possible to find a buried fortune on your property?" Adam asked. "Your ranch is only six kilometers from El Mezquital Del Oro. I looked it up online, and they used to mine gold in that village."

"You're still thinking about that?" asked Marisol, laughing. "I already told you it would be a waste of time. If you go looking for buried treasure, you won't find anything but trouble. Plus, you're not familiar enough with the area. All you're going to find are rattlesnakes poking around under rocks and boulders." Marisol scooped up a spoonful of ceviche and smeared it over her tostada.

"I guess you're right. If there had been anything to find, your cousins would have found it by now. It would probably be a big waste of time."

"That's right. It would be." She held out her tostada to Adam. "Want a bite?"

Drops of the mayonnaise-based sauce rolled off the tostada, melting in the tropical air. He thought about his recent bout of food poisoning and passed on her offer. After they had finished their meal, Adam picked up the check, and they headed for the truck. He hadn't done anything this spontaneous in years. Going to the beach for only one afternoon—he hadn't even gotten in the water, but it had been fun. They parted after Adam dropped her at the ranch, but he would return the following weekend. They hadn't made any plans, but both knew it to be true.

Chapter 17

Sophie

Parsley, sage, rosemary, and thyme—every American garden had to have them. Sophie and Rigo planted the herbs in a bed of peat moss and manure, edged by flat-fitted crags, but they would have to do better. Sophie peered over the stockade fence into the neighbor's garden. Besides the traditionally grown staples she had planted for the Colemans, Rich had cilantro, peppermint, lemongrass, and hot peppers.

She wanted to bounce some ideas off Rigo, but ever since their night out, he'd been giving her the cold shoulder, even after he'd sent her the flowers. She had forgotten to text a thank you. Some things just slip your mind when you're sick. It must have been too late when she'd thanked him in person earlier that day, but he couldn't stay mad at her forever.

"What do you think about planting something that would really wow them?" asked Sophie, trying to get some type of reaction out of him.

"Whatever you think."

"Come on, Rigo. This isn't fair. What's wrong?" She couldn't stand not being able to talk to him.

"Nothing."

"Please don't do this."

He began collecting the empty bags of peat moss. "No. I think I will do this. I'll never be anything to you other than an employee."

"That's not true, and you know it."

"Do I? I really put myself out there the other night, Sophie. I was hoping we could talk after that, but then you went out of town and I didn't hear from you until you showed up to work today."

"I said I was sorry. I wasn't feeling good." It wasn't a lie.

"Look. I'm not the kind of guy who needs thank yous. It just seems like you're not ready for anything, and that's okay. Maybe I was wrong, thinking we had more between us."

That wasn't it at all. "Do you really want to know what I think of you? How you make me feel?" These words came shooting out of her mouth before she could restrain them.

He dropped the bags on the grass. "What do you think of me?"

"I think—" Sophie started and faltered. The unwelcome fear of rejection had stolen her voice. *Just do it, you coward.* Things couldn't get any more awkward. "I think of … you. When I think of spending time with a man, I think of you. I've imagined us … together." The vocalization of her innermost feelings made her as vulnerable as a newly hatched bird that had fallen out of the nest.

"That's all I needed to know." He grinned and shrugged, as if it had been obvious. "I feel the same, and it's about time I started treating you like you should be treated."

Her body had turned to stone—stunned by his words. Rigo stepped closer and took her hands in his.

"Sophie, all of this isn't coming out of nowhere. We've been hovering on the edges of our feelings for one another for years, never crossing that line. You were married, and we worked together, but I'm crossing the line now. What I'm trying to say is … saffron."

"Saffron?" she repeated. "I don't understand?"

"Saffron—something that will wow the Colemans."

"Oh, right." She pulled her mind back to the task at hand.

"Sophie." Rigo placed his hand under her chin. "I aim to give you everything you want, and you asked me what we could put in the garden to wow the client."

"I did," she breathed.

"Saffron is the gold of spices." He squeezed her hands supportively. "Stay with me. I put some time into this. Saffron comes from the stamens of a purple crocus that blooms two weeks out of the year. Each flower produces only three stamens."

"How do you just know all of that?" asked Sophie.

"After I didn't hear from you the other day, I figured it would take more than ice cream and flowers to convince you to give this a chance. I did some research in case we needed something extra for the job."

"You researched herbs for me, just in case?"

"Yes," he said, "and as you can see, it wasn't a waste of time."

There it was again, his intoxicating smile. It was her turn to say something. "Why don't you come over tonight, and we'll order the bulbs together."

"Yeah?" he said suggestively.

Sophie had his full attention. It had been a long time, but this is how a man looks at you when he's interested. "If you're available, that is. We could have dinner and order the bulbs."

"I'm definitely available." He wrapped his arm around her waist and drew her close. "What time should I come over?"

•   •   •

Sophie rearranged the office for the evening. Rumpled blankets and dented pillows littered the sofa bed where she'd been sleeping. She straightened the sheets before folding it back into a couch. As she was arranging throw pillows, her phone rang.

"Hey, Harriet."

"Hi, honey. How are things?"

"Better. Much better, actually. How is everything with you?"

"Oh, I'm fine. I just wanted to make sure you were all right after our last conversation. I've been babysitting the grandbabies all week."

"I know. I saw the pictures on Facebook. It looks like they had a great time with you."

"We did have a great time, but I'm exhausted." Harriet let out a dramatic sigh. "I was glad to hear about you and Megan getting together."

Sophie swept some crumbs from her desk into her hand. "It was like we were back in college again. But listen, I can't talk long. I'm expecting company any minute."

"Anyone I know?"

"Yes, actually. It's Rigo from work." Sophie continued to bustle around the office with Harriet on speakerphone.

"That handsome man, who's always in the background in those pictures you send me of your projects?"

"That's him."

"I was wondering how long it would take the two of you to notice each other." There it was—the long pause. Harriet was waiting for her to catch up. "You've never been anything but complimentary of this young man …"

"I've never been able to keep anything from you, Harriet. Truthfully, he has been on my mind a lot. He may be … well, we'll see."

"Honey, it sounds both complicated and effortless, like so many things in life. Just try not to confuse your feelings for Rigo with your feelings about Adam."

Solid advice, as usual. Harriett knew her most vulnerable self, the one always searching for a place she truly belonged.

"I know you're expecting company, so I'll let you go, baby. Love you."

"Love you, too, and thanks again for checking in."

The doorbell rang, and Sophie went to answer it, catching a glimpse of herself in the foyer mirror—she could have passed for thirty. She greeted Rigo as his eyes roamed over her body.

"You look beautiful."

"Thank you." She should have also complimented him, but instead, she pointed at a black, plastic bag he held in his hand. "What's in the bag?"

"My mom wanted me to bring these to you. They're semillas de calabaza—pumpkin seeds. She grows the pumpkins herself."

"But your mom lives in Mexico."

"She does, but when I told her we were getting together today, she called my uncle and had him drive some over to my sister's house. My mom had just shipped a whole box to my uncle."

Had he spoken of her to his mother often? Often enough to receive homegrown pumpkin seeds, it appeared. "That was sweet of her." Sophie stepped aside and held the door open. "Please, come in."

"Thanks. You know, this is the first time I've been inside your house in all the years we've known each other."

Sophie caught him confidently eyeing himself in the mirror. "Well, I've never been to your house either."

"I guess you're right." Rigo glanced around the foyer. "Where are we going to work tonight?"

Sophie had almost forgotten the purpose of the evening. "Follow me." She led Rigo through the kitchen and down the hall to the office.

His cologne smelled of wood and spices, making it hard for her to concentrate, but it didn't take them long to get the business out of the way. Three kilos of crocus bulbs would be on the way from California that night. They had also found two recipes for rice dishes, both calling for saffron. It would be the perfect finishing touch to have the recipes written in calligraphy and set on the garden bench, next to where the flowers would bloom. The Colemans could rub it in their neighbor's face, as requested.

"That was easy," said Rigo, rising from the wheeled office chair.

"I know I probably could have done that by myself."

He leaned over her chair and spoke softly into her ear. "I'm glad you didn't."

His words sent tingles through her body. Sophie knew they were starting something, but it still surprised her to hear him talk like this after all the time they had spent working together.

"What smells so good?" Rigo held her hand, steering her toward the kitchen.

"It's lasagna. I hope you like Italian food."

"I do, very much."

Sophie pulled the casserole dish from the oven and placed it on the table next to a wooden serving bowl piled high with crisp vegetables. They slipped easily into conversation, fueled by their many years of friendship. He complimented her cooking and the house, but Sophie wanted more. The air in the kitchen pressed down on her, saturated with an invisible energy she was sure would electrocute her if she were to reach out and touch the gorgeous man seated across the table.

"You okay?"

He had caught her staring. "Yes." She shook her head, pulling herself back to their conversation. "I thought we could have dessert on the patio." Sophie pulled a lemon torte and a bottle of white wine from the refrigerator.

"That looks great." Rigo ran his fork across his nearly empty plate, collecting the last of the tomato sauce. He placed his dishes in the sink and followed her onto the patio.

Sophie passed him a slice of the citrus confection. "I've never had anything bad from the Amish market. I couldn't make it better myself."

Rigo took a bite. "I hate to say it, but maybe that's true. This is delicious." He licked the frosting from his fork.

"Would you like a glass of wine?" Sophie set her plate down and picked up the bottle, anticipating his response.

"No thanks. I want all of my senses intact this evening."

Maybe he *had* read her mind. She placed the bottle on the glass-topped end table. "Do you want to watch a movie after dessert?" If drinks and conversation were out, she wasn't sure what else to suggest.

"Not really." Rigo leaned back in the patio chair with his hands behind his head. "Why don't we sit out here and enjoy the sky? I don't need any wine to talk to you. You're my closest friend in the US."

This was news to her, but it shouldn't have been. Rigo knew more about her than Adam did, more than her sister, too.

Sophie collected the cake plates and brought them inside, then stopped in the bathroom to reapply her lip gloss before rejoining him on the patio.

"Come and sit with me." Rigo opened his arms to her.

Sophie's heart jumped into her throat, and she swallowed against the rising tension. He looked so enticing lying there with one leg crossed over the other, his dark-brown eyes soft and inviting. They lay together on the patio chair, her head cradled in his shoulder, talking about their families and what they wanted to accomplish in life. But was he going to make a move?

"Have you ever thought about traveling?" asked Rigo.

"Sure. I would have been super excited about the trip to Mexico if I hadn't had to go with Adam."

"It would probably be a better trip if *we* went together."

"Really?"

He touched his hand to her chin, gently lifting her face until their eyes met. "Really." He bent his head down, and their lips grazed ever so gently. She could feel his breath on her cheek.

Years of wanting and watching had led to this moment. She wasn't thinking of Adam at all, only of how good it felt to be pressed against Rigo. He enveloped her with his powerful arms and touched his full lips to hers, sweetly, softly, over and over. He rolled over and held himself aloft her body, and she ran her hands along his taut triceps. The pressure of his body pinned her down.

"Is this okay with you?" he asked.

She didn't know what *this* was, but she didn't want him to stop and nodded.

He slid his hand under her dress, exploring her soft skin. Her hands glided over the rippled muscles of his back, and he grew harder under his jeans, his bulge pressing into her thigh.

With his eyes closed, Rigo kissed her with a passion she hadn't felt since before she'd been married. The entire world melted away, and it was only the two of them, surrounded by the still night air and the clouds passing over the moon. Time and space dissolved, leaving only pleasure, nakedness, and bodies. Joined together, every lunge brought her closer to bliss. There was no going back.

"Why don't we go to bed?" he said, getting up and helping her to her feet. He led her to the stairs, their naked bodies hidden from her neighbors by frosted glass.

Warm under the covers, he caressed her breasts and her bottom. Their legs intermingled, and every brush against her skin evoked a desire for more. Sophie awoke several times during the night to view the sensual man sharing her bed. Hopefully, this would not be the last time. Had she made it too easy for him?

The sun shone through her bedroom window as Sophie stretched, when the memories of the night before came rushing back. Her heart sank as she rolled over to see the empty space beside her. Last night had obviously meant much more to her. Was it really such a shock that Rigo, too, had turned out to be a jerk? She had never met a guy who wasn't, but she would be fine. She always was.

Sophie walked to the bathroom, splashed water on her face, and thought about what had happened between her and Rigo. Had he worn a condom? She hadn't checked, too caught up in the moment. She wasn't looking forward to work that day.

Under a deluge of hot water, things didn't look any brighter. Sophie slunk down the steps wearing her robe with her hair wrapped in a towel, feeling like crap. The sad part was she had really believed him. She had been falling for him. How could she have been so easy to manipulate? Sophie rounded the corner to the kitchen.

"Good morning."

"Rigo?" His sudden presence filled the cavity of solitude in her stomach.

"Were you expecting someone else?" He cracked an egg into a bowl. "You looked so peaceful sleeping. I couldn't wake you, but I made breakfast for us. I hope you don't mind, but I cut some dill from your garden for the eggs."

He'd been there the whole time. After being with Adam for so long, it would take time to change her way of thinking. In the meantime, she would try not to confuse her feelings for Rigo with her feelings for Adam. Harriet had been right, again.

Chapter 18

Adam

The newfound balance between Adam's personal life and professional life was agreeing with him. He'd started the weekend at Marisol's ranch yesterday, unable to recall the last time he'd had such an instant connection with a woman. Today was golf day, and Adam was the first to arrive at the restaurant for their post-game dinner. The establishment didn't have a name, which wasn't uncommon. So many of the restaurants in Jalisco were simply called Restaurante. He would remember this one as the yellow Restaurante with stucco the color of the sun.

Chairs carved from rustic wood with leather seats stretched like drums occupied the bar lounge. Adam sat and ran his hands along the polished, oak arms of his chair. A server with a thick mustache and crisp, white shirt took his drink order immediately.

"Sí, señor, un Sol," said the server as he went to retrieve Adam's drink.

Supported by thick, hardwood beams, a vaulted ceiling towered above the dining area at the center of the building. A brick walkway bordered the dining room, open to the sky, lending an open-air feel to the restaurant. Potted palms and dwarf lime trees swayed in the downward gusts of fresh air from high above the city streets. The establishment showcased an open fire pit opposite the bar where the embers of logs burned red and smoky, slowly grilling the carnitas—pulled pork. The breezeway pulled the smoke up and out of the restaurant. By the time Adam had his beer in hand, the others had arrived, and he rose to greet them.

"Who knew the newest member of our golf tribe would be the winner after only his second game," said Sebastian.

"I just got lucky," said Adam, trying not to smile too much.

"I sure didn't," said Ruben, pulling out a leather chair next to Adam. "Dinner's on me *again*."

"Is the starving academic feeling the pain of losing?" asked Luis, who had stopped at home to change first. Everyone wore their golf attire, but Luis arrived freshly showered in a sport coat.

"Pendejo," responded Ruben. He gave the server his drink order.

"So what do you teach?" Adam asked Ruben. "I know you're a history professor, but what classes do you teach?"

"Are you a history buff?" Ruben responded, sitting up in his seat with interest.

"I'm starting to be. My friend, Marisol, has some wild stories about buried treasure. Actually, they're her cousin's stories."

"What kind of stories?" asked Ruben.

"Let's see. The most interesting one I've heard so far was about a family having to flee after a peasant uprising in Jalisco, the Hernandez Castañeda family, I think? Have you heard that one?"

Their drinks arrived, and the server set out a bowl of fresh guacamole. Small fans of dark cilantro leaves peppered the creamy appetizer.

"I don't recall that one in particular," said Ruben. "Everyone's families have those kinds of stories. They're essentially the Mexican version of the American tall tale, stories that take on lives of their own. They grow bigger each time new embellishments are added, but this is more of a literary topic."

"I don't mean to interrupt you guys," said Luis, scooping guacamole onto a chip, "but did you have time to ask your friend if she would like to have that genetic testing?"

"I did," said Adam. "She didn't really give me an answer, but I extended the offer to her, and she has the address to the clinic."

"We'll see if she decides to go ahead with it," said Luis. "Damn it!" A plop of guacamole fell onto his dress shirt, and he wiped it off with a napkin. "Are you guys ready to order?"

Adam decided on the carnitas, which he'd been eyeing by the fire pit ever since he'd arrived. The server took down their orders on a pad of lined paper, guided them to their table under the high ceiling, and hastened to the kitchen.

"So, to answer your question,"—Ruben cycled back to their previous topic—"I teach mainly recent Mexican history, the last two hundred years."

"That's an interesting period," said Adam.

"You think so?" asked Ruben, a little surprised. "People typically want to know about the Mexican indigenous populations like the Aztecs and the Mayans. I usually lose them at 'peasant revolt.'"

"You won't lose me. I'd like to know more about where these 'Mexican tall tales' originated." Adam poked a lime wedge into his beer and took another sip. "I've been looking online, but it's mostly just dates and politics."

"You asked for it this time," Sebastian said. "Once you get Ruben started on history, it's hard to stop that train." Sebastian finished his beer in two long pulls and flagged a different server for another.

"Callate, I'm trying to educate our new friend." The professor gestured to Adam.

Sebastian rolled his eyes, and he and Luis began talking sports. Once Ruben got going, it was usually a lengthy conversation.

"Okay then," Ruben began, "to fully understand how small fortunes came to be buried in the area, you need to understand why the Mexican Revolution took place and what changes it caused."

"Sure," said Adam. "I'm pretty much up to speed on the whole call for agrarian land reform and the social divide."

Ruben nodded approvingly. "You *have* done your research."

The others weren't paying any attention, still talking soccer, and attacking the guacamole.

"As you've probably read, the war lasted from 1910 to 1921," explained Ruben. "Peasant uprisings caused many wealthy hacienderos to liquidate their assets and try to flee the area with their fortunes. Banditos were everywhere for this very reason."

Adam sat up straighter in his seat. From his dive experience, he knew that folklore could easily become tangible fact when approached with enough perseverance and financial resources.

"It wasn't safe to have so much wealth in transit," continued Ruben, "and many buried their fortunes for safekeeping. In such a tumultuous time, many who buried their valuables were killed or unable to locate the places where they'd hidden their treasures in the war's aftermath."

The server set their plates on the table. Adam's carnitas came on corn tortillas with chopped cilantro, onion, and a mild green salsa.

Ruben didn't acknowledge the server. He took one bite of his sauteed shrimp and continued explaining. "This is where the line between historical fact and cultural storytelling blurs. I rarely get into this aspect of the Mexican Revolution, but because of your interest, I'm willing to delve into this topic."

"Are you still talking?" asked Luis.

"Just ignore him," Ruben said to Adam. "In the years that followed, stories circulated about poor farmers who had seen green fire escaping from the earth. When these farmers dug where they'd seen the fire, they would find gold, and it was termed the *green fire of gold*."

As Adam listened to the professor, the possibility of finding something truly valuable in los ranchos sent tingles through his limbs, and he had to sit on his hands to keep from fidgeting. "What kind of fortunes are we talking about? What would a find like that be worth today?"

"I doubt any of the fortunes remain uncovered, but according to Mexican folklore, it would be more money than you could make in a lifetime." Ruben popped two more shrimp into his mouth and continued lecturing.

"Watch out, though. If you feel tempted to go on the hunt, listen to this next part. There is said to be a magical property to the buried treasures, that they're meant for certain individuals only. One of my favorite stories is about a man who saw the green fire coming from the earth near El Mezquital del Oro. He dug down a quarter of a meter, but all he found was mulch. He thought it was strange to find a cache of mulch underground, so he put the mulch in a bag and stuck it on a shelf in the back of his general store. Days later, a woman came into the store and asked him why he had so much gold sitting in a bag on the shelf. The man looked at his bag of mulch and realized the gold was meant for this woman. He couldn't see what it truly was because it was meant for her, so he gave her the bag."

"Wow, I just got chills," said Adam, extending his arm with goose flesh visible.

"Anyway," Ruben said, "none of these 'tall tales' are based on evidence. These stories are a product of the hearsay of country folk spanning generations. I mean, green fire spewing from the ground? That's impossible. Plus, the fleeing hacienderos were usually in such a rush to hide their fortunes, the holes they dug were very shallow. You can see how it would be unlikely to find any that might remain."

Adam agreed with Ruben to his face as he made a mental note to buy a metal detector. He and Ruben eventually joined the soccer discussion and planned to meet in two weeks for their next golf game.

•   •   •

Adam had been finding it hard to concentrate on work. It was all he could do to stay until six o'clock. He worked on progress reports, logged purchase orders, updated the client, and checked his email from his laptop in the truck. Another crew of tradespeople had rotated through the job. The framers and plumbers had come and gone, and now he and Carlos were supervising the electrical workers. Carlos was his constant and his greatest asset on the job.

As long as he had Carlos, he would never have to be there another Saturday or Sunday for the project's duration. Carlos was extremely capable, and even though Adam didn't want to admit it, Carlos was a better manager. That was okay, though, because Carlos wasn't competition. Adam would let Carlos turn out a quality product and he would return to the States to claim his large bonus from Empire.

After work on Wednesday, Adam took a shower and went into the city in search of a metal detector. To his surprise, a Soriana stood only five kilometers west of the Guadalajara Cathedral. *Thank God*, he thought. Adam pulled into the parking lot and sighed. As he walked up and down the aisles, he noted that a trip to a big box store had never felt so luxurious. With its high ceilings, fluorescent lights, air conditioning, and limitless inventory, he could buy anything he needed, all under one vast roof. He quickly located the outdoor section and grabbed the only metal detector they had. He also seized the opportunity to load up on his favorite candy, having lost some weight between his visits to the ranch and working on the jobsite.

As he made his way to check out with an armful of chocolates, Adam passed the books and stopped to see if any were about the Mexican Revolution. Soriana really did have everything. He found a book on Mexican history with Spanish on one side of the page and the English translation on the other. Sure, he could look anything up online, but something about holding an actual book gave him comfort. Even though he filled his days with work and the friends he had made, he still spent most evenings alone, and it would be nice to have something to hold in his hands.

Back at the townhouse, Adam set up for a night on the balcony. The sun had set, and he turned on the porch lights. Iridescent green beetles knocked themselves against the glass bulbs, offsetting the electrical hum with intermittent clicking. He placed a bag of chocolates on the table, took a seat on one of the wrought-iron chairs with his Mexican history book, and skimmed the index until he found a section on the Mexican Revolution.

The book mentioned Guadalajara as one area from which hacienderos had fled during the time of civil unrest. He thought about the metal detector he had just purchased. Maybe it wouldn't be a waste of money. Next, he read the section on El Mezquital Del Oro. Investors from the United States had purchased the land comprising El Mezquital and mined it for gold in the late eighteen hundreds. During the Mexican Revolution, the Americans were stripped of this land, and ownership rights were given back to the indigenous people. The mines were shut down and branded as unsafe. The book gave further details about thieves having entered the mine shafts, never to return. It then said that in recent decades, the general population has come to respect the hazardous conditions of the mines and that the mines are now the property of the Mexican government. The government, in turn, has looked the other way, while local artisans collect gold nuggets from the nearby streams during the rainy season.

The volume explored multiple other villages and territories, but Adam knew exactly where to find El Mezquital, and it was close. So he decided to take the metal detector to los ranchos after work the next day. Even if he didn't find a fortune, the prospect of finding a nugget or two was tempting.

•   •   •

The following afternoon, Adam departed for El Mezquital with his new metal detector and a cooler full of bottled water. He had cut out a few hours early, but running a job in Mexico wasn't like running one in Baltimore. Mr. Greenberg wasn't going to show up in Guadalajara unannounced. Carlos was also professional, to his own detriment. He would never jump the chain of command and communicate directly with Adam's boss. To be honest, Adam was sure Mr. Greenberg wouldn't accept a call from Carlos, even if he did.

When Adam arrived in the village, the shop owners had rolled down the aluminum storefront doors for the afternoon, the employees home for lunch. A Meyer lemon tree grew from a tiny opening in a sidewalk edged with brick. Its branches arced down like so many rainbows, supporting the tart fruit. Adam parked next to the tree, wishing he'd arrived just a few minutes earlier. He'd forgotten his Orioles hat, and the sun's rays shone unobstructed by clouds. Nothing would be open again until at least four o'clock. Oh well, he kept sunscreen in his center console and applied some to his face.

Only a handful of people remained in the village square—a mother chased her toddler around a gazebo and a cluster of older men conversed under a shade tree. Metal detector in hand, he walked confidently away from the village, following the perimeter of a crumbling rock fence toward a neighboring valley. Once he was a good distance from the village, he donned his headphones and turned on the machine. The timeworn fence stretched all the way to a creek, and Adam left boot prints in the loose soil as he followed it. He waved the detector from side to side as he went, wondering if it might be broken. By the time he had reached the creek, the machine hadn't made a sound, not a single blip.

The current washed over a collection of rocks in the creek bed, and the rich colors of the submerged stones stood in stark contrast to their dry counterparts along the water's edge. Adam paused next to the stream, scanning the wet stones, hoping to spot something shiny, then continued his expedition. *Beep,*

beep, beep—his first find! He slowly moved the waterproof search coil over the hot spot, and it beeped again, so he carefully set the detector on a bed of pebbles and unhooked the sifter he'd looped to his belt. With a serrated hand shovel, he filled the sieve. The heavy soil had fixed the rocks in place, and Adam flicked the wet clumps of earth onto the wire mesh. He dipped the screen piled with mud into the flowing water and waited for the current to reveal the brilliant, yellow metal, but all he found after the dirt particles had been washed away was part of a can. *Fantastic*, he thought.

Even though it was just a can, the excitement he'd felt before he knew it was a can was like the feeling he'd had in Atlantic City. He and Sophie had gone there on a mini-vacation, and he'd won two hundred dollars from a slot machine their first night. He spent the rest of their vacation parked in front of the machine, and she spent the remainder of the vacation mad at him for not budging from the machine. Luckily, he didn't have to bother with Sophie now and could just have fun with his metal detector.

The hill he had descended blocked his view of the town as he walked parallel to the water's edge, stopping when he heard beeping and finding only trash. At least he knew the machine worked. Adam had his headphones on and didn't hear it when a man called to him from the far side of the creek. He continued to move the detector back and forth, waiting for another alert.

"¿Qué estás haciendo aquí?"

The muffled voice penetrated his headphones, and Adam looked up to see a man with a gun in an actual leather gun holster guiding a mule across the creek. Adam's adrenal glands infused his arteries with their heat, confirming on a primal level that Adam had placed himself in an undesirable situation. He pushed his headphones down around his neck and waited for the stranger to say something else.

"¿Por qué estás aquí y qué estás haciendo?"

It was hard for Adam to understand the man's accent, but his facial expression made it clear he wanted to know what Adam was doing there. Shit. It was obvious what he was doing there, with a metal detector in hand. Adam was too used to being the boss. He had given little thought to the fact that he might be trespassing. Well, he had thought about it, but it hadn't given him any pause. He'd just felt entitled to start treasure hunting wherever he wanted, which didn't seem like such a great idea now that a man with a gun was questioning his actions.

"Um, I was just—" Adam stopped to think. It was hard to find the right words under pressure. "Buscar cosas with detector—gold." He went with the truth. Anything else wouldn't have been believable.

To his relief, the man gave no indication he was planning to use the gun that hung at his hip, but Adam had overstepped his bounds with this excursion.

"Yo también," said the man. He was looking for gold, too.

"Have you found anything?" asked Adam, approaching the man with the mule.

The man took a plastic sandwich bag from his pocket and held it up for Adam to see. Inside, small, yellow pebbles about the size of Rice Krispies glinted in the sun.

"¿Oro?" Adam asked.

"Sí, son," said the man. They were pieces of gold. "¿Encontraste algo?"

"¿Qué? Could you say that again? Otra vez, más despacio—slower, please."

The man wanted to know if Adam had found anything, and Adam pointed at the assortment of trash he had unearthed. The man with the mule laughed heartily. Adam didn't appreciate being laughed at, but kept this to himself because this man was still a stranger with a gun.

"Sígueme." He gestured for Adam to follow him into the mouth of an abandoned mine across the creek. At least it looked like an abandoned mine. Thorny shrubs obstructed his view of the entrance.

Adam examined the man and the black hole in the mountain. The man smiled and waved Adam over, but something didn't feel right. It wasn't like when he had met Alberto. This guy gave him a bad feeling. Adam stepped backward, keeping the man in sight.

"Vamos a buscar mucho oro." The man pointed across the creek again. "Mucho oro," he insisted.

Now Adam knew he was in trouble. No one would intentionally invite him to share in a find, and no one would lead a complete stranger to "mucho oro"—a lot of gold. He wondered how many of this guy's friends were inside the mine. El Mezquital was known for its gold, and this was the perfect place for a setup like this, but Adam wasn't about to be one of their marks. He dropped his shovel in the dirt and stepped away, never turning his back on the man. It was about time for the village to come alive again. The man must have realized this, too, because he stuffed the sandwich bag in his pocket and led the mule across the creek, the way they had come.

Nothing had happened, but Adam could feel in his blood that it had been a close call. He had kept a level head, accurately assessing the situation, and promised himself he would not put himself in another situation like it. Did the creek in El Mezquital connect to the chor at Marisol's ranch? He would find out once he got reception. Adam didn't want to run into this guy again or anyone else like him and would stick to Marisol's ranch to use his metal detector in the future. This wasn't the United States, and he couldn't just be anywhere doing anything he wanted. He had to respect his new surroundings and proceed with more caution.

Chapter 19

Esmeralda
Los Ranchos, Mexico
September 1987

It had been nine months since the night of the festival in García—Esmeralda's last performance. She held her stomach in one hand and used the other to pivot around an oblong boulder. Grit rolled beneath her fingertips on the hot surface of the stone, and she could scarcely breathe in the muggy afternoon air. Loose earth gave way under her feet, sending sleek lizards scampering into the brush as she half hiked, half slid her way down the sloping hillside to the river. It was mid-September, and the river that had been nearly dry a few months ago rushed over smooth stones lining the bottom. The rains had returned. Low and strong to the west, the sun beat down on her. Jet-black hair clumped on her forehead, coated with perspiration, and her feet slid inside her leather sandals. Another contraction stretched its tentacles from her lower back to the dark line running down her swollen abdomen. Her knees buckled, and she landed, legs apart, on the gray pebbles littering the sandy banks of the river. She crawled into the water on her hands and knees, grabbing hold of rocks below the surface to propel herself into a calm pool, cut off from the current by a fallen mango tree.

The sturdy tree trunk lent support to her back, providing momentary relief from the painful crescendo of childbirth, but this reprieve was short-lived. Contractions returned with precipitating rectal pressure and an instinctual need to push. Her eyes rolled around, unable to focus on anything in particular—just moving. Whimpering moans escaped her mouth, only to be lost in the sound of fast-moving water pushing against the rocks.

Breathing, pushing, sobbing, and squirming in a puddle of water like a catfish cut off from the stream. One more deep breath—and push, push—the baby slipped into the pool. Murky water enveloped mother and child with blood and fluids. Esmeralda waved her hands between her legs and caught hold of a plump, little body. She pulled him to her chest—a boy. With the edge of her dress, she wiped his face, then waited for his cry. The new mother kneeled in the cool water. Dizziness engulfed her, and she sat back on her heels. The baby wasn't crying, his skin varying shades of purple and blue. What else did she have to do? She continued to wipe his face with her dress until— another contraction.

Her abdominal muscles solidified, and her lower back burned with pain. Teeth clenched, she leaned against the fallen mango tree, extended her legs, and let them float to the surface as the pressure built. She held the newborn above the surface and supported herself with one outstretched arm, pushing herself up from the rocky basin. A hard, bulging presence kept her legs apart. She felt *another* round head. Twins. She was having twins! She pushed forcefully with the next contractions and felt for the second baby in the red water. Blackness stole her vision, reducing her world to a small circular window. She clung to the waterlogged tree, fighting to remain conscious, slowing her breaths until her face stopped tingling.

As the outlines of objects in her surroundings returned, so did her alarm. Where were the babies? How long had it been? She swirled her arms, palms open, in the stagnant liquid. What was that? Something soft under the water. Esmeralda grasped the spongy cord and pulled her baby toward her, using the umbilical cord like a rescue rope. A girl. Was she alive? Esmeralda cleaned her nose and mouth and the infant yelped. Disoriented, she lifted her arm in which she had held her baby boy. Empty—but she already knew that. She jerked her head frantically, scanning the water for her baby boy. The new mother screamed and called to her baby boy, called for help, called to God, but no one came. No one heard. She waded in the river with her little girl pressed tightly to her chest, sloshing through the water, trying to keep her balance on the loose stones and leaving a trail of expanding blood in her wake.

There he was! She fought her way through the current to the other side of the river, clutching her baby girl, and scooped him up. His head fell backward, and his feet dangled with ten perfect toes. He hadn't made a single sound or taken even one breath. His life was over before it had even begun. In her other arm, her daughter grew cool. Esmeralda bent down and let her son slip into the water. The boy's placenta had passed with the birth of his sister. He and his placenta made their way down the river, banging against the occasional rock.

Esmeralda withdrew her knife from her pocket and cut her daughter's umbilical cord long enough to tie. She tucked her new little one inside her dress, close to her breast, and slowly followed the path to the ranch house.

Chapter 20

Sophie

Too much stonework in too small a space—by the end of the project, it was hard to distinguish between the Colemans' backyard and ancient Greece. The archway towered over the garden, grand to the point of foolishness, but no one could boast a more extravagant backyard.

"It looks great," said Rigo, lacing his fingers through Sophie's and staring at the Parthenon of a backyard they'd created together.

"It sure is … something," she said.

"It's exactly what they asked for," said Rigo, squeezing her hand.

"That's what's important." Sophie snapped a quick photo for Harriet.

The saffron bulbs had arrived on schedule. Amanda Coleman had not been as taken with the idea as Sophie had been, but this didn't bother her like it normally would have because that brilliant idea had completely transformed her relationship with Rigo. They had started the Colemans' yard as friends and ended as … well, they still hadn't labeled what it was exactly. Sophie pried her eyes from the grandiose backyard and asked Rigo if he wanted to do something that weekend.

"I had already planned on it."

There it was again, his playful smile. He was effortlessly good-looking, even in jeans and a T-shirt covered in cement dust.

"No, I mean get away. Do you want to travel somewhere this weekend?"

"It doesn't matter where we are, just as long as I can have you whenever I want." He kissed her on the neck, and she scrunched her shoulder up, pushing him away. "You can't do that here. Amanda could show up any minute."

Rigo brushed his hand through his hair, releasing a puff of cement dust into the air. "Are you afraid she'll think you're kissing her husband with my gray hair?"

"You're ridiculous. You know that?"

"Yes, but you love it."

Sophie's phone vibrated—a text from Amanda. "She's running late. If she has any issues, she'll call."

"That was too easy." Rigo ran his hands back and forth through his hair quickly to get the rest of the dust out and went to check on the last slab of concrete by the back gate.

Sophie's phone vibrated again, but she declined the call.

"Was that Amanda?"

"No, it was my mom."

"The slab will be dry by tomorrow, but I'll put a sign up so no one steps on it," he said after inspecting their handiwork. "And you shouldn't ignore a call from your mom. What if she needs you?"

That was it precisely. Her mom probably needed money. She should just block her number and be done with it. No need to drag old baggage into a new beginning, but now wasn't the time to open that box of old feelings. Sophie slid her phone into her pocket. "Why don't you come to my place tonight?" Hopefully, Rigo would allow the change of subject.

"Why not my place? My sister and her family went to Mexico—one last trip before she has the baby. So I have the house all to myself."

They had been meeting on her turf, on the jobsite, at her house. It was exciting to think of herself in his personal space, and she agreed.

•   •   •

Rigo greeted her at the door in sweatpants and a T-shirt. "Come in."

As soon as he shut the door, he backed her against the wall in the hallway, bumping her shoulders against framed family photos, and kissed her forcefully. The sweatpants made it easy for her to tell how he was feeling. Then he pulled away, took her by the hand, and led her to the living room.

"So why did you want me to wear yoga pants?"

"I'll show you." Rigo steered her around the corner into the living room, where three candles burned on the coffee table next to a fresh bowl of popcorn and a bottle of red wine. He had cued the TV to the opening credits of a telenovela.

"What's all this?"

"A cozy night in. I thought this would be a fun way for you to pick up some Spanish."

Even in sweatpants, she couldn't take her eyes off him. He stood there with his easy smile—black hair still wet from the shower.

"What are we watching?"

"Come and sit." Rigo sat on the couch and pulled her into his lap. "For your viewing pleasure, I've selected the best episode of *Corazones* ever made. This is the one where Hector returns from living on the deserted island for years, only to find that his third wife is remarried to his younger brother."

Sophie turned around on his lap and hugged him, laughing. "You know a lot about this series."

"Just give it an episode. Everyone thinks telenovelas are silly at first, but you'll be hooked. I guarantee it."

"It sounds like you're hooked."

"I'm not gonna lie. I am, but it's my abuelita's fault." He spread a comforter over the two of them. "Back when I was a kid, I would stop by her house every day on my way home from school."

"Aww, that's so cute—a grandma watching her afternoon soap with her grandson."

"To be honest, I wasn't super into it at first, but my mom told me my visits would be good for my abuelita after the Federales had torn her place apart."

"What? Why would they have done that? What were they looking for?"

"Anything of value." Rigo crunched on a piece of popcorn as if this conversation were commonplace. "A general lack of accountability makes for a lot of unauthorized searches."

Rigo passed Sophie the popcorn, but she set the bowl on the table without taking any. Poor Grandma. Sophie could only imagine how Harriet would have felt in a situation like that.

"Anyway, after the forced entry, my abuelita didn't like being there alone, and kept anything of value buried in her backyard."

"I can see why."

"She would always cook something before I stopped by, too. We would eat together and watch *Corazones*."

"That was so sweet of you."

Rigo delivered on his guarantee. By the end of the episode, she was invested. Even though she couldn't understand most of what was being said, the exaggerated facial expressions and the actors' commitment to the scenes made it impossible to look away—as cringeworthy as it might have been.

"Do you want to watch the next one?" she asked him.

Rigo held his hand over his mouth and opened his eyes way too wide. "¡Dios mío, es increíble! ¿Te gusta este programa estupenda?"

She laughed and gave him an exaggerated push into the couch. "Stop it."

"You'll have to accept leaving on a cliffhanger, because I can't take it anymore."

"Take what?"

"You know what I'm talking about." He looked her up and down. "I'd like to show you my bedroom."

"Is it time for a tour?" She would play along.

Rigo stood and held his hand out for her. "It is. Follow me."

His bedroom was simple—a nightstand with a lamp next to a full bed, neatly made up, and one dresser with a few scattered photos. He pushed her onto the bed and fell on top of her.

"Hold on." Sophie squirmed out of his embrace. "I want to have a look around."

"There's not much to see in here."

"I've noticed," she said, walking to the dresser, curious to see who meant the most to him. The room looked like a hotel room, save for the display of pictures. "Who's this?" she asked, holding an older photo of a man in an unfinished wooden frame.

Rigo joined her by the dresser. "That was my dad. This picture was taken six months before he died."

"I'm sorry." Sophie hoped she hadn't spoiled the mood.

"It's not your fault. I look nothing like him."

"Well, he was a handsome man, but not as handsome as you are." She coiled her arms around his neck and knocked him onto the bed this time.

Rigo pulled his shirt over his head, revealing his triangular-shaped upper body—so powerful. He was only an inch taller than her, but thick, hard, and macho. She wanted to breathe him in. Then he was inside of her, as physically close as two people could be, but she pulled him closer and squeezed, never wanting to let go.

"Hey." He brushed a piece of hair from her face. "Are you okay?"

She looked into his eyes, contemplating if she should say something or not, ultimately deciding he should know. "I need to tell you something."

Rigo rolled over and half-covered himself with the sheet. "Go ahead," he said, staring at the ceiling.

"What's the matter?" she asked. His mood had gone from sexy and playful to serious and somber.

"You tell me," he said in a measured tone.

What did he think she was going to say, that she had met someone else? It wasn't that kind of *I need to tell you something.* "Rigo, I didn't think about it until it was too late, but the doctor gave me some antibiotics when I was sick."

"Okay, but what does that have to do with anything? I figured you had taken something."

She propped herself up, resting her head in her hand. "Rigo, antibiotics can make birth control ineffective, and we've been … well, you know how we've been."

She saw him relax, rolling to face her. "Were you expecting me to be angry?"

"Aren't you?" she probed, watching him intently.

"Why should I be? We're a man and a woman making love."

He said this with such ease. *No one says things like that in real life.* "But what if I were to get pregnant?" She tried to understand how he wasn't upset with her.

"Didn't you say you wanted a child? As far as I know, you've always wanted children." His soft eyes still held some confusion.

"Yes, but we never talked about having one *together*. I'm in the middle of a divorce. I don't know where I'll be living. Are we even in a relationship?" Shit! Did she just ask him to define what they were doing? The conversation was spiraling out of control. She just wasn't used to this level of caring or lust or whatever it was.

Rigo brought her into his chest and hugged her. He just held on to her, and she let him. Their physical proximity and skin touching skin said what they were both thinking, even though she still wasn't entirely sure what that was.

"Cálmate, mí reina. No te preocupes. Todo estará bien." With his gentle hand, he combed the hair from her forehead and continued stroking as she lay on his shoulder. "I wasn't sure you were ready to hear it from me in so many words, but … I love you."

What? She hadn't been expecting that at all. She had just wanted to know if they were in a relationship. What they should call each other—boyfriend, girlfriend? Not that she didn't think she had those feelings for him. "How can you love me when you don't even know me?"

He laughed. "You think I don't know you? Believe me. I know you." He said this as if it were a scientifically proven truth, like the gravitational pull of a planet. "We've worked together for years. That's a lot of conversation, Sophie. Initially, I was rooting for your marriage to work out. I really was, but as time went by, my feelings for you as a friend turned into more. I watched you go home every evening to save a failing marriage, and I waited. I would have waited longer if I'd had to."

"But how did you know we would eventually be together?" She could feel him grow hard against her thigh.

"Just a hunch," he said.

Honest and casual with everything he said, he told the truth about how he felt. She had grown tired of hints and guessing, having navigated vague cues and unspoken, cryptic feelings for years with Adam. It felt good to know where she stood with her man. Rigo was now *her* man.

"What's going on up there?"

Why was it so hard for her to say? He was waiting, and she already knew how he felt. No risk in coming out and saying it herself. "I love you, too."

Chapter 21

Adam

Comp Zero was eight weeks from completion. They would be hanging drywall by the beginning of August. News of Adam and Sophie's separation had gotten back to Eileen, but Adam wasn't taken off the project. The partnership between Empire and Apex must have been competitive with what Eileen earned from her investments, and Adam was projected to come in under budget. Mr. Greenburg had gotten Comp Zero to sign with Empire for their next building in Canada, and Adam would again be project manager. Maybe the success of the Canada job would lead to a position as a senior project manager. Adam planned on telling Marisol the good news that coming weekend.

He left early for the ranch. A dense fog hovered over the road, and the farther Adam drove from the city, the thicker the fog became. He pulled onto the narrow shoulder to wait for the mist to burn away and held up his phone—three bars. Maybe he'd see how Ben was doing to help pass the time while he waited for visibility to improve. His nephew wouldn't be in class on a Saturday.

Ben picked up on the second ring. "Hey, Uncle Adam. I thought you'd forgotten about me."

"More like giving you your space, but I've missed you. How are your summer classes going?" Adam propped up his feet on the passenger seat and settled in for an update from his favorite nephew. Ben told him about classes, friends, parties, even the food in the dining hall.

"That all sounds great. Your dad would be proud of you." Adam grinned with pride. When his brother had died from cancer, he had taken Ben under his wing. "Are you keeping up with your mom? You should call her at least once a week, buddy."

"Don't worry, I am. She told me about your job in Mexico. How's that going?"

"I'm glad you asked. I thought you might be interested in some of what I've been hearing from the locals."

"What have you been hearing?"

Adam rolled down the truck window to let some fresh air blow through as he relayed everything he'd learned about the possibility of finding treasure in the area. "The general rhetoric is that anything buried has already been found, but how many times have we heard that before?"

"I support you one hundred percent, Uncle Adam. It's just like the diving. You took a whole lot of crap for it over the years from Aunt Sophie and my mom, but look at what you ended up finding."

"What we ended up finding," Adam corrected him.

"What we ended up finding," Ben repeated gratefully. "I still can't thank you enough for all the money you've put into my account at school. I have the scholarships, but they don't cover books or room and board. That stuff doubles the price!"

"Oh, I know. How's your account looking, by the way? Do I need to send more money?"

"Not until next semester."

"That's good. I'm still working on the next sale, but I did receive an email from a potential buyer recently. We've got two coins left to sell from what we brought up last summer."

"It's worth waiting on the collectors," Ben said. "The price of gold is nowhere near what the collectors are willing to pay."

"You're right," said Adam, as he looked through the window to check on the fog—still too dangerous. "Hey, guess what?"

"What?"

"I was close to Banderas Bay the other day, but they didn't have any boats available."

"Are you serious? Do you have any plans to go back?"

"Not without you." Adam paused. "What are you doing next spring break?"

"I guess I'm going to Banderas Bay with my uncle!"

Adam would end their conversation on a high note. "I don't want to hold up your Saturday, so I'm going to let you go, but call me anytime. The reception isn't great in most places here, but if you leave me a message or text me, I'll be able to get it once I'm back in Guadalajara."

"I will," said Ben before hanging up.

By twelve, the fog had dissipated, and Adam made the rest of the trip to Marisol's without incident. The curves in the road were familiar to him now. Even with the steep drop-offs, he drove the route with confidence. Young blades of green grass emerged from the brittle remnants of last year's brush along the roadside. Pitaya and nopal cacti were no longer the only green points on the mountains. Small shrubs and trees had sprouted their first leaves, and last night's rain had washed the dust from the houses in the valley below. Since the previous weekend, the ranches of Jalisco had gone from a barren desert to a land capable of sustaining and supporting life. When Adam unlatched the gate at Marisol's, she was tending the cookfire, and the scent of boiling beans filled the patio.

"How's the job going?" asked Marisol, setting down the piece of wood she'd been using to stoke the fire.

"Great," said Adam with a huge grin. "How did you know to ask?"

"Carlos and his family came to dinner at my aunt's house last night and told us how pleased Empire was with the progress. He said he played a large part in earning your company a new project."

Adam had given Carlos the good news earlier in the week. Talking to Carlos was the next best thing to talking with Marisol.

"Why don't you tell me the story in your own words," said Marisol. "You look disappointed that Carlos got to me first."

"That's all right. There's nothing more to add." Adam pulled a chair up to the fire. "Marisol, did you ever get in for the genetic testing?"

"Actually, yes. I couldn't resist."

"And," said Adam, "what did they say?"

"The nurse said it was a specialized test and the sample would have to be shipped to a lab in Mexico City for processing."

"So nothing yet."

"I should know something when I follow up for my results."

Adam felt he should offer to go to the appointment with her, but he didn't want to. "Want to see what I bought?"

She knew what he was doing—redirecting their conversation. "What did you buy?"

"Hold on. Let me get it from the truck." Adam hopped from his chair and quickly shuffled through the gate, scattering a group of chickens assembled in the shade of the crabapple tree.

"Not you, too." She laughed as he came around the corner, holding his metal detector.

"What do you mean, me too? I've been talking to this history professor, and finding gold in the area seems completely possible."

"It was possible years ago." Marisol corrected him, tending the beans. "Are you hungry?" She stirred the pot with a long, metal spoon while flipping tortillas on the comal. "Have a seat. The beans are almost ready."

He did as he was told, but first, he leaned the metal detector against the house. "So what's the plan for today?"

"We're going to start planting corn."

That didn't sound like much fun. They'd gone from day-tripping in Puerto Vallarta to planting corn. He wasn't even sure that would be possible. Her property had no fields, only mountains. Wouldn't they need some flat ground?

"But let's eat first." Marisol sat next to Adam, scooping pinto beans with folded pieces of tortilla. After lunch, she handed him his coa—a five-foot-long stick used to poke holes in the ground.

"What's this?" Adam started swinging the stick like a bo staff.

Unimpressed, Marisol waited for him to finish his childish demonstration. "Watch," she said, leading Adam to the edge of the yard where a fifty-gallon drum stood filled to the top with dried corn kernels from last year's harvest.

She dipped a metal feed bucket into the drum, and a cascade of kernels filled the pail, which she handed to Adam. Around her waist, she had tied a homemade seed pouch, and the rock-hard, desiccated kernels weighed heavily in the sturdy cloth. Using her coa, Marisol poked a hole in the ground and dropped some kernels into the hole without bending over. She got them right in, then pushed the dirt and gravel back into the hole with her foot, demonstrating the process for Adam.

He glanced at his bucket of seeds. The task didn't seem too difficult. He could finish with his kernels and still have time to use his metal detector.

"Let's try to cover at least half this side of the mountain all the way to the chor today," said Marisol. "I want to plant the corn crop before the wild grass grows tall enough to hide the snakes."

Snakes? Adam did not like snakes but didn't want to appear scared, so he didn't comment on the snakes. His new friend had some lofty goals for them. Adam looked at the metal detector leaning against the house. It would have to wait. With his coa in one hand and bucket in the other, he followed Marisol.

It wasn't as easy as she had made it look. Marisol made it into the hole every time. Naturally competitive, Adam aimed at the holes he made with his coa, but his kernels kept bouncing off the sides. He ended up having to kick most of the kernels into the holes with his foot as he covered them up. "Hey Marisol, where've your dogs been?" He asked, trying to pass the time.

"Oh, they're around. They stay gone most of the time, hunting in the mountains, only coming back when they've had no luck out there. Then I'll feed them, and they're off again."

They planted all afternoon, giving Adam's mind a chance to wander. The manual labor set his endorphins pumping, and as they covered the mountainside with the golden seeds, he kept an eye out for the glint of golden metal.

"Has your family always owned this property?" asked Adam, poking at the ground with his coa.

"As far as I know. Why?"

"Just asking." Adam knew Marisol knew what he was really asking. He wanted to know if her ranch had been a hacienda at any point, but she didn't bite. She had already told him not to waste his time.

Still, the possibility of finding gold had kept Adam interested in the day's activity. He had seen a few shiny objects that afternoon, but upon further inspection, they had turned out to be pieces of mica—pretty, but worthless.

It had taken all day to empty his bucket, three kernels at a time. They had barely made a dent in the fifty-gallon drum. The day's work had been just the beginning. Adam was sweaty and grateful when Marisol gave the word to stop for the day. Darkness fell as the sun sank behind the mountains to the west, heralding the cool of the evening, and their coas doubled as walking sticks on their dimly lit path back to the ranch house.

"I don't know about you, but I need a shower," she said. "I'm going to the chor. The river could be chilly after the rain, so you can start a fire to warm some water for yourself if you want."

"That sounds like too much work," said Adam. "I'm beat. The chor is fine for me, too."

"All right then, boys to the right, girls to the left." Marisol collected a bar of soap, a towel, and a change of clothes.

Adam retrieved his toiletries from the SUV. His leather travel case held miniature bottles of shampoo, conditioner, and shaving cream. Sophie had given it to him for Christmas two years ago. Adam took the case and a backpack with his clothes.

Intermittent gusts of cool wind swept down the mountainside into the valley through the mango trees to the chor, and Adam followed the path to the river. His hiking boots had been worth every penny. Dung beetles rolled their large balls of manure to discreet nests, retiring for the night while toads called to their mates in the dusk. Adam would wash off the day's work in the river and return, ready for some friendly conversation by the fire.

Under the mango trees, where he had first met Alberto, his eyes moved along the shoreline, searching for any telltale signs of treasure, but he found none. Adam deposited his toiletries on a broad, flat rock, then turned away from the river to hang his towel on a rogue piece of peeling bark. While facing the tangle of barren branches woven together on the hillside, he thought he saw something, but it couldn't be. This was the stuff of Mexican folk tales. It was probably a firefly or a flashlight. The *green fire of gold* was a myth.

"Hello," Adam called softly into the underbrush.

"Who are you looking for?" asked a voice from behind.

Adam's heart dropped into his stomach, and he spun around. "Oh, hey, Alberto." He attempted to make out the old man's features under the branches of the mango trees.

"I'm not Alberto. The name's Javier." Alberto's brother emerged from the shadows, stepping into the moonlight. "My brother told me about you. Adam, right?"

"Right," said Adam, still trying to identify Javier's defining features in the dark. He looked so much like his brother. "Alberto had mentioned you, too. Nice to meet you."

"Nice to meet *you*," said Javier, setting a paper grocery bag on the ground and coming to stand at Adam's side. He put his hands in his pockets. "So what are we looking for?"

"Nothing," said Adam, not wanting to appear foolish. Marisol had already laughed at him for his interest in treasure once that day. "I just thought I might have seen something. It was probably my imagination. The light is weird this time of day."

"It can be," said Javier. He broke rank to pick up his bag full of mangos.

"Do you mind if I have one of those?" Adam asked. The mangos that had littered the ground a few short weeks ago were gone—eaten, collected, or rotted. After his long day of farmwork, the sight of the juicy fruit had set his mouth watering, and ever since the food poisoning incident, he had been very cautious to avoid dehydration.

"Of course." Javier handed him the mango on top. "It looks like you're off to take care of some business, so I'll let you get to it."

"Yeah, thanks," said Adam. He wondered what Alberto's brother was doing wandering around in the dark, but wasn't going to question the man's actions on his own property.

Javier disappeared into the brush and Adam opened his travel case, extracting his shaving cream and a razor. Swirling currents washed the stubble-filled cream from the razor's tip as Adam held it beneath the water's surface. The white spot of cream traveled downstream, and he wondered if Marisol would see it. She was a friend and one of the most interesting people he had ever met, but at this moment, in the dark, he couldn't help but think of her as a *woman*. His mind painted a picture of Marisol downriver, nude. He thought of the cream from his razor running into the small of her back, clinging to her bottom, and wondered what she would do if he were to float downstream to have a look. Was she thinking of him as the current pushed past her thighs? Adam decided to wash his hair and maybe just float around the bend.

With his shaving cream and shampoo tucked safely in his travel case, Adam removed his boxers. No one would see him. The sliver of a moon cast minimal light as it moved in and out of the clouds. Exposed outdoors, wading in the water, he felt himself go stiff despite the cool temperature. As he rounded the bend, the water became increasingly shallow, and he thought he might have to stand up and walk back when he reached a long, open stretch of deeper water. Without boulders to form the lines of the current, its surface shone like black glass. From this pool of water, he saw her silhouette. Marisol's clothes hung from a bush near the river's edge, and her wet hair fell to the top of her hips. Thankfully, she was facing away from him. His good judgment had returned in time to reconsider his lecherous course of action. What would she think of him watching her? She had opened her home to him, fed him, shown him around Jalisco, and listened to him moan about his soon-to-be ex-wife. He hadn't felt guilty in years, but he had respect for Marisol. She didn't deserve a peeping Tom. She deserved much more. He did have a lot to offer presently, but sadly, it would have to go to waste.

Adam found his way back to the ranch house, using the coa as a walking stick. The fresh mountain breeze tousled his wet hair, and he took confident strides up the hillside, all the while watching the ground where he poked the coa.

Not far from the chor, he noticed something shiny in the dirt—probably more mica—but he couldn't resist the urge to bend down and find out for sure. Adam turned the flat object over in his hand and held it up to the limited moonlight. It was firm, round, and … golden—a gold coin. A gold coin! Holy mother! He could hardly believe it and performed an awkward dance of excitement right there on the trail, stifling a shout. *Get yourself under control*, he said to himself. Marisol was expecting him at the ranch house. He couldn't get sucked into the hunt this time of night. A rattlesnake could be coiled under a rock and he would never see it. Adam pocketed the coin. Coa in hand, he hiked toward Marisol's house. Every few seconds, he would stick his hand in his pocket to feel the coin and make sure it was real.

Adam was the first to arrive back at the ranch and started a fire in the pit beside the patio. River rocks had been fitted together to form the stone slab, which provided relief from the ever-present, muddy earth of the rainy season. He rearranged the plastic chairs next to the fire pit, where the smoke would offer protection from the mosquitoes. When Marisol returned from the chor, he asked if she wanted to sleep with him under the stars on the patio.

"It's going to rain again tonight," she said, hanging her wet towel to dry by the fire.

"How do you know?"

"Do you see that halo around the moon?" She pointed at the sky. "That means there's moisture in the air. You don't want to be caught out here in the rain. Scorpions wash out from under the rocks."

Adam looked down at his feet. Now, he would be scanning for gold and scorpions.

"Prima," called a voice from the side of the house. The two brothers rounded the corner and entered the yard, arms filled with provisions. "Prima," said Javier again.

"Primos,"—Marisol smiled—"it's good to see you. What're you doing out so late?"

"We brought some groceries," said Javier, placing the bag of mangos next to the fire.

Alberto also set his bags down. "Adam, my friend. How you are?" His English hadn't improved much since their last encounter.

"Good, thanks." Adam hadn't seen Alberto since the morning they'd gone fishing his first time on the ranch. "How've you been doing?"

"We been doing good. Things been good at the ranch." Alberto nodded toward the neighboring mountain. Adam hadn't realized their ranch house was so close by.

"Javier, this is Adam." Marisol introduced them. "Adam is here from the United States, working in the city with Carlos."

"We know each other already," said Javier. "I met him at the chor earlier this evening, but it's good to see you again, Adam."

"Thanks, you too."

Adam couldn't believe his luck. Marisol had told him about when these two would get together around the fire and the stories they would tell. There had to be a measure of truth to every folktale, and he hoped the cousins would be in the mood to entertain with some of their stories. Maybe one of their stories would lead him to more gold coins. He touched the coin in his pocket, not ready to reveal his find to anyone else.

"We hadn't thought about coming by this evening until late," said Javier, emptying the bags, "and the butcher was already closed. So we brought taco plates from San Cristóbal and some non-perishables for the ranch."

"We collecting the last mangos, too," Alberto added.

"Thank you so much," said Marisol. She went inside to get two more plastic patio chairs and set them by the fire for her primos.

Adam contributed by attempting to pass out the bottled water he kept in the SUV. "Here you go."

"Thank you, Adam," said Javier, "but I think this time of night calls for something a little stronger." He produced a small, round bottle of tequila. "I invited Don Edwardo to the gathering."

Fantastic, Adam thought. He had met Don Julio last time and looked forward to meeting Don Edwardo tonight.

Marisol pulled back the tinfoil on her Styrofoam plate and tucked into her chicken tacos. "Primos," she said, getting their attention, "Adam has become very interested in Mexican history." She didn't elaborate any further, continuing to scarf down the tacos. This statement had been a conversation starter for the sake of being polite.

"Yes," said Alberto. "I am teach him everything about this."

Adam thought back to his limited recollection of what Alberto had told him the night they had stayed up drinking before their fishing excursion. He couldn't remember much but agreed, also for the sake of politeness.

"Marisol love the story of the Hernandez Castañedas," said Alberto. "It was the favorite of all the little kids."

"So whatever became of the girls and their mother?" asked Adam.

"No one knows for sure," said Javier, distributing the rest of the warm taco plates. "There are a few different versions of the ending, and people have been searching for that treasure from here to Nayarit for over a century."

"Adam has a metal detector now," said Marisol with a mouthful of chicken.

"That won't help him with the Hernandez Castañeda rubies," said Javier. "Those stones were loose, not yet set by a jeweler. A metal detector is useless in the absence of metal."

"I guess you're right," said Adam, removing the tinfoil from his taco plate. He didn't need to find any record-breaking rubies. Simply finding a gold coin or two with his metal detector would suffice. The thrill of the hunt drew him in, not the need for money. Though the extra money came in handy for Ben's education.

"Nuestros treasure hunting days are over," said Alberto, taking a sip from his glass of tequila. "My brother and me, we too old for all the digging, right Javier?"

"Right," said Javier, somewhat unconvincingly. He stoked the fire, and a cloud of tiny embers rose from the flames.

"Marisol," said Alberto.

She had almost finished her tacos. "Yes, Primo?"

"Do you have your guitar?"

Adam liked the sound of that. Tequila and acoustic music by the fireside in the wilds of Mexico. No work tomorrow, and no Sophie to bother him.

Javier and Alberto could have taken their storytelling musical act on the road. They sang in Spanish, but their songs were corridos, the kind he had heard in Puerto Vallarta. Long after midnight, the fire died down, and los primos said their goodbyes, disappearing into the darkness. Marisol had invited them to stay, but they had declined. They knew these mountains and could find their way home on foot in the dark. *Amazing*, Adam thought.

Marisol showed Adam inside, where he spread his sleeping bag on the floor beside her bed—not much difference between being outdoors and indoors at her home. Three rooms stood side by side, unconnected to one another, lined up along the patio like a motel—a living room, bedroom, and dining room. None of them had doors, only thin lace curtains, which fell to the floor to keep the bugs out.

Adam lay there, unable to sleep. After the day's work, he should have been exhausted, but couldn't turn off, still thinking about the green light as he turned the coin over in his pocket. He *had* seen it. He was sure he had.

Adam's thoughts wouldn't let him rest that night. So he returned to the smoldering embers in search of Don Edwardo. He poured himself a short glass, hoping it would put some weight on his eyelids. As Adam drank, he scanned the horizon for the *green fire of gold*. Inwardly scolding himself for this obsession, he had almost pried his eyes from the brush when he spotted something, a flash in the distance, partially blocked by the mangled branches of shrubs. Had the flash been green? Maybe yellow? It was too late for fireflies, and the cousins were long gone.

Don Edwardo had given him the courage to crunch his way into the bushes, but before long, Adam had gotten himself turned around in the dark. Tree branches clawed at him from all directions, and he stopped in a small clearing to reassess his path. Which direction had the light come from? He tried to reorient himself, but nothing looked familiar. No nighttime noises filled the darkness, and an eerie silence reverberated in his ears. He spun in a circle, looking for anything recognizable.

Then he saw the flash again, but this time, he could identify it. Eyes—yellow eyes—four feet off the ground, give or take. He was being hunted. Nature had been astute enough to shut up, but he'd been snapping his way through the dry bushes. Where were the eyes? As quickly as he had seen them, they had vanished. He held his breath and stepped lightly, searching for anything he could use as a weapon. Where were fallen branches when you needed them?

He froze when a large body rose out of the stillness, looming toward him in the air. Brown fur occluded his visual field, and he readied himself for impact, but just before the predator made contact, it fell to the ground, dropping out of the air mid-leap.

The limp body of a mountain lion lay before him, eyes open, gleaming yellow in the pale moonlight. He jumped back as the dead mound of fur rolled over and an elderly woman crawled from beneath the once-powerful cat. This petite woman yanked a bloody machete from the dead beast, whose blood showed black on the sharp blade. She got to her feet and brushed herself off, muttering words Adam couldn't understand. Wiry hair tied into one long braid framed her face, and a calico dress covered her lean body. She wore leather sandals, typical of the region, and her face had more lines than should have been on a woman capable of killing a mountain lion with a machete.

"¡Muchas gracias!" said Adam.

"Mis niños necesitan comer," she said, taking a smaller knife from her pocket and kneeling over her kill. The woman removed the skin, ripping hide from muscle tissue. A drop of sweat slid down her face, and she wiped it away, leaving a black streak of lion's blood on her forehead. When she had finished, she draped the coat over one shoulder, hoisted the meat over the other, and walked off, leaving a pile of innards in the dirt.

Adam trekked back to the house in shock and lay on the floor, less concerned with the mosquitoes, but thinking about how much protection the lacy curtains would be if another mountain lion came in the night. He didn't remember falling asleep, but woke to the smell of pinto beans and corn tortillas. The damp air indicated it had rained.

"Good morning," said Marisol when Adam stepped out of the bedroom. "You must have pushed yourself planting corn yesterday. It's almost nine."

"Right. I didn't sleep very well."

"That's understandable. The rain kept me up half the night, too. I like to hear it on the roof. The dry season lasts so long by the time the rain returns, I'm too excited to sleep. Pretty soon, the mountains will turn from gray to green. You'll hardly notice it. Then, one day, you'll look around and feel like you're in the jungle."

Adam nodded, barely processing her animated morning chatter. "We'd better get planting before the grass provides cover for the snakes, like you said." He'd already had the run-in with the mountain lion and didn't want to add rattlesnake to his list of wild encounters.

"We've still got time before that happens. Have some breakfast before we leave." Marisol spooned some beans into a bowl.

"I'm actually not hungry yet."

She paused mid scoop. "You … not hungry. What's wrong?"

"You might think I'm crazy if I tell you," said Adam. "I swear I didn't have that much to drink."

"Just tell me," said Marisol, setting the bowl of beans beside Adam, just in case.

He took the bowl. "Don't judge." Adam relayed the story of what had happened last night, and, to his surprise, Marisol started laughing.

"What's so funny? I'm either going crazy, or I almost died! Either way, you shouldn't be laughing."

"That was my mom," she said. "I didn't know all that had happened when she dropped off the meat this morning. I have the lion salted and hanging from the laurel tree over there." She pointed at the tree.

Adam's gaze shifted between Marisol and the sinewy lion carcass dangling from the tree. He needed more of an explanation.

"Good news for you … I'm changing the menu for dinner," said Marisol. "I'm making birria. Remember the restaurant in Puerto Vallarta? Only I'm making my birria with fresh lion meat. It's very rare. There aren't many mountain lions around anymore."

"It only takes one lion to kill you," said Adam, still shaken from the experience.

"Every time a villager spots one, they don't stop tracking it until it's dead," continued Marisol. "It isn't safe to have mountain lions around with so many young children in los ranchos."

Adam hadn't taken one bite of his breakfast. "If you're not going to eat, we should get going." Marisol handed him a bucket of kernels and the coa, and they hiked to where they'd stopped planting the day before.

"I can't believe that woman was your mother," said Adam as they planted. He was getting better at planting corn and dropped more kernels directly into the holes than he had yesterday. All the while, he kept a lookout for the glint of golden metal, touching his hand to the coin in his pocket every so often.

"That was her, all right. Esmeralda couldn't take care of a baby, but she takes care of herself just fine," said Marisol.

"What do you mean?"

"She's lived in the mountains, without a proper home, for almost forty years now."

Marisol regarded him like this was no big deal. Maybe things circulated around los ranchos, but he wasn't from los ranchos and an elderly woman who could take down the kind of big cat he had only seen on TV warranted more backstory. Adam waited for Marisol to elaborate.

"Her head injury, while wiping away the essence of who she'd been, must have heightened her primal survival instincts. She's nearly sixty, but I don't worry about her out there alone. That old lady could bite the head off a rattlesnake." Marisol kept planting as she spoke, dropping kernels and kicking dirt into the holes.

"Occasionally, she'll catch something, leave me the meat, and sleep on the dining room table. Then she's gone again. She doesn't seem to recognize that I'm her daughter, but I think she feels something deep down. That's why she leaves the meat, or at least that's what I tell myself. And look,"—Marisol held out her hand—"she had this tucked into the lion meat." Marisol brandished a delicate ring. It was obviously fake, but pretty enough.

"What do you mean 'tucked into the meat?'" asked Adam.

"She uses the kills to deliver other items to me. I don't understand why and maybe never will, but I have to be careful when I'm cooking with her kills. The first time I made birria with one of her gophers, I got a mouthful when I bit down on a metal spoon hidden in the muscle tissue."

"What happened to her?" asked Adam. "How was she injured?"

"That's the thing," said Marisol, "no one knows. No one saw. All I know is she'd been singing as a Mariachi at the fair in García the night it happened to her. Her boyfriend at the time told police he'd gone to hang out with friends, and when he came back, she was gone."

"She was gone?" repeated Adam. "Obviously, she turned up again. Is that all anyone knows?"

"That's about it. She was found a few days later, wandering by the river. Her parents, my grandparents, could never get her to stay at home for any length of time after that, before she would take to wandering the mountains again. It took a while for my grandparents to accept this and stop trying to bring her back to the ranch. She's been surviving out here ever since."

Adam stopped planting. He waited expectantly for Marisol to continue, coa in hand.

Marisol spiked her coa into the ground and put her hand on her hip. "It's been a while since I told that story. Anyway, she must have been attacked that night because nine months later, I was born. She gave birth somewhere in the mountains and then dropped me off with my aunt."

"She gave birth to you alone in the mountains? She has to know who you are."

"Like I said, I think she does know me deep down, but it still hurts when she tells me she can't find her baby. I've stopped trying to explain that *I'm* her baby. It only upsets her. I just take the gifts, whatever they may be, and wait for the next time she turns up."

"Wow," said Adam. He was getting a different perspective on life. "It's impressive how you've been able to accept this."

"Lo que pasó voló," said Marisol.

The same saying again—*that which is in the past flies away*. They had been talking about the past, but *today*, they were planting, and they both got back to work.

Chapter 22

Sophie

Sophie and Rigo's new job was also in Alexandria. A well-to-do couple was hosting their daughter's wedding, and a complete backyard overhaul was in order. Unlike the Colemans' row home, this new project was a detached colonial with an expansive and well-manicured yard. The bride and groom wanted something small and easy, but the bride's parents had something else in mind. In Sophie's opinion, the backyard was already picture-perfect, but it was about achieving the client's vision for the space. All existing turf would be removed and replaced with shade-tolerant, blue fescue sod. Weeds were not on the guest list.

"You can drive the Bobcat, right?" Sophie asked Rigo.

Without hesitation, he climbed into the machine. "I told you I could." He drove the loader around back and parked it under a tall oak, awaiting further instruction.

Sophie met him under the tree. "I can't believe I did that."

"Did what?" He turned the engine off to hear what she had to say.

"I underbid the project, not thinking we would need to rent any equipment." She shook her head.

Rigo didn't respond right away, but sat in the driver's seat, eyes cast upward in thought. "I still have the house to myself for the next few weeks. If you stay with me, we can come in early and stay late, using all the same back roads I took for the Colemans' project. You could avoid your entire commute, and we could have this job done ahead of schedule."

When Sophie didn't reply immediately, he continued. "My sister's family will be in Mexico for at least a couple of months. Travel's expensive, and when they visit back home, they stay for a while. You saw how quickly we got here from her house the other day."

"Thanks for the offer, but getting the job done sooner isn't going to increase the profit margin."

"Right," said Rigo, "but finishing sooner allows us to move on to a more profitable project sooner."

"That's true," she conceded. As an added bonus, they would spend less time driving and have more time for … well … anything else. "Are you sure you wouldn't mind working the extra hours?"

"It doesn't feel like work when I'm with you."

No, it didn't seem like work, and after a few days of putting in those extra hours, she could see the project would not be as much of a disaster as she'd thought. Even though they were working longer days, they still had more time for each other in the absence of long commutes. They submerged themselves in tenderness and pleasure, making love and binge-watching *Corazones.*

As she lay beside her lover, Sophie wondered how Rigo had immigrated to the US. They had just finished an episode where

Hector's younger brother's visa had been revoked after he'd been caught laundering money through his chain of successful steakhouses. Rigo had a green card when she'd hired him, but she was curious to hear his story in his words.

"So how did you enter the country?"

"Do you really want to know?" He acted like the question had surprised him.

She caressed his waist and traced the line of muscle separating his abdomen from his groin. "I want to know everything about you."

"If you want me to tell you the story, you'll have to stop doing that."

"You mean *this*?" She pressed her body against his.

He closed his eyes, drew in a deep breath, and tried to remain in control.

"Sorry, I'll stop," she said. "I want to hear about it."

"Well, I was twenty-three years old." Rigo stretched out, folding his arms behind his head. "I can't believe it's been six years already."

A period of silence followed as he gathered his thoughts. Then he turned to face her and pulled a pillow snuggly under his head.

"There was this guy, José, who said he could lead people across the border. It was going to cost three thousand dollars—not pesos, dollars—but he said he knew the safest way to cross. José had previously helped my cousin cross the border. I knew my cousin had gotten there safely because he was sending his wife four hundred dollars a month."

Sophie didn't interrupt him, but patiently waited through Rigo's pauses as he recalled the details of his journey.

"My uncle lent me the money to pay José," said Rigo, "and I took a bus to Coahuila, one of the northernmost states in

Mexico, part of the Chihuahuan Desert. I'd never been out of Zacatecas before."

"Did you go alone?"

"In the end, yes. Another cousin of mine was going to cross with me, but his finances fell through at the last minute. I waited for José outside a family restaurant two miles north of the Coahuila military checkpoint. A group of people from Durango arrived by bus an hour later. It looked like the people from Durango knew each other, except for one Aztec woman with an infant. One other man traveled alone. His wife dropped him off and didn't stay long."

Rigo closed his eyes, picturing the scene and telling his story. "José had told us what we needed to bring. The most important thing was water, which I knew."

"Of course." Sophie curled her legs up, folded her hands under her cheek, and listened.

"We started walking, and after a few hours, we couldn't see anything but desert in every direction. It was different from the dry season in Zacatecas. In Coahuila, they had mangled palm trees with twisted limbs growing at random angles. They looked like the hands of the dead reaching out of the ground. After walking half the day, my calves were killing me but I didn't stop. If I had, they would have left me behind."

"What about the woman with the baby?" asked Sophie. "How could someone make that trip with an infant?"

Rigo smiled at her. It was the kind of smile people give a child who didn't understand something simple.

"The Aztec woman had her baby wrapped in a sling, tied to her back," he said. "She was like a wild animal that never tired, with one gourdful of water for the entire journey. Her strides were smaller than ours, and she couldn't have been more than four feet tall, but she was always at the front of the pack.

"I kind of paired up with the other guy who was traveling alone—the one whose wife had dropped him off. Christo was from some small village near San Cristóbal, Jalisco. You get to know someone quickly when you spend all day walking in the desert."

"What did you talk about?"

"Let's see. He told me about his wife and how they'd tried to have a family but couldn't. I told him about wanting to meet an American girl and make enough money to buy my own ranch in Mexico.

"Back then, I thought I would grow oranges on my ranch. The prices for citrus fruit that year had been phenomenal, but I've since found out that a lot of other people had the same idea. Now citrus prices are at an all-time low. It doesn't matter, though. You'd never be interested in starting a ranch in Mexico."

"How do you know I wouldn't be interested? I don't recall you ever asking me." She flashed him a playfully defiant look.

"Oh, come on. Look at your house," said Rigo.

She sighed and stared up at his bedroom ceiling. "My name may be on the deed, but that is not my house. It was the house Adam had to have, but I don't want to think about that now. Let's just stay in bed forever." She climbed on top of him and hugged him.

"Why don't we?" Rigo gently pushed her up by her shoulders, holding her above him so he could look into her eyes. "—move in together, I mean."

"Um, I know you think I have a lot of money," said Sophie, "but between the cars and that monster of a house, I'm all tapped out. I have no savings. Really, I have like nine hundred dollars in the bank."

"I didn't ask you for any money." He pulled away from her, and his eyes narrowed.

"But you wanted to move in together. Were you thinking I would move into your sister's house with you? Five people are living here already." She needed to stop talking. She was making it worse.

"What's the matter with you? I don't want any of your money, and I didn't mean for you to move in *here*. I've been saving everything I've made since I came to this country, waiting until I found a woman who was special enough to start a family with."

Stunned into silence, again. They had never had a true disagreement, and Sophie didn't know how to fix this. Finally, she spoke. "I'm sorry, Rigo, I didn't know. I wasn't thinking … I should go." She moved to get out of bed, but before her feet hit the floor, Rigo caught her and pulled her back against his bare chest.

"Please don't leave."

"I have to go. This will never work." She pulled away and stood from the bed. Rigo held on to her arm.

"What do you mean, this will never work? You haven't even tried. I'm not Adam. Don't you get it? I'm not Adam!" He let go of her.

"You're not Adam," she repeated back to him. "I know that. I'm not stupid. There's just no way it can work. Having a family is practically all I've ever wanted. My childhood wasn't exactly the greatest, and I had always planned on building something real, something lasting and safe, but as you can see, I'm a total mess." Tears spilled from her eyes. "You probably want to have other girlfriends and …"

"Your marriage really messed you up," interrupted Rigo.

"That's what I just told you. I'm not good for you. You deserve someone who has it together. Someone who—"

"But I want you! Can't you see that?" He jammed his legs into a pair of boxer shorts, walked around the bed, grabbed her, and hugged her so tightly a faint whistle escaped as she let out her breath. "I want you. I always have," he whispered.

"Do you know how much you pay me?" He watched her for a reaction. "I make twenty dollars an hour working for you. You're the cheapest, most beautiful woman I've ever met. So, as for other girlfriends, I haven't got the time. Sophie, I wait tables in the evenings and on the weekends, or at least I used to, until I quit so I could spend time with you. I've got enough money saved for a house. All I need is someone to share it with." Rigo gazed at her expectantly.

A lingering tear slid down Sophie's cheek, and she wiped her eyes. "I don't know what you're saying."

"What I'm saying is I want to be with you. Eventually, I want us to be a family, and I want you to trust me," he said, grasping her upper arms so she couldn't turn away.

She managed to squirm out of his hold and sank into a squatting position against the wall, wrapped in the sheet. "This is everything I wanted, and I don't know what to say." She hid her head in her knees. "I'm separated, but I'm not divorced yet. This is moving so fast."

Rigo sat in front of her. "Just say you love me. It's just you and me, like it's always been. Nothing's changed. I loved you yesterday, and I love you now."

After a long pause, she lifted her head and agreed. Nothing had changed since yesterday. They crawled back into bed. Sophie nestled her head on his chest. She would trust him. He cared. He wasn't going to hurt her. She fell asleep listening to his heartbeat.

•　　•　　•

Hand in hand, Sophie and Rigo walked along Baltimore's Inner Harbor toward Little Italy. They passed working professionals out for cocktails and couples from the suburbs having dinner. Rigo stopped and placed ten dollars into a homeless man's cup.

Sophie smiled and leaned in, pecking him on the lips. "Where would you like to eat?"

"There's this cozy Italian restaurant where they serve the best lemon butter sauce I've ever tasted."

"Mmmm. That sounds great." Sophie curled both of her arms around Rigo's bicep, giving him a squeeze as they walked.

She and Adam hadn't been out just for fun in ages before they'd split, but she couldn't see that happening with Rigo—settling into a boring routine. They had gotten over their first misunderstanding—a couple's milestone.

As they passed the singing fudge factory, beautifully harmonized voices wafted from the open door, along with the scent of sweet vanilla and maple syrup. Through the storefront window they saw a group of teen confectioners wearing aprons, smoothing fudge, and singing a cappella.

"Listen to that," she said.

"It takes talent for sure. I'd never be able to work there. They'd fire me in a second. I can't sing at all. How about you?"

"Me neither," Sophie said.

So much remained to learn about one another. Things as simple as singing ability were still new to them, even after spending years working together. Sophie loved learning new things about Rigo, no matter how trivial. Even the small details were interesting to her because *he* was interesting to her. She thought about his border crossing story and made a mental note to ask him to finish the tale at a more appropriate time. They continued down the city streets, past the National Aquarium, toward Little Italy. "Would you ever want to live in a city like this?" asked Sophie.

A cloud of steam escaped through the cracks of a utility hole in the sidewalk. "I would, but I wouldn't care to raise children in a city."

"Look at everything there is to do here, though."

"There's a lot to do," said Rigo, "but I need more open space. I'd like to at least be able to walk out of my house into a yard with some trees, somewhere I could run around with the kids."

"You seem fairly confident you'd like to have children." She steered him toward the metal railing lining the boat dock, where fluorescent pink clouds floated on the horizon, painted by the setting sun.

"I am," he said. "It's something I've always known I wanted—a family with children, that is."

Sophie let Rigo's words sink in, really seep into her conscious mind, thinking he might really be the one for her as she gazed at the prismatic clouds.

"Come on," said Rigo, pulling her away from the railing and her thoughts. "We're almost there."

They stopped in front of an attractive restaurant. Flowers spilled from its window planters against a light peach, stucco exterior.

"This is so cute." She approved of his choice.

Inside the dimly lit restaurant, the host seated them at a secluded table, tucked away for couples. Sophie hung her purse on the back of her chair. "I'm looking forward to trying the sauce you mentioned."

"You won't be disappointed. At least I hope you won't."

The server took their drink orders and set a basket of bread beside a plate of herb-infused olive oil.

"So where did you work before I met you?" Rigo took a piece of bread and broke it in half to dip.

"Let's see, I worked in an ice cream shop as a summer job in high school and the campus library in college. You already know about my job with the county before I went all in with my business. Nothing too exciting."

"Everything about you is exciting to me," said Rigo, reaching under the table and resting his hand on her knee.

"Scooping ice cream?" she said, and they both laughed.

"I'm serious, though," Rigo said, "tell me more about you … like, what's your favorite flavor of ice cream?"

She loved ice cream, especially when she was sick, but what *was* her favorite flavor?

"You're thinking too hard. What's the first flavor that pops into your head when I say, *do you want to get ice cream?*"

"Okay, okay," she said, stalling. "Peanut butter twirl."

"Really?"

"What's wrong with peanut butter twirl?"

"Nothing, I guess. It just pales in comparison to chocolate chip cookie dough."

Sophie laughed again. Anything they did, anything they talked about, was fun.

The server returned and asked if they were ready to order, pen poised, ready to record their dinner selections.

"Do you have any peanut butter twirl?" Rigo asked.

Sophie tried to stifle a laugh, but the server didn't think this was funny and repeated the question.

Rigo ordered the pasta he'd spoken so highly of for the two of them, and after the server left the table, they continued their lighthearted chit-chat. Things didn't always have to be so serious, and the pasta didn't disappoint.

Chapter 23

San Cristóbal, Mexico 1912
(Two years later)

Dusty from the trail, the group of riders approached the village of San Cristóbal. The lead rider pulled back on the reins, slowing her horse to a trot, then pushed the weight of her body through the stirrups. Her young mount snorted, stopping in front of the town church. Hungry and tired, the group dismounted, guiding the animals to the river. Clear water rushed over polished rocks, and the horses sucked in the cold liquid. The riders kneeled, cupping the fresh water in their hands, cooling themselves from the weeks they'd spent riding back from the Yucatan.

"So what's next?" asked Fidencio once he had quenched his thirst. He removed his wide-brimmed hat and ran his fingers through his thick, black hair.

"So we stay a while," said the lead rider.

"Why would we want to stay here?" Fidencio sat on a boulder and stretched his long legs as his horse picked at the scant grass sprouting along the bank.

"I need a break from riding," offered Teo. "We stay here because we are here." Teo sat beside Fidencio and removed his boots, revealing blisters on his heels. Nearly a foot shorter than Fidencio, Teo had one hundred percent Aztec blood running through his veins. When he stood, Teo was almost the same height as Fidencio seated on the rock. The Azteco waded calf-deep into the river, letting the crystal-clear water wash the sting from his broken skin.

"We're not staying because we're lazy," said the lead rider. "There's potential in every village. We just need to find it." She unraveled her long, dark hair that had been knotted into a traveling bun and quickly folded it into one thick braid draped over her shoulder.

"You're right," Fidencio said from his place on the rock, "but we should find something to eat."

"I agree." She flung her braid over her shoulder and grabbed the leather strap of her satchel hanging diagonally across her chest. "Teo, look after the horses while Fidencio and I familiarize ourselves with the village."

"Can't I come, too?" Teo asked, still standing in the river. He was softer than Fidencio, the newest addition to their band.

"Keep after the horses," said Daria. "That's what you were brought on to do."

Fidencio replaced his hat. Then he and Daria climbed the cobblestone road that split the village in two. Fidencio was smarter than Teo and handsome as well. He had a long, lean, youthful body. Not yet nineteen years old, his tall frame was still filling out with a horseman's musculature. Daria knew Fidencio yearned for her, which made him supremely loyal. She watched her back around everyone, but with Fidencio, she could relax … just a little.

"What is it you hope to find here?" asked Fidencio, squinting against the bright afternoon sun.

"First, let's see what kinds of businesses they have, then we can figure out who to target," she said.

Fidencio tipped his hat in agreement. They had met on the day she was taken from her family. Daria had not shed a tear on that day, nor any day after that.

"It looks deserted," said Fidencio.

The people of San Cristóbal had returned to their homes for the afternoon siesta. The empty streets amplified the occasional sounds of the resting village—a dog barking, the squeal of a toddler not wanting to take a nap, and the hum of elderly women gossiping on back patios.

"A good time to arrive anywhere," said Daria, eyes surveying the village square.

Fidencio followed her as she walked up the hill. He knew better than to take her hand. That type of open display of affection was a sign of weakness. She and Fidencio had been covert lovers for some time, but no one knew, not even their newest traveling companion. Daria would always have the upper hand. With nothing and no one dear to her, her enemies had no leverage, and she had no fear.

Her mother had taught her a great deal, but most importantly, she had taught her to know people—to know their thought processes—and to never let anyone surprise her. People were animals, and given the right set of circumstances, anyone was capable of anything. Daria never mixed emotion with navigating impossible situations, which is most likely how she'd survived her first few months as a captive. She waited, listened, watched, and learned. When the time had come, she made her move, stabbing her captors in their sleep. Everyone except Fidencio, that is.

"A restaurant. Good," said Daria. "Can you smell that?"

"Barbacoa?"

"My mouth is watering just smelling the smoke," said Daria. She stood in front of the restaurant, doors shut for the afternoon, but the tempting smells floated from the open windows.

"How much money do we have left?" asked Fidencio, yielding to her.

"Enough," she responded. They would eat well. "Let's continue our walk. The village should come alive again in the next hour."

Even with Fidencio, she kept her communication brief. It was better if no one knew exactly what she was thinking or what she was carrying. She touched her hand to the leather strap once more—a habit of hers, constantly checking to make sure it was there.

Fidencio had been taken in by the banditos who had taken Daria from her mother, just an add-on, a boy who'd had nowhere else to go. His presence in the group had been a matter of his survival. Violence didn't suit him and he did all he could to avoid it, which had been evident on the night they had first met. Held at gunpoint, robbed, and tossed around, it was Fidencio who had whispered his intentions to keep her safe.

As they walked the streets of San Cristóbal, Daria tightened her grip around the leather satchel. She never took it off, even in sleep, just like her gun—ready for anything, at any time, from anyone.

The three rubies and most of the metal chains remained in the satchel. Of course, no one knew this. As far as Fidencio knew, the men he used to ride with had spent everything within weeks of Daria's capture. She wouldn't even open the pouch at night while her riders slept. The beauty of the stones meant nothing to her. They were security and nothing more.

The two of them passed the schoolhouse and a modest playground. "This is a nice place," said Fidencio. "Could you ever see yourself staying in one place?"

Daria wouldn't look at him, but could appreciate the question. Once upon a time, she could have, but now … having been forced into this nomadic lifestyle. Initially, she'd longed for her freedom—to stay in one place, in peace, but life on the trail offered excitement she'd never known she would like so much. There was no good answer to his question.

Fidencio ignored her silence. "I know I could, and I know you don't like to hear things like this, but no one's around." In the middle of a side street lined with quiet houses, he stopped and held her in place, forcing her to acknowledge him. "I love you."

Daria looked directly into his eyes. She cared for him but felt none of the antiquated physical sensations that would typically accompany a young woman's affections—no butterflies in the stomach or secret wishes to marry. She wasn't sure she could love anymore, not after losing everyone she had once loved, all in one night. Fidencio had helped her try to find her mother and sister for months, but they had never arrived at Primo Romualdo's. They had never even made it to San Pedro. No, she wasn't interested in love or staying in one place. She just needed to keep moving. Perpetual motion ensured the grief could never catch up to her. "Fidencio," she said.

"Yes." He looked at her expectantly.

"Go get Teo and bring the horses."

Fidencio's face fell, but all he said was, "Okay." She knew he'd been hoping for more, but you can't give what you don't have.

They were all hungry, that was all. A full belly could make people strong. Daria returned to the main square and rested her back against the stucco wall of the restaurant. She would feed her men well, and perhaps that would be enough to redirect Fidencio's feelings. Emotions were dangerous, distractions that made people vulnerable. If he was going to ride with her, he could not be distracted.

Teo and Fidencio clomped along the cobblestone street on horseback, leading Daria's horse by the reins. When the men reached the restaurant, Fidencio's boots clacked against the stone street as he dismounted his colt. With a new rope, Teo tied the horses to the trough outside the restaurant as the proprietor opened the door. She hadn't seen the rope before. Where had it come from?

"Pasense, por favor. Bienvenidos." The restaurateur held the door open and gestured for the group to come in and be welcome.

Welcoming it was. After two weeks of salt-cured campfire fare, fresh vegetables were the best part of meals prepared by people who "stayed in one place." Pico, salsa, and guacamole—the colorful, crisp food came in stark contrast to the dusty trails they'd been riding.

"Would you like something to drink?" the restaurateur asked the group with his hands folded neatly in front of him.

"Water, please," responded Daria, never partaking in the presence of people she didn't trust.

The owner busied himself, filling glasses with water. He set a bowl of warm tortilla chips in the center of the table.

"I'd like a drink," said Teo.

Daria shot him a stern look but said nothing.

"Water's good." Teo corrected himself, stuffing chips into his mouth.

Daria ordered barbacoa for all—a generous platter of fresh, unsalted meat accompanied by refried beans and tortillas. Thinly sliced, raw cabbage garnished the meal, which was unexpected and well received. They ate and talked, famished from the long ride, absorbing the savory smells and flavors of this long-anticipated meal. No one saw the proprietor leave the restaurant, though Daria saw him enter again. The restaurateur's face led her to believe something was amiss. Maybe it was how he held his mouth, uncertain of how to relax his facial muscles—the face of someone holding a secret. He returned Daria's eye contact, but only for an instant before diverting his gaze.

Daria stood in response to the man's suspicious behavior. She placed a stack of pesos on the table. "Let's go."

Fidencio rose immediately, but Teo couldn't tear himself from the meal.

"We're leaving. Now!" said Daria, hastening to the door.

Fidencio followed. She swung the door open wide, revealing a line of men on horseback, barring their path to their horses—locals doubling as law enforcement. The leather-clad men carried guns.

"We don't harbor banditos in San Cristóbal." A man with a badge spoke for the group.

"Then we'll be going." Daria knew not to argue the semantics of their status with these men, their faces cemented in permanent scowls. They must have had dozens of groups like hers pass through their village since the Revolution began. The three of them would leave, which would suit Fidencio just fine—avoiding any unnecessary violence. Daria made for their horses, but the men closed ranks.

"You can *walk* out of here," said the officer. "We're keeping the horses and the rope you stole."

She had told Teo to stay by the river with the horses. That idiot was always trying to prove himself. She should have asked him about the rope. Now, the stolen cordage was going to cost them their horses. But that wasn't going to work at all. They lived a life on the trail, and she would not be leaving without their horses. "Let me pass."

"I'll give you one last chance to leave without a fight," said the officer. He spurred his horse and drew closer to Daria.

She would not let them intimidate her. Setting out on the trail without horses was suicide in these times of revolt. They would have to kill her before she left without them. Calm and measured, with iced water running through her veins, Daria readied herself for what she might have to do. Fidencio flanked her to the left. Where was Teo? It didn't matter. The time was now. She took her gun from the unbuttoned holster at her side and shot the officer squarely in the chest. Daria didn't wait to watch him fall as she darted between their blockade of horses, freeing her own from the trough. Fidencio followed her lead, and the two of them rode toward the river. The river valley would take them out of the village. If they went in any other direction, not knowing the terrain, they could end up trapped at the edge of a foothill, too steep for their horses to climb.

The villagers turned law enforcement officers rode behind Daria and Fidencio, firing their guns, but missing so far. They were farmers and merchants, not fighters. Daria prayed their luck would hold out long enough for the men to exhaust their ammunition.

She kicked her horse, pushing the animal to bound forward, faster than it had ever sprinted before, when a searing pain pierced her like the molten end of a fire iron. Daria felt her abdomen, but found no wound. The horses raced along the sandy bank. Holding the reins with one hand, she probed her back. Warm, wet blood bathed her fingers. Her braid beat down on her wounded back in time with the horse's strides as she spurred the beast to run faster.

Fidencio galloped past on his Spanish colt, a full hand larger than her own. He raced on without looking back, as Daria grew weak. Her body sank into itself under the extreme weight of fatigue, lungs begging for air. Her legs couldn't kick. She fingered her wound once more—so much blood. The ball in her throat brought back distant memories of her childhood, when feeling came naturally, and she swallowed hard against these destructive emotions. With her remaining strength, she gripped the cold steel of her weapon, shooting at the men and missing.

The day grew brighter. All who had been dear to her, everyone she had lost, crowded together in the brilliant light obscuring her view of Fidencio galloping away. The wall of white stole her world, as if she were riding into the face of the sun. She removed her satchel from her shoulder. It was too heavy, pressing her down, slowing her down. She couldn't breathe with it on. An overwhelming urge to sleep flooded her senses, but she willed herself to keep going. The reins became slick noodles and slipped from her grasp as she splashed into the cool water. Bubbles rose into the light, and the leather satchel sank beneath her, coming to rest on the river bed next to her gun. Her eyes fluttered closed, shutting out the pain in her back and the pain in her heart. With her last breath, river water rushed into her lungs, extinguishing her soul and setting her free.

Chapter 24

Marisol

Behind the tinted glass doors of the medical clinic, a lab report held the answer to the question that had changed the course of Marisol's life. She would have brought Adam with her, but hadn't seen him in a week. She was used to doing things on her own, though. It had been that way ever since Christo had left for the US. Not wanting to arrive at a private clinic in the city looking like a ranchera, she had borrowed a skirt and flat, black dress shoes for the appointment. Today, she would finally have answers.

A flood of cool air funneled past as she stepped into the waiting room. The door closed behind her, and Marisol hesitated in her flats on the pristine, marble floor, taking in the elegance of the room. The receptionist smiled and greeted her kindly, but it was superficial. Marisol had not achieved the look of sophistication she had envisioned. Her borrowed clothes hadn't fooled anyone.

"Buenas," Marisol said, after reaching the reception desk. "I have an appointment with Dr. Lopez."

"Y cómo se llama, señora?" The receptionist asked for her name.

"Marisol Valdez Avila."

"Sí, señora." The receptionist marked her as present and offered her a seat before disappearing into the back to let the doctor know she had arrived.

Marisol strolled to the opposite side of the waiting room and sat next to a table full of fashion magazines, making her feel even more out of place. *Who actually lives like that?* she thought. Her time to ponder this question was short. Dr. Luis Lopez promptly entered the waiting room, hand outstretched.

"It's so nice to meet you," the doctor started. "I'm glad you could make it. You should find our meeting enlightening."

"I hope so," said Marisol. She met him halfway and shook his hand.

The receptionist watched as Dr. Lopez led Marisol to his office and closed the door.

"Can I offer you anything to drink?" asked Luis.

"No, thank you," said Marisol.

"Okay then, let's get right to it. Please, have a seat." He gestured to one of two leather chairs opposite his desk. Today's visit was not for an exam but to review the results of her lab work.

Dr. Lopez took a file from the far side of his polished desk and opened a folder. "Archaic, I know, using paper files like this. We are electronic, I can assure you, but they haven't scanned your file yet."

He smiled at this last comment of his, but Marisol's facial expression showed only apprehension. She twisted her purse strap anxiously.

"If I go too quickly or if you have questions, feel free to stop me at any time," said Dr. Lopez.

"Thank you," was all Marisol could manage. Why had all of her sons been stillborn? She was about to find out.

"My initial suspicions were correct. The trait is, in fact, a recessive one carried on the female sex chromosome. In your situation, we're dealing with one recessive trait in particular, and that is the trait linked to Flanner Syndrome, which causes fetal death for male offspring in the womb."

"Flanner Syndrome," said Marisol. "What is that?" She leaned closer to the desk in anticipation of an additional explanation.

"Flanner Syndrome is characterized by multiple missing organs. Fetal death occurs so early most parents of a child with the disorder report never having felt the baby move during gestation."

"I never did," said Marisol, touching her hand to her abdomen.

"Exactly," said Dr. Lopez. "How many children did you have, Ms. Avila?"

"Three. Three sons—none of them living."

"I'm sorry to hear that," said Dr. Lopez. "To be quite honest, it is very rare for any woman to pass along this recessive trait three times to her male offspring. Statistically speaking, you should have contributed the dominant gene on at least one of these three occasions. Should that have been the case, your male child would have been completely healthy and would not be a carrier for Flanner Syndrome."

Marisol's heart sank, but Dr. Lopez was unaware of this and continued with his science.

"Also, if you were to have had a baby girl, she would have been healthy with only a fifty percent chance of being a carrier." Dr. Lopez paused, taking stock of his patient's current mental state.

"So what you're saying is that I had a chance all along of having a healthy baby boy or a healthy baby girl?"

"That's exactly what I'm saying. It was a statistical anomaly that you had three male offspring and passed along the recessive trait all three times."

Marisol sat back in her chair. She stared across the room while her imagination played an invisible film of how different her life could have turned out.

"Would you like to see the lab report?" asked Dr. Lopez. "I can have Daniela make you a copy."

Marisol didn't need a report. Her life was a copy of the results. Alone. Childless. She wasn't sure if this information had been helpful or hurtful. She had her answer, but now she also had regrets. Why had Christo given up so easily? Why hadn't she fought harder to get him to stay? Was he really dead? If not, where was he? Even if she could find him, was it too late now that she was approaching forty?

"Ms. Avila, you don't look so well." Dr. Lopez took a bottle of water from a mini-refrigerator in the corner. "Here." He gave her the bottle. "Drink."

She followed his instruction and drank the water. As she sipped the cool liquid, her swirling thoughts settled, and she realized she had another question. "How did I end up as a carrier?"

"That is an excellent question," Dr. Lopez responded. He brought out a whiteboard and drew a pedigree.

Marisol watched him, but it was like he was talking in a vacuum that sucked all of his words away before they hit her ears. He talked and drew circles, lines, and squares.

"So," said Dr. Lopez, "the only way you would be a carrier would have been if there had been some type of inbreeding in the family in the past." He paused as this taboo information registered. "Can you recall any incest in the family?"

"I really can't. I'm not trying to hide anything. I just can't think of any time this would have occurred in our family." Marisol sat silently, and Dr. Lopez left the whiteboard, sitting once again opposite Marisol at his enormous desk.

"There is one thing, though," said Marisol. "I don't exactly know who my father is. This is the only piece of family history I don't know."

"I think you've found the answer then, or the question, rather. Do you have any clues about who your father might have been?"

"My story is a little complicated," Marisol began. "My mother had abandoned me when I was a baby. The woman I call my mother is actually my aunt. My birth mother suffered a head injury as a young woman and later turned up pregnant with me. No one knows the complete story."

"That's truly unfortunate," said Dr. Lopez.

"My aunt said that my mother was engaged to be married to her high school sweetheart," Marisol continued with the information she knew. "They were supposedly in love, and her fiancé was looking toward a career as an attorney. After the injury and unexplained pregnancy, he dropped her in a matter of weeks. No one blamed him. They blamed my mother's promiscuity."

"But you said she had sustained a head injury. How could people blame *her* for someone taking advantage?" asked Dr. Lopez.

"I don't know. You know how things are in the mountains."

"Of course." Dr. Lopez inclined his head as he stood. "I've got another patient waiting, so I have to excuse myself, but feel free to stay as long as you need. I know it's a lot to take in."

Marisol took another sip of water, and the doctor was out the door before she could thank him. If no one had been able to figure out who her father was back then, how would she ever find out forty years later?

Chapter 25

Sophie

Bright and clean on the inside, the Mexican restaurant was tucked into a dingy strip mall, sandwiched between a twenty-four-hour laundromat and a vacant convenience store with bars on the windows. A whimsical rooster towered over their table, peering at Sophie from its fixed position in the mural.

"I hope you like it," said Rigo. "This is where I used to work."

"Do you miss working here?"

"Not really. Well, maybe the food."

"What kind of peppers are these?" Sophie pointed at the centerpiece—a small bush covered in what looked like upside-down Christmas lights.

"These are Thai firecrackers, but they're just for decoration. Jalapeños are hotter."

"Would you eat one for me?" asked Sophie, resting her elbows on the table and leaning forward.

"One of these?" Rigo pointed at the potted pepper plant.

She dared him with her eyes. "I bet you can't do it."

"So that's how it's going to be." Rigo accepted the challenge. He picked a ripe pepper and began to chew. His eyes teared up.

"Are you okay? I can go to the bar and get you something." Sophie started to get up.

"I'm fine," Rigo choked. "Here comes Nicandro."

A young twentysomething, dressed in matching sweats and high tops, approached their table with a swagger, carrying a tray. "What's wrong with you?" said Nick, placing two glasses of iced water on the table along with the complimentary chips and salsa.

Rigo popped a chip into his mouth and washed it down with a cold glass of water.

"I miss this shit," said Nick. "What've you been up to?"

"Nick, this is Sophie. Sophie, this is Nick." Rigo reached for Sophie's water. "Nick and I used to work together."

"Damn, you guys are together now?" Nick and Sophie shook hands. "It's nice to meet you. When we worked together, this guy would talk about you all the time. He would—"

Rigo cut him off midsentence with a wide-eyed, forceful stare. "Nick, how's school going?"

"Oh, right, school's going great." Their server beamed. "I just took my last skills test for clinicals."

"What are you going to school for?" asked Sophie.

Nick slid into their booth. He sat so close she could smell his cologne. "I'm in nursing school and I'll be graduating in a month." Nick helped himself to their chips and salsa. "I think my wife is even happier than I am."

"Oh, really. What does she do?"

"We have four kids, so she's been doing it all while I've been in school." Nick turned to Rigo and gestured to their surroundings. "But what'll happen to this place once I'm working in the hospital? Do you think they'll be able to get by without either one of us?"

"I'm sure they'll manage," said Rigo. "Seriously though, Nick, congratulations."

Rigo's friend thanked him and told Sophie about how Rigo used to quiz him in the back of the restaurant while they washed dishes at the end of their shifts together.

"All right, Nick. That's enough. Don't you have other tables? You're sitting a little too close to my girlfriend."

"Damn, Rigo. Yeah. I'll leave you and your lady alone, but what can I get you guys to drink?"

"Vamos a tomar dos tequilas de Herradura con hielo," said Rigo.

"Perfecto, señor." Nick performed a mock bow and went to get their drinks.

"What did you order?"

"Tequila with ice—my favorite kind, Herradura."

"What does it mean? Is Herradura someone's name?" Sophie asked.

"It means horseshoe." Rigo pushed the two empty water glasses to the edge of the table. "Sorry, I drank all your water."

"It's okay." She stifled a laugh, picturing his face after he had eaten the pepper. "But why name a tequila horseshoe?"

"Surprisingly, I have the answer to that question." Rigo explained how the Herradura factory sat next to a curve in the road that, when viewed from the air, had the distinct shape of a horseshoe. "Christo told me about it."

Their drinks arrived. "I gave you guys doubles but only rang them in as singles." Nick flashed a sly half smile. "You're welcome." Before they could thank him, Nick left for another one of his tables.

"Christo was the man you were walking with in the desert, right?" Sophie asked.

"Exactly," said Rigo. "Christo told me about the time he and his wife had taken a tour of the Herradura factory, and I told him I'd try it someday if we ever made it to the US."

"What do you mean, 'if?' Weren't you following a guide?" Sophie tasted her drink. "This is very good."

"I thought you might like it." Rigo held his glass up, admiring the double shot before taking a long swallow. "Just because we pay a guide doesn't mean our safety is guaranteed. A lot can happen in the desert. It's not like buying a vacation package."

"Of course not," Sophie agreed.

Rigo's friend returned to their table and took their orders. "Sopa de mariscos and pollo a la crema—solid choices," said Nick. "Everything'll be out soon." He placed an extra bowl of chips on the table and left.

"You should tell me the rest of the story," said Sophie as they waited for their meals. "You never finished telling me how you crossed into the US."

"I'm surprised you're so curious."

"Why wouldn't I be?"

"I don't know. I guess I just don't think of myself as that interesting."

"That's crazy," said Sophie. "You're way more interesting than I am. I've never done anything dangerous like that. I've never had to, I suppose."

"You have an unusual take on it." Rigo pulled a napkin from the metal dispenser and placed it under his glass. "Emigration is just so commonplace where I'm from. You make the decision knowing there's an inherent risk that comes with taking a chance to better your life."

"Very true." Sophie thought about how she had taken a risk separating from Adam, although it was only a financial risk—not the same thing at all, but a risk nonetheless. "So will you tell me the rest?"

"Sure, but remind me where I left off."

"It was the end of the first day. The sun was setting, and you were all getting tired."

"That's right. Christo and I had been talking to pass the time when José yelled for us to hide. I hadn't seen anything, but Christo and I did what he said. We ran, assuming it was border patrol."

Rigo's eyes were far away as he recalled the events in his mind's eye. "When we came to a ravine, I tripped and rolled down the slope. Christo had slipped too, but caught himself on a boulder. José and the rest of the group had run in another direction, and from the bottom of the ravine, it sounded like whoever we were hiding from had followed the larger group." Rigo ran a tortilla chip through the house salsa.

"How long did you stay down there?"

"It seemed like hours, but it was probably only minutes. When I started to move, I saw a beam of light sweep across the gulley, so I closed my eyes, praying they wouldn't see me."

Sophie leaned in closer. "Weren't you afraid of scorpions or snakes?"

"That's the thing. People are much more dangerous than animals. Well, people are animals, actually—the most dangerous kind of animal."

Also true, Sophie thought.

"Eventually, I opened my eyes and the group of men with flashlights standing at the top of the ravine moved on. When I found Christo, his body was sprawled on a rock ledge. He didn't have a pulse, and he wasn't breathing. I couldn't make out any injuries in the dark. They were probably internal. Anyway, I felt completely helpless. There wasn't anything I could do for him, so I closed his eyes and went to find the others."

Rigo took a slow sip of his drink. It couldn't have been easy for him to dredge up these memories. His story was like something from a movie, something far removed from her suburban life. "You left him there? What about his wife?"

"I know it sounds bad, but we would never have made it carrying the weight of a dead man's body. Besides, we wouldn't have been able to do anything for him."

What a choice to have to make at such a young age. Sophie thought about the decisions she was making when she was twenty-three. She had never had to decide to leave a dead body behind in the desert.

"I couldn't find anyone else," Rigo recollected, "and figured they had either been caught or were still hiding, so I just headed north. It wasn't until morning that I found the others. They had also traveled north through the night. After rejoining the group, José said we should be prepared in case the men came back. He didn't ask what happened to Christo, and I didn't tell him. We just kept walking, but the whole time all I could picture was Christo, lying there on the ledge."

"That could have been you," Sophie said.

"It could have been any one of us. I got lucky, I guess. No, I know I got lucky." He looked meaningfully into her eyes.

Usually, these looks of his made her melt, but she was too invested in the story. "What happened next?"

Rigo obliged her and continued. "We were all so hot, and it was hard to keep going. I had started with two gallons of water and was down to half a gallon, sweating more than I was taking in."

"How much longer did you have to walk?"

"You mean run," Rigo corrected her. "A gunshot sounded, and everyone dropped their waters. We ran for miles. My muscles burned, and my mouth was dry, but I couldn't stop. We had crossed into the United States through the ranch of a private US citizen."

"Who was shooting? Was it border patrol?"

"Sort of. The US government allows its citizens living on the Mexican border to act as militiamen for the border patrol. That was the first day I felt less than human. A man was hunting me like a deer, and he had every right to do it. He saw me as an invader."

Sophie had no words. She placed her palms on the table on either side of her drink and listened.

"We ran for hours through the desert," Rigo recounted, "dodging thorns and diving through barbed wire fences. The Aztec woman stayed in front. She slid under the wire with her baby, and I never heard it make a sound. We didn't stop running until after dark."

"And what about water?" Sophie took another sip of her drink. She was thirsty just thinking about it.

"We ended up coming across two troughs of stagnant water, the kind used for livestock. My traveling companions drank from the troughs, but they were full of mosquito larvae. I couldn't bring myself to swallow the water, so I swished it around in my mouth and spit it out. José counted everyone in the group—only seven of us left. We were missing Bartolo too, but nobody went back to find him. He had most likely been shot by the rancher or had collapsed from dehydration. Either way, everybody had come too far to turn back and look for a dead man."

The food arrived. "Here you go," said Nick. "We have a new cook, but I think he does a better job with the sopa."

Rigo pulled a crab claw from his soup, cracked it, and sucked out the sweet meat. "It is better," Rigo agreed. "Who's cooking now?"

"It's the owner's nephew. He's like sixteen, but everything he makes is so good. If you need anything, just let me know. We're getting pretty busy."

Nick was right. There wasn't an empty table in the restaurant, and Sophie could see why, after cutting into her pollo a la crema. "Keep going," she said to Rigo.

"That was all the exciting stuff. After that, we waited in a ditch until José came back with a truck. He drove us to Phoenix, and I called my cousin from there. I stayed with him for a few days and then took a bus to my sister's house in Alexandria."

"I can't believe you went through all that to come here." Sophie had always known Rigo was something special, but every new thing she learned about him seemed to elevate her opinion of him that much more.

"When I want something, I'm very persistent," he said, looking into her eyes.

Sophie lowered her gaze, focusing on her rice and beans. She was still getting used to being treated so well.

"You can look at me when I say things like that. I'm not embarrassed." Rigo hailed a different server to bring them two more drinks, while Nick sat at another one of his tables, actively talking with another man's wife.

"I know we haven't been officially seeing each other long, but we've known each other for years. Sophie, every time I look at you, you wake me up and make me feel alive with desire. You're the most beautiful, kind, and interesting woman I've ever met—everything I ever wanted in a partner. You challenge me, but more than that, you see me. I want to build a future with you." He produced a small velvet box. "You deserve the chance to have everything you've ever wanted—love, children, success, adventure—everything, and I want to give it to you."

What was he trying to say? Sophie froze, like a statue carved from petrified emotion. She needed to get off this speeding train … only, she didn't want to.

"I know you just got out of a bad marriage, so I'm not trying to rush you into anything. I only want you to know exactly what my intentions are." Inside the velvet box, an opal ring shone with a myriad of iridescent colors. "It's not a diamond because this isn't a proposal. It's a promise, my promise to love you—all the colors of you. This relationship can be anything we want it to be. It belongs to us."

Rigo's steady and supportive words guided her off the speeding train, leading her to a soft meadow where her fears and anxieties could not take root. This relationship could be anything they wanted it to be.

Chapter 26

Adam

It was only Tuesday, four more days until Adam could return to the ranch. He sat inside his truck at the construction site with his seat pushed back, making room for his laptop. In his mind, the image of a woman's face smeared with lion's blood danced among green flames, threatening to take his attention away from his responsibilities.

"Hey, boss?" Carlos knocked on the glass, startling Adam and sending his laptop banging into the steering wheel.

Adam rolled down the window. "Yeah, Carlos. What's up?"

"We should have most of the skimming done by the end of the week," Carlos said, trying to start a conversation.

Adam had been leaning hard on his site supervisor, so he gave Carlos the courtesy of getting out of the truck to take a tour of the site, which he should have been doing, anyway. He didn't recognize any of the laborers, all of them interior tradesmen. Adam had been doing the bare minimum for weeks now and Carlos must have been feeling the weight of his negligence.

"When do we have the lighting fixtures scheduled for installation?" Adam asked, even though Carlos had everything under control. Asking was merely a way to show interest and appreciation, and he hoped his site supervisor wouldn't see through this ruse.

Carlos consulted his notes. "In two weeks, after the painters."

They took the elevator to the fourth floor, which would house the executive suites, and made their way to the future president's office. Blueprints for all project phases leaned against the metal framing in the corner. On top of a stack of drywall, the two men spread out the blueprints with the drywall specs.

"The design called for three-quarter inch drywall, but I was able to get half-inch drywall for one-third the price," Carlos explained.

Adam's bonus got larger every time Carlos made a decision like this. "That's great, and it won't make a difference with the soundproof insulation we're installing."

"I would have asked you first, but my call wouldn't go through. The reception in the mountains isn't great."

"Not to worry," Adam assured him. "You made the right choice, as usual."

The site supervisor knew exactly what Adam was doing. Carlos probably hadn't even tried to call about the drywall, but had to make it look like he was yielding to Adam's direction. Whatever. As long as they stayed on schedule, and as long as Carlos kept making decisions that improved the bottom line, Adam was happy. They could continue paying each other contrived courtesies indefinitely.

"I think I'm going to cut out early today," Adam said after finishing their impromptu meeting.

"Okay." Carlos's tone gave nothing away. "I've got everything under control."

"I can see that. Keep it up, and if you have any questions, call me."

"Will do."

Adam wouldn't be receiving any calls from Carlos, and it wouldn't be because of the reception. He thanked his site supervisor again before heading for the elevator.

The metal detector had found a new home in the back of the SUV, so he didn't have to stop by the townhouse first. Adam would have brought a change of clothes, but honestly hadn't planned on leaving early.

He bypassed the turn to Marisol's ranch house, bound for the river, where he had first met Alberto, the same spot where he thought he had seen the *green fire of gold*. Fresh, young runners studded with thorns stretched across the trail, ready to snag any unsuspecting hikers on their way to the water. Not long down the path, his leather shoes fell victim to the triangular assailants, and he used the metal detector to free himself from the line of thorns lodged in his footwear. Adam stepped gingerly over the emerging greenery growing wild in the rainy season, but the closer he came to where he'd seen the light, the less concerned he was about his clothing. By the time he had reached the river, loose loops of string covered his work clothes, snagged by the new growth encroaching on the path.

Adam gripped the metal detector and switched the setting to ultrasensitive. Still new to treasure hunting on land, he wasn't sure if the machine could detect gold through stone or just dirt and sand. A few blips sounded near some of the smaller boulders but yielded nothing significant, which left him wondering if the sand had a metallic element.

By the time Adam had looked under a dozen heavy stones, he felt a familiar high, like when he was underwater blowing sand on the ocean floor, wanting to get a few more feet uncovered before surfacing for a new tank. Today, it was one more rock, then one more rock. But who was there to stop him or scold him? He had all afternoon to look under as many rocks as he wanted, and he didn't have to answer to anybody.

Adam put his back into it, literally, leaning against a massive boulder. With the weight of his body, he pushed through his legs into his back, pressed squarely against the stone. Beads of sweat dripped from his temples, but it didn't budge.

To hell with it. He picked up the pace, shoes scraping and scuffing against stone as he traversed along the river's edge, until a loose rock sent him tumbling to his knees. From the ground, he could see he might be losing perspective, and took a moment to get his emotions in check. The all-too-familiar feeling of losing control was overtaking his better judgment. He had learned to recognize when he was in this frenzied state and tried to pull himself out of it. There had been too many occasions where he had found himself underwater, cutting it too close with his oxygen reserves, risking decompression sickness on his ascent. He needed to pack up his gear and head back to the jobsite, where he should have been from the beginning, but he didn't want to leave. Maybe he just needed to work smarter, not harder. No, he didn't have to leave. Just one more boulder. He pushed himself onto his feet again.

If I were to bury a fortune, not knowing when I would be back to claim it, I would do it above where the water would rise in the wet season, well above. Adam talked himself through it. Following this logic, Adam surveyed the valley and noticed a distinct change in the texture of the rocks. At a certain distance from the river, the stones transformed from smooth and contoured to jagged and bumpy—smarter, not harder.

Now that he had established where the water would flow at its peak, he began a new search. Where would someone hide something in a hurry? Once again, Adam scanned the riverbank, looking for markers, and found a boulder that was significantly darker than the rest. It couldn't be that easy. He laughed out loud. No one was around to hear him. *Those poor old men, all they had to do was put a little brain power into their search.* He pushed the boulder, but it didn't budge. He repeated the same efforts on countless other stones possessing distinguishing characteristics with no luck until he pushed on one oblong boulder roughly resembling a pear. He leaned against the stone and it budged slightly. Crouching down, Adam pressed his shoulder against the large rock and pushed with all his weight. It rolled—too easily. Someone had to have moved the stone recently. If not, the slow erosion of dirt from the mountainside would have acted like cement, fixing it to a permanent resting spot at the river's edge.

He adjusted the setting on his metal detector and waved it over the newly exposed earth. *Beep, beep, beep, beep, beep.* Using the slender shovel, he began digging, but after removing two feet of soil, he still had nothing to show for his efforts. Adam waved the machine over top of the dig spot again. The beeps sounded faster this time—louder too, and with a renewed sense of purpose, he kept digging.

The pointed shovel clanked against something round and solid. Adam stuck his hand into the hole and brushed the loose dirt away, uncovering a clutch of small rocks and one larger rock he must have hit with the shovel. Great. He had just wasted over an hour digging up a bunch of rocks, the same rocks that were absolutely everywhere in los ranchos. Then he thought back to the tale of the buried mulch Ruben had told him, and like an excited grade school boy with a head full of stories, decided to save the rocks.

He jumped up from the hole to retrieve the metal detector's canvas carrying case. It would be strong enough to hold the rocks. Back at the edge of the hole, Adam lay on the ground, collecting the stones. The larger rock fit neatly into the palm of his hand, and he brought his arm out to get a better look. *What the?* It wasn't a rock! Three gaping pits and a toothless fissure stared blankly over his shoulder—a human skull, but it was so small. The reality of what he had uncovered sank in as the skull slipped from his grasp, rolling down the dusty slope toward the river and coming to rest face-up against a tree stump.

Had anyone seen him? Adam combed the mountainsides with his eyes. Neither one of Marisol's cousins had explicitly given him permission to be there, and now he'd disturbed a child's grave. He scurried down the hill to get the skull and, bone in hand, wiped the sand from the cranial cavity onto his white shirt, creating streaks of red clay and wet sand. Hollow eye sockets watched him, judging him, as he delicately lowered the remains back into the hole. Cascades of sandy earth quickly filled the burial site as he bulldozed the dirt with two hands into the hole.

With his scratched leather shoes, Adam tamped down the disrupted burial plot before jogging up the mountainside. The clatter of equipment ruined his chance at stealth, but he didn't see anyone on his way back, just as he had seen no one on his way to the river. It would be okay. Marisol's cousins would never know, and he would control his treasure-hunting urges moving forward. One gold coin would have to be enough. He was in Mexico for work, and that is what he would focus on—construction work.

Shaken from the afternoon's events, Adam wasn't eager to drive out of los ranchos. The roads were treacherous enough without driving distracted, but Marisol's was close. When his

SUV came bumping down the unpaved road, Marisol was milking the cattle.

"What happened to you?" She left her cow tied to a branch and met Adam at the gate, carrying a bucket of milk.

"You're going to think this is ridiculous, but I thought I saw a green light at the river the weekend we planted corn together. I didn't tell you about it because I didn't want to sound crazy." His explanation tumbled out like a handful of dice.

Marisol shot him a thin smile and set the bucket down. "You mean you wanted to keep anything you found for yourself." Her comment met with silence. "I told you it was pointless. If there was anything to find, my primos would have already found it."

"But I did find something." He took the coin from his wallet and showed her. "And that's not all. Today, I found something else."

"You're joking." It was a statement but also a question. "Where is it? What is it?" Adam's find had revived the childlike excitement she'd set aside years ago. "Did you find the Hernandez Castañeda jewels?"

"No! Definitely not."

Marisol's expression fell into a calm indifference. "What then?"

"Bones," said Adam as he tucked the coin into his wallet.

"Bones? So what? There are bones all over this place. Burial sites in churchyards are expensive. You probably just found someone's great-great-grandfather." She returned her attention to the task at hand and picked up her bucket of milk. "Here, take this to the fence."

Adam didn't reach for the bucket. "Marisol, it was a baby."

She dropped the pail on its side, and the warm, frothy milk soaked into the dirt. "Was it a boy or a girl?"

"How am I supposed to know?" said Adam. "When I realized I had a baby's skull in my hand, I put everything back as fast as I could."

"I can't think of anyone who buried a baby by the river." Marisol mentally sorted through everyone living in los ranchos.

"I'm sorry. I should have thought about how difficult this would be for you." Adam righted the empty bucket. "Like you said, the bones probably belonged to a family of farmers who lived a long time ago. We should just forget about it."

She ignored what he said. "If it had been a boy with the same genetic abnormality as my sons, I might have Dr. Lopez construct one of his drawings with the circles and the squares. Maybe I could find out who my father is."

"What are you talking about?"

"I got the results of the blood test, Adam."

"And …?" He had forgotten to ask about that.

"And I carry the recessive trait for Flanner Syndrome."

"What's that?"

"It's some kind of rare disorder that … It's not important. The point is, I could have had healthy children, Adam. We just gave up too quickly." Sadness pulled at the corners of her mouth, aging her.

"But how could finding out who this baby belongs to lead you to your father?"

She shook her head, eyebrows drawn. "I guess it couldn't. I would need to know who the parents were and why the child died." She vocalized her thoughts as quickly as they came to her. "I would need to have a DNA sample tested for the disorder …" She covered her face with her hands, rubbed her eyes, and let her arms drop to her sides. "It would be too expensive, and in the end, it would most likely give me no clue as to who my father is."

"Luis might help with the testing again." Adam shouldn't have said anything about the bones.

"Don't pay any attention to me." She wrapped her arms across her chest and around her sides in a self-soothing hug. "Knowing the truth wouldn't solve anything. I'd still be here on this ranch, alone."

Adam scrambled for something to say, some comforting words.

"It's just so hard sometimes, the not knowing," she continued.

"I'm sorry you've had to deal with so much." There—a simple statement showing compassion. He didn't try to relate his situation to what she was going through. He couldn't.

"Thanks," she said. The cow Marisol had been milking shuffled from side to side as far as the rope would allow, prodding her to finish and untie it from the branch.

"Why don't we take another trip and forget about all this for a while? How about this coming weekend?" Adam suggested.

"You're too used to distracting yourself, Adam."

Her armor was cracking, and through her independent and self-reliant exterior, showed vulnerability, which Adam found alluring. He slowly pulled her toward himself. Marisol hesitated, but laid her head on his chest.

"Thank you for being my friend, but you know, and I know, this could never work. Besides, I could never bring myself to cheat on my husband," she said, lifting her head and taking a few steps back.

Adam hadn't meant to suggest they would be a couple or anything. He intended to offer her some comfort, a distraction, in this moment, but maybe he was the only one feeling the sexual pull. "I'm sorry, I should get going." He gave her an out. "I've got work tomorrow."

Marisol needed to untie the cow, but didn't avert her eyes from his. They stared at each other. Adam knew it would ruin everything. They said all the practical things two people in their situation should have said, yet they were still watching one another, not moving, breathing faster, each waiting for the other to make a move. They waited for something that would allow them to fulfill their physical desires, the gold coin forgotten for the time being.

Adam stepped toward her and held out his hand. With every step he took, he knew he should walk the other way, but he didn't have the strength of character. Marisol accepted his outstretched hand lightly and dropped her eyes submissively. She let him guide her to the bedroom. Amphibians and insects called to their partners in the twilight as he laid her on the bed— their bodies joined. The skin of his chest stuck to her breasts, and his thrusting would leave her delicate skin chafed in the days to come. Her nails dug into his back, and he grabbed her wrists to pin them over her head. With his eyes closed, Adam lost himself in his personal pleasure, climbing an imaginary mountain, and hurling himself off of its tallest peak.

Chapter 27

Sophie

Sophie bent to lay a piece of sod on the exposed earth. The grass wouldn't have much time to take root before it would be trampled by one hundred fifty of the bride and groom's closest friends and relatives.

"Doesn't this place look great?" asked Rigo, glancing across the yard at the wisp of a tree they had just planted. "I think it was brilliant of you to suggest planting the walnut tree. Imagine them picking fresh walnuts with their grandchildren."

Sophie admired the wiry sapling growing by itself, surrounded by the new patchwork of grass. "I know it looks a little funny now, but in fifteen years, it's going to need the space."

Scattered throughout the yard, Rigo had stacked piles of sod with the Bobcat. Sophie reached for another roll, and a wave of dizziness washed over her. She side-stepped, touching her hand to the pile of turf, and lowered herself into a seated position.

"Hey." Rigo dropped his crumbling roll of dirt and roots, rushing to her side. "What's wrong?"

"It's nothing." She held up her hand, asking for some room to breathe. "I've just been feeling a little tired all day, pushing myself to keep up with you." Sophie rested her back against the wall of sod. Dirt particles sprinkled onto her hair.

"Can you describe how you're feeling?"

"Just tired. That's all." She didn't want to make a big deal out of it.

"Stay here. I'm going to get you some water. Don't get up." Rigo jogged across the yard, to the truck parked on the street, and returned with a bottle. He let her rest, taking small sips of water. "It looked like you lost your balance. Do you want me to take you to the doctor?"

"No, I'm feeling better." She squeezed his hand, appreciative of his concern.

Rigo leaned against the dirt wall beside Sophie. "When was the last time you had your period?" He saw the puzzled look on her face. "I'm only asking because we've been together for a few months now and …"

He didn't finish his statement, but she could fill in the blanks. "Maybe I've been doing too much physical labor."

"*Or* you could be pregnant." He turned his head toward her, disturbing the pile again, causing more dirt to rain down on them.

"You think so?"

"Maybe. Remember what you said about the antibiotics?"

Sophie drew her knees up, wrapped her arms around them, and dropped her head into the hole they'd created. "I didn't plan this. We didn't plan this." She lifted her head and regarded him. "Are you upset?"

"Upset? I could never be upset with you. It's not like we haven't talked about having children, and we're writing our own story—for us. Remember?"

Sophie studied the opal on her finger as it refracted light from the sunny backyard. Each angle of the stone showcased some colors while hiding others. She wondered which color represented an unplanned pregnancy.

"Just try to relax. I'll lay the rest of the sod and start the sprinkler. We can pick up a pregnancy test on the way home." Rigo helped her to a lawn chair under the shade of the large oak and finished the day's work on his own, all the while glancing lovingly at her every chance he got.

Could she be pregnant? It was possible, but what were the odds that she would get pregnant inside of such a narrow window? It wasn't likely, but she would take it easy and let him finish up. The dizziness had subsided, but the exhaustion remained.

When they arrived at the pharmacy, he helped her from the truck. She didn't need any help, but Rigo was a mixture of progressive and old-fashioned. This was one way he showed her he cared. Ever since their conversation earlier in the day, he had been treating her like she was a fragile orchid, as if a touch from his rough hands would tear her petals. This made her feel considered, but it was more than that. He made her feel … important.

"You're smiling," he said. "I'm so glad to see that."

Of course, she was smiling, but she had to keep her feelings in check. They knew nothing for sure. She had always wanted to be a mom, but she could just be coming down with something. Maybe she belonged in the cold and flu aisle instead of family planning.

Rigo pulled a box of pregnancy tests from the shelf. "This one has two tests, in case we need an extra."

Sophie took the box. After everything they had shared in the bedroom, this moment should've been natural, but standing under the fluorescent lights of the pharmacy didn't evoke any romantic feelings. She kept watch as if, at any moment, someone she knew would round the corner and ask her about the box she held in her hand.

"Do you need anything else while we're here?" asked Rigo.

"No, nothing from the pharmacy, but what do you think about Chinese takeout?"

"There's never a bad time for Chinese takeout. I know a fabulous place close to the house."

•   •   •

Rigo set the takeout on the kitchen table, and Sophie disappeared into the bathroom. It was simple enough—pee on the stick, but she didn't want to make any mistakes, so she read the directions. Yellow fluid migrated up the absorbent tip, and a vertical line appeared in each window. She checked the directions—negative, but as she stared, a faint line appeared next to the first. It wasn't as dark as the first line. Was it positive? She consulted the directions yet again, and … yes. The second line could be lighter than the first, meaning the test was positive. She was pregnant!

Adam would have been livid, but Rigo wasn't Adam. Test in hand, Sophie opened the door, but her words wouldn't come out.

"And?" Rigo nudged.

The words "I'm pregnant" pushed past her fears and hung in the air like a saturated cloud, releasing a shower of emotion when Rigo took her in his arms, pulled her close, and cradled her head against his shoulder.

"*We're* pregnant," he said. "This is wonderful news, mi reina!"

She squeezed him back with one arm while holding the testing stick with the other. Everything she had ever wanted was happening, but all so fast and not the way she had planned. Tears escaped her eyes as she imagined her family together on Christmas morning, opening gifts they would never have to hide, a family where everyone always came home at night.

"Come," said Rigo, guiding her to the kitchen. "You have to eat something." He spooned heaping portions of the Chinese takeout for the mother-to-be.

"This plate must weigh five pounds," she said. "I can't eat all this. The baby is probably only microscopic at this point."

"You don't have to eat it all if you don't want to, but you have it just in case." He pulled her chair out.

"It doesn't seem real." Sophie dipped an egg roll into the sweet and sour sauce. "Mmm. This is the best Chinese I've ever had."

"I know. The Mandarin Tree does it right." Rigo made himself a plate. "I agree, though. It doesn't seem real—like a dream or something."

"Exactly. I wanted to be a mom the whole time I was married, and now it's finally happening." Married. She was still married, to Adam, that is, and carrying Rigo's baby. She and Adam were separated, but this was hardly how she'd planned to start a family.

Rigo recognized Sophie evaporating into her thoughts. "What's wrong?"

She didn't want to spoil the mood. "Nothing."

"Don't do that, Sophie."

"What am I doing?"

"Shutting me out," he said. "We're in this together. This baby is as much a part of me as it is a part of you. I want to make this pregnancy as easy as possible, and if something's bothering you, I want to help you in any way I can."

She didn't want to hurt his feelings. "I know we're doing things our own way, but right now, I'm still married to Adam, and I'm carrying *your* baby. It's not a good feeling. I mean … it is a good feeling … but I just wish the timing was better, that I was already divorced. Do you understand what I'm trying to say?"

"I do," said Rigo. He set his fork down. "But there are some things that we can't change or rush—the legal system, for instance. You two have to be separated for one year before the state will grant a divorce.

"Sophie, the good thing is that the separation period started months ago. This can't be disputed. Adam's been in Mexico, and you've been here. Flight records, emails, and witnesses can all attest to this if he tries to dispute it, and he may not."

"That's true." Sophie still hadn't returned from her private place of condemnation.

"The best thing we can do is start the paperwork. Let's visit a lawyer. They'll probably advise you to move out of the house so the two of you will no longer share a residence. That way, when Adam returns from Mexico, there'll be no confusion about when the separation period began."

"I must've forgotten to tell you. I had the separation papers drawn up weeks ago."

Rigo smiled. Good. He was happy about her trip to the lawyer, but all of this planning and scheming on top of the pregnancy was too much for one day. It wasn't really scheming, though. It was just moving forward. Yes. She would call it moving forward.

"Let's not worry about any of this now, Sophie. There's nothing we can do at eight o'clock at night. After dinner, we should just shower and go to bed."

"I think I might go to bed now. Between the Chinese food and everything we've been talking about, I'm feeling a little nauseous."

Rigo collected their mostly full plates from the table as she headed toward the bedroom. "Sophie." He caught her by the waist. "Everything's going to be fine."

She didn't respond, continuing past him as his fingers slipped from her belly. How was he so sure of everything? She had never been supremely sure of anything … until now … maybe. She wanted this baby. Rigo was right. They would take it one step at a time. The legal system couldn't be rushed. No point in stressing over something she couldn't change. The passage of time would fix all of her problems, but she didn't want to rush a moment of this pregnancy.

Chapter 28

Adam

Adam sank into a chair by the fire and let his arms hang over the sides. "Is that all of them?"

"I have two kernels left." Marisol stuck her hand into her pouch, producing the last two golden seeds. She held them out for Adam to see, then tossed them by the gate for the chickens. They went unnoticed by the poultry, who had already tucked their heads into their feathers for the night.

Adam had worked on construction sites, clearing trash as a teen, and had also been an avid basketball player until recently, but he could not remember a time he had been this physically tired at the end of a day. "You do this every year on your own?"

"I do everything on my own."

Marisol had been throwing these digs out all day. He knew last week had been a mistake, but why couldn't she just let it go? They weren't married, and he didn't have to put up with this stuff from her. Adam had placed his hands on the arms of the chair to get up and go when Alberto and Javier came through the gate, followed by Marisol's dogs.

"It's so good to see you, my babies!" In her dusty work jeans, Marisol squatted and opened her arms to welcome her prodigal companions. "Where have you three been?"

They knocked her over, playfully pawing at her shirt. Pepe took her thick braid in his mouth, but this was where she drew the line. Marisol scolded the ringleader, and Pepe skulked off to the side of the house to lie against the cool stone.

"I hope you have some of your homemade tortillas handy," Javier said, with his arms full.

"Here, let me help you, Primo." Marisol jumped to her feet and took the plastic bags dangling from Javier's hands.

"Thank you," said her aging cousin.

Adam stood but wasn't planning on leaving now that these two had shown up. Their presence would be the buffer he needed to shield him from Marisol's undertones. Adam helped Alberto with his load. "What did you guys bring?"

"We bring everything for the dinner," said Alberto, holding a clear, plastic bag crammed full of blood-red meat.

"We enjoyed our visit so much last time, we thought we could do it again," said Javier. "This time, we planned ahead and have everything for fajitas." He produced a bottle of dark tequila—Cazadores Añejo. "So who wants to hear a story?"

"I'm not sure I'm in the mood for any more stories, Primo. I'd like to hear something real for once," said Marisol, returning the somber mood to the fireside.

"Then I have just the tale. It's a true story, this one. It's about a farmer, his daughter, and her boyfriend."

"I've always liked that one, Primo." Marisol dragged two more chairs closer to the fire and motioned for her cousins to have a seat. "But happy endings aren't that easy to come by."

"Marisol speaks the truth." Javier poured the amber liquid and raised his glass of tequila to the group. "I've been looking for my happy ending for over forty years."

"I'd never known you were so sentimental when it came to love," said Marisol.

"Not love, my dear. Treasure." Javier righted the conversation.

Marisol shook her head. "And here, I thought you were about to get emotional."

"I am no such thing," confirmed Javier.

"Don't worry." Marisol raised her glass and took a sip. "I won't spread any vicious rumors."

"¿Tienes un tazón, Prima?" Alberto asked.

Marisol disappeared into the kitchen and returned with a sizeable, metal bowl. "¿Está bien?"

"Sí, gracias, Prima."

Alberto placed the bright red cuts of flank steak into the bowl, sliced three limes in half, and squeezed the acidic juice over the meat.

"Have you really been treasure hunting for forty years?" asked Adam.

Javier raised his eyebrows before calling himself out. "It's an addiction."

Adam could relate. "But you're not hurting anyone."

"That's what I tell myself. If you get down to it, it's actually decent exercise, hiking and digging, but it is getting harder as the years go by."

Alberto sprinkled garlic, cumin, and chili powder into the bowl, massaging the spices into the meat as Marisol's dogs hovered close, watching his every move.

"Are you still looking for the Hernandez Castañeda fortune?" Adam asked.

"I am," said Javier. "The rubies are said to have belonged to Spanish royalty, passed down through generations—the largest of the three measures two inches in diameter. I dream about those stones. Sad, I know."

"Adam, you want look for the treasure tomorrow?" asked Alberto, his attention temporarily diverted from his culinary creation. "With my brain and you muscle, we are good team."

Even though tomorrow was Sunday, Carlos would be on site, pushing to finish ahead of schedule. Adam had been thinking about making an appearance at Comp Zero, if only for the sake of his professional relationship with Carlos, but the opportunity to get back to the hunt pulled at him like a fishing line. "Yes, that would be great. Are you coming, Javier?"

"No. I'd like to come. There's nothing I like more than having someone younger do the heavy lifting for me these days, but I have an engagement in the city."

"Suit yourself. More treasure for us. Right, Alberto?"

"Sound good to me, my friend." Alberto passed the marinated meat to Marisol. "Ready for the fire!"

After the incident with the skull, Adam had promised himself he was done with treasure hunting, but as is true with most addictions, this promise to himself was short-lived.

The following morning, Adam woke with a headache. Why did he keep doing this to himself, and how come no one else ever felt bad the morning after a night of drinking? The tequila had done its job, at any rate. Last night had been fun, and it had earned him permission to use his metal detector all day. He scooted from his sleeping bag on Marisol's floor and ventured out to the patio through the protective curtain.

Marisol must have woken up early. The cattle weren't making a sound, and their udders hung high. With the morning milking done, she was probably avoiding him at the chor. He found Alberto asleep on top of his afghan beside the fire pit. "Hey, Alberto, are you ready to go?"

"What you want?" Alberto rolled away from Adam and covered his face with the blanket.

"It's nine thirty. Javier's gone already. Do you still want to go treasure hunting today?" No response. "If you do, we should probably get started soon. It's supposed to get pretty hot today." Adam chugged a bottle of water he'd left next to the fire. He couldn't start out dehydrated. "Alberto?" Adam nudged him on the shoulder.

"Go away. My head is hurt."

Aha! He wasn't the only one this time, but this didn't give Adam much satisfaction because now he didn't have a partner. He had no desire to cajole this elderly man out of bed on a Sunday morning, so Adam gathered his equipment, sucked down another bottle of water, and set off on his own. He should have returned to the city, but Javier and Alberto had given him their blessing to roam the ranch, searching for buried treasure. Adam laced up his hiking boots and swung his backpack over his shoulder. A quarter of a mile later, Marisol's house was out of sight.

•   •   •

A reddish scorpion, no longer than an inch, scuttled away as Adam lifted a precariously placed boulder. Nothing—again. After having been at it for nearly two hours, he sat on the closest rock, massaging his shoulder. If he wasn't careful, he would end up wasting his entire day out there with nothing to show for it but a scorpion sting.

"Watch out for the red ones. Their venom is stronger than the others," said a voice with a heavy accent from behind.

A portly police officer had his gun drawn, breathing too quickly. Adam would have asked if he was all right if there hadn't been a gun pointed at his chest. How had he missed the lumbering footsteps of this out-of-shape man? This obsession of his had led him into trouble again.

"Come with me. You're under arrest," coughed the officer, holding his gun with one hand and using the other to cover his mouth.

Adam couldn't resist. "Are you okay?"

The officer hacked up something nasty onto a rock, which dried almost immediately. Then he made a few more disturbing noises before repeating himself. "You're under arrest."

Adam rose and held his hands in the air. "But I haven't done anything."

"You're trespassing."

Adam assured the officer he had permission to be there.

"Of course, you have permission. Now come with me."

"No, I do have permission. I know Marisol, and her cousins said it was okay for me to use the metal detector on their ranch today."

The officer started coughing again, keeping his hand with the gun steady through the entire fit.

"You need some water?" Adam reached into his pack for a bottle.

"Keep your hands where I can see them." The large, uniformed man composed himself. "I'm not going to say it again. You need to come with me. You're under arrest. If you resist and try to run, I'll be forced to discharge this firearm."

Oh, shit! Adam's eyes widened. He had never been in a situation like this before. So he went along with it. He had nothing to hide and was sure he could explain everything after the officer lowered his weapon.

The police officer directed Adam to a dated Honda and cuffed him to the dry-cleaning hook in the back seat. The tiny car bounced along the gravel road, vibrating and humming. Adam wasn't even sure they would make it to the station.

•   •   •

Exposed brick showed through the peeling plaster exterior of the aging precinct in San Cristóbal. The officer had thrown Adam into one of two holding cells beside his desk. Anyone who walked through the front door would be able to get a good look at Adam behind bars. He paced back and forth, then stopped to ask about a phone call.

The officer sat at his desk with a ham sandwich, inhaling a third of the sandwich with his first bite. "Sit down and relax," the officer said through a mouthful of salty meat.

"Charo." Javier entered the modest government building and greeted the officer.

Adam's spirit took flight at the sight of Javier. What were the odds? The very person he needed to explain his presence on the ranch had just walked through the door of the police station with what looked like a bag of pastries for his arresting officer.

"What's in the bag?" Charo asked from behind his desk.

"Cinnamon buns and conchas from the panadería." Javier handed them over. "I was going to bring some coffee, but I figured you'd have some here."

Had Javier not seen him? "Javier!" Adam called to his acquaintance from his cell. "What are you doing here? You're just the person to get me out of this misunderstanding."

Javier didn't respond. Why? He just watched as Charo unrolled the paper bag and smelled the pastries.

"Thank you, Javier. We do always have coffee, but I used the last of it yesterday. Do you mind watching the place for a minute while I go to the abarrotes to get some more? The new guard should be here in about fifteen minutes."

"Not at all. I've got plenty of time," said Javier.

These guys seemed like friends. Why was Javier still ignoring him? Adam waved his hand through the bars. "Hello?"

Charo made a grizzly noise in his throat, spat into a piece of tissue, and headed for the door. "Be back soon."

Once Charo had cleared the doorway, Javier finally acknowledged Adam as he approached his cell.

"Javier! It's so good to see you. You have to help me. Please tell him you gave me permission to use the metal detector on your property. Someone called the police on me."

"Adam," Javier said calmly, "that was me."

Adam didn't understand. He clutched the bars in his hands and eyeballed Javier between the metal poles. "What? Why?"

The person staring back at him wasn't the old, retired man he'd spent time with around the fire. No one had ever looked at Adam like that before, a smiling face with vicious intentions.

Javier narrowed his eyes and homed in on Adam. "You knew I had found something."

What? Adam's eyebrows shot up. "What are you talking about?"

"I just don't know how you figured out where I'd hidden it." Javier put his hands in his pockets and paced in front of Adam's cell. "How did you find it, Adam? I'm curious."

What was he talking about? "The only thing I've ever found in the mountains was a gold coin, but that was the day Marisol and I were planting corn."

Javier smiled an unfriendly smile and made a show of slowly shaking his head back and forth. "You took it when you unearthed the remains." Javier didn't rush the conversation. Instead, he let the silence stretch out before asking, "Was it your doctor friend in the city who helped you put the pieces together?"

"What are you talking about?" Adam really didn't know. He was telling Javier the truth. What had kept Adam looking was the prospect of finding something. If he had found the Hernandez Castañeda jewelry or whatever it was Javier was talking about, he wouldn't have been using his metal detector with a hangover. Javier just needed to stop messing with him and tell the police officer this was all a mistake so he could get the hell out of there.

"I would be willing to look past your apathy for the deceased if you would just tell me where you've hidden the treasure," said Javier.

"What treasure? Again, I don't know what you're talking about." Did Javier have something to do with the bones?

"Look, I don't have time to sit in this jail with you all day. Just tell me where it is, and I'll leave Marisol enough money to get you out. The jailer is a friend of mine."

That much was obvious. "I swear I don't know what you're talking about. I went down to the river, where I thought I'd seen the *green fire of gold*, started digging under this boulder, and found bones. Once I realized what I'd done, I tried to put everything back the way I'd found it. I'm sorry!"

Javier stared him straight in the face. "I don't believe you, Adam."

"I'm sorry. It was an accident. What do the bones have to do with the treasure, anyway?" asked Adam.

"Don't be stupid with me, pendejo! You're in a Mexican jail for trespassing on *my* land. If you don't want to be in here for the next ten years, tell me where you put it. The case I buried beneath the bones is gone, and Alberto told me he had seen you there with your metal detector."

"You hid the treasure under a grave. But why?" It was hard enough to play catch up but nearly impossible with the added stress of his current situation behind bars.

"These aren't items you can entrust to the banks in a safe deposit box, Adam. They would have been gone as soon as I made the first call to a collector. I've been through this before. I thought an infant's bones would be enough to keep out the thieving Federales while I found a buyer, but you've taken greed to a whole new level."

What Adam thought had been a slight misunderstanding was spiraling into a major problem. Adam pushed on his forehead with both hands and rubbed his eyes, but when he took his hands down, he saw the situation had not changed.

"I don't have whatever you buried. I swear to you. Just get me out of here. I have to be at work in the morning," begged Adam, pressing his face between the bars.

"I think you have more to worry about than missing a day of work." With that, Javier left the building to wait for the new guard on the steps of the precinct.

Adam stepped away from the bars and sat on the cot. Why did he have to go looking for treasure? Why had he been so greedy? He had everything he had ever wanted—a great paying job, a huge house, and finally, his freedom from Sophie. What good were any of those things to him now?

But if *he* hadn't taken Javier's find, who had? Adam thought back to the dig site. There had to be something that could offer a clue as to who had really done this, but everything had looked the same out there—rocks, dirt, shrubs, the same stuff that was everywhere in los ranchos.

Adam closed his eyes and imagined himself holding the skull in his hand. He pictured it rolling down the hill. With his eyes clenched shut, Adam squeezed his brain, trying to extract any minor detail that could help him. He held the recalled picture in his mind, watching the skull as shadows danced across the frontal bone. Shadows on a day when there had been no clouds in the sky. He remembered looking up and seeing vultures feeding on something beyond the tree stump where the skull had come to rest—an animal carcass with smooth contours, skinned by a practiced hand. Flies had been landing on his neck. He remembered the hum of their wings and the distinct smell of rotting meat. His senses had stored these details for him—primal memories brought to the forefront by his olfactory system.

Rotting meat? Adam said to himself. *Rotting meat … rotting meat!* "Javier!" Adam's shout went unanswered. Javier had either left, or he was ignoring Adam again. "Javier! Anyone out there?"

"¿Qué quieres?" asked a new guard Adam didn't recognize. A young man with closely cropped hair repeated his question as he walked across the lobby to Adam's cell. "¿Qué quieres?"

"Perdoníme señor, puedo llamar a un amigo mío. ¡Solamente una llamada telefónica, por favor!"—He needed to make a phone call.

"¿Y por qué, guey?"

"Por favor. Es muy importante. ¡Por favor!" Adam shouted.

"What's in it for me?" asked the guard.

Sure, now he speaks English. Now that he thought Adam had something to offer him.

"I'll give you everything I have." Adam pointed to his wallet on Charo's desk and the guard pulled out an assortment of pesos and dollars. He hadn't seen the coin tucked behind Adam's credit card.

The guard reflected on what he held in his hand and nodded. It was enough to buy a phone call. An antique rotary phone sat on Charo's desk—a landline, sure to get service in the mountains. The guard opened the cell door. Adam made the phone call as the guard stood by with his hand resting on the handle of his pistol.

"Carlos."

"Sí. ¿Quién es? Adam, is that you?"

"It's me, Carlos. It's Adam. Listen, I don't know how long the guard will let me talk, but I need you to come and bail me out. There's been a huge misunderstanding, and I'm in the San Cristóbal jail. Will you come?"

"Sí. Yes. I'll come, but you'll have to pay me back," said Carlos.

His site supervisor sounded pissed, and rightfully so. "Fine, of course, whatever you want. Just get here, okay?" Adam gripped the phone so hard his knuckles turned white.

"Okay, I'll be there in a little while," said Carlos before the line went dead.

The guard hung up the phone for Adam. How long was a little while? How long would he have to sit there with all the answers and no way to clear his name?

As it turned out, a little while was about an hour, and for a certain price, Carlos would keep the news of Adam's brief stint in jail from getting back to the folks at Empire. Adam had already given his cash to the young guard, so when Carlos showed up, Adam handed over his ATM card and told the site supervisor he was welcome to the entire balance, minus bail money. With well over ten thousand dollars in the account, he had enough to buy his silence.

Adam paid the jailer, collected his cell phone, and thanked Carlos as they left the outdated police station, but Adam still needed one more favor. He knew he would be pushing it, but asked Carlos for a ride to Marisol's, so he could pick up his truck.

"Adam, I don't know what this is all about, and I don't want you to tell me. I'll drive you to Marisol's, but that's as far as I get involved. Understand?"

"Completely. You're a lifesaver." Adam knew he had lost Carlos's respect, but he really didn't need it. He just needed a ride. When they arrived at Marisol's house, Adam got out of the car without saying a word, and Carlos drove away.

Before Adam took his truck, he felt he owed it to Marisol to tell her his suspicions about Javier possibly being the decedent's father. How else would Javier have known about the grave? But why would Javier have kept this a secret from Marisol? Wouldn't this have been something that family shared with one another, especially since Marisol was so close with her cousins? Maybe Javier was hiding more than what was buried beneath the grave. And, if that were the case, maybe Adam shouldn't get involved any further. Then Adam thought about the last time he and Marisol had spoken about the grave. It had upset her. It would probably be best for everyone if he just left. As Marisol had said before, knowledge wouldn't change her current situation. It wouldn't bring Christo back or change what had happened to her sons. Adam decided to keep his suspicions to himself and leave, but as he climbed into the SUV, Marisol emerged from the ranch house, followed by Javier.

"I told you, Primo. No one else has been out here over the past few days except for Adam."

What was Javier doing there? The two men locked eyes. Then Marisol's cousin grabbed her from behind and raised a hunting knife to her throat.

"What are you doing, Primo?" She squirmed in his embrace, but Javier cinched his arm tighter around her waist. "Stop playing around! This isn't funny!" Javier pressed the cold metal into the pulsing skin of her neck.

Adam shut the door, put his hands in the air, and called out, "Javier, you don't need to do this. I didn't find anything."

"I'll let her go as soon as you tell me where it is."

Adam recognized the look in Javier's eyes. He'd seen that look before reflected in his own mirror—the face of someone in a frenzied state, blinded by greed. Just one more rock. Just one more pass over the ocean floor.

"Adam, what is he talking about?" Marisol choked out. "Just tell him whatever he wants to know. He's been asking about what you found out here. Give him the coin!"

"He comes into my country, onto my land, and digs up the grave of my child." Javier's acidic words seared the air. "Everything he has isn't enough for him. He wants what's mine, too."

"What are you talking about, Primo? You had a child. Why didn't you tell me? When?" Even the sharpened blade of Javier's knife couldn't curb Marisol's need for the truth. "Was it a boy?"

Adam crept closer during their exchange. Pebbles rolled like marbles beneath his feet as he tried to remain steady. "Let her go. I don't have any weapons."

"I'll let her go when you give me what's rightfully mine. How did you get out, anyway?" Javier shook his head, cursing Charo.

"What is he talking about, Adam?" asked Marisol.

Adam continued moving forward, slowly approaching Javier and Marisol. He kept his hands high, feeling them turn alternately hot and cold from their prolonged time above his head. "Javier found someone's buried fortune," said Adam, "then *he* went and buried it under the bones I dug up the other day, and he thinks I took it."

"Did you?" she asked.

"No!" he shouted. "What kind of person does everyone think I am?"

"Just give it to me, Adam. Are you really willing to sacrifice Marisol for money?"

Adam wanted to punch the smug look off his face, but he had to be careful. Javier cared more about the treasure than his own family, and without actually having the treasure, Adam had nothing to trade for Marisol.

His only chance at finding what Javier had hidden was finding Esmeralda. Marisol's mother had been leaving fresh kills for her daughter all these years. It had to be her. The wild woman he had seen in the clearing had stripped the lion's skin with the precision of a skilled hunter. Adam thought about everything Esmeralda had hidden for Marisol inside the animal carcasses she would leave. If meat lay by the gravesite, Esmeralda had to have Javier's find, but this woman roamed the mountains like a cougar. She could be anywhere. Adam searched his surroundings desperately, and there it was, their ticket to safety—a fresh kill hanging from the laurel tree.

"I have a pretty good idea where it might be, but I'm not sure. Promise not to do anything crazy if I'm wrong."

Javier fixed his eyes on Adam. "You'd better not be wrong."

"Marisol," said Adam, "has your mother been by lately?"

"Last night," she whispered from behind the blade. "Why?"

"I'm going to go to the laurel tree, Javier," said Adam, walking slowly, still holding his hands in plain sight.

Adam stepped cautiously to the tree supporting the deer, which had been gutted, skinned, and salted. He felt the striated muscle tissue, searching for signs of an incision—and there it was. Bloody juice oozed from the meat as Adam used his hand to probe inside the animal's flesh, finding jagged items—foreign bodies like hard bullets lodged inside a soldier. Adam pulled out a handful of loose diamonds coated in pink-tinged fluid.

Javier let go of Marisol, and she fell into the dirt, holding her hands to her throat where the knife had been. Adam threw the gems on the ground and started toward Marisol. His legs felt unnaturally light, as if his adrenal glands had pumped them full of helium. In only a few long strides, Adam was at her side, pulling her up from the ground. Javier removed piece after piece of jewelry from the dead animal flesh, while Adam and Marisol fled to the SUV.

Safe inside the truck, Marisol told Adam, "I have to find out if the death of Javier's baby has anything to do with why I ended up like this."

"Like what?" asked Adam, locking the doors.

"A middle-aged woman with no husband and no family. Whoever crossed the line with a family member years ago has ruined my life. They're the reason why my sons were all stillborn. I work alone. I sleep alone. I'll die alone, Adam. Don't you get it?"

"You can't go out there. He has a knife. We have to get out of here." Adam started the engine.

"You're such a coward."

"I'm not a coward. I'm looking out for our safety. That knife was just at your throat!" Adam put his arm on the back of Marisol's seat, preparing to back up.

"You weren't man enough to be a good husband, and you're not man enough now to help a friend. I knew you wouldn't change, but I never thought I would need you to." Marisol unlocked her door.

Adam squeezed his hands into fists with his foot still resting on the brake. "God, Marisol! Where is this shit coming from?"

"Stay here if you want. I need answers. My cousin has what he wants already. I'll be fine." She left the safety of the vehicle, leaving the door open. As she approached Javier, Adam heard her ask who the child's mother was.

Through the open door, Adam heard Javier say something but couldn't make out what it was. Javier continued to root through the deer at an odd angle, so Adam couldn't read his lips, either.

"Who was the child's mother?" Marisol repeated.

Why was Marisol willing to risk getting killed searching for information that wouldn't change anything, anyway? And how could she put *him* in this situation? Now, Adam had to get out of the truck. He couldn't just let her walk into a dangerous situation like this. If something happened to her, he would never forgive himself. Adam put the truck in park and left the engine running to go after his friend. He followed Marisol, watching her long braid sway from side to side as she marched toward the answer to the question that had mapped out her life's pain.

"Just leave it alone, Marisol. I don't want to hurt you." Javier turned from the carcass, knife in hand. "If you go poking under boulders, you'll find rattlesnakes."

"Who was the child's mother?" she asked again.

Javier glanced over Marisol's shoulder, letting Adam know he'd been seen. The metallic scent of hot deer blood jammed under Adam's fingernails was making him nauseous.

"You are my prima. So I'll ask you to let this go one last time." Javier squeezed the handle of the knife.

"Who was the child's mother?" she asked, unflinching.

Javier pulled his shoulders back, knowing she would never let it go. "It was your mother."

Adam couldn't see Marisol's expression, but imagined her face frozen like the rest of her body. Her braid hung, unmoving, down the length of her back. Then Javier delivered the final blow—a powerful left hook to the soul.

"I was the one at the festival in García."

After hearing these words, Adam pushed his boots against the dusty terrain, propelling himself forward. Javier was going to kill her! Why hadn't Marisol let it go? Why hadn't Javier lied to her? But Adam already knew why. Greed had poisoned Javier's heart, pumping tainted blood throughout his body, feeding the hand that held the knife.

"But I can't risk you turning me in for rape—not now that I'm exceedingly wealthy." Javier leaned toward Marisol and pushed the knife deep into her abdomen, angled upward— another choice he could not take back.

Marisol coughed and fell to her knees with her hands clutching the knife's handle. So many things went unsaid as her lungs filled with blood.

"I told you to let it go," said Javier.

"Oh, God!" Adam found his voice and raised his hands to his head, threading his fingers through his hair—so much blood. "Don't pull the knife out, Marisol. It's stopping the bleeding."

"I am sorry." Javier kept talking as if Adam weren't even there. "I'd been out of the country for years and didn't recognize your mother, but I never abandoned you. I was there when she had you and your brother. She left him floating in the water, but I pulled him out and gave him a proper burial."

What the hell? Javier had seemed like such a normal guy. This couldn't really be happening. Marisol gurgled as blood spilled from her mouth. They had to help her. She lay beneath the laurel tree as tears mixed with the blood on her beautiful face.

Adam waved his hands, discouraging the old man from pulling out the weapon. "No, Javier. Leave the blade. We can still save her." Adam stepped toward Marisol. "Help me lift her into the truck. We need to get her to a hospital." Adam's hands shook as he awkwardly pulled at his friend.

Javier placed his hand on the handle of the knife and yanked it from his daughter, then turned toward Adam. Blood welled up from the cavernous wound and saturated Marisol's clothing. Could she feel it? Was she in shock? Adam couldn't help her now, but he could save himself. Javier would kill him, too. Not only did he know Javier's secret, he had seen him murder Marisol. Adam backed away from Javier and raced toward the SUV without looking back. He jumped in and slammed the door. With the vehicle locked, he backed up as fast as he could navigate the curves of the gravel drive.

What had just happened? It wasn't his fault. Marisol had been safe in the truck. He had asked her not to get out. What more could he have done? She had put *herself* in harm's way. He had nothing to do with her death, but would the authorities see it that way? Adam watched Javier through the windshield. Strangely, Javier hadn't moved from Marisol's side. He hadn't even tried to chase Adam down. What was he planning?

Adam maneuvered around the curves in the road, getting as far away from los ranchos as possible. He wanted desperately to hop a plane out of there, but it was time to work on damage control. His friend was dead. He had to let the authorities know. Maybe he should go to the American Embassy. The laws wouldn't be the same in Mexico as they were in the US, and the people at the embassy would know what to do. He held his phone up while the SUV whipped around the mountain roads. Only one bar, but it was enough to see that Mexico City had an American embassy. He tapped on "Mexico City." *Three hundred miles away!* That was way too far. He had to let someone know now.

Beeeeeeep, beep, beep! Adam swerved back into his lane. He was in no shape to drive, but what else was he supposed to do after having just witnessed a murder? Once he got back to Guadalajara, he'd figure out who to call. Adam placed his phone face down on the passenger seat. He had seen too many movies about Mexican law enforcement and didn't have any faith in going to the police. Javier's police officer friend had just arrested him that morning. The last thing he needed was something like that on a larger scale, in one of those federal jails Marisol had told him about, like the one in that song with the scorpion and the sombrero.

His racing thoughts distracted him, taking his attention from the road. Adam mashed on the brakes, and the SUV screeched around a tight curve, his wheels barely keeping contact with the road's surface. *Breathe, Adam. Breathe,* he told himself.

"Oh, shit!" Adam flung his arms up, crossing them in front of his face, as the truck slammed head-on into a pile of fallen earth and rocks that had not been there yesterday. Adam looked up from the inflated airbag as talcum powder rained down inside the vehicle. His eyes showed him only fuzzy images, and he blinked. Adam pocketed his phone and stumbled from the truck, making his way to the side of the road. With a trembling hand, he touched the jagged rock wall to steady himself. Next to his bent fingers, a harmless trickle of water trailed down the hot stone. He pressed his back to the rock wall and lowered himself to the ground, hoping the world would stop spinning. His phone had no more bars—no way to call for help. Dry heaves brought up nothing from his stomach, and he laid his head against the mountain, fighting the urge to sleep.

Chapter 29

Sophie

Rigo leaned against the granite countertop in Sophie's kitchen. "My sister and her family should be coming back from Mexico any time now. What do you think about getting a place of our own?"

Sophie's divorce attorney had advised her that moving out of her shared dwelling was a necessary step in finalizing her divorce. "I think it's a great idea." Letting go of the house was easy. It was really about letting go of Adam and the life they had shared, and she had already done that.

Sophie peered into the fridge, but it was empty except for a bottle of ketchup and two round pickle slices floating in a glass jar. It didn't make any sense to keep a full refrigerator when she was never there. They were only there now to print the invoice for their latest job on company letterhead. She could have emailed it, but the client wanted a paper copy.

"He still doesn't know you've started divorce proceedings?" asked Rigo.

"No, and he's going to be pissed. Not because he cares, but because I will have been the one who made the first move."

Sophie scoured the pantry for a bag of chips or something, but the only things in there were stale marshmallows and a bottle of wine. Currently, she had no use for either one.

Rigo pulled her into a warm embrace. "He'll be surprised, all right." He kissed her on the mouth and held her close, their noses touching, until she wriggled from his snare. Rigo took the hint. "You're obviously hungry. What can I get you and the baby?"

"I don't know why I'm so hungry. Our baby is only the size of a grape, but I'm ravenous all the time. It's weird."

He held up his hands. "No judgment. Just think of me as your own personal DoorDash. So what do you and our baby need?"

"Do you remember that lemony pasta we had in Baltimore?"

Rigo looked at his phone—five o'clock. "I'm happy to get whatever you'd like, but why don't we go together? It'll take the same amount of time for us to go to dinner as it would for me to drive in and out of the city during rush hour. What do you say? Will you be my date?"

"You know what? That sounds good. I'll jump in the shower."

"I'll keep you company." Rigo tugged her back into his arms.

"Oh, you will?" Sophie bit her lip seductively.

"Is that a problem?"

"No, sir."

Rigo stood behind her in the shower and ran his hands through her hair, then over the small bump forming below her belly button. He kissed her neck, and she sighed contentedly.

"Where do you want to move?" Sophie asked, eyes closed, enjoying his lips on her wet skin. She felt him grow stiff behind her.

A guttural noise escaped his lips as he tried to focus on their conversation. "I was thinking about the Eastern Shore." He took a step back to curb his arousal. "The rent would be reasonable while we look for something to buy."

"You've really thought this through, haven't you?" Even after all of his consistency, his automatic answers still surprised her, as if he'd been considering them for months, waiting for *her* to catch up.

"I have been thinking about it for a while," he said, confirming her suspicions as he massaged her scalp with peppermint shampoo.

She flashed him a devious smile over her shoulder, with one eyebrow raised. "Were you that sure of yourself?"

"You fell for me, didn't you?"

She rolled her eyes, turned around, and wrapped her arms around his neck. "Yes, I did."

After so many years of stagnation, her life continued to move at a clip. In a matter of months, she'd fallen in love, become pregnant, and now she was moving in with a man who cherished her and their baby growing inside of her.

Sophie didn't want to keep much from the house and the life she had shared with Adam. She needed her office furniture and supplies, but everything else had memories attached—best to start fresh.

•   •   •

The garden-style condo in Easton backed to a private inlet off of the bay. Sophie and Rigo leaned against pillars on a weatherworn, wooden dock while minnows swam in schools below their dangling feet. Every so often, a minnow broke the surface, sending expanding rings of water across the quiet inlet.

"It's peaceful here." Sophie rested against Rigo.

"I never knew you were such a nature lover."

"There are so many things we don't know about each other, and I'm looking forward to spending a lifetime figuring them out."

They watched the sunset over the brackish water as Sophie thought of the life growing inside her. She would soon be a mother. They would be parents, and this was what it felt like to be a family.

Chapter 30

Adam

Hello. Hello?" Charo smacked Adam on the shoulder after confiscating his cell phone. "Wake up!"

Adam's eyes fluttered open against the strong sun, and his dry tongue stuck to the back of his front teeth. What time was it? How long had he been sitting on the side of the road? Where was Javier? Where was Marisol? Why did his head hurt so much? Adam looked around and saw the crunched hood of the SUV hissing white steam in response to his questions. He felt the back of his head, tender and swollen, like someone had inserted a water balloon under his skin. The airbag must have saved him from hitting his head on the steering wheel, but the back of his head had taken the brunt of the countercoup force. What had he run into? His memories leading up to the accident were fuzzy, but at least his vision was clearing.

Adam opened his mouth to ask some of his questions, but Charo tapped his thigh with the tip of an ostrich skin cowboy boot. "Get up," grumbled the out-of-breath officer.

Adam put his palms on the pavement and tried to push himself up, but his elbows gave way, and he lay down on the roadway.

Charo hitched his belt up, bent down, and pulled Adam by the underarms. The two hobbled to the police car, and Charo deposited Adam into the front seat. The officer must have wanted to monitor Adam's injuries. From the passenger seat, Adam wondered what had caused the accident. Why had he been driving so fast? Had he hit another car? Was anyone else injured? Hopefully, the more the swelling went down, the quicker the answers to these questions would return to him. Adam rolled his head to the side and reached out to get Charo's attention.

"Whoa!" The officer grabbed Adam's wrist so forcefully it could have snapped in two. "Keep your hands to yourself. Understand?"

Adam withdrew his arm and cradled his wrist. "Are you taking me to jail?"

"Same place as this morning," said Charo.

"Okay," was all Adam said. The sun shone hot on his face through the car window, and the motion of the vehicle put him to sleep again. He slept until dusk and awoke lying on a cot inside the jail cell in San Cristóbal.

Charo had a cup of cold water and an ibuprofen waiting for him. "Here, take this." The officer placed the ibuprofen through the bars onto the floor with one of his meaty hands, then set the water next to the pill.

Adam's head throbbed, but it was different than it had been earlier in the day. The pain had been at the back of his head, but now an elephant stomped on his forehead. He had some type of head injury, probably a concussion, but he needed fluids. So he chased the small, brown pill with the entire glass of water and lay down on his one lumpy pillow to sleep, praying he wouldn't throw up.

•   •   •

"Wake up."

Something cold and hard hit Adam in his eyelid. Someone told him to "wake up" again as another round object bounced off his cheek. Adam opened one eye and then the other to see the concrete floor of his cell littered with green grapes. He wasn't sure if his neck was stiff from the accident or from sleeping on the squeaky, metal cot, but he carefully slid his elbows under himself, raising his torso. He cautiously lifted his head, expecting pain, but felt a bit better.

"Good. You're awake."

Through the bars, Adam saw Javier holding a cluster of grapes by the stem. Adam sat up, happy to see a familiar face. "Javier, do you have any water?"

The old man made no move to refill Adam's cup as if the request had surprised him, but why? Adam covered his eyes with his hands, taking long breaths and trying to bring everything into focus. The events of the past twenty-four hours were a blur, but maybe if he could focus, really think, he could remember what had brought him to his current situation behind bars. There had to be something that would jog his memory.

"Could you tell me what's going on?" Adam concentrated on Javier's face from his seat on the edge of the cot.

Javier plucked another grape from the cluster and popped it into his mouth, chewing slowly. "Why don't you tell me what you remember? We should start with that."

It sounded like a good idea. Adam would tell him everything he remembered, and Javier would help him fill in the blanks. So many images swam in his head, but they were out of sequence, and some so unbelievable Adam wasn't sure if he'd dreamed them. But why hadn't they taken him to the hospital? He needed medical care—a doctor.

"Javier, can you take me to a hospital? I was in a car crash." Adam touched his hand to the back of his head, inspecting the swelling. "I think I have a brain injury."

"We had a doctor come to see you already," said Javier.

Adam's mouth hung open as he pondered this statement. "You did?" Adam closed his eyes and rolled them around in his head, inspecting each dark corner, looking for memories of a doctor, and he saw one. "I remember Dr. Sebastian. I did see a doctor."

Javier set another grape on his tongue and smiled at Adam, his face framed by the lead-gray bars of the cell. Adam had been there before, but when? So many images floated in his head. He needed to catch one, just one, and examine it.

As Adam attempted to zero in on Javier's face between the bars, Charo stole his attention, stomping his boots on the floor mat at the entrance to the precinct. The officer stepped through the threshold with his mouth turned down, eyebrows furrowed, holding his hat in front of him with two hands.

"What did you find?" Javier asked his friend.

"It wasn't good." Charo dropped his eyes to the floor. He wouldn't look at Javier. Dust had settled into every fiber of the officer's uniform. Adam recognized the dust. Charo had been to los ranchos.

"Charo, whatever it is, tell me." Javier insisted.

Adam's eyes snapped back to Javier's face. He had caught one of the memories. Well, it was more of a feeling than a memory. Adam glared at Javier's profile, framed by the metal bars, listening to the detachment in his voice play repeatedly, like the call of a gull.

"Javi, your cousin has passed," said Charo

"What do you mean, passed? Weren't you called to the ranch for a disturbance coming from Marisol's dogs?"

Adam's eyes moved between the two men. Maybe something one of them said would help him remember.

"The dogs were going crazy because of your cousin's body. By the time I got there, they had her pretty well ripped apart."

"What do you mean, 'ripped apart?'"

"Please don't make me describe it in any more detail." Charo covered his mouth with his hand as his eyes glassed over, filling with tears.

Was Charo crying? Adam closed his eyes again. He had to remember what happened.

Javier straightened up and put his grapes on the wooden desk. "You're going to have to do better than that, Charo. What happened?"

Charo didn't answer right away, and before he did, he snorted up what sounded like a gigantic ball of mucus and swallowed. "Well, I called the team out there. We needed the manpower from Guadalajara." Another long pause. Adam could tell Charo wasn't used to these kinds of things happening in his jurisdiction. "Their detectives said it was a stab wound that had killed her and that the dogs had moved in after she was already dead."

Red. Blood. Tears. Adam saw Marisol's wide eyes mixed with other images that slipped past one another in his subconscious mind. He had been chasing her, then running away. Memories, like puzzle pieces, slid through his mind, searching for their partners, wanting to link together and form a coherent picture. Adam waited for his brain to filter these images, smells, and feelings. He waited for the truth. Why was it taking so long? He reached around to feel the water balloon deflating under his scalp—that was why.

Javier dropped into Charo's office chair, staring into space. "Who could have done this?"

"There's more." Charo looked at his friend, then at Adam. "This involves you, Adam."

Heat radiated from Adam's scalp as he willed himself to put the pieces together. How was he involved?

"They've made Adam their number one suspect, driving as recklessly as he was away from the ranch." Charo walked to his desk and pulled out a paper cup. Then he made his way to the small bathroom in the back. Once he had returned, Charo passed the cup of water through the bars to Adam. "They'll be coming for you soon. Any murder suspects are automatically transferred to the state prison in Guadalajara."

"Wait. What?" Adam's heart punched him in his chest, hard and fast, like a boxer on a speed bag.

Javier rose from his chair. "I can't stay here. I can't be near this man." Without saying goodbye, Javier swiftly left the station, leaving his grapes in an abandoned pool of condensation on the wooden desk.

"I'm going to the men's room." Charo addressed the prisoner. "You hang tight, and the guys from Guadalajara will be by to transport you." Charo's arms hung limply at his sides as he shuffled toward the restroom in the back.

Adam drank his water, hoping it would lubricate his memories or, at least, quiet his racing heart. He lay down to think.

He must've fallen asleep because when he opened his eyes, two new uniformed men stood in his cell, staring at him as he lay on his cot. He squinted his eyes to read their name tags: Sergeants Juarez and Gutierrez. Both had dark, wavy hair brushed back from their foreheads, toned muscles, and shoulders about to burst through the binding material of their uniforms, but only Sergeant Gutierrez wore sunglasses. His dark glasses shielded his eyes above the hard line of his mouth. His expression gave nothing away, but the forceful grip he used to pull Adam from his cot told him everything he needed to know. This was real. He was being taken to a real jail with more than two holding cells. Adam wriggled in his newly applied cuffs, knowing his memories were the only things that could unlock his shackles.

The officers led him down the front steps of the small jailhouse. Each officer held one arm. This time, they secured the metal cuffs to an iron bar in the backseat of a black Tahoe. Reggaeton bumped through the speakers, and Adam's headache pulsed in time with the music. The base from the sound system knocked against his tangled ball of memories, and Adam hoped the deafening music might knock one of them free like autumn leaves raining down on a blustery day.

Adam leaned his head against the glass as they drove. It was still too painful to lay his head on the headrest. He watched the countryside go by through the tinted glass, but where were they taking him? They weren't headed to the city. Adam recognized the streets they were taking, having driven them countless times to Marisol's. They were headed toward los ranchos. Were these men even with the Guadalajara police department?

"Hey guys, could you roll down the windows?" asked Adam. "It's getting hot in here."

"¡Callete!" said Gutierrez, without turning around.

"¿Tienes confianza en lo que estamos haciendo, amigo?" Sergeant Juarez asked his partner.

Gutierrez didn't give his partner the courtesy of a response. He kept his eyes on the road, behind his sunglasses, with one hand on the steering wheel and his other arm draped over the center console.

"Where are we going?" asked Adam.

"To jail." Gutierrez turned the music up louder.

That was a lie. If only the truth were as easy to identify. Adam wouldn't let himself fall asleep again. He couldn't with the music as loud as it was. If they weren't taking him to the jail in Guadalajara, then he had to figure out where they were going.

They passed El Mezquital del Oro, and a short distance after the village, the sergeant turned onto a familiar gravel drive, the one Adam had taken so many times to Marisol's ranch. Only she wouldn't be there this time, so why were they going?

The Tahoe pulled up at the ranch house. Gutierrez got out of the driver's side and greeted Javier with a handshake and a smile.

Adam's stomach dropped into his large intestines. *What?* Sergeant Juarez had turned off the music, but with the windows up, Adam couldn't hear anything Gutierrez and Javier were saying outside. What were they saying?

Then an acorn fell from the sky—a memory—clear and complete. Adam had been there before, watching Javier from a locked vehicle. If his current situation had not mirrored his recent run-in with Javier so closely, he wasn't sure he would have been able to pull this memory out of the cluster of events that hung in his mind. Electrical signals traveled through Adam's brain, whispering their secrets, and he processed these truths as quickly as he could. Javier had killed Marisol. Adam had seen him do it. He had tried to help his friend, and then there was the accident, but what good would knowing any of this do him now? Marisol was still dead. He still had a traumatic brain injury, and Javier was still calling the shots.

Adam ran his fingers over his eyebrows, stroking the pain in his head and lamenting what he'd just remembered. The haunted look in Marisol's eyes right before she died suffocated him like someone wringing the air from his lungs, twisting them with two hands.

Javier and Gutierrez returned to the Tahoe, and Sergeant Juarez opened the door for their prisoner. Adam and Javier locked eyes. Did Javier know he knew? Yes, he did. Adam could tell. Javier's piercing eyes hung above a thin smile. Adam knew what that smile meant. No matter what he said, these men belonged to Javier. It wasn't about finding the truth. It was about escaping Javier.

"All you have to do is show us where you've hidden the rubies, and all your troubles will be over. It's that simple," said Javier.

He had found the Hernandez Castañeda fortune! But why hadn't the rubies been in the carcass with the rest of the jewelry? Adam had nothing else to offer. He had no idea where they could be, but he couldn't let Javier know this. He needed time to think.

Gutierrez drew his gun and aimed it at Adam's chest. "Maybe this will remind you of where you put them."

"Okay, okay," said Adam. He didn't know where the rubies were, but Gutierrez was the kind of guy who would shoot someone for the fun of it, and Adam didn't want to give him a reason to shoot. Adam trudged slowly toward the river, needing to devise a plan, hoping this brief hike would buy him some time. Even though the events of the past twenty-four hours had returned to him, he was still in rough shape. His balance was off, and he held his cuffed arms out in front of him to steady himself like someone who'd had too much to drink.

"I knew you'd remember eventually," said Gutierrez, following him with the gun. Adam could hear gravel crunching as Javier and Sergeant Juarez followed behind.

Adam led the group of men along the dark path to the chor. He wished he had his coa with him for balance. The pebbles and the sloping terrain made it hard to find secure footing as the group descended the mountainside. When he reached the stretch of deeper water, Adam stopped, and Sergeant Gutierrez bumped into him, probably on purpose, any excuse to be even more of an asshole. Adam thought about jumping into the water and swimming his way out, but wasn't sure he could make it with his hands cuffed. The key was not to stop. He would do anything he could to keep them thinking he was leading them to what they wanted. Adam bent over, saw black, and rested his palms on his knee to recover. Then he lifted a large rock and threw it to the side. The clattering of the stone echoed in the river valley.

"That's more like it," said Gutierrez. "Keep digging."

"If you want them so badly, you dig them up." Adam stared obstinately at his captors. He had to drag this out, needing more time to come up with some sort of plan.

"Help him, Gutierrez," said Javier.

The arrogant smile slid off the sergeant's face and landed in the shallows with a splash. Adam had never guessed Javier would have this much pull. What exactly had he done before he retired? Gutierrez reluctantly leaned over to move the stones, holding his gun loosely at his side.

This was Adam's chance. Without hesitation, he picked up a rock, swung it into the side of the sergeant's head, and the brawny officer toppled onto the pebbly shoreline. Adam didn't know he'd been capable of so much violence, but his own life was at stake. The gun lay at his feet, but Adam wasn't about to shoot anyone. He didn't even know how. Fortunately, the burst of adrenaline that accompanied smacking another human being in the head with a rock had cleared most of the brain fog that had settled in after the accident. He homed in on the heavy, metal weapon and flung the gun into the bushes.

Sometimes, first ideas turn out to be the best ideas, or in this case, the only idea. Adam splashed into the river, wriggling along the rocky bottom like a catfish, afraid to surface for air. He sensed someone coming up behind him underwater and hoped it wasn't Sergeant Gutierrez. Strong hands clasped Adam's leg and dragged him to the riverbank, where Adam got to his feet. His saturated hiking boots had taken on pounds of water, and his wet clothes stretched toward the ground, pulling on his shoulders like a lead vest. Sergeant Juarez had pulled him from the river basin. Adam didn't have the information they wanted and knew if they found out, they would kill him. They were probably going to kill him, anyway. How had he ended up in this situation?

Juarez placed one veiny hand on Adam's shoulder. Javier had chosen wisely. These guys were young and strong. If he were to run, especially soaking wet, he wouldn't get far. Adam's face tingled. His breaths came too quickly. Panic narrowed his field of vision, but out of the shadows, he saw something, or someone. Adam blinked his eyes, and there, holding Sergeant Gutierrez's gun, which he had thrown into the bushes, was Alberto. What was he doing there? It seemed Alberto was always lurking about the ranch, seeing everything that went on, quiet as a mountain cat. Marisol's docile cousin pointed the gun at the group as he spoke.

"It obvious no one has the rubies. They are a myth. They are legend, and no one else need to die for them."

Adam took advantage of the distraction and hurried down the shoreline. He hoped his wrinkled fishing companion wouldn't shoot.

"What are you doing?" Javier asked. "Give that to me."

Alberto wasn't going along this time. "You killed Marisol."

Hope welled inside Adam's chest cavity, and his heart leaped with joy when he heard Alberto utter those words. It was no longer his word against Javier's, but even with the extra burst of energy that came from finding out there had been an eyewitness, his legs were moving way too slowly. Dizziness overtook him and he sat, taking cover under a clump of scraggly bushes to remove his boots. He would never be able to climb out of the valley if he didn't free his legs from the extra weight. Adam pulled at the knot in his lace, wishing for better dexterity in his fingers in his anxious state.

"What are you talking about?" said Javier, confident in his ability to control his brother.

Adam could hear everything from the bushes and repositioned himself, peering through a thin gap in the branches. He couldn't stay there long.

"I see you kill Marisol," Alberto clarified.

"You don't know what you saw," said Javier, feeding Alberto the facts.

"Guys," said Sergeant Juarez, gesturing in the direction Adam had run.

Gutierrez sat in a few inches of water, blood dripping down his temple from a scalp laceration. Disoriented from the blow to the head, he was of little use to Javier.

"I saw you take stones from the deer," said Alberto. "I saw you kill our little Marisol and takes the jewelry."

"Jewelry? Is there something you're not sharing with us, Javier? I thought we were just dealing with a set of rubies," said Gutierrez from his seated position. He touched his fingers to his scalp and winced.

"Our murderer is escaping." Javier pointed downstream in Adam's direction.

Adam held his breath. He hadn't gotten nearly as far as everyone thought.

"You all need to do what I hired you to do!" shouted Javier.

Sergeant Juarez took out his handcuffs. "Javier, this is not what we discussed, and I can't be a part of it anymore."

"You can't arrest me," said Javier. "I could tell your chief about how you kidnapped the murder suspect and how you were willing to accept a bribe."

Javier's words could not penetrate the sergeant. "We have an eyewitness who saw you murder your cousin, Javier—your own brother."

"I could tell them about how you made a deal with me for a cut of the rubies," said Javier, scrambling for threats. For the first time, his unflappable demeanor had cracked.

"What rubies?" said Juarez.

"It is over, brother." Alberto shook his head in disappointment. "Just go with him. Nothing is worth what you do to Marisol."

Cuffed and in desperation, Javier reached into his pocket for his knife, but before he could pull it out, Alberto shot him, only once. A dark, wet patch spread across Javier's pant leg as his lips pulled back from his teeth like a rabid dog.

"¡Pinche guey!" Javier grabbed at his leg.

The officers confiscated the knife, checked Javier for the rubies, and found nothing. Things had shifted again, this time in Adam's favor, but how long would it last? Adam wasn't going to stick around to find out. Finally! Both of his boots were off. He scrambled up the hillside from the chor, headed for the main road that cut past El Mezquital. Climbing on the rocky terrain presented a challenge with the handcuffs, even more so now that he couldn't use the path, but he wasn't slowing down. The road to El Mezquital would be coming up soon.

Barbed wire—a good sign. It lined the country roads and … wait, was that a car crunching along the gravel road? Adam dropped to the ground. He stared through the underbrush, looking for the Tahoe, but saw a pickup. He got to his feet again and slid through the barbed wire fence onto the road. The truck had passed him, but they were moving at a slow crawl. In the back of the truck was a couch, and on the couch sat a woman as wrinkled as a pug. A sheer, black scarf covered her wiry, gray hair, and she rode in the truck bed with two white goats.

"Hey there," shouted Adam. He tried to keep his handcuffs from view. "Hey, could I get a ride?"

The old woman banged on the back window with a flat palm, and the truck came to a stop.

"¿Qué pasó, Ama?" asked the driver as he stepped out of the cab to see what his mother needed. He didn't look much younger than she did. Years of working in the sun had transformed this man's face into lined leather. "¿Qué quieres?" asked the man. "Tenemos que transporter estas cabras al matadero."

"Sí, sí, pero mira a este quey." She pointed at Adam. "Se parece que tiene un problema."

Adam couldn't understand anything they were saying. They spoke with thick country accents, and he couldn't pick out any of the words.

"Yo no quiero los problemas de este hombre, Ama." The man turned to get back into the cab. "Vamanos pues." He turned the key, but the engine wouldn't start. He tried again.

The old lady in the back beckoned Adam with a slender, bent finger while her son wrestled with the ignition. Adam approached the old woman. She leaned toward Adam and asked him. "¿Problema?"

"Sí." Adam nodded. He tried to be polite and agreeable, still hoping for a ride.

"Entra." She motioned for Adam to climb in.

Great! "Thank you," said Adam. "I mean, gracias." He climbed in and sat on the rusted truck bed next to the goats.

The old woman smacked the glass again with her palm, and laughed as one of the goats raised its tail, releasing a shower of fecal marbles in Adam's lap. The man drove the truck painfully slow. Adam willed them to go faster. He sat next to the goats, and the old woman continued to stare.

"¿Qué pasó?" She pointed at his handcuffs.

It was amazing how much he understood based solely on her hand gestures. "Oh, these?" said Adam, holding up his cuffed wrists.

She formed a toothless smile and nodded. Then the old woman smacked the window again.

"¡Para, Ama!" shouted her son. The man saw Adam in the rearview mirror and frowned.

"You wouldn't believe the story if I told you," Adam said.

She stared at him. Hand gestures would take them no further in the conversation. Adam stayed low and kept an eye out for Javier or any blue lights. Every time a vehicle came into sight, Adam's muscles tensed like a coiled spring, ready to jump from the truck bed into the brush.

They wound their way around the roads Adam had come to know so well. He wouldn't be using these roads again. His friend was dead. Marisol was dead, and so was the freedom he had felt while he was with her. He wasn't sure if it was his head injury or genuine emotion, but he fought to hold back tears, not wanting to make the trip in the truck bed any more awkward than it already was. Maybe he could have done more for Marisol, but right now, he needed to focus.

"It looks like we're headed for the city," said Adam.

The woman on the couch leaned toward him, cupping her hand around her ear.

"Guadalajara?"

"Sí, Guadalajara," said the woman. "Vamos al matadero."

She gave the goats a sinister look Adam didn't understand until they drove up to an enormous, metal warehouse soaked with the rancid smell of blood and spoiled organ meats. A rusted sign hung above the loading bay, but Adam couldn't make out any letters.

The man parked off to the side, unlatched the truck bed, and clicked at the animals to jump out. Once the livestock had touched down on the cement, the man clicked at Adam, who climbed down, joining the goats.

"¡Vete!" said the old man. "You go!"

Adam would get no further with the goat man. His traveling companions clacked their hooves on the hard ground as they waited for a commercial cattle truck to finish unloading. Under bright floodlights, brown bovines paraded single file down a sturdy ramp into a holding pen, already crowded with cattle. When the last bull was secured in the holding area, the commercial truck roared to life, pulling away from the slaughterhouse. The powerful engine momentarily drowned out the hum of the stable flies.

The man led his two goats to the main building and pushed the buzzer next to a heavily insulated door. Adam kept his distance, dodging piles of fresh manure as he went. There had to be something inside he could use to free his hands.

Minutes later, the door swung open, and a laborer leaned out, his white uniform spattered with blood. "¿Qué quieres?"

"Tengo dos chivas en venta." The man pointed at the goats.

"No compra chivas, señor." The uniformed man let go of the door, and an automatic lock engaged with a loud snap.

Adam leaned against the slaughterhouse in the shadows and pressed his lips together, blowing air from flared nostrils. He slammed his cuffed hands against his thighs. After all he'd been through, he had to get his cuffs off so he could get a ride back to the city. He couldn't risk asking for a ride from anyone else still wearing them. He didn't even have shoes on. Whoever picked him up might take him right back to the police.

As the man directed his goats to the pickup truck, a second worker opened the door, placed a brick between the door and the frame, and jogged into the yard after the goats.

"¿Cuánto cuestan?" asked the meatpacker, pulling some paper bills from his pocket.

Adam glanced around the cement yard. The two men were occupied, haggling over the price of the goats, so he slipped through the door in search of something to cut his cuffs. A long line of split cattle hung from a conveyor belt on the ceiling, and his breath formed white puffs of moisture in the cold warehouse. Adam didn't see anyone else in the white uniforms, but he kept out of sight, sliding behind the animal carcasses, searching for anything he could use to pry the cuffs from his wrists.

Past the lines of flesh were tables outfitted with electric saws—quiet and clean. Good thing they had come after dark.

This place would have been teeming with people in the daytime, judging by the number of workstations. He decided not to try to use the saws, afraid he might end up sawing his hands off. Plus, anyone still in the building might hear him.

Adam kept walking until he reached a wall of tools, each one with a unique purpose for slaughter. He scanned the wall until his eyes found a pair of industrial clippers. He kneeled on the cement floor, inserting the ring of one cuff into the tool and applying force with his knee until the metal split. He repeated these steps to free his other hand.

After replacing the tool, he stuffed the cuffs into his pocket and quickly left the warehouse. Outside, the man with the goats had gone, and the meatpacker herded the goats into the employee parking lot. Adam left the brick in the door and made for the surrounding underbrush. He would have to sleep in the mountains that night and try to find a ride back to the city in the morning.

Chapter 31

Adam

The plane from Guadalajara to Baltimore landed at three in the afternoon. Before disembarking, Adam unzipped his carry-on and took out a blister pack of pills Sebastian had prescribed. He dry-swallowed the tablets, trying to combat the persistent nausea he'd had since the car accident.

"Uncle Adam." Ben met him at the terminal. "I'm glad you're back!"

"Ben!" Adam let go of his rolling suitcase and threw his arm over his favorite nephew's shoulder. He drew Ben in for a hug. "I'm glad to be back, and thanks for picking me up. I haven't been able to reach your aunt." Adam gripped the handle of his suitcase and pulled it behind him as they walked through the terminal, headed for the parking garage.

"Would you like something to eat?" Adam gestured to an airport bar and grill crowded with patrons. "It's pretty packed. Their food must be all right."

"Sounds good to me," said Ben. "I've got some things to talk to you about."

"Oh, yeah? Like what?" said Adam. "You ready to buy your books for the upcoming semester?"

"I am, but that's not what I wanted to tell you about." Ben smiled.

Adam knew that look. Ben had met a girl. "Tell me about her."

Ben's eyes lit up. "How did you know that was what I was going to tell you?"

"Come on. Let's go inside." Adam ushered Ben through the entrance to the bar and grill, where they caught up between bites of their double bacon cheeseburgers.

•　　•　　•

Adam walked through the front door of his own home before six and parked his suitcase in the foyer. "Sophie?" he called up the stairs.

No answer. Strange. Both of the cars were there. "Sophie," he called again, taking the stairs two at a time.

He couldn't wait to see the look on her face when he told her his story—how he was arrested *twice* and almost shot, how he flagged down a truck in handcuffs, and managed to finish the most important project of his career two weeks early.

She hadn't left him a note, but why would she? They hadn't communicated since he'd left. He had tried calling and texting every day since he had escaped death, but she must have blocked his number. She hadn't responded to any of his comments on her social media, either. She had been posting pictures of various stages of her projects, so he knew she was okay, just ignoring him.

Inside the main bathroom, crisp air streamed in through the open window above the Jacuzzi tub. God, he loved the smell of autumn approaching. Adam stripped off his traveling clothes, threw them into the corner next to the sink, and filled the tub. Under the open window, he added hot water periodically, turning the spigot with his toes. Ever since the day he'd almost lost his life, it had been hard for him to turn off his thoughts. Whenever things were still, he found himself sorting through various regrets, and Marisol's death was at the top of that list. He hadn't killed her, but he hadn't been able to save her.

By the time he had gone through everything he could have done differently to save his friend, the tips of his fingers were pruney. Adam let the water out of the tub and dressed. Almost eight o'clock, and Sophie still wasn't home. Where could she have gone? She was always home by seven. Adam went down to her office and found exactly nothing—no desk, no computer, no scanner, not even a paper clip. In disbelief, he paced around the room, his footsteps echoing on the hardwood floor.

He dialed her number again, but it went straight to a default voicemail greeting. So he sent a text. *Where are you?* She didn't text him back, which was nothing new. He marched to the window to check the driveway again, then slammed his phone on the windowsill. This was ludicrous. They were both adults. If she didn't want to talk to him, she could at least give him the courtesy of a response.

Adam strode from her office, running his hands through his hair. He surveyed the kitchen and the living room, finding everything in its proper place. After checking her side of the walk-in closet and seeing that practically everything was still there, he reasoned she had finally taken his advice to rent an office space and turn her gardening into a legitimate business. She was probably driving that broken-down, stake bed truck.

Maybe she was staying over at Harriet's. She did that sometimes.

He sent her another text. *Dinner tomorrow? We need to talk.* Still no answer, but he had expected as much. Adam pushed his feet into a pair of crocs he used to take the trash out and knocked on the neighbor's door.

"Hey, Adam." His retired neighbor, Jim, looked surprised to see him.

"Hi, Jim. Listen. I just got back from an extended business trip and Sophie's phone must have died. I haven't been able to get a hold of her. Have you seen her today?"

"Actually, yes. I was washing my car earlier, and I saw her with that young guy she works with. She was carrying a folder, or maybe it was an envelope."

"Thanks, Jim. I just wanted to make sure she was okay." You could always count on older folks to spy on their neighbors. Retirees were better than a security system.

"No problem." Jim looked at Adam's feet. "Nice crocs. I have the same ones."

Adam gave Jim his best fake smile and returned home to fix himself a bowl of stale Cheerios with water before going to bed. He would have to stop by the grocery store on his way home from work the next day. Sophie must have been very busy with the new office to have let the shopping go as long as she had.

·   ·   ·

Adam's first day back at the office was everything he had hoped it would be, though he still hadn't heard from Sophie. Mr. Greenberg greeted him outside the door to the conference room.

"Well done, Adam." Mr. Greenberg gave Adam a firm handshake.

"Thank you, sir."

"The client was pleased with the project, and *I* was pleased you came in two percent under budget. What did you do, lay the bricks yourself?" Mr. Greenburg held his fingertips together, chuckling.

"How are the negotiations going for the manufacturing location in Canada?" asked Adam. He wasn't in the mood to think about the recent past, even if it came with praise.

"Just fine. We should have all the subcontractors' contracts signed and returned by the end of next week. Pack your bags. We're sending you to Canada next month."

"Wonderful."

"Don't get too excited. There's a mess down the street you'll have to clean up first." Mr. Greenberg's voice dropped an octave. "Fleet Street has been dragging on. It should have been completed almost two months ago, but the client keeps coming back with problems. We've had to back charge a lot of the subs and they're getting upset. It's all stuff Kevin should have caught. I think he's drinking again."

"That's too bad," said Adam, trying to keep the edges of his mouth from curling into a smile

"Anyway, I'm meeting with him later today to recommend he take a leave of absence. He's been with the company for a long time, but I can't have this kind of liability. If he can't straighten himself out, I'll need you to take his place as Senior Project Manager of the mid-Atlantic region."

Could this day get any better? Adam sucked his lips in to conceal his smile and somberly furrowed his eyebrows.

"Fleet Street is your responsibility from here on. Just knock out everything on the punch list. Understand?"

"Yes, sir." Adam waited for more details about the timing of his impending promotion, but that was it for now. Mr. Greenburg excused himself and stepped into the conference room.

•   •   •

On the front porch, with his hands full of brown grocery bags, Adam tapped on the door with his shoe. When no one came, he put the bags down and found his keys.

"Sophie," he called. "I know you're still mad, but I picked up some ravioli and pesto sauce from the market." She was probably upstairs asleep. The stake bed truck still wasn't in the driveway, but that wasn't unusual—Rico or Ricky or whoever probably took it after dropping her off.

Adam boiled the water for the pasta while putting the groceries away. He thought of what he would say to smooth things over. She wouldn't want to hear about his career, so he decided to ask her about the office and how her business was going.

Half an hour later, Adam had everything set. A fresh cherry cheesecake sat on the dining room table, but Sophie hadn't come down from the bedroom.

"If you want me to keep cooking, you'll have to show some appreciation." He entered the main bedroom and found it empty. His clothes were still in a pile on the bathroom floor. What was going on? Had she moved out? She couldn't have left him. She needed him. Plus, all of her stuff was still there. What was she going to do for money without him? He dialed her number. It went straight to the default greeting again. Bold as ever, he called Harriet.

"Hi, Harriet," said Adam, "Sophie didn't come home last night and hasn't been home all day today. Is she with you?"

"Sophie's whereabouts are her own business, Adam."

"What's wrong? Aren't you worried?"

"I know where she is, Adam. She's just fine, happier than I've seen her in years. I don't want you to ruin it for her. If she wants to contact you, she will."

"All of her things are still here. Did she say when she would be back?"

"She said she left some papers for you to sign on top of the washing machine."

"What papers?"

"Just look in the laundry room. I'm not going to get into any of this." Harriet hung up.

Papers? He stepped into the laundry room and opened a manilla envelope with his name on it. A separation period? Beginning on May fourteenth? Why hadn't she contacted him about this? Adam's heart tapped out an angry rhythm in his ears. Didn't his opinion matter? A divorce hearing had been scheduled for the same date the following year. She wasn't wasting any time.

Adam took out his phone and checked her social media accounts—blocked! She had blocked him from all her accounts. She must have done this while he was at work. Megan would be able to tell him something.

"Megan?"

"Who wants to know?" Sophie's sister answered in the same brick wall fashion Harriet had.

"This is Adam, your sister's husband."

"Go ahead," she said dryly, not acknowledging his sarcasm.

Adam dropped the separation papers onto the washer, then picked them up again to reread the dates. Unbelievable. "Do you know where she is?"

"Yes."

"Will you tell me where I can find her?"

"No."

"What's with all the secrecy?" he demanded, irritated by her unwillingness to enlighten him.

"Look, Adam. Just let it go. She's come such a long way since you've been gone. Yeah, she's still married to you, but she's with somebody else, and she's going to have a baby. If you care about her at all, you'll sign the stupid papers and move on."

"What!" Adam grabbed the bottle of laundry detergent and flung it against the wall so hard the top burst open, spewing blue liquid all over the room. It's like he'd been gone for years instead of months. Things didn't happen this fast. "Who's the father?" It was a logical question. He deserved to know.

"Are you that clueless?"

Adam's face grew red. Why did they keep messing with him like this? "Who is he?"

"You really don't know anything, do you?" said Megan. "I thought you were just playing dumb, trying to harass my sister. I didn't want to be the one to tell you all of this."

"I have to talk to her, Megan. Could you just give me her number? I think she might have a new phone because my calls keep going to this generic greeting."

"There's no way I'm giving you her new number." Megan ended the call.

Adam stood in the laundry room, phone in hand, staring at it as if it would somehow come to life and explain everything to him. Eventually, he sat down to a plate of ravioli. Sophie had to come back for the rest of her things. He would just wait.

•   •   •

It had been two weeks. Sophie wasn't coming back.

Adam had rectified the outstanding concerns on Fleet Street. He had the Midas touch. Everything he had a hand in was turning to gold, except when it came to his marriage, and the residual headaches he was still experiencing. Adam checked the calendar. He would follow up with the neurologist next week. Maybe they would be able to give him something stronger for his headaches.

From his spot on the sofa, Adam picked up the legal documents from the coffee table. Sophie would expect him to sign. It wasn't so bad living alone. He liked it, but eleven years of marriage. How could he just throw that away? It was one thing planning on doing it and another thing entirely to actually do it.

His phone rang—an unknown caller. "Hello?"

"Adam?"

"This is Adam. Sophie, is that you?"

"Yes, it's me. I can't talk long. I wanted to make sure you received the preliminary divorce papers." A long pause. "Adam, are you there?"

He imagined himself squeezing Sophie's skinny arms until they turned blue. "Yes, I'm still here, and I have the papers in front of me." He tossed them back onto the coffee table.

"Fair enough, don't you think? You get the house and the cars. I keep the stake bed and my office furniture. You can do what you like with my other things. I'm starting fresh."

Fair enough? Adam was still trying to catch up. Even though he had never wanted to have children, it was hard to think of his wife carrying someone else's baby. "How did all of this happen?"

"That's none of your business. Will you sign?"

"You're sure about this?" he asked.

"Very sure."

She was all confidence—keeping it brief. What had happened to his Sophie? "If this is really what you want, I'll sign." This couldn't possibly be what she really wanted.

"Great. I'll see you on May fourteenth. My lawyer will take care of everything on my end. I hope the job in Mexico went well for you." She hung up.

"Thanks," Adam said to the dead phone line. He would have to find a lawyer. He would sign the papers, but not before he had someone review them. Adam wished he could use the lawyer he'd used to represent him in Mexico. Sebastian had referred him to one of his lawyer friends from college, who had done an outstanding job of protecting Adam's rights after Marisol's murder. Adam might not even have to return for the trial. His lawyer made sure to provide the prosecution with everything he thought they might need before Adam left.

•   •   •

The following May, inside the Baltimore County courthouse, Adam spotted his soon-to-be ex-wife. "Wow, Sophie, you look … different."

"Thank you, I think." Sophie waddled past him to the only available seat in the lobby.

Adam scanned the room for Rigo. One drunken happy hour in a Pittsburgh bar and he had gotten all the inside information from Megan. His buzz had vanished when she'd told him

Sophie had left him for Rigo, a laborer, *head of the mulch division*. It was embarrassing, but it was happening.

Rigo entered the lobby and pocketed the keys to a mini-van he and Sophie had purchased together. The two men made eye contact, acknowledging each other with succinct nods, and Rigo joined them in the waiting area.

Once their case was called, the three of them followed the corridor to room 212. Adam walked behind the couple and watched as Rigo escorted a pregnant and past due Sophie, arm in arm. This man's baby was growing inside of *his* wife. How could he have let things go this far? It wasn't until he had actually seen her, seen Rigo, seen them together, seen her belly, that the finality of it all registered. This was it. He'd come to a divorce hearing today, and he was going to get a divorce. She looked at this … laborer with love and adoration. She used to look at *him* that way—she must have. What did this guy have that he didn't? What could Rigo offer her in the way of financial security? Wasn't she thinking about any of that? Didn't she care at all about the life they had built together? How could she throw it away on this guy? It was at this moment he knew he would truly miss her. This would be the last time he would ever see *his* wife.

Chapter 32

Mexico, Present Day

A tour bus rumbled along the winding mountain roads. Magnificent views of the turquoise water two thousand feet below filled the windows of the rickety bus as it rounded the curves on the narrow highway. Stucco houses clung to the mountainsides and wildflowers dotted the landscape with brilliant colors. The bus was filled to capacity and headed to Puerto Vallarta. The hum of a dozen conversations filled the air as people talked excitedly about their vacation plans. A small child lay on his mother's lap in the back seat, eyes growing heavy as the motion of the bus rocked him to sleep.

The bus rounded another curve, and the driver slammed on the brakes. Conversations transformed into screams. The child flew from his mother's arms, striking his head on the seat in front of them. The bus skidded but regained purchase, coming to rest in the middle of the road.

"What's going on?" a passenger shouted to the driver over the clamoring confusion of a busload of people displaced.

In the center of the highway stood an elderly woman, wearing nothing but a tiny skull strung around her neck. Bright red shone from the nose and eye sockets of the bony sphere. She clutched the strings of the necklace. Her mouth moved, but the roar of the aging engine smothered her words.

The driver pulled the handle, opening the door slowly as the naked woman ambled to the edge of the road. He turned off the engine and engaged the emergency brake before following the woman cautiously, not wanting to spook her. High in the Sierra Madres, a fall from this height would be fatal. "Señora," the driver said calmly.

"Tengo que irme con mi hijo." She held the skull out for him to see.

The bus driver examined the charm, seeing that the hollows of the nose and eye sockets had been plugged with rubies. The precious stones caught the light, reflecting red onto the pavement, but the woman's black eyes were deep canyons, formed by a turbulent river of sorrow.

"Señora," he said again, extending his arm to her. "You don't have to go with your son. You can come with us."

Esmeralda looked into the driver's eyes, backing up to the steep ledge. She wrapped her fingers around the skull, closed her eyes, and willingly tipped backward over the cliff. The driver lunged for her but missed. His fingers grazed the surface of her skin. He had been too slow. A crowd of spectators stepped off the bus, gathering behind him, but the woman's body had disappeared under the canopy of the trees below.

"Everybody back on the bus, please," the driver said, herding the passengers onto the bus. If they stayed parked in the road, hidden by the curve, they would be the next ones over the edge.

•   •   •

Esmeralda

Why was the man digging? Why was he digging in the bones? The bones needed rest. The bones needed meat. She knew the man, but who was he? Who was the digging man?

Scratching at the ground like a stray dog, Esmeralda pulled a box from the dirt. Smash—with a large stone, she crushed the box, revealing a drawstring bag with chains and jewels. She would deliver these treasures to her baby girl, and she would save some for the bones. Esmeralda would keep the fiery stones until they could be together.

She grasped the miniature skull hanging from her neck. They were falling, just like in the cornfield. No more digging—only falling. She had given to her daughter, and she had given to the bones.

Chapter 33

Sophie
Four Years Later

Sophie and Rigo lay in bed together. "Are you sure you want to do this?" she asked.

Rigo pressed his body against her back and wrapped his arms around her. "Are *you* sure you want to do this? It's not too late to change your mind."

She met his gaze with confidence. "We've already shipped everything we own to Mexico. I think it's a little too late to change my mind."

"There are few things in life that can't be undone. This isn't one of them," he said. "Will you be happy there?"

After four years of marriage, her happiness mattered to him just as much as it had when they first started dating. "Being with my family makes me happy, but if I had to choose again, I would still choose to move to Mexico," she said. "We made the right decision. I want the kids to speak Spanish and to learn about the other half of their culture."

"I feel the same," Rigo agreed.

He lifted her T-shirt over her head and peeled off her panties. His hands explored her breasts and slid around to the small of her back. She inhaled sharply with pleasure as he entered her, and the two of them made love, then lay together in the quiet night. It would be morning all too soon. She would move to a foreign country, and although Rigo knew the language, her working knowledge of Spanish was rudimentary at best, but she would learn. She would have to learn.

•   •   •

The following afternoon, they checked into a brick hotel in García after a day of travel. In the center of the village stood a towering tree whose peeling bark revealed a cream-colored trunk. Shops lined the perimeter of the square, giving it a small-town feel. Sophie and Rigo's little girl had been born only a few days after her divorce, but Emma wasn't so little anymore—now a big sister to two-year-old Bryce. When Rigo turned off the engine, Bryce and Emma stirred from their slumbers in their car seats.

"Are we there?" asked Emma.

"We are here, my love," answered Sophie.

"Where's my blanket?" asked Bryce sleepily.

Rigo pulled the matted, yellow blanket from the traveling pack. "Here it is."

Bryce grabbed the blanket, tucked it under his chin, and closed his eyes once more. Emma unbuckled herself from her car seat and slipped her sandals on, ready to jump out of the van as soon as anyone opened the door.

"Okay, guys," said Sophie, "I want you both on your best behavior. This means no shouting or running, and you have to stay with Mommy and Daddy until we get into the room. Does everyone understand?" She waited for a reply from the children.

Emma voiced her understanding immediately, but Bryce was asleep again. Rigo opened the van's sliding door, and Emma quickly jumped down, skipping over to Sophie. Bryce rested his head on Rigo's shoulder, clutching his blanket. Inside the room, Rigo laid Bryce on top of a bed with a thick, embroidered comforter, and Sophie flipped on the window unit to get some air circulating.

"We're really here. We're really doing this." She held her shirt out and let the window unit blow cool air onto her skin.

"Yes, we are." Rigo held his arms out, inviting Sophie for a hug. "Come here. It's going to be great."

He couldn't possibly be sure of that, but she decided to believe him. "I know. We just have a lot of work to do."

"Yes, but once we build the house and the ranch is functional, things will settle down again." He squeezed her tightly and smiled. "Why don't we do some exploring?"

•   •   •

Once Bryce had finished napping, Sophie called everyone to the front door. "It's time to take a walk around the village square and check out some shops."

"Can we climb the tree?" asked Emma.

"That tree isn't for climbing, baby. It's for decoration and shade," said Sophie.

"Can we have a picnic under the tree?" Emma asked.

"We sure can," Sophie responded. "That's a wonderful idea."

Rigo collected Bryce into his arms. "Okay then, a picnic it is."

Emma left to find her princess dress-up clothes, which her mother had put away neatly in the bottom drawer of her dresser. She came clickety-clacking back into the common area, wearing her plastic, high-heeled princess shoes.

"You can't wear those shoes, Emma. The streets are cobblestone, and you could fall," said Sophie.

Luckily, Emma didn't put up a fight, changing into her sandals before they left. A path wound around the backside of the hotel, through a tight alley, depositing the family into the village square. Although García wasn't big, the town center could accommodate sizeable crowds, and shops of all kinds bordered the square—a shoe store, a grocery store, a bakery, a doctor's office, and even a tack shop, each with an open storefront equipped with roll-down doors, similar to garage doors. Atop a model horse, a craftsman worked stitching a leather saddle for all to see. It was like going back in time to a time Sophie couldn't even recall. She had only seen towns like this in the movies.

The paletería—popsicle shop—drew the children's eyes. Made from freshly ground fruit instead of frozen sugar water, a rainbow assortment of the frozen treats stood proudly in the cooler. From pineapple to mango, coconut to kiwi, they had every flavor and combination one could dream of.

Bryce pressed his nose to the glass on the cooler. Sophie gently pulled him back and wiped his tiny smudges from the glass.

"I like the purple one," said Emma. "What kind is the purple one?"

Her dad told her it was prickly pear.

"Ew, what's a prickly pear? I don't want to get spiked."

"It's just a kind of fruit, but what about a strawberry paleta?" Rigo suggested.

"Oooh yeah," said Emma, clasping her hands together in anticipation of the frozen dessert.

"Queremos unas quatro paletas, por favor," Rigo said. "Una de fresa, otra de mango, la tercera de coco, y la última de …" He paused and asked Sophie, "What would you like, mi reina?"

"I think I'd like to try the prickly pear."

"Ew, Mom is going to try the prickly pear. Be careful, Mom," said Emma.

"I'll be careful. Thanks for the warning," Sophie said with a smile. She touched her hand to her abdomen, and her sea-green eyes met Rigo's loving gaze.

Emma took her pink pop from the lady behind the counter and pointed at a black-and-white photo of a woman and a child hanging above the cash register. "Who are they?" she asked her mother.

"I'm sorry, but I don't know, baby."

The shop owner came around the counter and leaned down in front of Emma to answer her question. "That is a picture of my great-great grandmother, Ivette, and her mother, Catalina. They started this shop over one hundred years ago when that big tree you see over there was only a little sapling, just like you."

"I'm not a sapling." Emma frowned, and her parents laughed.

The shop owner returned to her post behind the counter. "Catalina and Ivette traded one silver necklace for this very lot and started a juice stand. They didn't have refrigeration back then, but now look at what this place has become." The woman gestured to their colorful, air-conditioned surroundings.

"That's a wonderful story," said Rigo, acknowledging the shop owner's family history.

They enjoyed the pops under the shade of the giant tree. Rigo's hand hovered close to Bryce seated on the brick wall, ready to catch him at any moment. This was Sophie's life now, and she loved every minute of it. From the time they woke up in the morning to the time they put the children to bed, their days revolved around the kids. It was hard for her to imagine life without them. She finally had everything she had always dreamed of having. The diamond ring on her finger sparkled as she ate her prickly pear paleta, and Sophie knew no matter where they lived, they would always be home together.

If you enjoyed
DOUBLE-CROSSING THE BORDER
look out for

SOUTHERN
Souls

A HAUNTING STORY

COMING SOON FROM

SARAH LAUER
NAKAWATASE

CHAPTER 1

AMOS
Georgetown, South Carolina
1828

The buttery aroma of boiling rice clawed its way up through the humid air to the children playing in the live oak tree. Last night's rain had unfurled the tender, green leaves of the resurrection fern, carpeting the hardwood boughs of their natural jungle gym. Emerald fronds mingled with tangled fibers of Spanish moss, cascading from the sprawling branches down to the sandy soil of the South Carolina coast.

Amos planted his bare feet on a cushion of moss and inhaled deeply. Rays of light glinted off ocean waves, visible from his perch high in the giant tree, and a salty breeze mixed with the earthy tones of the rice. Cradled on a long limb, Amos tilted his head to the sky. Ocean air pushed past his face, and he listened to waves crashing on the shore, watching waterfowl swoop down over swarms of mullet and rise into the morning sky with beaks full of the small, shiny fish. In the canopy, his thoughts were as free as the birds, gliding on the warm currents of air that traveled with the ocean tides.

Boom! Boom! Boom! Boom! The rhythmic pounding of rice reverberated through the cook yard below, pulling him out of the sky, away from the birds, and back to the Chapin Plantation. Amos looked past his feet at the other children descending from the lower branches. The rumbling in his stomach challenged the thunderous beating of the rice, but he wasn't ready to come down.

On the ground, whole grain rice filled immense mortars carved from the bald cypress trees that thrived in the Lowcountry swamps. Wooden pestles crashed into the hollowed-out logs, grinding chaff from yellow grain—Carolina Gold. These small pieces of rice, encased in their fibrous coats, demanded year-round labor, and the overseer ensured production was never interrupted.

Amos stole one last glance at the ocean before stretching his toes down to the next branch. If he waited too long, he would miss the morning meal, and it would be a long time before supper.

Slash pines, with their tufts of green needles as rigid as their naked trunks, separated the big house from the tattered rows of slave quarters, and bent saplings filled the gaps between these lines of softwood soldiers. Horace, the overseer, emerged from the tangled greenery, and a hush fell across the cook yard, punctuated only by the pounding of rice. The booming pestles marched out the staccato rhythm of their lives from October through January, when the rice was processed for shipping. Only moments ago, the cook yard had been a place of fellowship, conversation, and a shared meal. Now the men and women cast their eyes toward the packed soil.

The overseer wore a long-sleeved shirt, stained yellow with sweat, and he kept a full beard, even in the unrelenting heat of the South. At seven thirty in the morning, his breath reeked of whiskey and decay that drew the mosquitoes out from the shaded edges of the woods. He strolled down the milling line and headed for the climbing tree. Amos hugged the trunk of his beloved wooden giant—his stairway to freedom—but the dark skin of the tree couldn't shield him from the overseer's bloodshot eyes as they traveled up the ribbed bark of the trunk to where Amos stood on the lowest branch.

A gap-toothed grin spread across the overseer's blotchy face. "Ain't you a little old to be playin' in trees, boy?"

"Yes, sir," Amos said, quickly averting his eyes from the devil's stare that held him frozen on his branch.

"Then why don't you come down here and start to millin' like the rest of 'em?" Horace gestured to the long line of enslaved people driving their cypress pestles into the rice like the knowing gears of a clock.

"Yes, sir." Amos wanted to climb back up the tree and leap into the air, letting it carry him away, down the beach, but climbing would only make things worse. The cruelty that had freely come from this overseer was unmatched by any who had come before him, so Amos continued his descent. With his feet on the ground, he found a place in the milling line and took up a pestle. His thin arms shook as he lifted the heavy piece of timber.

"Get this Negro some more rice," Horace said with a humorless chuckle, scanning the milling line to see who would be the first to come to the boy's aid. The overseer stood with his thumbs in his pockets, watching as Amos struggled with the weight of the pestle, pushing the tiny capsules of rice over the edge and into the dirt.

Halfway down the line, a man with powerful arms, the color of dark mahogany, glistened with his efforts in the wet morning air. He worked pounding the rice and kept his eyes on his task like everyone else in the line.

"Well, who's it gonna be?"

The overseer asked a lot of questions, but no one was supposed to answer them. Amos concentrated on controlling his pestle, stabbing at the grain in his mortar.

"Now I know y'all ain't gonna like what happens next if I have to ask again." Horace laughed and made a display of shaking his head from side to side in disapproval, moving his hands to his hips.

Amos never knew what Horace found so funny, but nothing good ever came of the smelly man's uncomfortable laughter. The heavy, wooden tool, almost as tall as himself, threatened to tip his mortar with every strike, but Amos clenched his jaw tight and contracted the sinewy muscles of his upper body, directing the pestle as best he could.

Horace's eyes bore into him, and the silence that stretched out was worse than the overseer's unfounded laughter. Relief from his blistering stare came when the strong man laid down his pestle and hastened to the mountain of raw grain. This giant of a man pushed a tin bucket into the mound of unprocessed rice, and the hard pellets flowed into the vessel like water droplets hitting a tin roof. He approached Amos with caution, pouring the Carolina Gold into his mortar.

"And who told you to stop workin'?" asked the overseer, glaring at the man with the bucket.

It was another of Horace's questions no one was supposed to answer. The man silently took his place in the milling line again, lifting his pestle and bringing it down on the dry grain in time with the ensemble of plantation hands. Horace stepped sideways down the line, creeping closer to Amos as he held his pestle with trembling arms, lifting it and smashing it down on the rice.

"Hey boy, you're breakin' the grain!" Horace ran his hand through his greasy hair, leaving clumps of dirty, blond locks in its wake.

Amos couldn't help it. The pestle was too heavy. Once it started to drop, he couldn't slow it down. He *was* breaking the grain.

"I think this boy's a little slow," the overseer said, reaching for the whip hanging from his right hip. He unbuttoned the coiled weapon from his belt, took the molded grip in his hand, and snapped the leather rope in the air. A deafening crack echoed in the yard, bouncing off the tree line.

Water filled his eyes, but Amos blinked back his tears. He wasn't strong enough. He had damaged the rice, and now someone would pay for it. Amos was supposed to be looking down, but his eyes followed Horace as he homed in on the man who had filled his bucket.

Horace held the whip up for all to see, making a spectacle of his power, turning slowly in the cook yard next to the pot of boiling rice. "Y'all just don't know how good y'all have it." Horace snapped the whip in the dirt, releasing a cloud of dusty earth from the packed yard. "Ain't nobody better ever question me!"

Amos jumped back, and his pestle fell to the ground with a thud, drawing the overseer's attention. Horace tightened his grasp on his weapon of choice, squeezing the blood from his knuckles as he turned toward Amos. "It's always you, ain't it?"

As fast as a cobra strike, the leather tongue of the whip reached out and bit Amos on the shoulder, cutting through his shirt and splitting his skin. Blood erupted from the deep laceration. Only six years old, Amos fell to the ground, holding his shoulder, writhing in pain. He kicked his legs and screamed but couldn't stop his tears. They flowed down his cheeks and landed in whole droplets on the dusty ground. The muggy, Carolina morning air soaked up his cries for help, extinguishing his howls like sand kicked over the orange embers of a dying fire.

Satisfied with his morning's work, Horace looped up the whip and fastened it back to its rightful place on his hip. He sniffed and wiped his nose on his shirtsleeve. Without looking back, the overseer left through the narrow wood, headed for the rice fields past the plantation house.

CHAPTER 2

JAMIE
Present Day

Three interlocking loops embellished the time-worn handle of the iron skeleton key Jamie used to turn over the lock. The heavy, wooden door, slathered with a fresh coat of white paint, stuck in the frame. With her arms full, Jamie pressed on the kitchen door with her foot, and it came free, ripping a strip of tacky paint from the frame. The kids ran past into the dated room with a pea-green refrigerator, across matching linoleum, and through a swinging door. This move would be good for them. It'd been almost two years since they'd lost their father in the accident.

"Mom," said Maddie, running up to her with her younger brother, Jackson, in tow.

"Yes." Jamie placed her bags on the counter, pushed her long, honey-brown hair over her shoulder, and bent down to meet her daughter at eye level.

"Jackson and I went around the whole room, through that door, but the lights won't come on. Can you help us? It's too dark in there."

"Are you scared, baby?" she asked Jackson, who'd just turned four.

He looked at her with wide, brown eyes but didn't answer, so Jamie pulled him into her arms and lifted him up. "Follow me, guys."

Jamie pushed through the swinging door into the living room and felt along the wall for the light switch. Her fingers followed the grooves of the wooden paneling until they hit the familiar shape of the switch. She flicked it, but nothing happened. The property management company had described the Chapin Plantation as updated. Jamie wasn't sure that was an accurate description anymore, but she had already signed the lease. They would have to make the best of it.

Maddie darted through the maze of cloth-covered furniture to a fringed lamp balanced on an end table. She swiped her stringy, brown bangs to the side and waved to get Jamie's attention. "Look, Mom. Can I turn it on?"

"Please." Jamie nodded her head in approval.

Maddie turned the knob, and pale light fell across the living room. The power was intact. They would just need to replace some bulbs. Dust caked the sheets covering most of the furniture, and cobwebs hung from the corners of the rooms. Even the spiders had moved out long ago, their webs weighed down with years of grime.

"I'm scared." Jackson buried his face in her neck and hugged her tightly.

"You don't have to be afraid, sweetie. This is just a big, old house. No one has lived in it for a long time, and all it needs is a good cleaning. After we move this dirt out and set up your toys, I think you're going to like it here." She squeezed him back. "Tonight, though, we can all sleep together in my room. It's too late to start cleaning."

Darkness had fallen before they'd arrived at the house that evening, but the days would soon grow longer. The holidays had passed, and Jamie was glad they were over. The past month had been filled with cookies, parties, and family, but the hollow feeling in her stomach had been ever-present. Since the day they'd lost Andrew, nothing could satiate the black hole carved into her core.

"Let's go to the car and get our overnight bags from the front seat. They have everything we need for tonight." Jamie smiled encouragingly at her children.

"Okay, Mom." Maddie was mommy's little helper and would start first grade at her new school that week.

They returned to the kitchen through the swinging door, whose hinges groaned. Years of vacancy had left them begging for grease.

"It's too dark out there," said Jackson, peering out the window above the kitchen sink as Jamie carried him to the back door. The black window showed only their reflections from inside the kitchen.

"Don't worry," said Jamie. "We'll get a better look at the yard tomorrow morning. The property manager said there are acres upon acres where you guys could play. She also mentioned some huge, live oak trees on the property we could use for swings and an old garden to plant vegetables and flowers if we wanted."

"Mommy, I can see the big trees for the swings," said Maddie as they descended the cracked, concrete steps from the kitchen door. "Look."

She pointed beyond the driveway toward the ocean, where a cluster of trees stood sentinel, silhouetted by a waxing moon. Hundreds of years old, these trees had seen everything.

Jackson lifted his head from her shoulder and craned his neck to see the trees. "I see them, too."

"Can we go over there, Mom?" asked Maddie.

"No, not tonight. It's too dark." Jamie put Jackson down and leaned into the van to grab the overnight bags. She loaded her shoulders with luggage straps and passed Maddie two pillows that had wedged themselves between the two front seats. "Maddie, can you hold these?"

"Yes, I can." Maddie took the pillows under her arms and followed her mom back into the house and up the back staircase connecting the kitchen with the second floor. Jackson touched his hand to one of the duffel bags hanging from Jamie's shoulder and kept pace with his family.

With clean sheets on the mattress and everyone in their jammies, they piled onto the main bed. Jackson and Maddie snuggled into her arms on either side, and in their mother's protective embrace, their worlds were right. Love radiated from their little hearts, and Jamie soaked it up like rays of sunlight.

Ever since the accident, she hadn't been able to feel much of anything. The numbness that comes with losing someone you love so quickly is all-consuming. It was as if her heart had been dipped into a vat of wax ... burned at first, then coated until it was as hard as a candlestick. The only remedy she'd found—the only thing that could melt the wax—was spending time with her children. It wasn't taking care of her children on her own that was difficult. It was the time they spent apart. Time alone allowed the blackness to creep out of her stomach and into her thoughts, but she couldn't let the sadness into her mind. She had a job to do. She had children to raise.

Acknowledgments

In the fourth grade, I had the privilege of having Mr. Tom Conroy as my English teacher. He assigned a 2-4 page writing journal every week to a room full of nine-year-olds. We would brainstorm on Mondays, outline on Tuesdays, draft on Wednesdays, and write our final copies in our best cursive on Thursdays. He encouraged us to be creative! Mr. Conroy is one of a kind, always drawing out the very best from his charges.

Thank you, Mom! My mom has always been my best friend and my favorite person to butt heads with. This fabulous woman is also my co-author for our science fiction novel, *Dormant Diversion*. She has been my editor since the fourth grade when she would find me under the covers with my flashlight, going over the final copy of my writing journal just one more time.

To my kids and my forever husband, thank you! Brian, Beverly, Josefina, and Saburo, you have always supported my dreams! I am thankful every day to live in a house with such love and positive energy!

Thank you to Black Rose Writing! This is my second published novel with Black Rose Writing. The encouragement, support, marketing, editing, cover designs, and networking opportunities this publishing company provides are unparalleled.

Thank you, Jackie Hernandez, for your extensive knowledge of Mexican culture! I am grateful for your unique perspective and appreciated working with you to ensure that *Double-Crossing the Border* represents Latin American culture respectfully.

Authors need a community of readers, editors, and other authors to help point out the flaws we can't see in our own pieces. Thank you to editors, Samantha Wekstein and Laura Pulaski, and to all the beta readers for helping transform a three-hundred-page manuscript into a market-ready novel.

Finally, thank you to the readers! Whenever someone reads one of my books, my dream comes full circle. I hope you have found some relaxation and entertainment in my pages.

About the Author

Photo by Small Seed Photography

Sarah lives by the beach with her forever husband, three children, and one chicken. Over the years, family hikes, Little League games, and big family dinners have kept her smiling. Her spice rack occupies twelve square feet!

She earned her Bachelor's degree in Public Health Studies from Johns Hopkins University and her Registered Nurse (RN) license from Horry-Georgetown Technical College. Presently, she works as a cardiac nurse.

In her twenties, she started an agave farm in Jalisco, Mexico, with her first husband, lending accurate details to *Double-Crossing the Border*. In her teens, she worked as a dairy farmer, drawing upon this experience while writing *Southern Souls*.

Sarah also provides her local community with a yearly creative writing scholarship—details available at sarahlauernakawatase.com.

Other Titles by
Sarah Lauer Nakawatase

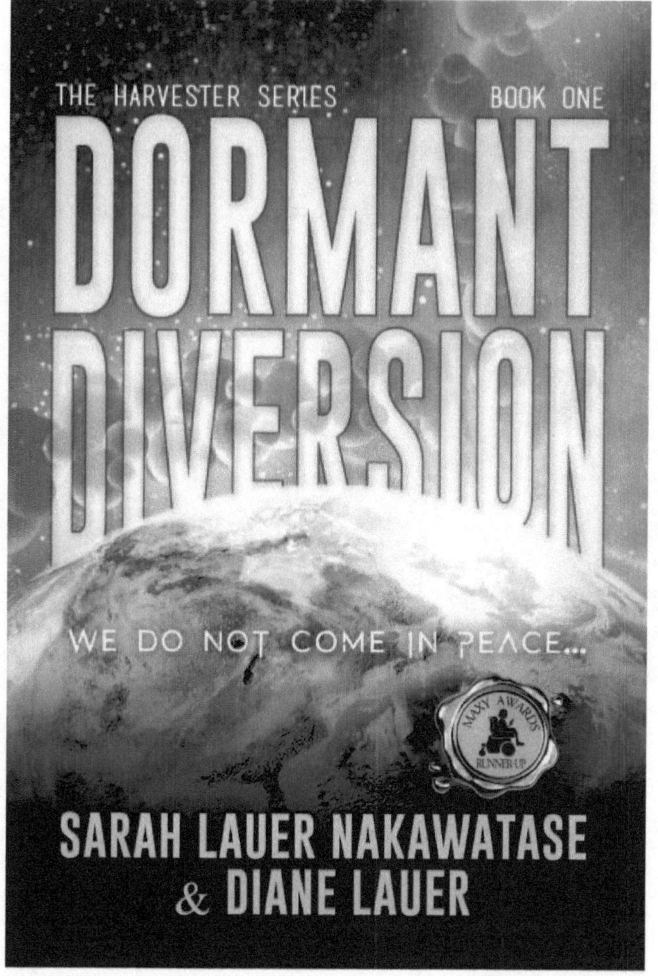

Note from Sarah Lauer Nakawatase

Word-of-mouth is crucial for any author to succeed. If you enjoyed *Double-Crossing the Border*, please leave a review online—anywhere you are able. Even if it's just a sentence or two. It would make all the difference and would be very much appreciated.

Thanks!
Sarah Lauer Nakawatase

We hope you enjoyed reading this title from:

BLACK ROSE writing™

www.blackrosewriting.com

Subscribe to our mailing list – *The Rosevine* – and receive **FREE**
books, daily deals, and stay current with news about upcoming
releases
and our hottest authors.
Scan the QR code below to sign up.

Already a subscriber? Please accept a sincere thank you for being a
fan of Black Rose Writing authors.

View other Black Rose Writing titles at
www.blackrosewriting.com/books and use promo code
PRINT to receive a **20% discount** when purchasing.